Beyond & Within

THE OPEN HEART

Stories and Fiction by

Catherine Wells

Edited by

Emelyne Godfrey & Patrick Parrinder

Beyond & Within

THE OPEN HEART

Stories and Fiction by

Catherine Wells

Edited by

Emelyne Godfrey & Patrick Parrinder

FLAME TREE
PUBLISHING

Publisher & Creative Director: Nick Wells
Editorial Director: Catherine Taylor

FLAME TREE PUBLISHING
6 Melbray Mews, Fulham,
London SW6 3NS, United Kingdom
www.flametreepublishing.com

25 27 29 28 26
1 3 5 7 9 10 8 6 4 2

Hardback ISBN: 978-1-83562-255-1
ebook ISBN: 978-1-80417-179-0

The cover image is created by Flame Tree Studio. Frontispiece illustration and cover detail is based on *Cold Spring in Bloom* © Broci 2024.

A copy of the CIP data for this book is available from the British Library.

Printed and bound in China

Contents

Introduction

Patrick Parrinder and Emelyne Godfrey

DURING HER LIFETIME, only her closest friends knew of Catherine Wells the writer. To most people she was 'Jane', the gracious and indefatigable hostess, expert gardener and devoted mother who stood loyally by her husband H.G. Wells as he rose from obscurity to worldwide literary fame and fortune. 'Jane' – one of several pet-names given to her by her increasingly errant husband – acted for many years as his personal assistant, business manager and sometime collaborator, as well as maintaining the family home which her husband, often away during the week, loved to fill at weekends with boisterous house-parties, largely made up of his fellow-writers. At least two of these, Arnold Bennett and Frank Swinnerton, became Catherine's intimates. Another friend was her old schoolfellow the novelist Dorothy Richardson. She portrayed Catherine as Alma Wilson (married to 'Hypo') in several volumes of her experimental novel-sequence *Pilgrimage*. But it was not until after her death from cancer in her mid-fifties that it became known that Catherine (not 'Jane') had herself been a serious writer – the author of a number of published short stories and of an unfinished novella, *The Open Heart*, which we are now able to publish for the first time.

Amy Catherine Robbins was born on 8 July 1872 at Shadwell, London. Her father died in a railway accident during her adolescence and she was still dressed in mourning when in 1892, shortly after she had turned 20, she and her friend Adeline Roberts found themselves in H.G. Wells's biology class at the Tutorial College in Red Lion Square, Holborn.[1] Their teacher was a thin, moustachioed 26-year-old. Hard-working and perpetually hard-up (he was, he had told a friend, 'fired by the furies of necessity'),[2] he had married his cousin Isabel a year earlier. Wells held a London University B.Sc. and had a small biology textbook (destined to remain in print for some 30 years) in the press. If he had literary ambitions, all there was to show for them was a handful of articles, mostly in obscure educational journals. Yet in the next four years he would publish *The Time Machine*, *The Island of Doctor Moreau*, *The Wheels of Chance* and

1 The Tutorial College, owned by William Briggs, was an offshoot of his University Correspondence College (1888–1964), eventually absorbed into the National Extension College in Cambridge. It was a major precursor of the Open University.

2 Letter to A. T. Simmons, 13 November 1891, in *The Correspondence of H.G. Wells*, ed. David C. Smith (London: Pickering & Chatto, 1998), vol. 1, p. 179.

many of his best-known short stories – works that, in themselves, would establish his reputation as something new on the cultural horizon.

How much Catherine glimpsed of H.G. Wells's potential we shall never know. Their mutual attraction was immediate, however, and Wells was soon looking to her for an understanding and sympathy that he had failed to find in Isabel. He later recalled Catherine as a 'fragile figure, with very delicate features, very fair hair and very brown eyes'; she was studying for a London University B.Sc. degree in order to take up high school teaching.[3] Just over a year later the two of them took the decisive steps that led to his divorce and to her becoming 'Jane' Wells. The story of their love affair and subsequent marriage has been told many times, beginning with H.G. Wells's own accounts in his Introduction to *The Book of Catherine Wells* (1928) – reprinted at the end of this volume – and in his *Experiment in Autobiography* (1934).

During their early years as a married couple, Catherine was occupied with her husband's bouts of serious illness, with his rapidly expanding literary career and his many enthusiasms (including their joint riding excursions on a tandem bicycle) and with bringing up her two sons, George Philip Wells ('Gip') and Frank, born in 1901 and 1903 respectively. On a night in 1911 the family moved

3 H.G. Wells, *Experiment in Autobiography* (London: Victor Gollancz and The Cresset Press, 1966), vol. 1, p. 362.

into the rectory on the grounds of the Countess of Warwick's estate in Little Dunmow, Essex, which Wells named Easton Glebe. It was in the later years, when her sons were at boarding school and Wells himself was increasingly absent from Easton Glebe, that Catherine found time for her own writing.

Meanwhile the Catherine Wells who would be remembered by her contemporaries and by her children came into her own: the lively, sympathetic mother who controlled the practical side of family life; the outdoor person and devoted skier who took her sons on regular trips to the Alps; the confidante of male writers such as Swinnerton (whose first glimpse of H.G. Wells was while working as a clerk at the publishing firm run by the formidable J.M. Dent) and George Gissing; and the affectionate friend recorded (after some initial hostility) by the social reformer Beatrice Webb. Of the Wells's house-parties at Easton Glebe, the biographer David C. Smith has observed that if people came to see H.G., they stayed to admire Catherine. An outstanding tribute came from her neighbour, the socialist Countess of Warwick. In the closing sentence of her memoir *Life's Ebb and Flow* (1929), she declared that of all her intimates 'the sweetest nature and finest character is the friend whose loss is irreparable – Catherine (Jane) Wells'.[4]

4 Frances, Countess of Warwick, *Life's Ebb and Flow* (London: Hutchinson, 1929), p. 276.

H.G. Wells, too – for all his absences, and the philandering that led to his fathering children by two other women, Amber Reeves and Rebecca West – found her loss irreparable. In 1928, the year after her death, he published *The Book of Catherine Wells*, a selection of her short stories and poems together with an introduction describing their first meetings, their marriage, their life together and then her other life as a writer. This life seems to have flourished in the 1920s, when she rented a flat in London as what their acquaintance Virginia Woolf would have called a 'room of her own' – a flat that H.G. never visited until after her death. During her lifetime, Catherine had published the odd short story, but now he found a great deal more. What H.G. put in print was, he thought, 'everything she ever completed that conveys her quality'. Yet, as he added, there was 'a much greater bulk of unfinished work', most of which belonged 'to a long fantasy of difficult design called "The Open Heart"' which had 'some fine and tender passages' – but nothing that was better than what could be found in her finished stories.

There is a sizeable number of histories of H.G. Wells's life, not to mention his own autobiographies. However, very few biographies consider Catherine in any detail. She is frequently depicted orbiting her husband and ministering to his requirements, while her subjectivity remains relatively unexamined. This limited view of Catherine leads in turn to an incomplete view of Wells. In fact, during the course of his research, David C. Smith came to realise that one could only really attempt to comprehend Wells by understanding his wife.

It is easy to see traces of Jane Wells, the quiet social facilitator and observer, in Catherine's depiction of the overlooked governess in 'Night in the Garden'. Even Frank Swinnerton, who recounted her with great fondness and acknowledged her depth of character, nonetheless focused his praise on the roles she took on to cater to the needs of others: as her husband's typist and proofreader and the researcher for *The Outline of History*; host and potential First Aider to her guests, pianist and costume designer. In his introduction Wells, when discussing Catherine's direct input in his career, is careful to credit her with administrative and secretarial roles, telling us that she was 'more realist' and 'less creative' than he was. Her 'wistful' creativity is apparently tied to, and limited by, her motherly and wifely instinct to help creatures in need. As Wells reminds us, it is he himself who thinks in more cosmic terms and sees beyond the sentimental walled garden of the everyday – and whose work therefore constitutes a higher art form. But like H.G., Catherine was also interested in significant matters such as deep time. In 'Cyanide', 'April in the Wood' and 'Night in the Garden' we encounter repeated references to such phenomena as the 'crepitations' and 'flutterings' of nature. With subtle adjustments of tense, Catherine invites us, in sections that are almost word-for-word, to look up and around into nature and to take a microscope to the natural world. Whether deliberate or not, the repetition of these passages gives us the impression that we are being stalked by images of a world which is noisy with productivity, mirroring the clamour of her protagonists' thoughts as they grapple with desire, fear and wonder. Here, the dominant and lush tree is imperceptibly hollowed out by the 'remote progeny' of mere maggots, those harbingers of mortality. And just as H.G. exposed the complacency of the British Empire in *The War of the Worlds* (1898), Catherine reminds us that we humans, who stride through nature, matter intensively, at least for now.

Categorised by Wells as an 'absurd fairy story', 'The Last Fairy' was written by Catherine and her younger son Frank. It is a tale that can readily be converted into a pantomime; Catherine even suggests sound and musical effects. When a fairy, who is out of practice, decides to venture into the world of human beings one final time, she accidentally transforms a horse into a dragon. Slapstick encounters abound, reflecting the wild, playful dressing-up games enjoyed by the family and friends.

Frank was particularly interested in theatre; he acted alongside Daisy Warwick's daughter Mercy, a year younger than him. Daisy, the Countess of Warwick, had transformed an old barn on her land into a vibrant local theatre. Events were organised there by a local committee whose members included George Bernard Shaw, Arnold Bennett and Cecil Sharp, who helped to revive Morris Dancing. Ellen Terry famously treated audiences to scenes from *Romeo and Juliet* and also brought her coterie to Little Easton. A photograph of the cast of *The Taming of the Shrew,* performed at the Barn Theatre in 1919, attests to the vibrant community of actors and writers who had gathered around Daisy Warwick and Catherine Wells, the indefatigable theatrical costumier.

Catherine was also adept at employing more subtle types of humour. We see this reflected in the Swiss attempts at English on the Alpine notice boards in 'Everymother' and the understated banter in 'The Dragon-Fly', particularly in the lawyer's admission that he had never seen such creatures which, as the story's young protagonist says, "livvinther-Worter and kummowtan Bust"! Catherine understood children and spent much time in their world. Like the mother in this story, one can easily imagine her reading 'Nature books' with her sons. Having once illustrated Wells's own scientific work, she adorned a book of fairy tales which belonged to Felice Spurrier, granddaughter of Daisy Warwick. Adeptly mimicking children's delightful speech, Catherine's stories try to represent the way in which children see the world. Their perspectives are valid, she argues, and children should be heard as well as seen. For instance, in 'The Dragon-Fly', Michael's wise warnings are unheeded by his inattentive mother. In 'The Emerald', Midge's feeling that the jewel is indeed valuable is dismissed by her slightly older and self-proclaimed worldly explorer friend, Peter-next-door.

When Peter and Midge skive off school and go on an adventure, they are carving out a sense of freedom from their parents for themselves. 'Everymother' is the product of Catherine's climbing holidays with her sons. It shows the grown-up child, still watched by his mother, flexing his muscles and taking delight in his scrambles in the Alps, unaware of the extent of his mother's silent terror with each ascent. She attempts to ward off images of torn ropes: the Matterhorn disaster of 1865, in which four climbers died when a rope snapped, continues to cast a long shadow over mountaineering history.

Death, the loss of love, fear of injury and health anxiety are subjects which readily occur in these stories. Catherine was Wells's steely nurse early in their marriage; she had also tended to their older son Gip when his grumbling appendix became an urgent case and had to be removed when he was a boy. Her observations of the Great War, when she spent much time attending to the sick and dying, show that the experience was not only deeply distressing; it also seemed never-ending and tedious. The otherwise fit and healthy young man in 'The Oculist', an apparent embodiment of the principle of *mens sana in corpore sano*, learns that his sight is threatened. The photophobia and floaters from which he is suffering suggest that the protagonist has intermediate uveitis, a normally self-resolving inflammation of the uvea, the pigmented layer of the eyeball; soon, however, his mind disintegrates too. Feeling dehumanised, he questions his own continued existence in a sightless, shifting world in which he feels he has no purpose. Suicide beckons him, as it does the female protagonist in 'Fear' – an unsettling tale set on the cliffs and probably inspired by Catherine's and H.G.'s time living at Sandgate, Kent.

This anthology contains many stories which critique the institution of marriage and complement Catherine's observations on the subject in *The Open Heart*. 'Fear' echoes the ending of *The Wing of Azrael* (1889), the triple-decker novel written by one of marriage's strongest opponents, the First Wave Feminist Mona Caird. Just as Caird's innocent heroine senses that her fiancé is too handsome to be trustworthy, Mary's nocturnal presentiment in Catherine's 'The Beautiful House' uncovers the fiend behind Evan Hardie's stalwart appearance and knightly facade. Caird and Catherine represent women who strive to live independently of male influence, but their happiness is threatened by those (often women) who allow the male to dominate and conquer. It is a woman in 'The Fugitives' who betrays a fleeing wife. In the wake of the Clitheroe Abduction Case in 1891, it was ruled that a husband could no longer incarcerate his wife. This makes 'The Kneeling Image' – reminiscent of the way in which the lifelike image of a wife is imprisoned in a work of art in Robert Browning's 'My Last Duchess' (1842) – all the more horrific.

Stories such as this have an echo of her husband's work. The narratives of H.G. Wells are scattered with purloined bodies and souls that are trapped and living the wrong lives. Like the leisured, domestic 'queen' idealized in John Ruskin's influential *Sesame and Lilies* (1865), Rosalind Bray, the heroine of 'In a Walled Garden', leads a comfortable and sheltered life that is superficially as pretty as a painting. That is, until an encounter with a stranger shows her that her life has actually taken the form of, as H.G. might put it, 'that colourless contentment that replaces happiness'.[5]

Written during the Sandgate years, Catherine's confessional letter to Wells reveals that she too could feel trapped. We also have the impression that she experiences overwhelming sensations of guilt for expressing her emotions:

> I feel tonight *so* tired of playing wiv' making the home comfy, & do [sic] if there was only one dear rest place in the world. & that was in the arms & heart of you. [...] The high bright ambitions one begins with, the dismal concessions – the growth, like a clogging hard crust over one of house & furniture & a lot of clothes & books & gardens, a load dragging one down. If I set out to make a comfortable home for you to do work in, I merely succeed in contriving a place where you are bored to death. [...] Well, dear, I don't think I

5 H.G. Wells, 'Zoological Retrogression', reprinted in *The Fin de Siècle: A Reader in Cultural History, c. 1880–1900*, edited by Sally Ledger and Roger Luckhurst (Oxford: Oxford University Press, 2000), pp. 5–12 (p. 9).

> ought to send you such a letter. It's only a mood you know, but theres [sic] no time to write another & I have been letting myself go in a foolish fashion.[6]

By contrast Wells (as he confesses) did have outbursts. One wonders if Catherine's experience of these flare-ups found their way into her story 'Fear'. 'The Last Fairy' also seems to reflect the random occurrence of fun and games and unnerving displays of temper.

It was never really possible to know a person completely, her fiction implies, for the human soul was comprised of so many sides – just like the metaphorical 'solid polyhedron' of *The Open Heart*. The unpredictability of human nature was encapsulated in Richard Mansfield's performances on stage, in which his transformation from the stunted Hyde to the respectable, upright Dr Jekyll both stunned and troubled audiences at the end of the 1880s, the time of the Whitechapel Murders. It is not then surprising that the teenager in Catherine's 'The Ghost' thinks that the entity she sees before her is the man whose theatrical performances she admires. This horror, for which we are unprepared, together with Catherine's other works, demands us to ask ourselves how much of the person we see before us is real or just a brilliant piece of stagecraft?

---

6 Smith, David C. (ed.), *The Correspondence of H.G. Wells: Volume I, 1880–1903* (London: Pickering & Chatto, 1998), letter dated 26 April 1906, p. 456.

The Open Heart

The Open Heart is a work of mixed genres, almost impossible to classify. It begins with an elaborate framing narrative: a Preface, signed 'J.G. Williams' (not his real name), explaining that the manuscript that follows was left to him, with instructions for its publication, by his friend Edgar Crawshay who had committed suicide. How the manuscript came into Crawshay's possession is not revealed, but Williams believes his friend had travelled to the Pacific 'to answer its human cry' – or, in other words, in an unsuccessful search for its author.

What he knew of her is quite unclear. Williams describes Crawshay as an 'indolent, leisure-loving man' and does not mention his age, but he sounds significantly more mature than the 27-year-old author, who addresses what she affirms is an imaginary reader, the 'spiritual brother of my soul'. Could Crawshay have convinced himself that he was her 'spiritual brother'? That is just one of the text's unsolved mysteries. In any case Crawshay and the framing narrative are forgotten as soon as we begin the manuscript's opening chapter with its cancelled title, 'Letter from a Lost Island'.

At first the narrator tells how, having suffered shipwreck on an ocean liner bound for Auckland, she found herself alone on a deserted island which to her seemed like 'fairyland, or the Utopia of dreams, or perhaps… some distant, forgotten part of Heaven'. The harrowing details of the ship's foundering, and of her survival in an open boat from which her fellow-passengers have somehow disappeared, are deliberately passed over. Far from being traumatized by these experiences, once she comes ashore the narrator is overwhelmed by the beauty of the 'enchanted island' and by her wonder at what she finds there. At its centre is a large, abandoned palace with extensive gardens, apparently 'built by some incredibly wealthy, half-mad monarch of the past, some bygone Ludwig or Shah Jehan, a place accidentally forgotten by humanity' (though still, it seems, equipped with the necessities of life). In front of the palace, very briefly, she glimpses a 'vision of people, silken-clad or naked in the sunlight', but she very soon realises that she is the only person there.

The palace and its surroundings are the implicit setting for the rest of the story, although for long passages this is forgotten as the author reflects on the tribulations, the violence and the unhappiness of the world she has left behind. We are indeed reading a utopian text in some ways reminiscent of an H.G. Wells novel such as *Men Like Gods* (1923), where the narrator's chance relocation to an ideal world becomes a vehicle for devastating criticisms of the society we know.

During the weeks or months of her solitude, the author records her thoughts in a diary addressed to a single reader who may or may not be 'the invisible genius of this paradise'. The physical reality of the island setting soon fades, since the author shows no interest in going down to the shore, let alone in gazing out to sea or looking for boats on the horizon. Later, when she leaves the palace to wander down long 'allées' and to observe the wildlife of the surrounding forests, there are times when we seem no longer to be in the South Seas but in an English parkland with its birch and willow and bluebell woods – an atmosphere suffused with a poised, expectant silence which we encounter in 'April in the Wood'.

Much of the manuscript's opening chapter consists of introspective essays exploring the nature of love, the reasons for its failure and the barriers to full understanding and mutual equality that have poisoned relations between the sexes throughout human history.

Here, too, there are hints of internal contradiction; the author longs for a mate 'who shall answer to our spiritual needs as Echo to our voice', yet rejects the Platonic notion of the divided soul seeking to reunite with its other half. She tries to persuade herself of the superiority of an imaginary and disembodied love while clearly registering this as self-deception. Soon the diary becomes a spiritual autobiography, telling of the childhood and adolescence of a figure whom it is tempting to see as Catherine Wells herself, even though (since the author remembers the death in 1898 of the British prime minister William Gladstone as a significant event of her childhood) we are reminded that she is some 20 years younger than Wells. Above all, she describes how 'We of this generation...have had to come out of the shelter of those religious beliefs into which we were born and bred' – an experience doubtless shared by more than one generation growing up in the late Victorian world.

The author of *The Open Heart* outlines her spiritual development through several phases, tracing the conflict between religious (specifically Anglican) piety and her growing desire for sexual love and excitement. The religious life, as she saw it, offered a refuge from the world's complexity and disappointments at the same time that it harshly rejected the beauty of nature and the promptings of natural instinct. In these passages the diarist vividly recalls her youthful emotional states while also showing evidence of wide reading and philosophical reflection: there are allusions to the myth of Danaë (imprisoned by her father in a bronze chamber under the court of his palace), to Cicero's essay *De Senectute*, to the Book of Revelation and to the *Imitatio Christi* of Thomas à Kempis, as well as to now forgotten Victorian figures such as the fashionable evangelical novelist Susan Warner (pen-name Elizabeth Wetherell) and the Jewish writer Grace Aguilar.

In addition to the mysteries of religion and sex, in another section of the diary she tells of her fascination with a third 'mystery', the field of scientific knowledge. This she began to explore when, as a girl, she started to collect items of potentially scientific apparatus and to dream of conducting chemical experiments way beyond her means. It is not hard to connect the author of this highly amusing passage in Chapter Two with the keen would-be science teacher who had once turned up in H.G. Wells's biology class. The author says nothing of her professional aspirations, however. Instead she speaks of the hopes and the profound disillusionment involved in her engagement to be married, a future that was thwarted when her lover died prematurely – though not before their love had passed its first intoxication and had become tainted by jealousy and mutual reserve. In part of Chapter Three, the diary expands into a powerful feminist essay on women's need for freedom from their subjection to men, and on how marriage deprives (presumably middle-class) women of their liberty by excluding them from the world of work. The author sums up her aspirations for the personal life in the following terms:

> To strive one's utmost towards intelligence, to open one's heart to its widest to love and to measure one's conduct constantly against the standard of one's sense of beauty is to live religiously and not in vain.

Chapter Four, with its opening fable of the old man who refused to sell his beloved songbird, marks another abrupt shift of focus and a return to the celebration of the natural beauty of the author's deserted island. Increasingly, she explores the experience of solitude and probes the ambiguity of the 'little brother' to whom every section of the diary has been addressed. Is he, as at first implied, a wholly imaginary figure? Or might he assume corporeal form and come to join her on the island? As her loneliness intensifies, the author's consciousness becomes all-pervaded by fantasies of his possible presence there. The mind-games played by one who (in the words of a poem by Catherine Wells inspired by Chopin's Prelude no. 6, op. 28) 'listens for a footstep/Knowing it will not come'[7] lead to her final *cri de coeur*, which is marked as 'The End' of her story – though whether it was the conclusion that Catherine Wells intended we shall never know.

As to the identity of the 'little brother', whether in the diarist's or in Catherine Wells's own imagination, we are (no doubt deliberately) left in the dark. Some readers have found him to be an idealized version of the all-too-absent H.G. Wells; others may reject that interpretation vehemently. *The Open Heart* was left unfinished. While it may be read as a most haunting and memorable exploration of Catherine Wells's private and inner emotions, it is also a fiction which aims to keep that privacy intact.

Patrick Parrinder and Emelyne Godfrey

7 *The Book of Catherine Wells*, p. 286 (p. 276 in this edition).

The Book of CATHERINE WELLS: Prose

The Last Fairy

IN THE LATE SUMMER of a few years ago the last of the fairies looked over her wardrobe of disguises, selected that of an old apple-woman as the least threadbare, and went walking along a country road. Having yet some remnants of her magic power, the fairy did not find the apple-basket heavy. But she knew she was growing old. She had not been out in the world for a long time, and when she put on her disguise she had much the same feeling that our grandmothers had when they would say: "My dear, this is the very last summer I shall wear a *hat*." (In those days there were bonnets for the mature.) She had it in her bones that it was probably the last time she would go adventuring among human beings.

They were getting a bit beyond her. Her latest appearances on earth, though her memory was not so good as it used to be and she was not very clear about them, had been, she knew, uncomfortable on the whole and socially unsuccessful. She had got a young kitchenmaid into a lot of trouble by sending her magically to a ball, where in a hurry of coming away she dropped her shoe; and it being traced home to her, the poor girl lost her situation. Another time she had met a bright young Boy Scout who, in the course of business, had helped her across a crowded street, and to whom in return she had given three magic wishes; he had used the third wish to wish for three more and so on, until the poor old fairy had had to retire hastily to fairyland in a bankrupt state, and live very quietly and economically for several years to recover herself.

Such experiences had shaken her nerve. She resolved as she walked along the road to be careful this time, to remember that she wasn't young any more, and not to try anything difficult or dangerous in the magic way. Her Rodeo days were over. To-day she was just out for a little exercise in the sunshine; perhaps she might bring off a few pretty surprises among these mortals, perform a few kindly acts. That was the idea. That, she insisted, really was the idea. Nothing like – and the old fairy's eyes brightened maliciously at a memory or two. No, no, of course not! Nothing like that. *That* was ages ago.

She looked about her. During her long life she had seen a good deal of the world, and this bit of it, she thought, looked uncommonly Dutch. She was approaching a small town, a little town neatly planted on a landscape of neat fields; there was no untidiness about its outskirts, no dust heaps, no sheds or *débris*. It hung on a neat canal like a bead on a string. Presently she would see some people. It was quite a long time since she had met human beings; some of them were delightful, but some of them were very odd. Occasionally one simply had to use extreme measures with them in self-defence. All sorts of things one had to do. Change them into toads, for instance. *Had* to. A most useful device.

A qualm of anxiety came into the old fairy's mind. Did she remember now how that toad charm went?

Not far along the road in front of her was the hind part of a horse. It protruded from a stable; she could not see its fore part, nor the ostler who was inside, putting a collar over its head. Just to see if she had got it right the old fairy pronounced what she remembered as the Toad Charm.

The result surprised her. The hindquarters of the horse dropped about a foot in height, the legs bent to an acuter angle, great claws spurted from the hoofs, and the short stump of hairy brown tail shot out into a great scaly blue and green and gold appendage some six feet long. The dragon breathed for the first time in that character, and the ostler was badly burnt.

The ostler squealed and dropped the harness, and the dragon, backing out of the shed, snorted more fire, unfurled great leathery wings, and flapped heavily away over the red-tiled roofs with a noise like books being slapped together at spring-cleaning time. The fairy was slightly disconcerted for a moment, and then she laughed very heartily.

The ostler, rushing out of the stable, saw an old apple-woman. "Seen my horse, missus?" he called out to her.

Now one of the fairy's maxims was "Never explain, never apologise." Feigning deafness, she merely plodded on, and the ostler, wasting no more time on her, ran off in the direction he supposed his property had bolted.

The old fairy followed, a little uneasy at what she had done. Letting loose a dragon was, after all, a serious matter. It was exactly the kind of incident she had been determined to avoid. Funny how old habits— Anyhow, it was done now. With genuine regret she tried her best to think how she had gone wrong. She believed she knew what mistake she had made. The two charms were alike – up to a point. She was sorry about it. Sometimes these dragons did a lot of mischief. She must follow it up, and put things right again. She would find the dragon, change him into a toad first for convenience of carriage, take him back to the stable, and there restore his horse shape.

The incident, however, though unsuccessful in its main intention, had refreshed her and increased her confidence, and given her that natural satisfaction that follows the exercise of one's gifts. She went up a narrow cobbled street – looking for trouble, a harsh critic might say. It was a cheerful street. Its houses were painted brightly in green and white and red and blue; they had high-pitched, gabled roofs, and pinks and geraniums dangled gaily from their window-boxes. A man in a white linen overall came round a corner trundling a barrow of big round cheeses coloured like huge oranges. She passed the canal over a low bridge, and met more and yet more white-clad men trundling and carrying these orange-coloured cheeses. And then she came into a market square so piled about with glossy, golden cheeses, on stalls, on barrows, on the ground, that it seemed as if the sun had suddenly burst out, though indeed it had been shining all the time. There were ruddy apples too, and bright green cabbages, and tethered in temporary stalls were black and white cows with velvety skins. At one side of the market square was the canal, and barges loaded with flowers and more orange cannon-ball cheeses were moored by a flight of steps.

The old fairy was delighted with the pretty place. She felt that she might find her chance here to do a lot of nice magics, little things people couldn't do for themselves, and that they would be grateful to her for thinking of. She would be the most wonderful Good Fairy that ever was. She thought that she wanted to do good out of the sweetness of her own nature, but, as a matter of fact, it was partly a way of smothering her uneasy conscience at having let loose a dragon on these innocent townsfolk, and partly it was a way of shirking the extreme difficulty of her immediate duty, which was plainly to find the animal. But she let herself be distracted. People were standing about gossiping to one another, and glancing up every now and then at the big clock in the turret of the Town Hall. Suddenly it boomed ten times, and above its brazen face a large gilt angel raised a trumpet to his mouth and blew a clockwork blast. A door sprang open, a procession of wooden soldiers on horseback came forth, jerked round a platform, and went in again, the door slammed upon them, the angel blew his trumpet once more, and with a burst of noise and chatter the market opened.

Women in snowy lace caps bought the cabbages, and men in baggy trousers chaffered the cheeses, and carried them to and fro piled on wooden trays. The old fairy put down her apple-basket at a convenient place where she could sit on a low parapet, and turned over her stock-in-trade. It was a long time since she had taken out the apple-basket, but it looked all right. There were some apples of particularly delicious flavour, she knew, suitable for good children, and there were some others equally pleasant to look at containing maggots for bad children. There were some that were just apples, to give to the police, and there were a few that were very special, one that sent you to sleep for a hundred years, one that contained a dose of the precious Elixir of Youth, and a small poisoned one for ogres. The old fairy put these at the back, arranged the others to her satisfaction, and sat down looking very simple and countryfied and old-world indeed.

Presently she noticed that an aged woman with a market-basket had singled her out. She was a chubby old lady with cheeks like rosy apples themselves, and she smiled at the fairy as if they were two people who were sure to get on together. She was accompanied by an old man in a large, flapping felt hat and a gay crimson waistcoat, and hanging on to them was a pigtailed child with a freckled face. Directly the old fairy saw her she knew that she wasn't a good child. She had hooked her arm into her grandmother's, and was lugging the old lady back to a sweet-stuff stall.

"Presently, Priscilla," said the nice old lady, with her eye on the apples.

"No! want it now," whined this unpleasant child.

"Silence, Priscilla!" said the grandfather sternly, and looked so awful for a moment that even Priscilla was cowed. The old lady turned to the fairy.

"And how much might you be asking for these?" she said.

The fairy named a price rather less than she heard the other apple-sellers asking, as a kindness to the nice old lady. Being a fairy, she knew nothing about the wickedness of underselling.

The offensive Priscilla crept up to a cat sitting on the parapet, pulled its tail hard and suddenly, and jumped back to her grandparents out of reach. There was a piercing "miaw" and the cat flew along the parapet and up a wall. The fairy saw all this, but the grandparents did not. Grandfather was greeting a friend with long sweeps of his dignified hat, and grandmother was buying the apples. The bad child then sidled up to a near stall where a milk churn was standing full of milk. She gave it a push, it went over the back of the stall with a terrific clatter and deluge of milk, and Priscilla was back beside her grandmother gazing at the apples before anyone except the old fairy realised what was happening.

The purchased apples were now in the old lady's basket. Priscilla caught sight of them, snatched one out of the basket, and bit it in half before anyone could stop her.

Very properly it was full of maggots. A nice child could not have had such an apple, but if it could have, it would never have behaved with the explosive vehemence of Priscilla.

"Pris-*cilla*!" cried her grandmother, snatching away her skirt.

Priscilla yelled with nausea and fury, and stamped her feet. Her grandfather was diverted from his conversation and turned round upon this scene. He aimed a smack at Priscilla, but missed.

The old lady turned apologetically to the fairy. "It wasn't a very nice apple, was it?" she said reproachfully.

The fairy was sorry to have hurt the old lady's feelings. "It looked quite sound and sweet," she said. "And I don't think *you'll* find a bad one among them, ma'am. Let me give you another to make it up." She turned over the apples in her basket to pick out a fine one. But a great disturbance broke out.

Grandfather had been scolding Priscilla, and Priscilla had kicked him. Whereupon grandfather grabbed at Priscilla and tried to shake her. This all made a lot of noise.

"I'm afraid she's a naughty little girl," said the fairy to the old lady, sympathetically. "You have a deal of trouble with her, I can see."

"Well, we mustn't be too hard on children," said the gentle old lady. "I'm sure I wish I was young again myself sometimes, that I do. And I dare say I was a trouble enough to my poor mother."

The fairy had picked out the best apple she could find to give the old lady, but now she had a sudden idea. Here surely was a chance to give this delightful old personage the wish of her heart. She took out the apple containing the Elixir of Youth.

"This is the one I'd choose for you, my dear," she said. "Do taste it now."

The grandmother laughed. "Too hard for my old teeth," she said.

"Just try it," urged the fairy, magically softening the apple.

The old lady bit the apple gingerly, and looked surprised. It was soft and very juicy, like a ripe peach, and broke in her hand so that she had to push it nearly all into her mouth for tidiness' sake. And then she disappeared!

The dear old lady had suddenly and completely disappeared, and in her place stood a duplicate Priscilla, the two children standing side by side like a pair of pictures for a stereoscopic view. At this surprising sight the grandfather uttered a cry of rage. "Magic! Witchcraft!" he spluttered, shaking his fist at the fairy and waving his stick, and he turned round and called out to everyone about him.

"There's a witch here!" he shouted. "A witch!"

People turned their heads and stared. The fairy realised with a touch of panic that things might be awkward for her. "Witch! Witch!" yelled the old man, beside himself. All the crowd was now turning round on the group, but at first, seeing the duplicate Priscillas, they thought he was shouting "which?" – a very natural mistake – and merely wondered aloud and jocosely at the excitement displayed by the grandfather of twins. "He dunno which is which," explained a bright-witted cheesemonger with a happy laugh.

But the fairy saw there was not a minute to lose. She grasped all her forces and wished the old gentleman's mouth stopped with – with—

What could she stop it with? He was opening his mouth to shout again. "Oh – the nearest thing!" she completed hastily.

It was a cheese. It happened to be the bottom corner cheese of a pile that was arranged on the next stall in the shape of a truncated pyramid. It was the critical key cheese, so to speak, in the base of the heap. When it hopped off the stall into the mouth of Priscilla's grandfather the cheeses above it began to slide and dollop one by one off the stall to the ground and roll along the sloping pavement of the market-place to the stone steps. Under the steps was a convenient barge. Dollop, dollop, down the steps they went, one after the other, very nicely and methodically on the whole, into that barge. The bargee had just finished unloading his cheeses into crates on the quay. He was at the farther end of the barge with his back to the steps; he stood upright and stretched himself, and wiped his mouth expectantly on the back of his hand. "Ah-you-ay!" he called to a small boy who might run the necessary errand. As he did so the first of the travelling cheeses entered the barge and rolled between his feet. He stooped again and picked it up and added it to his pile on the quay, and as he did so another rolled into its place, and in its turn another.

"Oo-*er*!" said the bargee, at the twenty-third cheese.

It occurred to him to look round.

His head was beneath the level of the pavement. All he saw was a walloping rush of cheeses into his barge, coming quicker and quicker until they descended in spate and were bumping him heartily about the knees.

There is an expression sometimes used in musical notation – *cadenza*. It means that trills and ornamental roulades may be indulged in at that point to the limit of the singer's accomplishment. So instead of putting down here what the bargee said, I will just write: *Cadenza*.

Meanwhile a happy crowd rejoiced at the amusing coincidence that, on the collapse of a stall piled with cheeses, one of these had bounced up and sideways, hit a choleric old gentleman in the face, and embedded itself between his teeth. The stall-keeper was annoyed at first at this accident to hit his stock-in-trade, but he became convulsed with merriment as he realised what had not, as a matter of fact, happened.

"Don't you be troubling yourself," he spluttered to the old man, who had grasped the cheese with both hands and was trying to wrench it out of his teeth. "I'll give it yer!" He turned to the crowd. "He can keep it now, I don't mind."

"'Tis a good breakfast you've got there, Mynheer," shouted someone.

The old gentleman tugged away at the cheese, but he could not dislodge it. He could not even see over it; a baleful eye came sideways round its glossy curve, and glared at the fairy. The newly created Priscilla wept, but her prototype was looking interested and happy.

"'Tis a fresh one," said the stall-keeper, amid new roars of laughter.

That, thought the perturbed fairy, is something. And, she continued, applying one of her most used maxims, things might be worse. In a moment she would be able to think of some way of keeping his mouth shut more comfortably.

That first, and then something could be done quickly to straighten out this Priscilla muddle. But before there was time for thinking, her first mistake added itself to the confusion. A noise up above them, like the imitation off-stage of a galloping horse in a provincial theatre, grew in volume and interrupted the innocent merriment of the crowd; a great shadow swept across the sunny market-place, volumes of smoke came over the Town Hall roof, and the dragon sailed into view. It tried to alight on the roof ridge, missed it, and scrabbled about to get a foothold, dislodging several tiles and breathing sootily as if its wick wanted trimming.

"'Tis a big bird and no mistake," said a matter-of-fact person.

"Look at the smuts on my apron!" said a good hausfrau.

"Ooooh, how bew-tiful!" said the original Priscilla, awestruck.

"Now that," said a naturalist looking out of a third-floor window through his spectacles, "is not a heron."

"Why are they all making such a fuss about a cloud?" said a short-sighted old lady. The dragon looked down and realised that a long time had elapsed since its last meal. "Thunder!" said the old lady. "I *said* it was a cloud."

Now this dragon, that had been so abruptly called out of the limbo of legendary and discredited animals by the old fairy, was about as rusty and out of practice at its business as she was herself. It clung awkwardly to the roof, bewildered by the clamour from below. Dim instincts stirred within it. Something, it knew, was expected of it – but what? It must have felt rather as one does when, to amuse the company, one is led into a room blindfolded and 'willed' by tittering friends. The dragon caught sight of the gilt angel on the clock tower. Was that it? He plunged at it, grasped it in his claws, tore it easily from its anchorage, and sailed off with it across the red roofs. He spoilt a lot of tulips just outside the town, where he sat for a time forcing this indigestible meal into his mouth. It was a tough morsel. The angel's pedestal disappeared at last, very like the end coach of an overladen train struggling into a tunnel.

But the fairy was immensely relieved by this turn of affairs. She felt that there might have been an accident here that would really have spoilt her day. The dragon might have taken off the wrong Priscilla and eaten her. Or anybody. Something too difficult even for a fairy to put right again. Whereas now, if they would only give her time, if they would only stop pushing and shouting and give her time to think—

"Hi, stop him!" shouted the ostler, appearing suddenly running from the end of a street and pointing to the trail of smoke that wound up the dragon's exit. "That's my horse."

"No, no, mister, that warn't no *horse*," explained a bystander kindly.

"Corse it was my horse!" shouted the ostler. "Bolted. Why couldn't you hold him, somebody? You see a horse running away and nobody's got the gumption—" (*Cadenza.*)

He was so insistent that one or two men standing round began to wonder why indeed they hadn't somehow thought of holding the animal until its rightful owner came.

"I dunno," said one.

"Seemed a bit wild-like," said another.

"Thought it was a bird, maybe," nearly said another – till he realised half through the sentence what palpable nonsense he was talking, and ended with a helpful clearing of the throat.

"Which way'd it go?" demanded the ostler; and then he caught sight of the old fairy. The fairy had not liked the look in the ostler's eye; she felt she couldn't think while he was there so near to her, and so she was very busily and quietly packing up her apples and preparing to slip away without bothering anybody.

"That's the old woman!" he shouted, leaping towards her. "That's the old woman who scared my horse. Mischievous old witch! She come along behind my horse, wot's as quiet usually as any animal could be, and she made it jump."

He threw out his hand to grasp her by the shoulder.

The fairy was alarmed. "Go back!" she thought she said, but without knowing it she spoke those simple words in her native tongue.

The effect was immediate. The ostler recoiled even as he touched her, stood for a moment shouting:

"Jump – it – made – she – and – be – could – animal – any – as – usually quiet as wot's horse my behind, along come she, witch, old mischievous, horse my scared who woman old the that's!" and then started running backwards very rapidly across the market-place with his eyes glaring at her until he reached the end of the street and, still running backwards, disappeared.

"Dear, dear!" said the old fairy, and sat down again behind her basket. "I must have said the Backward Spell." The lighter-minded portion of the crowd, convinced that the ostler was a merry fellow escaped from a travelling circus, laughed and slapped each other and ran after him out of the square. This relieved pressure and removed a good deal of noise, and the old fairy was just getting her breath again when the dragon came flustering back over the roofs and dropped limply into the market-place. Its throat ached, it was thoroughly uncomfortable, it felt a queer disposition to get alongside human beings and have its nose rubbed and be given a hot bran mash. Then perhaps this nubbly feeling inside would disappear. Down among all these people there must be someone of importance who could do this thing. And as if in answer to the helpless instinct of this dumb animal, a personage in a long robe and gold-laced hat came pacing with great dignity just at that very moment out of the Town Hall. The dragon precipitated itself towards him.

"Oh! It's going to eat him!" cried the fairy in a panic. "Now for it! The Toad Charm!" She began it hurriedly – too hurriedly. The red and rolling eye of the dragon, the fiery breath, the yawning and terrible jaws studded with pointed, glittering teeth, peeled off its head like a plum skin, and revealed the placid visage of a thoroughbred Dutch cow. "That isn't right!" flashed through the fairy's mind, even in mid-sentence, and she altered the end of her spell. The black and white splotches that were spreading rapidly along the back of the animal were stopped midway, its hindquarters collapsed to half their size, and a mass of spiky quills shot out and enveloped them.

Priscilla, alone of all the spectators, possessed that simple directness of intellect to know what she was seeing when she saw it. "Cowcupine," said Priscilla.

Cowcupine, or whatever the *mésalliance* might be, it had no powers of flight, and its bulky form hurtled down on the top of the unfortunate personage and pinned him to the ground.

"Horses like that oughtn't to be allowed about," said the matter-of-fact person.

"Somebody will get knocked down," said the short-sighted old lady.

The naturalist heard a noise and glanced out; but as it only came from the ground he turned back to his bird-stuffing.

"Now I've made another mistake," thought the fairy. And then she had a flash of insight. "Am I perhaps doing more harm here than good?" she wondered.

People were laughing. The fairy could not see what they were laughing at, but it seemed to be at the struggles of the creature that still wallowed helplessly over the gold-laced and important personage. No one understood its peculiar difficulty. For as a cow gets up hindquarters first and a porcupine gets up forequarters first, it follows that this unfortunate combination could not get up at all. The naturalist would have been able to explain this to everyone, if he had not been so busy stuffing.

"They oughtn't to laugh at that gentleman," said the fairy. "They mustn't laugh at him." But they went on laughing and the gold-laced personage went on struggling.

"If only it hadn't been something so silly!" she said, stamping her foot. "If it had been some splendid, noble animal that had run up to him trustingly. Like an elephant, or—"

The important personage was none too pleased when the bulk above him heaved, swayed, and resettled itself, and getting his head twisted round he peered up and saw that it was an elephant that encumbered him.

"I didn't mean that!" cried out the distracted fairy, though no one was listening to her. "Stop! I didn't mean it! Oh, I am losing my head!" she wound up.

She made a great effort to collect herself. "You," she said, concentrating on the elephant, be smaller, *smaller*, the smallest animal there is."

And the elephant disappeared…

"I had just got hold of the bridle when the horse bolted again," said the matter-of-fact person over his mug of ale that evening, telling the whole affair just as it did not happen to his neighbour. "Bolted right out of the Square, and we never saw it no more."

"Went back to its stable most likely," said his neighbour, knocking out his pipe, and thinking it a dull tale.

The personage was helped up. He stood for a moment while his hat was looked for and brushed up and given to him. As soon as he was erect again the crowd became wonderfully silent and respectful. He looked at them as if he was going to make a speech. Then he seemed restless…

And disappeared into the Town Hall hastily, scratching.

"Bother!" said the fairy, realising his trouble. "I couldn't even manage that business properly."

She sat down by her apple-basket, and the people who had crowded together about the various disasters she had caused began to disperse and drift away and turn back again to their own affairs. The old fairy looked at them all, and suddenly she felt very tired. Things hadn't gone quite as she intended. That dragon business was over, anyhow, thank goodness; she had put that mistake right. Now she would like a rest. It wasn't so warm and sunny in this world nowadays as it used to be. The world had changed; there were not the hot summer days now that she remembered in her youth. It was no good catching cold; she had better go home. To-morrow, if it was finer—

She covered up the apples, keeping very resolutely out of her mind the thought that this was her last good-bye to earth. She got up slowly, and prepared to go.

There was a touch upon her arm.

She turned, and there was a Priscilla, looking at her pleadingly. Ah! Yes, she had forgotten that little disaster. But which Priscilla was this?

"Do you believe in fairies?" asked the old fairy.

The Priscilla nodded, and her eyes were brimming with tears.

A happy inspiration came to the old fairy, and she remembered what to say. The grandmother flashed back into existence, looked a little confused for a moment, and said, hesitatingly, as though she did not quite know why:

"Thank you!"

And then she smiled a farewell and turned away.

Well, that was better. One wasn't so played out, after all. The old fairy looked round the market-place again, and it came to her that it would be an effective and altogether splendid end to her visit to turn all these hundreds of piled yellow cheeses into solid gold, as a farewell present to these people who had been so amusing, and whom, without intending to, she had rather knocked about. It would astonish them to see an old apple-woman do that, a simple old woman who had been sitting there all the afternoon without their noticing her. And then she would depart, amid the plaudits of the populace. They would remember her always, gratefully and wonderingly. They would tell their children about her, and write a legend about her in long verses.

Now how did the gold charm begin?

And then just in time she saw Priscilla's grandfather. He was sitting leaning on the parapet not far away, and he had given up tugging at the cheese in his mouth, and he was just crying big tears.

It would kill him. It would certainly kill him.

Well, well, she supposed she had better spend the little force she had left in releasing him. So she wished his cheese away, and as it happened that just then Priscilla's grandmother had come back to him and given a pull at it herself, he thought to the end of his days that it was by her cleverness that he was set free.

Was there anything else? The fairy looked round, and the big door of the Town Hall reminded her of yet another duty. Let the smallest of all animals be dead!

And then she went.

"Did anything happen at the market today?" asked Mevrouw van Teulype that evening of Mynheer van Teulype.

"Nothing out of the way in particular," he replied. "There was a horse got loose and knocked over a stall of cheeses."

"People ought to be more careful," said Mevrouw.

"I shall keep a horse when I'm big," said Priscilla to herself with her eye on a yellow-haired boy in the next garden...

"After just the beginning," said the grandmother to a neighbour, "Priscilla was no trouble at all, all the morning."

"Well, so that's all blown over," said the fairy, at home again, tucking up her feet on a toadstool and putting a little, just a *very* little, drop of old nectar in her tea.

She had forgotten the ostler – still running backwards – for ever, who knows? But being in Holland, he was probably stopped before long by a canal. And water, as everybody knows, will wash away any charms but those which are naturally one's own.

The Beautiful House

MARY HASTINGS at thirty-five looked older than her age, not by any line in her handsome face but by a dignity of carriage that went beyond her years, and by the early grey that had touched ever so lightly the waves of her abundant dark hair. Spinsterhood suited her temperament and had not faded her vitality in the slightest degree, indeed her independence and the passage of time had marked her only with a finer gravity of bearing. Her occupation gave her abiding content, she was an able and even distinguished landscape painter, and her sufficient income was increased by the sale of the sketches that she liked least. Her best work she either kept, or gave away.

Behind her open manner she had reserves of shyness, and although circumstances and her generous nature had made her rich in friends, it was thus comparatively late and when her youth was gone that she formed a relationship with anyone which shone supreme. This made it all the more precious to her. It happens to most human beings to love at least once with the love that finds no flaw, and that experience came to Mary Hastings through her friendship with a quite young girl, Sylvia Brunton, an intimacy which had its birth and ardent life, and faded and died at last like other human things.

They became acquainted at one of those large miscellaneous art schools at which English girls with a sense of the beautiful are so prone to mark the time between the ages of twenty and thirty. Sylvia was one of those time-markers, a girl with that overpowering sense of the responsibility of life which comes to the serious young, a trust of years and opportunity which must be met, it seemed to her, and met instantly, and which she had all too hastily supposed was an obligation to paint pictures. She was fair and as slender and lovely as a stitchwort flower in a hedge, and Mary Hastings saw her, and in a manner fell in love with her on an occasion when she went back with the sudden fancy to sketch the place where she had worked so many years before. In her lonely way, Mary Hastings had a sharpened and fastidious enjoyment of scents and sounds and visual impressions; she went back to soak in the atmosphere of the shabby familiar place and its distinctive reek of paint, exactly as a man might roll port wine under his tongue.

With a few meetings their mutual liking flamed to intimacy.

Like all congenialities it was largely inexplicable. They liked the same things. They discovered in each other the same passion for the country and the old life of the country, the quiet interiors of eighteenth-century houses, flower-gardens, the smooth surfaces of fine china and polished wood. They liked the same books, the same poets. And between them there was that sense of *rapport*, that effect of rapid mutual understanding that finds some of its happiest examplars among women. Their sense of intimacy embraced even the large part of each other's mind that was left unexplored. Their conversation became as confident as a player's touch upon a tuned instrument, it left many notes unstruck, and yet they were secure that the most probing search would discover no jarring string.

And then to intensify their communion, they found the house, which gathered together the threads of their love, and held it as a body should its soul.

Mary Hastings had a four-roomed cottage in Sussex which she called her sketching tent, and there Sylvia came to her for a midsummer visit. It was adjacent to a farmhouse from which the farmer's wife came over to cook and clean for them. They became more and more delighted with each other. Sylvia imported a note of gay picnicking into the cottage that had never appeared there before, and a touch of adventure into their daily meals and walks that was delightfully novel and amusing to Mary. They took long rambling walks, invaded cottages and pleasant farmhouses for meals of that egg and jam nature so attractive to women, and in their long evenings discovered the peculiar satisfactions of reading aloud. It was on their last day together that they found the house. They had taken their lunch, and raided further in their walk indefinitely southward than they had ever done before; and in the full beauty of a July afternoon that had been cooled by a brief and exquisite shower they emerged from a little wood of willows upon an open park-like space, with gentle grass slopes that fell away in gracious sweeps, set here and there with fine beech-trees and oaks. At one side the trees thickened and arched over a rising glade, its grassy floor sunbespattered; before them the slope rose to a trim hedge, and over the shoulder of some trees showed a chimney stack.

"If we are going to have the luck we deserve," Mary had remarked, "that will be an inn where we can get tea."

They came round the hedge to find a white gate, and then they saw the house.

They might perhaps have found it difficult to convey to anyone but each other how supremely beautiful the house seemed to them. At the sight of it Sylvia gave a little cry of rapture, and grasped Mary by the arm. It lay long and low to the south like a happy cat stretched to the sun; it was roughly of that E shape dear to the Elizabethans who had built it with an ample porch and little square room above marking the letter's middle stroke, and extending forward at either end as if with arms to embrace them. Its old brick walls were covered at one side with a great ivy that sprang from the earth with a gnarled trunk like a tree, the other was hung with a tangle of vine and wistaria and passion-flower wonderfully intermingled. Great bosses of green moss clustered on the old roof of red tiles that were stained too with grey and ocherous lichens, and on either side of the bricked path that ran between the gate and the brown nail-studded door was a space of green grass edged neatly with clipped box, with an apple-tree or two slanting their trunks to the ground.

They leant over the gate taking it in. "It is, it really is, the house of my utmost dreams," said Mary softly, as if too loud a tone might blow the vision away.

"If we could only look inside," said Sylvia desirously.

"I wonder. We might perhaps ask them if there is any place where we could get tea."

They unlatched the gate and went up the bricked path together. At the door Sylvia with a faint murmur of ecstasy laid her cheek on the sun-drenched stone that framed it. It was one of those spontaneities that freshly enchained Mary's heart. The bell clangoured gently and remotely. The door stood already ajar, and softly treading feet came unhurrying along stone flags behind it. It was opened by a silver-haired old man in neat spare black.

He was most sorry. There was no place for tea. There *was* an inn, a mile away… He conveyed that he thought the inn unworthy of them.

"Has this house a name?" asked Sylvia. "I think," she added extenuatingly, "it's the most beautiful house I've ever seen."

The old man smiled. "Acridge Manse it is properly called," he said. "But my master, he will have it called 'Love o' Women.'"

"Love o' Women!" wondered Sylvia. "Is it as beautiful inside?"

For answer he fell back with a charming gesture of invitation. "My master is away, ma'am," he replied to their hesitancy. "I live alone here with my wife. If you would like to come in…"

"Could we?" Their eyes consulted.

"The house is to let, as a matter of fact," the old man added.

"Oh! then…" and their scruples died.

It was quite as good inside, Sylvia said. It was far better, insisted Mary. They examined the low-beamed, ample rooms at first tentatively and then exhaustively as the allurement of the house enfolded them. It couldn't have been touched, Mary rejoiced, for a hundred years at least. The floor of the stone-flagged hall spread itself wide and ample, the hospitable heart of the house; opposite the door by which they had entered stood open a garden door, an oblong enchantment of translucent leaves of hanging creeper and distant, shining flower colour, framed in the deep cool browns of the hall. Right and left opened low-ceiling, wide rooms, gravely walled and floored with dark old wood, and one that was larger was delicately gay with white panelling and chintz. From a corner in the hall mounted a broad staircase, barred with slenderly twisted rails.

The little library, recessed with deep window bays and deep window-seats, added a fresh astonishment, for dear familiar books were gathered there like welcoming friends. "What could we have done more," said Mary, "if we had chosen them ourselves?" "Everything we've ever talked about seems to be here," marvelled Sylvia. They passed into the garden. And the garden was the garden of their dreams, grave with still lilies and sentinelled with evening primrose, and gay with honeysuckle and roses that swayed and shook falling petals upon them as they went, with wide borders riotous with larkspur and poppies and bell-flowers and pinks and pansies clustering low. A little lawn led them across its soft thick turf to a seat of old stone.

They sat down there in silence.

Mary began to speak softly. "This is very wonderful," she said. "I have never been here before, and yet it is as familiar as if I had known it always. It feels, my dear, as if I had left it years ago, and now come back. Or as if I had already dreamt it all as clearly as I see it now."

Sylvia nodded. "As if one had been a child here," she said. "Oh, look at that old chap!"

That old chap was a laughing head and bust of stone wreathed with carven leaves, that pushed its way out of the ivy beside them and caught the sun full on its face. "Feel how warm and human it is!" said Sylvia, with her slender hands clasping his either cheek.

Mary thought of nothing else but how adorable Sylvia looked, with the transparent pink of her fingers against the grey stone head.

The old butler met them again at the garden door, and smiled. "I've taken the liberty, ma'am," he said, addressing Mary, "of putting tea in the drawing-room." His "ma'am" had a quaint leaning towards "marm" in its intonation.

"But really we mustn't," began Mary Hastings.

"My master would wish it, marm," he said deferentially, but as though it clinched the matter.

They abandoned themselves completely to "the spirit of the thing", as they called it. They had tea in the white-painted, chintz-furnished room, and in the midst of that Sylvia gave a sudden little cry of discovery.

"Mary!" she cried excitedly. "This house is to *let*!"

Mary looked at her aflush with sudden daring. "Shall we take it then?" She tried to throw a note of facetiousness into her voice.

"We *could*, you know," said Sylvia. Her voice dropped. "Our hearts have taken it!" she said.

"We could come here together," she went on. "Just whenever we wanted to. Just you and I. Mary beloved," she almost whispered, "wouldn't you like it?"

Her slender hands lay out along the table, palms turned up. Mary gathered them in her own hands and kissed them.

"I should – like it!" she said, whimsically insistent on the moderate word.

"If only the rent isn't monstrous," said Sylvia. "It ought to be, in fairness."

They put that to the old butler. But he named an astonishingly low sum.

"My master would like it occupied," he said, as if he saw that an explanation was needed. "And there" – he hesitated – "there are conditions. My master wishes me and my wife, marm, to remain and do the service."

"As if," said Sylvia afterwards, "we could possibly imagine the place half as nice without the old dear."

His master, he explained, was travelling abroad; for an indefinite period. He himself would undertake, he said, to get his consent to a simple form of agreement. There would be no difficulty, he was quite sure. Meanwhile they might really consider the house quite at their disposal. "I'm so glad, marm, if I might say so," he said, "that it's you and the young lady."

"Why?" smiled Mary.

"The people I've had over it, marm! If you're fond of a place, it's cruel. Like showing the blind, I say. And then after they've seen every stick and stone they've said it's too far from a station, or not big enough, or too big, and I can't say I've been sorry, marm."

Sylvia was reminded suddenly of a forgotten question. "Why does your master call it by such an extraordinary name?" she asked.

The old man looked away above the trees, and the shadow of a smile twisted his lips. "He says it won't last long, miss," he said.

They left at last. "It's literally tearing ourselves away," said Sylvia. "We've so grown here in this one afternoon, that it feels as if we'd always been here."

They walked on in silence for a moment, Mary with her hand slipped through Sylvia's arm.

"There was never any fear of the other people taking it," said Sylvia. "It wasn't for them, and if it has a soul – and what could have a soul if that house hasn't – it knew it was waiting all the time for us."

Their minds apart and very much of their talk together after that were concerned with the house. Whatever else might be about them in their daily life when separated, there together they agreed to share a fastness, have there the things they both cared for most, live the kind of life they loved best, talk out their intimate thoughts. It was Mary, although she did not perceive it, who, so much the elder of the two, could picture their relationship to one another so crystallised and enduring, whose idea of the happy life was such a collection and intensification of the beautiful things she knew. Each, they agreed, should gather together that woman's litter of significant souvenirs, old letters, a photograph or so, little gifts and relics that had memories, and send them to the house. It was Sylvia's idea to keep clothes there that they would wear nowhere else; clothes that should be quaint and lovely and of the fashion of the house, that they would choose and send there in readiness for their coming. Each went about with eyes awake for little beautifications they might acquire for it, and they bought and sent it now a china bowl, now an old book, a bit of material, an old quaintness of needlework and such like. At last they went there together and stayed in the house ten days, arranging these things in it and fondling it in its utmost detail.

The house and its surroundings, and Sylvia within it, filled Mary's horizon. She could never have told what it was about that young girl and about no other that so entranced her, what it was that she had and no other had for her that so filled her eye with pleasure, what mysterious alchemy touched to delight the most commonplace "something said, something done" of this particular other human creature. And Sylvia devoted herself to a half-whimsical adoration of her friend, squandered before her all the treasures of tenderness and imaginative rich affectionateness that were stirring and growing and coming to flower in her youth and womanhood like the swelling of buds in spring. In a hundred ways then Mary knew what it might be to have a lover. She loved to caress Mary's hands, look and look at her, anticipate her trivial needs, surprise her by gifts.

What wonder if Mary grew daily to feel for her much of what she would have felt as a lover for a lover, as a mother for a child, as one perfect comrade for another. She joyed so much in the sheer youth of her, she even liked and felt tender to her soft immaturities of thought. In those ten days her mind unconsciously stored a hundred happy pictures, of Sylvia coming round the turn of the old brown staircase, singing, and the leap of a sunbeam to her golden head as she passed; of evenings when it had been chilly enough to have a fire and the old butler had brought great logs, and Sylvia lay firelit at her feet while she read; of Sylvia somewhere in the garden against the translucent screen of greenery suddenly turning her face to her all alight with response to something she had said. She did not know that each of these moments held its memory within it like a secret sting.

They schemed the good times they would have together at the house. They would come on the first day of every month for at least a week. "Besides every other chance," said Sylvia, "if we don't appoint some definite time that nothing shall be allowed to interfere with we shall end by getting here hardly at all." Mary agreed instantly. "And I can't possibly live, my dear," said Sylvia, "without seeing you at least as often as that."

Mary's heart sang within her. For her own part she intended to live at the house altogether, and it had come into her mind as at least a possibility that she might prolong Sylvia's visits indefinitely, until there should be a visit at last that did not end.

Their last morning came. "Why are we going away?" said Sylvia half plaintively more than once. "When we've got such a good thing as the life we're living here, why don't we stick to it; stick on like limpets, Mary?"

"It won't run away," said Mary with the happiest certainty. "Is anything in the world going to stop us from being here again on the first of October?"

"Nothing," vowed Sylvia, and struck an attitude, hand upraised in the act of swearing to this promise.

During the rest of September Mary did not see her. Sylvia flitted about England on a series of visits, and wrote fitfully, sometimes more than once a day and sometimes not at all for several days. She touched off the members of various households in phrases that painted them for Mary to the life, and elaborated a portrait of which Mary had had indications from her before as "my idle, beautiful relative". That was Evan Hardie, and some kind of elaborately removed third cousinship was their blood tie. Mary wondered what kind of a man could possibly be tolerable and fit Sylvia's allusion to "that winsome grimacer". But Sylvia evidently liked him. A snapshot of a house-party showed him even by that unflattering medium, tall and a handsome youth. "Squirrel-brown hair" was another of Sylvia's phrases.

The last days of September came. Mary went down to her cottage to make arrangements for dismantling it;

now that they had the house, she declared she had no further use for it. Sylvia was to join her there, and go on with her for their week at the house.

Sylvia came, and after their separation was more than ever radiant to Mary's eyes, more than ever enchanting and adorable. She brimmed over with the history of her past three weeks, and in and out of her talk laced the name of Evan Hardie. "I have seen a lot of him", she said at last with an air of having just realised it, "and talked to him no end. He's been delightful."

"You don't mind, Mary darling?" she said on the heels of this avowal, catching her by the shoulders and looking suddenly into her eyes.

"*Mind?*" Mary's tone banished almost fiercely the faintest suggestion of possible jealousy.

"I'd like you to see him," Sylvia insisted. "He's the prettiest thing, and you adore good looks, Mary. As a matter of fact" – her voice became disingenuous – "he's staying not far from us now, at his uncle's."

"Which uncle? I'm getting so mixed, Sylvia."

"Sir Steven Hardy. He isn't *my* uncle, anyhow. Evan might come over."

And later, talking about the house, Sylvia said: "It will be delightful to show it to Evan. I expect he'll come over."

Mary had a sudden spasm of astonishment at the idea of showing it to anyone.

"I've told him about it," said Sylvia happily, taking Mary's concurrence for granted.

Mary had told no one. No one could have understood.

The following morning Evan Hardie did come over, and they walked to the house together.

Mary was alive with scrutiny of this handsomely-built, square-faced, clean-shaven youth. She felt at once attracted and antagonistic to him. Actual beauty is so unusual in a man that the startling effect of him almost put out Sylvia's light. Mary looked at him again and again. She recalled Sylvia's whimsical phrase. He was, undeniably, the prettiest thing, he had a sheer delight in movement that revealed the supple strength behind it, his colouring was made up of endless subtle shades of reddish and golden brown, he was hatless, and the rough russet-coloured clothes he wore confessed an awareness of effect which Mary conceded was justified. She set out to make the acquaintance of this attractive person, but she found herself, as they walked along, constantly dropping out of the three-cornered talk. It kept going out of focus for her, and alluding to things he and Sylvia had done or seen together in the month just past. There was a running ripple of merriment between him and Sylvia, almost a frivolity of give-and-take chatter that did not fit into Mary's habit of talk; her intercourse with Sylvia had a graver note; and she realised with surprise that this new tone, just like the one that had seemed so peculiarly and specially their own, also seemed to fit Sylvia's mind like a glove. She was naturally versatile.

Mary was amused at first, and then a little wearied. Listening to them was like watching the charming and purposeless play of very young animals. She was waiting so keenly for Hardie to reveal himself; in the light of Sylvia's liking for him she was so eager to appraise him and find him worthy. And to that desire of hers he opposed a froth of chatter and high spirits that was as impalpable and impenetrable as thistle-down.

They reached the house, and Mary found herself reluctant to the last to see him enter it. If she could have thought even then of any device to stop him she would have done so. The whole place had become so intimate to her. She shrank from the roving glance, the careless question. But indeed, she found, she need not have been afraid.

Mary thought she had never seen the house so beautiful before. The late September sun was low in the sky, and streamed deeply into the rooms, lying on the floors in golden pools of light. With the passing of the hall door Sylvia began to point out this or that special beauty that she loved, but Evan failed to respond. He strode through the rooms with his light quick step, and became very amusing when he discovered that by tip-toeing to his utmost he could just brush the ceilings with his hair. Through the doors which Mary had never known before were low-pitched he had to bend his head, which he did with a quaintly puckered grimace that sent Sylvia into peals of laughter. "Of course I'd rather live in a house where I didn't have to crawl about on all-fours," he said with a comical plaintiveness, and made much of stretching himself erect and being able to breathe naturally when they got out into the garden. He seemed to take the garden for granted as the sort of garden that does hang about a country house, but at a corner where two walls ran at right angles, and the great old ivy had stretched round its thick arms, he stopped and became serious.

"If you were to strip down that ivy," he said with animation, "you could have a fives court here."

"You're an unutterably brutal and philistine person," said Sylvia, and seemed to like him no whit the less.

Hardie and Sylvia talked on the way back, but they radiated satisfaction in one another. The sun had reddened the sky and was sinking fast when they reached the farmhouse by Mary's cottage, and the tall stone gale pillars that faced it, and gave it the air of an old French château, were throwing long shadows on the grass. They crossed the yard by a hayrick, ankle-deep in sweet-scented straw that shimmered in the fading sunlight, and in a corner stood the silent kine waiting motionless for the opening of their byre. Down the quiet air sailed a homing bee. A farm lad crossed the yard, swinging an armful of hay on the fork over his shoulder, and chanting a scrap of song in his Sussex drawl.

"If you want to choose a wife,
Choose in the morning air-r-ly,"

he droned in the evening stillness.

"Good idea!" said Evan Hardie, as if to himself.

"Coom oop there!" said the farm lad with a resounding thump on the flank of the hindmost cow...

For all that evening Evan Hardie remained very much on Mary's mind; she felt that whatever lay beneath that engaging exterior, she hadn't in the least penetrated it, and she was troubled by not being able to take hold where Sylvia seemed to have an easy grasp. And other things puzzled her and filled her mind with a vague unrest. He seemed to threaten the very existence of their exquisite solitude together, and Sylvia did not seem to know it, nor if she knew it did she appear to mind. And Sylvia was preoccupied and rather silent; her eyes were bright, a little smile curved her lips and a little tune hummed in her throat. Again and again Mary began to talk, and could not touch Sylvia to response. It was like trying to throw straws across a gulf. Mary watched her, and wondered uneasily and dared not ask what held her thoughts.

The next morning Mary woke early, woke suddenly as if she had been called. The sun was shining into her room, and outside a bird was singing, very sweetly. She got up and looked out of her open casement into the garden beneath. It was very early, and the sunshine was so thin as yet that it scarcely picked out the shadows below, but it shone keen and bright into her face. Everything was very silent. Across the grey grass-plot below, grey with heavy dew, someone's feet had already brushed a green track. And all the garden was a wonder to see, sparkling and glittering with a thousand prismatic colours, that shone from the dewdrops on the grass and from the glistening web of morning-spun gossamer that laced together every leaf.

She started. Treading on the thickly-dewed grass almost as silently as ghosts, Sylvia and Evan Hardie stood beneath her window. They were looking up at her, their faces alight with youth and happiness. Something gripped Mary by the heart.

"If you want to choose a wife,
Choose in the morning early,"

sang Hardie softly up to her, and put his arm round Sylvia's shoulders.

There was no mistaking the meaning of that, nor the look in Sylvia's eyes, nor the kiss with which she presently greeted Mary good morning.

Evan stayed to breakfast, and made a hilarious meal. He was in the wildest spirits. "Hungry?" he said to Mary's enquiry. "I don't believe I can ever have eaten before from the feel of things. Coffee! what a ripping idea! Here, Sylvia child, don't stand and look at it; pour out the coffee, or make way for your betters. Eggs! bacon! honey! I *say*, Miss Hastings, what a time we're having... Another egg! I've never eaten three eggs, but, by Jove, I will today." And Sylvia laughed and ate, and was lit by a sort of radiance that made her seem to Mary more lovely than ever.

There followed a curious day for Mary. She saw these two young creatures absorbed in one another, and yet she could not get out of the background of her mind the obstinate idea that presently this dazzling irruption into her happy solitude with Sylvia would somehow cease; that somehow Evan Hardie would go away as suddenly as he had come, as if he were some bustling bumble-bee that had fallen into and would presently fall through and out of their delicately spun web of intercourse. She could not grasp yet the thing that had happened. Sylvia was amazingly tender to her when she did not seem to have forgotten her altogether, and discovering with sudden contrition that she and Evan had left Mary alone nearly all the morning, she made an especial point of her going with them for a walk in the afternoon. But as a trio they achieved no mutuality; Hardie was constantly tempted to drop his voice and murmur little things to Sylvia that curved her cheek in a smile or turned her face to his. It was to Mary as if she sat and shivered in the shadow while the warm sun shone on those two and wrapped them about.

In the evening she and Sylvia were left alone again. They sat by the fire, and Sylvia settled into her old place at Mary's feet, and asked her to read. But presently Mary looked up to see Sylvia's eyes spellbound in dreams.

She stopped. Sylvia started, and looked round at her and laughed. "*Oh* Mary!" she said with a comical air of remorse.

Mary could not speak. She let the book fall on her knee.

Sylvia looked up into her face, regarding her. "I'm very happy, Mary," she said softly.

"My dear!" and Mary put her lips to the golden head against her knee.

Sylvia turned round again and looked into the fire.

"What do you think of him, Mary?" she said abruptly.

"Think of him?" repeated Mary, startled by the suddenly searching question.

"I want to know really what you think," persisted Sylvia gently.

"I hardly know him yet," fenced Mary.

"No," said Sylvia, slowly. "And you won't. I don't know whether I do."

"Sylvia!"

"Tell me what you think of him, anyhow." Mary probed her own mind. "He's utterly delightful to look at," she said. "He's charming in all sorts of ways…"

"Yes?"

"And – I suppose I must say it, Sylvia – it would be something I had hidden from you if I didn't – I ask myself still, *why*—"

"I know," nodded Sylvia, with her eyes on the fire. "I know. *Why?* I wonder if I know why."

"What do you mean?" said Mary.

"I mean I wonder why it is that I am happier with him than I have ever been before in my life."

"Are you?" said Mary, steeling her heart.

"Yes. What is it makes the difference, Mary? I don't talk to him as I do to you. We've really hardly talked – real talk, I mean – at all. I don't believe I shall ever talk to him in the way you and I have talked. When we talk about impersonal things we don't get on particularly well. I mean, talk doesn't flow – it's almost as if we were trying to walk towards each other through something thick and entangling. And it doesn't seem to matter."

"Doesn't it?"

"No. When we are together we don't want to talk; we want…" She turned her head, and, resolute to create no shadow on their mutual frankness, she forced out: "Mary, we want to kiss!"

Mary leaned forward over Sylvia and laid her cheek very gently on her soft hair. She felt suddenly old. "That's right," she said, a little huskily.

Sylvia was silent for a moment. "He's such a beautiful, beautiful thing," she said slowly. "He's all light and colour and movement. To see his hair blowing in the wind— Oh, Mary!" she broke off, "what is the good of trying to tell you!"

"I know," said Mary. "My dear, I understand."

She understood. Something far stronger than she had claimed her beloved for its own. She told herself that she understood, that it was overwhelmingly right that it should be so, and that if it were in her power she would not change a jot of what had happened. And yet she could not sleep that night. She lay still and awake, in the weary state of one who feels the dull discomfort of oncoming pain. And when she fell asleep at last she slept uneasily and dreamed. She dreamed that she stood before the house, the dear house that enshrined her life with Sylvia. It was night, and a full moon shone that turned the ancient walls to silver and the trees and shadows to velvet black. She heard a rustling among the creepers on the wall and on the roof, little noises of snapping and breaking and falling, and, looking closely, she saw that there swarmed over the house numbers of little elfish creatures, their faces pallid in the moonlight, who busied themselves with frantic haste. They were tearing the house to pieces; some were throwing down the chimneys brick by brick, others pulling off the tiles. Great dark rents gaped and widened in the roof as she looked. She tried to cry out to stop them with that voiceless agony of the dreamer that can make no sound. She saw one impish form low down on the wall stripping off the ivy with peculiar zest; one after another the long, wavering strands fell back limply with their pale, flattened rootlets stretching out like helpless human things in pain. She ran forward and seized the little wretch by the arm. He turned his face to her, and it was Evan Hardie's face, twisted into an expression of diabolical malice. He clawed viciously at the hand that held him, and stung by the pain of it she saw a long scarlet scratch start out upon her wrist.

With a cry upon her lips she woke.

There were voices under her window, voices that passed, and hurrying feet.

She got up and looked out. It was still dark, perhaps about three o'clock, but the farmer and two or three other men were out by the gate and in the road beyond, with hastily gathered garments, it seemed, huddled about them, looking up at the sky. She looked, too, and over the dark tree-line to the south there was a red glow upon the clouds, angry and lurid.

"'Tis a fire, sure 'nuff," she heard the drawling voice of the farmer.

"'Tis too far to help 'en, then."

"'Tis likely old Baxter's ricks," said one of the men, after an immense interval.

"Na-ow," said the farmer. "'Tis two mile and more beyond 'en."

The glow reddened and faded, and reddened again. Her dream that had embodied her thoughts with such fierce symbolism was still vivid enough to make her intensely unhappy. That reddening sky, signal of loss and disaster and distress, the careless, gigantic spoliation of some human pygmy's labours, seemed to her all of a piece with the colour that her world had taken on. She sat and watched it long after the farm-men had gone, watched it until its brightness faded and the soft grey wings of the dawn at last brushed it out of the sky.

She did not tell Sylvia of her dream, but as they sat at breakfast she told her of the distant fire. Sylvia had slept through the night serenely and dreamlessly, and she hardly seemed to credit that all the world had not done the same.

There came a gentle knocking upon the door of the cottage. Mary opened it herself.

In the doorway stood the old manservant from the house, and for a moment Mary did not recognise him, he was so infinitely aged and beaten and worn. He looked at her with a white face and reddened eyes and tried to speak, but the muscles of his mouth were shaking past his control. In an instant she knew what had happened.

"Oh!" she said, needlessly, putting her hand upon his arm; "tell me – what is it?"

He looked at her, his face working with his effort to speak and stay the dull grey tears that ran down his cheeks. At her touch he collapsed, leaning his head on his hands upon the door, and trembled and sobbed.

"All, all gone," he said huskily – "all gone," then the word "Fire".

For the moment all that this meant to Mary was swamped by the tragic figure before her. Wrenched so rudely out of the house that had held him, that he had cared for and tended so long, he was infinitely pathetic, pitiful as a shelled snail.

"Is your wife safe?" she asked.

He stood up and nodded, trying to speak. "At the inn, marm," he said. "Every one...very kind. I had to...come and tell..." and his voice broke again.

Mary took his wrinkled, quivering hand between her own. "Thank you for that," she said. "Come in and sit down now and rest."

But he would not. The farmer's trap he had come in was waiting out in the road to take him back. "Come to me if you want anything," was all that remained for Mary to say.

He thanked her shakily. "Don't mind me, marm," were the last words she heard from him as he turned away down the path, huddled and bent.

With his disappearance beyond the hedge the full sense of her own loss fell upon her like a swooping bird. She stood still where she was, trying to bring her mind into relation with this immense disaster. Sylvia's voice same from the parlour, humming a little tune.

"Sylvia," she said, going in. "It was *our* house!"

Sylvia, surprised by her tone, turned round from the flowers she was arranging. "What was?" she asked.

"The fire."

"*Mary!*" she exclaimed. But it bit into Mary's heart that her voice was astonished rather than dismayed.

It was by Sylvia's suggestion that they presently set out for the house. Mary checked the excuse upon her lips and braced herself to this necessity. It was an exquisite autumn day. The air was very still and full of the woodland scents of fallen leaves, and in the flood of sunshine the trees shone red and gold. At last they stood again upon the familiar slopes of beech and chestnut-trees by the house. Mary stopped in a wide space of green grass, leaf-scattered, from which radiated glades of yellow-leaved trees. She looked over the trees where they had seen for the first time the chimneys of the house rise up. They were gone, and the leafy crown of the trees against them had gone too. In its place blackened twigs stood spectral against the sky.

Mary shut her eyes in sudden pain. She wanted intensely to see no more. In one swift, horrible vision she had imagined the charred, smoking ruins that lay beyond those trees.

Sylvia broke the silence.

"Isn't it dreadful to have lost it? *Our* house. We shall never live there now, Mary."

"No," said Mary.

They were silent, standing side by side, Mary craving with every fibre of her being for something from Sylvia, something said, she knew not what, that should touch her misery with healing.

"After all, you know, dearest, as I'm going to marry so soon, we shouldn't have come here again so very much."

The words, and still more the light melody of Sylvia's voice, fell between her and Mary's heart-aching with the steely separation of a guillotine.

Sylvia exclaimed. Up the glade in front of them, arched over by the golden-leaved trees and floored by the gold that had fallen, sat Evan Hardie, motionless upon a chestnut horse. The sunlight struck through the thinned branches and turned him to a figure of beaten gold. As he sat there, conquering, triumphant, a still figure astride the shining, satin-skinned horse, he looked to be a robuster pagan Saint George, whose coat of mail was all of woven sunshine.

Sylvia ran forward to him where he stood and laid her cheek against the horse's neck. Her hair loosened as she ran, and fell about her. Her gesture had the happy security of a bird that drops upon its nest.

A sudden pain seized Mary by the throat. She did not know what it meant at first, for weeping was unfamiliar to her then. But from her strained, longing eyes fell slow tears.

She told herself how glad she was, how very glad.

The Dragon-Fly

THE HOT SUMMER SUNSHINE poured down into a sunken garden isolated by high hedges of crimson roses. Rosebeds in their first extravagance of bloom and paths of crumbling red brick tufted with little flowers, went down in the steps to a lily pool of golden, sun-drenched water. Here and there, beneath the brown shadow of the floating leaves, palpitated a scarlet fish tail; and over the water darted blue dragon-flies or came to sudden rest that would transfix leaf or blossom with a sapphire pin.

There came distant voices and laughter, and presently through a rose-covered archway appeared half a dozen people carrying tennis racquets or sunshades; two men, hatless, with white flannel shirts open over sunburnt necks, a man in a soft felt hat and tweeds, a girl with an orange handkerchief twisted round her head, a woman in white with a shady hat, and a rather older, lace-trailing lady. Prancing about their heels came a small restless shock-headed boy, wearing almost invisibly short white pants and a white woollen jersey that either through washing or growth looked tighter than his own skin could possibly be.

"I want you to see Perkins. He's grown enormously," the lady in white was saying to one of the tennis-playing men.

"There's Perkings," squealed the small boy, darting down the steps to the water and pointing to a vanishing flash of ruddy gold.

"Shall we all sit here on the steps and cool?" said the white lady. "That was the hottest set I've played this summer."

"We'll want our revenge soon. We'll take them on again, won't we, Betsy?"

"Michael, you'll fall in if you lean over like that."

"I won't, Mummy."

"Come and sit up here."

"I want to see Perkings."

"Have you tried a steel-strung racquet?"

"Mummy, can I put some crums in the water?"

"The fish won't come out now, Michael."

"*Peraps* they would if I put *crums*."

"Take care, child, you are treading on my dress."

"Wait a second, I'll get you a cushion, Mrs. Potter."

"Oh, Mr. Willoughby please—"

"All right, there's one just here."

"Mummy, where are the *crums*?"

"That boy is devoted to animals. He's just perfectly happy if he can get animals to play with."

("Of course I don't say the upkeep isn't heavy, but with the one thing and another raising the subscription now seems to some of us jolly bad business—")

"I have always loved animals. That pond is full of the most charming creatures. One day we saw a water rat there – such a darling. Oh, he's thrown it all on the leaves. Michael, give it to me. You can't throw it far enough."

"Na-oh-oh!"

"Well, throw it on the water then. When one lives in the country one gets to be such friends with all the animals. I don't mean just one's own dogs and horses, but all the little helpless things."

"*You* frow it."

"Hullo! You've hit a dragon-fly."

"Mummy, I've hit a *dagon-fy*."

"Poor dragon-fly. Aren't they exquisite? We read all about them in your Nature book, didn't we, Michael?"

Michael, incoherent with excitement: "They livvinther-Worter."

"Now I shouldn't have thought that, old chap, judging from appearances."

"He means when they are beetles, Mr. Bernard. Before they turn into dragonflies, they live in the water."

"I never knew that."

"They livvinther - Worter and kummowtan Bust."

"Oh, Michael! Miss Bates found one, didn't she? Haven't you ever seen a dragon-fly split its beetle skin and crawl out and sit and dry its wings and fly away? It's a perfect entertainment for a summer afternoon."

"Mrs. Willoughby, I confess I've missed it. I've led such a quiet life, getting called to the Bar and one thing and another..."

"Mummee. Come here quick."

"Hush, child. And I suppose you don't see many dragon-flies in the Temple."

"Mum*mee*. Here's one, crawled out of the water."

"Where, Michael? Take care, you'll fall in. On the lily leaf? Oh! that's just the old skin of one, child. He's come out of his skin and flown away. Look, Mr. Bernard. Isn't it perfect? Feet and all."

"Mummy, I see the dagon-fy."

"Where? Yes, there it is. Doesn't it look shivery and frightened? Poor thing. It's frightened of the water underneath. It might fall back and get drowned. I'll get it."

"Don't touch it, Mummy. Miss Bates said not to touch it."

"Because you might have hurt it, Michael. But I shan't."

"What's the fuss, Mabel? Oh, *that*. My wife, Mrs. Potter, doesn't think any animal can take care of itself or its young, and she always wants to do it for them. She wants to go round putting hot-water bottles on the birds' nests on cold nights."

"Robbie, don't make fun of me. I'm only saving this lovely thing from a watery grave. I want him to be happy like the others. Think if you'd spent all your life in a cold dark pond waiting and looking forward to being a glorious green dragon-fly flashing about in the sun, and then you'd got drowned before your wings were ready. There. He loves being on my finger. See how he's looking all round at the new world he's come into."

"And you've got a good day for it, old chap. Rotten for him if he'd waited two years and then had a wet day."

"Look, he's crawling. O-o-oo, it feels so funny. Do let him come on your finger, Mr Bernard. Let's make a bridge – you put your finger against mine. Look at his big serious eyes!"

"Partner's pushed to three no trumps and he's got left with it."

"Don't make me laugh; now he's coming on to your finger."

"Mum-*mee*, he'll fall off."

"No, he's quite safe. Don't shout, Michael, you'll frighten him. One wing is getting quite stiff and dry. Think what he must be feeling now, Michael, looking forward and forward to today for two whole years, and now waiting just a few minutes till he can stretch out his lovely wings and fly right up into the sky."

"Ummm. Will he fly up in the sky, Mummy?"

"Of course. Wouldn't you if you had wings? Don't you think he's feeling excited?"

"He's getting fearfully active. He'll take off from my hand in a minute. Mrs. Willoughby – Help! Am I to let him?"

"But his wings aren't expanded. Do give him to me, and I'll put him down on the grass—"

"Mummy," (with deep, impatient reproach) "you've *dropped* him."

"He's all right. He jumped on the soft grass. Oh, Mrs. Potter, must you really be going? It was delightful of you to look us up. Do remember we shall be here for another two months anyhow... Lunch on Sunday? Of course we'd love to. Robbie! Mrs. Potter is asking us... Good-bye. Good-bye, Mr. Potter."

"Mummy, his wing is all twisty."

"Hush, child. Good-bye!...Half-past one? Thanks ever so much. We won't be late. Well – I'm ready for the revanche set – are you? Robbie will be back as soon as he has seen them off."

"Mummy, look, do look."

"What *is* it, Michael?"

"His wing's broken. Where he fell down on it."

"He's all right. That wing hasn't got so dry as the other yet, and it still looks soft. See, he's walking."

"His wing's all twisty, Mummy."

"He's just got it caught in that bit of leaf— I'll straighten it out for him."

"Oh, it's stuck, Mummy. You've *torn* it."

"Michael, don't *shout*. How can one do anything? You'll terrify the poor thing. Look, now we'll lift him up here and leave him to get properly dry."

The damaged insect dragged itself to the edge of the little brick wall, planed off, tilted sideways and fell to the ground.

Exclamations followed it. "Off he goes. Isn't he lovely? Crashed, poor chap. Bad luck, old man. Try again."

"Here's Robbie. How we can have the return match. Come along."

"I'll stay here, Mummy."

"No, Michael, not by yourself, my treasure. You might fall in the pond."

"I won't, Mummy. I want to stay with the *dagon-fy*."

"No, Michael. Now we'll put the dragon-fly up here in a nice shady place, and then he'll get properly dry before he tries to fly again. See? Leave him comfortably there. Now he'll be happy. Come along."

The party trooped out of the little rose-garden again, their talking voices fading away into a diminuendo of sound. Last to be heard was a treble tone barren of conviction:

"Will his wing get quite well, Mummy?"

May Afternoon

A VERY PERSONABLE young man, in the flannels and straw hat that responded to the sudden summer heat, sat by one of the outer tea-tables in Kensington Gardens, his tea, ordered some half-hour since, neglected and bitter by his side. The tables had been crowded that afternoon, gaily dressed people had frothed up against them out of the park, and broken into bright little groups that chattered and chinked cups and laughed, and presently passed away again into the outer greenery. Crawshay sat almost alone at last, with the gravel round his feet scored and criss-crossed by the idle patterns he had drawn and redrawn with his cane. Just in front of him he had jabbed some deeper holes.

Spring had come late; that year she had been sulky, the jade! and reluctant. Now at last she had been given notice to quit by the young summer and had rushed forth, hot and impetuous, spilling out flowers with prodigal hurry in the park, blistering the new green paint on the chairs with fierce sunshine, and turning the very sparrows silly with the sudden intoxication that she poured into the air. Crawshay had come into the park in search of some quiet corner where he supposed he might sit and think out his peculiar trouble. And before he noticed it, his feet had taken their habitual way northward in a direct line for Mrs. Lacey's house, he had discovered himself all at once almost within sight of her terrace, had damned impatiently, and turned back to face a direction that was as empty of interest for him as a drained cup.

His acquaintance with the Laceys had begun when at eighteen he had been left to Lacey's guardianship by the death of both his parents. His father and mother were elderly people who had spent their last ten years in the irresolute pursuit of sunshine about southern Europe, keeping him with them in his school holidays; and so it happened that at their death the Laceys were almost his only friends in England. On Lacey's advice he had gone to Oxford, and he spent his vacations with parties of other young men, or at the Laceys' house. He felt shy of both the Laceys then, although Mrs. Lacey was much younger than her husband, barely thirty at that time, and warmly kind and friendly. But Crawshay was of opinion that Lacey had outgrown any charm his father had found in him. He was an authoritative museum official, a heavy pipe-smoker, and tacitly autocratic in his home, with one of those richly inexpressive stammering minds that contain their learning like a shut box. The most wonderful treasures of knowledge were known to be hoarded there, but the lock was rusty and the key seemed lost, and so in the end it really mattered very little if they were.

The lock, it is true, occasionally creaked a little. It was understood, for instance, that out of the continuum of Lacey's slippered evenings there would some day exude a book. To the adolescent youth he had seemed as dull and unimportant as most middle-aged men.

But when he was one and twenty Crawshay had discovered that in one direction at any rate there was a streak of the adventurous in Lacey, and that he had been an astonishingly unconventional trustee. There were explanations, an encounter so uncomfortable to Crawshay that it ended to his own surprise in his practically asking his defaulting guardian not to mind. He came away from that interview with mixed feelings. He was reasonably annoyed at having his patrimony reduced by a third, but he was young enough to think that what remained to him, since it was in its moderate way sufficient to start him in a profession, was almost as good as it had been. But whereas Lacey had seemed to him hitherto only dull and negligible, he now recognised something in his quality that he found contemptible. The manner of his explanation had done much to give that impression.

He hoped Mrs. Lacey didn't know what Lacey had been up to. It would be humiliating for her, he thought, and he didn't want her to experience anything so disagreeable; she had always been so jolly kind to him. He liked her very much. And boy that he was, he didn't want her to know how poorly Lacey had behaved. For the first time in his life he had penetrated behind a much older man's front, had found him out silly in action and shuffling in conduct. It made him feel important and responsible as he had never felt before; he felt that this scandal of damaged manhood must be hushed up but the next time he saw her alone Mrs. Lacey had let him understand that she did know, and even how generously she thought he had behaved. That had embarrassed him. He muttered something about its not mattering at all, and blushed and changed the subject awkwardly.

It was a step in the intimacy of their friendship. With no further words between them it put them on a footing of knowing, together, all about Lacey. Mutually they avoided criticism of him.

Crawshay went back to his college, finished his course in an economical spirit, went on for a couple of years to a German university, and when he came back to England he was a grown man and in some mysterious manner he and Mildred Lacey had become contemporaries.

Mrs. Lacey was a woman with an extreme prettiness that had ripened, with firm muscles and quick movements, and frank, alert grey eyes that looked straight at her interlocutor. She ran her household and mothered her three brightly pretty children with an easy cleverness that impressed Crawshay profoundly.

She was by nature clear-headed, and inside the limits of Lacey's departure at nine-thirty and return at five, she had done quite a considerable amount of reading and thinking, talking and seeing. Crawshay began to find her a delightful friend. She had none of that series of unsubstantial shows that is harshly called a shop-window; her interests and curiosities had been for their own sake and not for their conversational usefulness; she was as frank in her deficiencies as in other things – politics for instance had never interested her and she had never troubled to smatter them. But she must have had a touch of French blood in her veins, her interest in life, art, and humanity was so lively, her mental attack so direct. After the assertive, egotistical talk of his college contemporaries, Crawshay found her clear-cut honesty astonishing. In a hundred ways she grasped firmly where he only seemed to fumble. And she was continuously amusing and interesting. For six months he had taken unthinkingly as much of her companionship as he had wanted, then three weeks without her, while she had been with her children in the country, had jerked a discovery into his mind that was like something being flung up through a trap-door on to a stage.

At first – he could not help it! – it was an altogether delightful and exciting discovery. A hundred scattered memories of her rushed together, clung about this new central fact, and were changed and coloured by it. He remembered with delight contacts with her hand, her hair, her shoulder, scarcely apprehended at the time, that now thrilled him. For a day or two he remained thinking of her simply and ecstatically. Lacey, it was true, lurked behind this radiant picture like a little black thing in a corner, but dull and unimportant as he had always been, a thing unimaginable in connection with these iridescent emotions that swept through his mind. But he began to want very much to see her again, and as the days passed the little figure of Lacey struggled to come out of its corner and take on a greater value. He thrust it back. It was almost unbearable when he presented himself at her house at the punctual expiration of the three weeks to be told that it would be yet four days before her return.

He came away a little chilled.

There had been something concrete about the hall door, the door which Lacey entered daily with a latch-key, and the porch in which Crawshay had seen the children grouped with hoops and mailcart, that had abruptly touched his imaginings with conflicting reality. They were so fragile as to shiver at that touch of matter of fact as flowers shiver at the frost. The irreconcilability of his dream with her assured position enthroned in her family stared him blankly in the face, no longer to be evaded; it surprised him that he had not appreciated this before, he wondered simply and shamefacedly whether really he wouldn't have been considered rather a cad to let such thoughts as he had had concern themselves with Mrs. Lacey. He began to be troubled by the knowledge that by the accepted code of honour, he was a dishonourable friend. But the thought of her still lay obstinately warm at his heart.

He wanted to do the right thing. He decided that he had one obvious duty; he must never, never let her know. If she never knew, would it matter that he loved her?

His first state of simple emotional delight passed. Directly he had decided that he must not tell her his mind became a blank. Correct as that course of conduct might be, his imagination refused it as his feet might have refused tight boots. His imagination indeed kept on persistently scheming situations and anticipating conversations quite incompatible with never, never letting her know. To devise his further behaviour towards her wearied him, it was not so much like fitting a puzzle together as trying to combine two halves of two puzzles of different sizes into one cohering whole. He went to see her at last, no longer in the happy state in which he had mounted the steps half a week before, but bothered, more than anything else bothered, by the confusion in his attitudes.

At first he had talked and listened to her with only half his mind, and thought about her with the other. Without knowing it he was looking at her intently, so that her frank serenity became faintly clouded, one might almost have thought her nervous. A silence fell between them.

She had even coloured a little. He really had not meant to speak to her at all of what had stabbed into his heart, he had come to see her meaning that very honestly. And then face to face with her that idea seemed suddenly absurd. She looked so safe and solid a friend, there was such capacity for counsel in her kindly eyes. The impulse had overwhelmed him to put the difficulty to her as he would any other simple trouble.

It seemed to him as if he jerked his voice forcibly into the silence. "I wonder if you would mind very much if I told you something," he said.

She laughed, not quite naturally. "I thought there was something the matter," she said.

He leant across the little table that was between them. "I didn't mean to tell you," he said, and hesitated and found it more difficult than he had believed.

"Well?" she said valiantly, trying to look him frankly in the face, and failing a little.

(How beautifully the sun and sea had tanned her cheek!) "Don't you know what it is I want to tell you?"

"How can I know?" she almost stammered.

Her confusion fired him suddenly. "You do," he pleaded. "You've got instincts. I bring it to you as I bring all my difficulties. You're the wise one." His voice broke to a whisper. "Dear wise one! What am I to do?"

The words that he could not say shone out of his voice and eyes. She looked up at him quickly, and pretended no longer not to understand. She flushed intensely, for a moment he thought she was going to cry. All at once, it seemed to him an enormity that he should have spoken as he had, that now a stern angel would turn him out of his garden of friendship with her and slam the gate upon him for ever. Very humbly he bent his head to kiss her fingers as they gripped the arm of her sofa.

She moved her hand before his lips could touch it. "Don't," she whispered.

He thought her offended, and drew back. "I beg your pardon," he said, with mortification in his voice.

"Oh my dear!" The cry broke irrepressibly over her lips, and he looked at her, startled at her tone, waiting. But her eyes were downcast. She was silent for a moment.

"What do you want?" she asked him.

Crawshay's eyes dropped; he sat with intertwined fingers, wrenching his knuckles together. Everything went from him save his bald fact.

"I want to love you," he said slowly, and at her silence looked up at her.

Her clear-shining, courageous eyes met his. "And I want to love you," she said gently.

He was astonished beyond measure. "Mildred!" he cried, and across the little table he caught her hands in his.

She looked back into his eyes very steadfastly. "And we live in the world we live in, and we mustn't and we can't."

"I love you!"

She shook her head slightly. Her voice trembled. "This is a beautiful thing we can't have, dear."

"It's – endlessly beautiful. I love you."

"I'm married."

"I know. I don't care."

"You must. A woman puts her heart in harness when she marries."

"You own your own free soul."

"Do I?"

The simple irony of her challenge tore his fine phrase to pieces.

"You – you ought to," he stammered.

She laughed. "I dare say," she said. "But I don't. And that's why you mustn't be in love with me, Guy, or I with you."

"How can I help it?"

"Stop it."

"I can never stop loving you."

"Oh, there are ways," she said with a note of wisdom in her voice that nettled him. "If you don't see me for a long time—" She got up and went to the fire, and, looking into it, went on speaking. "We – we can stop it. You'd better not come and see me again at times when you're likely to find me alone. Better perhaps if you don't come at all for a time."

"Not come!" he said blankly. "But I—"

He got up too, and came to the fireplace, leaning his elbow on the mantleshelf, and spoke with his head on his hand, "I wish I could explain," he said. "You know, Mildred, it seems so – so jolly to love you. It feels like the most natural thing in the world. I know really I'm a mean cad – at least I suppose I'm a mean cad – I suppose I've got no moral sense or something..."

She looked at him with a smile. "Oh nonsense!" she said heartily. "That's all rubbish dear, and you know it is."

He smiled back. "It feels like rubbish," he said in a comforted voice. "But it's what people would say."

"Oh, it's what people would say. But it's nonsense all the same."

"Then" – he had felt his way to argument – "why shouldn't I love you?"

She looked into the fire, weighing her answer. "Because marriage is a pretty straight bargain for a woman really, it has got no place in it for this love you bring me, Guy. I don't undervalue it, my dear" – he flushed with pleasure – "you bring it as you might bring flowers; to me it's as sweet as flowers, so sweet that I've told you the truth, I love you back. I won't smirch your gift with lying. I love your youth and yourself, and your hair and eyes and all the pretty things about you. I'd love you so gladly. But some other woman will have to love you, Guy, not me. I can't run any risks. I'm married to a man who'd not excuse me – if he saw you – holding my hands – as you did just now. Do understand me, my dear. All this life I have led so long has come to fit me like my skin. If it was torn off me, I should bleed to death. There's my children. In the long run my children and their happiness mean far more to me than you do. And I'm more important to them than I am to you. I wouldn't for all the world give them as hostages to luck – to chance. And that's – why."

He was silent for a time. "It's like killing something beautiful," he said at last.

She nodded. "I know. It feels like – cruelty. It can't be helped. It's got to die this time. I suppose, in the history of poor men and women, it has died, thousands of times."

He looked at her unhappily, and presently she too turned her eyes from the fire and met him. They softened very tenderly and she laid her hand upon his arm. "There is one thing," she said. "I think I will take from all the beautiful possibilities that we're not going to have. Why shouldn't I? Something I've wanted so much." And she had bent forward unexpectedly and kissed him full and sweetly on the lips.

He had clasped her then, and kissed her again and again, and said passionate, wild things. "No, no," she said imploringly.

And then they both heard the front door slam, and Lacey's heavy tread coming up the stairs.

He hadn't come into the drawing-room. Heaven knows what would have happened if he had. Starting apart, she trying in desperate haste to assume a casual attitude in an easy-chair, he drawn up stiffly, feet planted apart on the hearthrug, they heard Lacey turn into his study on the half landing. They were saved from discovery. But that moment had given them the quality of their relationship, their first and last embrace had ended with a poor scuffle for the positions in which they now hung so limply. The uncompromising facts of the situation stared Crawshay in the face. There was nothing more to be said. What had happened had taught him more than hours of discussion. His honest young heart had never imagined the sting of hypocrisy. "Good-bye," she had said, holding out her hand; and whispered, "Don't come again," and he had held it tightly for a moment with, he hated to remember, his ears on the stretch. And then he had come away.

That was all. The whole episode had been as sweet and fragrant and honest – as hay.

He had come away in an heroic mood to embrace almost eagerly the separation that was to be his penance. The disgust of his sensations when he had been so nearly "caught" by Lacey – the vulgar word occurred to him, and he could not rid his mind of it – contributed not a little to that readiness. And for a time, too, it was a wonderful thought, and filled his mind, that she was away there on the other side of London, in love with himself. The sweet taste of her candid avowal lingered with him. It was a sufficient satisfaction for quite three days. For those first days he was not at all unhappy.

But it was a satisfaction that had only itself to feed upon. What next? is the incessant cry of the insatiable human heart. He began to find out that there was to be no "next," that that bitterness was enfolded in the fine flower of their sacrifice. Then at once he wanted very badly to see her again. How could their intercourse be broken off with that snatched insufficient conversation? He began to think of other considerations, qualifications, aspects that he might have put to her, that it was only reasonable to put to her. They had parted on an impulse. There were plenty of arrangements they might have made to keep their friendship, at any rate; he would have given his word never to cross that boundary again if she had wished it so. Slowly and surely he began to forget the cogent argument of Lacey's footsteps heard upon the stairs. And in this manner, creeping up here, swirling forward there, flooding and swallowing all his thoughts at last, like the tide running in over long reaches of unresistant sands, came the unconquerable conviction that this truncation of their friendship was absurd and unnecessary, and then everything else in his mind went awash in that like seaweed wrack upon the flow.

With that, a curious change came over his thoughts of her. Many times since their last meeting he had gone over in his mind all that had happened, all that she had said. Indeed that occupied him mainly. On that afternoon of spring as he sat in the park alone at the tea-table with his tea cold at his elbow, he thought of it all again. But the life had gone out of that remembered talk. Under the wear of his repetition the realities of their interview had lost their saliency like a fingered coin. He had ceased to feel her honest candour, he gave her no longer any credit for her own share in their renunciations. He did not know it was so, but insensibly his thoughts of her had soured. His mind had travelled far when he sat there, prodding his cane into the gravel; it was insisting ill-temperedly that it was nothing but cowardly of her to have shut her doors upon him as she had. She knew that he had made no other friends half as intimate, that he depended on her. And she had just turned him out. She wouldn't trust him. Wouldn't he have given her his word?

He was irritated, annoyed. He wished he could wipe out the whole thing. He told himself that it had been a crowning mistake to tell her, to trust her, confide in her at all. Here he was, stranded alone on this wretched afternoon, with everybody in London, it seemed, about him, meeting, smiling at one another, flowing into friendly groups. He might have been having tea in that pleasant drawing-room now if he hadn't been such a fool as to tell her. Why not? What a fool he had been! And hadn't she led him on, with her show of open-minded tolerance, to suppose that she wouldn't take the conventional line as she had done, scuttle back to orthodox defences at his first attempt to strip their relationship bare to its truth. She had let him come and see her constantly, let him fall in love with her, and then thrown him over to scramble back to peace of mind again as best he could. He made hard phrases about her as one might swear; that they were untrue, that wherever was the folly of his present position it wasn't in him or in her, lay submerged in the flood of his hurt vanity like a thing drowned.

He was aroused at last by the waitress. She stood beside him and smiled down upon him engagingly, and getting no response, clattered the tea-things together and conveyed by an offended manner that he had been there long enough. He saw with surprise that the crowd that had surrounded him when he sat down, was gone. As he walked away the shadows lay long on the grass, the sunshine fainted, something that was more like a creeping sweetness than a breeze stirred among the flowers. Nearly all the promenaders were gone, gone to their homes to dress, to forgather again in smiling, animated clusters round dinner-tables. Presently lights would flicker up in the big stone houses, windows would shine out, people would come out cloaked, to get into carriages in twos and threes and fours, and be driven swiftly to theatres and parties. Across the crowded, humming theatres they would nod and wave friendly hands, from bright, compact dinner-tables they would troop up into drawing-rooms, gossiping and laughing.

He had to spend his own evening somehow.

He dined alone at a place where there were little candle-shaded tables for two people in a balcony, and downstairs larger ones for four. No one else was there alone. He had chosen it haphazard, he had never been there before, and there was an air of surreptitiousness about more than one couple who dined together at the screened tables in the balcony that penetrated him with torment. Everybody did these things! Towards the end of his dinner he perceived that immense spaces of evening still stretched before him, and asked for an evening paper. He ran his eye down the list of theatres, and picked out a play whose name had been flung at him lately from every hoarding in West London. The plot of the play touched obliquely and absurdly on his own preoccupation; its three acts of irritating false issues rushed at last to a glib solution.

Crawshay came out into a pressed and squeezing, chattering crowd. Before the theatre an intense light, a stupendous flare of electricity fell on their faces, on brilliantly coloured cloaks, diamonds and sweeping feathers. In the glare every face was ghastly white, he saw the women black shadowed, heavily lined, powder-encrusted, ugly. He struggled out of the pressure and fell into a side turning as into a pit of darkness.

Life was ugly – ugly and stupid. That was what he had found out. And one had to take it as one found it.

He went on, through gloomy side streets, almost deserted, through busy main thoroughfares blazing with lights and crowded with hurrying, hustling people. Cab whistles shrilled about him, swishing motors whirled outward from the glittering cluster of theatres like sparks from a firework. At one corner he was held by the crowd.

A woman in a big hat drifted nearer to him, and murmured the battered formula of her trade.

A spasm of disgust shook him with anger. "No fear!" he replied roughly, and moved on.

She turned away sharply with offence. He went on, angry with himself for his brutality, but indeed he knew in his heart that that rough rebuff had been the measure of the nearness with which he had come to snatching her offered company.

He felt that in that woman's approach the very spirit of civilisation itself had spoken, and pointed out in one crude coarse gesture that it had not been unmindful to provide for his commonplace case and that of thousands of similar others. He did not mean to be beaten, he did not mean to conform to the spirit of civilisation's standard of conduct, but meanwhile—

Meanwhile! Meanwhile he walked solitary through the night, tormented in body and mind. Meanwhile the theatres, restaurants, hotels, and all the busy, brilliant forgathering-places of great London turned out their guests, clapped together their doors, and flicked out their lights. The fewer and fewer people on the pavements melted into the darkness, the rarer and rarer taxis flew away into the night, the humming roar of London's pulse grew quieter, quieter, and stopped. He was left alone.

The Ghost

SHE WAS A GIRL of fourteen, and she sat propped up with pillows in an old four-poster bed, coughing a little with the feverish cold that kept her there. She was tired of reading by lamplight, and she lay and listened to the few sounds that she could hear, and looked into the fire. From downstairs, down the wide, rather dark, oak-panelled corridor hung with brown ochre pictures of tremendous naval engagements exploding fierily in their centres, down the broad stone stairs that ended in a heavy, creaking, nail-studded door, there blew in to her remoteness sometimes a gust of dance music. Cousins and cousins and cousins were down there, and Uncle Timothy, as host, leading the fun. Several of them had danced into her room during the day, and said that her illness was a "perfect shame," told her that the skating in the park was "too heavenly," and danced out again. Uncle Timothy had been as kind as kind could be. But— Downstairs all the full cup of happiness the lonely child had looked forward to so eagerly for a month, was running away like liquid gold.

She watched the flames of the big wood fire in the open grate flicker and fall. She had sometimes to clench her hands to prevent herself from crying. She had discovered – so early was she beginning to collect her little stock of feminine lore – that if you swallowed hard and rapidly as the tears gathered, that you could prevent your eyes brimming over. She wished someone would come. There was a bell within her reach, but she could think of no plausible excuse for ringing it. She wished there was more light in the room. The big fire lit it up cheerfully when the logs flared high; but when they only glowed, the dark shadows crept down from the ceiling and gathered in the corners against the panelling. She turned from the scrutiny of the room to the bright circle of light under the lamp on the table beside her, and the companionable suggestiveness of the currant jelly and spoon, grapes and lemonade and little pile of books and kindly fuss that shone warmly and comfortingly there. Perhaps it would not be long before Mrs. Bunting, her uncle's housekeeper, would come in again and sit down and talk to her.

Mrs. Bunting, very probably, was more occupied than usual that evening. There were several extra guests, another house-party had motored over for the evening, and they had brought with them a romantic figure, a celebrity, no less a personage than the actor Percival East. The girl had indeed broken down from her fortitude that afternoon when Uncle Timothy had told her of this visitor. Uncle Timothy was surprised; it was only another schoolgirl who would have understood fully what it meant to be denied by a mere cold the chance of meeting face to face that chivalrous hero of drama; another girl who had glowed at his daring, wept at his noble renunciations, been made happy, albeit enviously and vicariously, by his final embrace with the lady of his love.

"There, there, dear child," Uncle Timothy had said, patting her shoulder and greatly distressed. "Never mind, never mind. If you can't get up I'll bring him in to see you here. I promise I will... But the *pull* these chaps have over you little women," he went on, half to himself...

The panelling creaked. Of course, it always did in these old houses. She was of that order of apprehensive, slightly nervous people who do not believe in ghosts, but all the same hope devoutly they may never see one. Surely it was a long time since anyone had visited her; it would be hours, she supposed, before the girl who had the room next her own, into which a communicating door comfortingly led, came up to bed. If she rang it took a minute or two before anyone reached her from the remote servants' quarters. There ought soon, she thought, to be a housemaid about the corridor outside, tidying up the bedrooms, putting coal on the fire, and making suchlike companionable noises. That would be pleasant. How bored one got in bed anyhow, and how dreadful it was, how unbearably dreadful it was that she should be stuck in bed now, missing everything, missing every bit of the glorious glowing time that was slipping away down there. At that she had to begin swallowing her tears again.

With a sudden burst of sound, a storm of clapping and laughter, the heavy door at the foot of the big stairs swung open and closed. Footsteps came upstairs, and she heard men's voices approaching. Uncle Timothy. He knocked at the door afar. "Come in," she cried gladly. With him was a quiet-faced greyish-haired man of middle age. Then Uncle had sent for the doctor after all!

"Here is another of your young worshippers, Mr. East," said Uncle Timothy.

Mr. East! She realised in a flash that she had expected him in purple brocade, powdered hair, and ruffles of fine lace. Her uncle smiled at her disconcerted face.

"She doesn't seem to recognise you, Mr. East," said Uncle Timothy.

"Of course I do," she declared bravely, and sat up, flushed with excitement and her feverishness, bright-eyed and with ruffled hair. Indeed she began to see the stage hero she remembered and the kindly-faced man before her flow together like a composite portrait. There was the little nod of the head, there was the chin, yes! and the eyes, now she came to look at them. "Why were they all clapping you?" she asked.

"Because I had just promised to frighten them out of their wits," replied Mr. East.

"Oh, how?"

"Mr. East," said Uncle Timothy, "is going to dress up as our long-lost ghost, and give us a really shuddering time of it downstairs."

"*Are* you?" cried the girl with all the fierce desire that only a girl can utter in her voice. "Oh, why am I ill like this, Uncle Timothy? I'm not ill really. Can't you see I'm better? I've been in bed all day. I'm perfectly well. Can't I come down, Uncle *dear* – can't I?"

In her excitement she was half out of bed. "There, there, child," soothed Uncle Timothy, hastily smoothing the bedclothes and trying to tuck her in.

"But *can't* I?"

"Of course, if you want to be thoroughly frightened, frightened out of your wits, mind you," began Percival East.

"I do, I *do*," she cried, bouncing up and down in her bed.

"I'll come and show myself when I'm dressed up, before I go down."

"Oh please, please," she cried back radiantly. A private performance all to herself! "Will you be perfectly awful?" she laughed exultantly.

"As ever I can," smiled Mr. East, and turned to follow Uncle Timothy out of the room. "You know," he said, holding the door and looking back at her with mock seriousness, "I shall look rather horrid, I expect. Are you sure you won't mind?"

"Mind – when it's you?" laughed the girl.

He went out of the room, shutting the door.

"Rum-ti-tum, ti-tum, ti-ty," she hummed gaily, and wriggled down into her bedclothes again, straightened the sheet over her chest, and prepared to wait.

She lay quietly for some time, with a smile on her face, thinking of Percival East and fitting his grave, kindly face back into its various dramatic settings. She was quite satisfied with him. She began to go over in her mind in detail the last play in which she had seen him act. How splendid he had looked when he fought the duel! She couldn't imagine him gruesome, she thought. What would he do with himself?

Whatever he did, she wasn't going to be frightened. He shouldn't be able to boast he had frightened her. Uncle Timothy would be there too, she supposed. Would he?

Footsteps went past her door outside, along the corridor, and died away. The big door at the end of the stairs opened and clanged shut.

Uncle Timothy had gone down.

She waited on.

A log, burnt through the middle to a ruddy thread, fell suddenly in two tumbling pieces on the hearth. She started at the sound. How quiet everything was. How much longer would he be, she wondered. The fire wanted making up, the pieces of wood collecting together. Should she ring? But he might come in just when the servant was mending the fire, and that would spoil his entry. The fire could wait...

The room was very still, and, with the fallen fire, darker. She heard no more any sound at all from downstairs. That was because her door was shut. All day it had been open, but now the last slender link that held her to downstairs was broken.

The lamp flame gave a sudden fitful leap. Why? Was it going out? Was it? – no.

She hoped he wouldn't jump out at her, but of course he wouldn't. Anyhow, whatever he did she wouldn't be frightened – really frightened. Forewarned is forearmed.

Was that a sound? She started up, her eyes on the door. Nothing.

But surely, the door had minutely moved, it did not sit back quite so close into its frame! Perhaps it— She was sure it had moved. Yes, it had moved – opened an inch, and slowly, as she watched, she saw a thread of light grow between the edge of the door and its frame, grow almost imperceptibly wider, and stop.

He could never come through that? It must have yawned open of its own accord. Her heart began to beat rather quickly. She could see only the upper part of the door, the foot of her bed hid the lower third…

Her attention tightened. Suddenly, as suddenly as a pistol shot, she saw that there was a little figure like a dwarf near the wall, between the door and the fireplace. It was a little cloaked figure, no higher than the table. How did he do it? It was moving slowly, very slowly, towards the fire, as if it was quite unconscious of her; it was wrapped about in a cloak that trailed, with a slouched hat on its head bent down its shoulders. She gripped the clothes with her hands, it was so queer, so unexpected; she gave a little gasping laugh to break the tension of the silence – to show she appreciated them.

The dwarf stopped dead at the sound, and turned its face round to her.

Oh! but she was frightened! it was a dead white face, a long pointed face hunched between its shoulders, there was no colour in the eyes that stared at her! How did he do it, how did he do it? It was too good. She laughed again nervously, and with a clutch of terror that she could not control she saw the creature move out of the shadow and come towards her. She braced herself with all her might, she mustn't be frightened by a bit of acting – he was coming nearer, it was horrible – right up to her bed…

She flung her head beneath her bedclothes. Whether she screamed or not she never knew…

Some one was rapping at her door, speaking cheerily. She took her head out of the clothes with a revulsion of shame at her fright. The horrible little creature was gone! Mr. East was speaking at her door. What was it he was saying? *What?*

"*I'm ready now*," he said. "*Shall I come in, and begin?*"

The Oculist

ON A BENCH in the sunshine in Hyde Park sat, one morning in late summer, a young man of twenty-seven, and at a discreet distance, a hospital nurse in a dark-blue uniform. He was fair-haired and fair-skinned, athletic and well-grown, but his eyes were invisible behind densely black glasses that fitted tightly to his brows and cheek-bones. He had been brought there, as had been his routine for two weeks, by the nurse; his hand had lain within her arm as he walked, she had guided his steps. She brought him always, by a convention that stung him by its folly, to a fresh place to sit down; in reality it mattered nothing to him where he sat if he were free from the patter of passing feet; it mattered nothing since he looked only into the eversame blackness of his glasses.

But he could not bear the sound of those invisible feet, the murmur about him of a crowd that he could not see; it tortured him so that at last he had to fight against the impulse to hit out suddenly with his arms, if only so he might feel those bodiless presences. He did not explain this to the woman who accompanied him, nothing of this nor of the hundred other things that hurt and tormented him. They had often an almost wordless struggle for the objective of their two daily walks, she for the thronged promenade that she considered cheerful for her patient, he for the silence of the turf stretch where the sun fell upon him warmly, a gentle caress that smarted his eyes in their darkness with tears.

He had lived in the darkness for two weeks.

Before that he had had an enforced holiday for three months. That holiday, the oculist he had consulted had told him, would probably cure his trouble altogether. But he had received impressive warnings. No reading, no eye-strain whatever, no late hours – the stout, slow-moving old man confronted him, as he had confronted the great ones of the earth, with ultimata. There was a scarcely hidden threat if these instructions were not followed. If there was further inflammation— The stout old man's voice tailed off. Well, there mustn't be any more inflammation.

To the young man the shock was severe. When he entered that roomful of apparatus presided over by the stout old gentleman, he had anticipated nothing more serious than the prescription of an elegant pince-nez. He had gone to keep his appointment, rather flattered by the prospective pince-nez, as he might have gone to buy a new hat in March.

He had to tell his father what the specialist had said. He made light of it to his mother; and to his sisters, who at the moment were superlatively interested over costumes for a fancy ball, he said nothing about it at all. His father, a prosperous solicitor taking this only son into partnership, assented grudgingly to the prescribed holiday. The young man went down to lodgings in a Sussex farmhouse.

It was a charming holiday. He found himself near a hospitable household of friends, welcoming and gay; it was summer weather; one young girl of the party seemed to him beautiful, and the most sympathetic and intelligent being he had ever dreamt of. He fell in love. His headaches vanished, and at the end of three months had had almost forgotten the reason why he was idling so happily in that pleasant place. On the eve of his intended proposal to her he remembered. He realised that as a matter of form, he must make that all right. He would get a clean bill of health.

He raced up to London the following day by the earliest train. He bought a day ticket; he would return in the late afternoon, and walk over to her home that evening. It would be dusk; and then moonlight, summer moonlight, would make the world still more wonderful than it was already. It would be the perfect scene.

He walked buoyantly up Harley Street; he knew the house by some absurd streaky orange flower-pots that decorated the windows of the stout old gentleman, who had no time for aesthetic susceptibility. But the stout old gentleman was abroad. His partner offered him, through the medium of a pallid girl secretary, an appointment for half-past five.

That was a nuisance, but it would do. The last train down left at seven-fifteen.

Meanwhile he had all the afternoon to kill. He lunched early, and after his three months of Sussex and bare down stretches the very streets were amusing. He felt superbly well, he wanted to leap and shout. He walked along familiar streets ablaze with sunshine, down Shaftesbury Avenue, down Charing Cross Road. A bustle of approach and arrival at the Coliseum. He saw brilliant posters. Of course! Down there in Sussex they had talked of *Sumurun*; she had loved it.

He went in.

He was in luck, as usual. They were just beginning. All through, he knew he'd be in luck that day. He sat down. A youth in Turkish dress stood before the curtain and declaimed a prologue, the curtain parted and rolled back, and the East, that magical, romantic, humorous East of his boyhood, that wonderland of the *Arabian Nights*, began to live before him on the stage. And not only remote upon stage; out of a blinding light edged by black nothingness at the back of the theatre came the people of his childish imagination running down a flowery pathway straight across the auditorium to the stage, as if they had been born in the sun and ran to earth along a rainbow. Their feet ran or danced or marched along that pathway at one point not ten feet from his head; a trick that touched them with magic and mystery and reality at once. Shining brown bodies, glittering black eyes, and flashing white teeth, they swayed and swung and danced to jolly music; beautiful veiled women slipped about the bustle of the bazaar followed by a pageantry of attendants, were loved passionately and died for dramatically; female slaves with laughing eyes smuggled contraband lovers into their mistress's presence; he saw the inner splendours of an Eastern palace, whose music was slender fountains that splashed and tinkled into their basins, and where Sumurun danced for her lover. Crimsons and purples, green and blue, azure, topaz, cloth of gold and silver, hues of the peacock and golden pheasant – a wonderful web of colour intensely lit, a very glut of colour! He had looked so long on the grey Sussex Downs. And then vengeance pursued those lovers, and an angry sheik struck with his gleaming scimitar at the great brass shield uplifted to protect them – Crash!

The curtain fell. He sat back, aware once more of himself and of the theatre about him.

He discovered that his head ached, and that there was an aching pain behind his eyes.

He stumbled out, seeing dancing spots of light on a crimson mist.

He took a taxicab to Harley Street, and sat nervously in the oculist's dreary, shadowed waiting-room, watching every palpitation of his pain as if he watched a living thing. He waited half an hour, three-quarters of an hour, an hour. Two other people came, sat in the shadows, passed out to their interviews. His pain increased.

He was taken at last into the presence of a buoyant young man, inclined to be stoutish, with a manner whose cheerfulness affected him like a noisy laugh. He found himself trembling suddenly, and sat down. His voice cracked as he gave his name, and the young oculist glanced at him, slightly surprised, before he turned to look up his case in a card index.

There followed the usual questions. "Been to a theatre, have you?" remarked the buoyant young practitioner. "That was a pity, eh? Now let me look into your eyes."

A searching light was focussed into his eyes. "H'm," said the young specialist, looking into one eye. "Hah!" switching aside the direction of the searchlight and looking into the other. "Oh! what a pity, eh?" laying down his lens and looking at his patient as if he joined him in commiserating a spoilt hat.

"Is there – inflammation?" asked the patient. After what he had been told three months before, he knew that his future depended on the answer to that.

"Oh dear yes. In your right eye," said the young specialist, turning to his bureau for pen and ink. He scribbled with momentous pauses of thoughtfulness; the thin cloth of his grey frock coat wrinkled across his fat back. His patient sat in silence, tense with the terror of a further question that must be asked.

The specialist swung half round on his revolving chair and held out his prescription. "You'll get this made up, won't you?" he said. "Rub it in twice a day over the brows – I mean once a day over each brow and once a day behind each ear," – he became trivially explicit. "Then here is the formula for your glasses – they'll be black, you know. Till you get them—" he rummaged in a drawer and produced a hideous shade of black card – "wear this. You must rest your eyes a bit. You'll have to have a nurse—"

"A nurse!"

"Take you about for a bit, you know. I'll send you one if you'll allow me; excellent woman. She'll take care of you all right. And you'll come and see us again when Mr. Priestley's back."

The buoyant young specialist got up to indicate that he had done all he could.

The young man rose to his extended hand, and tried to ask his supreme question offhandedly. "Do you think I'm in a bad way then?" he got out.

The doctor looked at him confidently. "I think we'll save the other eye," he said with cheerfulness.

Save the other eye!

"Do you mean I'm likely to become – blind?" He was holding his voice steady as if with a physical grip, but it snapped at that last word, snapped to a falsetto.

The young specialist looked at him with surprise, as if he had committed the gravest indecorum. "Oh!" he protested. "Mustn't look at it like that, you know, really. I think it's all very hopeful." He charged his voice with increased warmth. "You mustn't get depressed. That *would* be a pity. That never does any good. You'll probably see quite well with the other eye. Plenty of people only use one eye, and never know it," he went on anecdotally, and humouring his patient doorward. "I'm told I do it myself."

He was in the hall, and the parlourmaid, with a manner adequate for any disaster, was saying, "Taxi, sir?"

He told the man to drive to Victoria Station, and not until he was halfway there did he realise the change that had become necessary. He stopped the cab and gave his father's address in South Kensington.

In that cab, and for all the sleepless night that followed, it was as if he fought a black canopy that was falling, and covering him thickly, fold upon fold, depth upon depth.

During the night he tried to write a letter to that beloved one in Sussex. He tore up what he had written at last and wept with rage, with passionate anger, beat his fists upon the table and set half a dozen things dancing and clattering to the floor. A moment after came a tap at his bedroom door, and his mother's voice.

"Is anything the matter, dear?"

He controlled himself. "Nothing, mother," he called back. "Only upset something. Sorry."

"Oh!" he heard her. "Good night, dear."

"Good-night, mother."

He sat down and presently began a fresh letter...

He imagined that some emotional scene would occur in his family when they knew what had happened to him, but by modern standards they indeed behaved very well. He told his father, who received his statements uneasily, and assured him that specialists always made too much of things; and through his father the fact filtered to the others. They adopted a convention of speech – "Edward is resting his eyes" – and after that had been said once or twice it might have been they who were blind and not he, so completely did they appear not to see the cardboard shade that he wore. After a day had passed in this manner he on his side could not have borne a commiserating word from any of them; he began to avoid his mother; for sometimes he heard in her voice a tremulousness that might soften to speech about this stark fact they were all covering so decently.

A strange existence began to be his. The nurse arrived, and the black glasses closed him in with darkness. His days became a routine of trivial happenings that concerned himself and his parasite, the nurse, and left others untouched. It was the strangest thing in his experience, that this colossal misfortune could thus single him out. It was like a murder being done in the midst of a tea-party that ignored it. They left him to the companionship of the nurse; they seemed a little afraid of him. They were afraid of their own inadequacy, they had no words ready. He felt they were all oddly, curiously embarrassed.

Mealtimes were the worst part of his day. Then indeed their presence was hard to maintain; his tragedy was a great raw-boned naked thing which the rags of their convention could not keep covered; constantly at something said, or some disability of his, disguise slipped from it and it glared upon them. As day followed day this became so great a stress upon him that he longed to shatter their fine-spun web of behaviour with one blow of his fist upon the table, shout out, "I am blind! I am blind!" and force them to live with the clean and dreadful truth. And then some little thing, the decorous footfall of the parlourmaid behind his chair, the offered helping on a plate, discreetly named as she brought it, would shut him back into the silence.

As the days passed on a hundred trivialities hemmed him in and held him from the shouted truth, as the fine threads of the Lilliputians bound Gulliver to the earth. The nurse, cool and indifferent, took control of him in endless petty ways, regulated his hours with ridiculous precision as if that were germane to his recovery, meticulously carried out the oculist's instructions, and was conscientiously cheerful until her patient's silence aggrieved her. More than anything else, the perverted nature of this woman struck him as amazing. Her cold self-possession in the presence of his human tragedy had an almost dreamlike quality to him, it was so strangely impenetrable by his overwhelming disaster. At first he did not know that this was so, he credited her with a sympathy which she could not express, and then he began to realise that to her he was nothing very exceptional or extraordinary. He had never had a serious illness in his life, he had never before been attended by a professional nurse. To her, he wasn't a human being in voiceless torment, he was a number in an oculist's case-book, he was at the moment her unexhilarating means of livelihood. He was not an individual victim of a dire and unique tragedy, but one of hundreds. The mechanical excellence of her devices for the care of him frightened his soul. So might a caught bird, had it the wit, thrill with new terror at the final captivity implied by the perfection of its cage. He saw her as the frigid concierge of a dreadful part of the universe, an organised corner of the world whose existence he had hardly apprehended, whose doors yawned slowly open to receive him. She and the oculist and the world about him were ready with a routine into which he could be dropped. God! That was the appalling thought! it was ready for him. A routine – a prison! Out of the world of light into the world of darkness. They only asked of him to behave, according to their prescription, "well." If he accepted their provision for him, went through that door without a sound, took his appointed place in that nether world without a sigh, they would give his behaviour their recognition, they would call him "plucky".

In his darkness, he thought much of courage, and how its quality has changed in the life of man. It had come to mean this silent endurance of terrible things, things in themselves great and gaunt and awful. Blindness and slow disease and death, and loss and separation from a loved fellow-creature; he saw that these things sat among family circles and with groups of friends, silent, dark, enormous faceless presences, dreadful ghosts to whom the living must speak first before their voices can be heard. And in these days in which his life course was set, it was courage not to look at them, not to speak of them, to pretend with passionate earnestness that they were not there. It was not always so that man had dealt with grief. He thought of Job and his affliction, and the three friends of Job who "lifted up their voice, and wept; and rent every one his mantle and sprinkled dust upon their heads towards heaven." Thus they sat with him seven days and seven nights.

"Wherefore is light given to him that is in misery, and life unto the bitter in soul;

"Why is light given to a man whose way is hid, and whom God hath hedged in?..."

That was an ennoblement of great sorrow. But, he reflected, in those ancient days the griefs and troubles of man fell upon him by no chance, they came invested with a high splendour, they were the anger of God made manifest. Now these things were stripped of that dignity. The rich promise of the life that had been unfolding before him could be smashed as idly by a chance encounter with bacteria as his own unconscious foot might smash a fly upon the road.

He had had a reply to his letter from Sussex. Through it shone plainly her readiness to adapt herself to his disaster. Perhaps his misfortune had made him supersensitively critical; it was as if he missed something in her letter he had expected to find there. He reread it for that invisible something. What was it that it lacked so cruelly? He hardly knew; he knew only that her self-orientated sentences of sympathy left him utterly uncomforted. She made it evident how completely she envisaged their future, herself the limelit figure, his slave and link with the world, tender, ministering. It seemed to her a not undesirable life. She would add her effort to this business they were all about, this stifling of reality. He imagined her with the first freshness of their union evaporated, devoting herself to the endeavour to make him just as happy as if he could see; while his part would be to pretend that she was his sight and his eyes. He felt that for such a vision to be possible her imagination of the life they might have lived together must have been thin indeed. He rebelled, with every fibre of his heart he rebelled against this poor substitute offered him.

No. He had not realised it before, but it seemed that foolish things might happen in the world he was in, things that made his life worthless and void; and that he had run up against one of them. He held one liberty still, the liberty to leave it.

As he sat in the sunshine on the bench in the park that late summer morning with the nurse beside him, he reflected that while he could still see he would be wise to safeguard that way out. Presently that might be more difficult to do. With the increase of his malady they would hem him in still more effectually from every exercise of his will.

It was the nurse's evening off duty. About seven he pleaded fatigue and went to his own bedroom. And then he took off his black glasses – in the dusk, his eyes did not feel the shock of the light very much – and waited hovering about his door like an escaping criminal. He slipped successfully downstairs, and by using his latchkey opened and shut the hall door without noise. In spite of his gruesome errand he felt happier for the adventure.

"I want something to kill an old dog with," he said to the chemist's assistant.

He was in considerable spirits by this time, and became anecdotal about the dog. It was all surprisingly easy. By the chemist's advice he bought sixpennyworth of prussic acid.

He went out of the shop, resisted with enormous difficulty the temptation to walk on instead of returning home, and with the same precautions got back into the house quite successfully. No one had seen him.

He locked up the bottle with its innocent looking lumps of white stuff, in his writing-desk, and felt he had done a prudent thing.

In the night he was visited by a new fear. He realised that once his sight was gone he might not be able to find the bottle again. His head ached, it seemed to him that his eyes ached intolerably, and that he was paying for their brief exposure in the dusk. In his closed eyes began a chase of spangled stars, a fiery rain of falling pinpoints of light, an interminable dance of dazzling intricate patternings from which he was helpless to escape. He had suffered that torment before, he groaned now to realise its fresh onset. Over and over again, try as he would, his burning eyeballs rolled to follow the track of those glittering constellations till they fell into the corner of the field, to sweep up again as his eyeballs rose, and drag them down once more. And then, holding his eyeballs still by sheer will, they danced and spun and mocked him and shone with fiercer light.

He got up. He took out the bottle, pushing aside the bandage that the nurse arranged for him nightly before he slept. It seemed to him that his eyes hurt him much more, and that his sight was blurred. He held the bottle in his hand. Surely the time was already come. He broke the seal slowly.

Mysterious clutch of life! He put it back into its place.

Two or three times after that he took it out and looked at it, telling himself that he must familiarise himself with its exact whereabouts. He would not acknowledge that he took it out with intention; unless he had gone through with the business he would have had to admit himself a coward…

One morning an appointment card came for him from the secretary of the slow-moving old gentleman in Harley Street, who was back again in his room full of apparatus. He knew then, what he had not realised before, that he hoped still, hoped like a fierce pain.

He was led into the presence of the stout old gentleman by the nurse and left. He answered a string of slow deliberate questions. In the shadowed room his dark glasses were taken from him.

"You don't feel any pain now?" suggested the stout old gentleman.

"No," said the young man judicially, "not exactly now."

The usual scrutiny of his eyes followed, punctuated with more slow questions. "And how long have you been using the dark glasses?" for the second time.

He put out his hand to replace the glasses. "You need not put those on again," remarked the oculist as if he were saying the most commonplace thing in the world. "I see nothing much the matter with your eyes at present—"

"Nothing the matter—" the young man's voice broke hysterically. "Do you mean – I shan't lose my sight?"

"Tt, tt," said the old gentleman impatiently. "I can find nothing very much the matter now with your eyes at all."

"But—" said the young man, and then turned away. He realised he was going to burst into tears. He put his hands to his face and leant upon them for a moment.

The old gentleman, who was putting away his lenses in their place in a nest of drawers, turned sharply at the sound and was exceedingly astonished. He turned his back and fiddled with the contents of the drawer to give his patient time to recover himself.

The young man could barely await the opening of the consulting-room door. The nurse remained forgotten in the waiting-room. Almost at one bound he was in the street – joyful street, glorious street! striding along on feet that did not seem to touch the pavement, laughing with joy, seeing, seeing, seeing...

The Emerald

§1

MR. MOONEY'S SHOP in the High Street was wedged between a tobacconist's and a pastry-cook's. They were both flourishing concerns, and long ago their proprietors had rebuilt their old frontages and put in large windows of glossy plate glass to replace the little square panes that still protected the curiosity dealer's varied stock. Altogether there must have been between three and four hundred objects of the most miscellaneous kind and origin crowded on shelves against those small panes, and if one had included the mother-of-pearl card counters, engraved and shaped like fish, the mixed plateful of old coins, and some foreign postage stamps stuck on sheets of browned paper, they would have totalled a couple of hundred more. There were rows of plates of oriental china, vases of every kind and shape, two stately figures of Kwannon, a little gentleman of white porcelain with whiskers of real black hair, seated in great dignity with his hands tucked up into his long sleeves, three barometers, some ivory carvings, weapons, an Indian god writhing his astonishing equipment of arms, a lot of miscellaneous jewellery and old watches – but the catalogue is too familiar for repetition. There are still, thank heaven, many such shops. Behind the window, lit by such daylight as could slip through the crevices of this display, was more of Mr. Mooney's stock-in-trade, heaped on shelves, on tables, or packed onto and inside a chest of drawers and a book-case. A customer had to move warily; and when the dimensions of Mr. Mooney, coming forward slowly from his little back room to answer the jangle of the shop-door bell, were fully exhibited, the possibility of the arrangement became more remarkable still. It was easy to infer that Mr. Mooney had not made a hasty movement nor had an irritable impulse for many a long year.

Mr. Mooney had closed his shop for the night. His outside shutter was pulled down, his modest supper was spread on the table round the lamp in his back room, his cat, as placid and as circumspect in movement as her master, was seated before the fire, and the three old ledgers in which Mr. Mooney kept his accounts were laid out beside his supper things for his monthly inspection. He was turning the pages of the book devoted to his purchases, and he had paused in the turning. His large begrimed forefinger was pointing to one item on the crowded page of sloped writing:

I Emerald. ?

That was the entry. It had a line to itself.

He had found the emerald among a litter of small rubbish in a lacquer box that he had acquired in the same sale lot as some Indian weapons that he had bid for. He had bought the whole lot for twenty-three shillings. When he got the things home, he had turned out the lacquer box, and among beads and shells and scraps of carved sandalwood and so on, was the emerald. It puzzled him from the first, but to begin with he assumed it was a piece of green glass. It was oddly shaped, not geometrically true, but a kind of lopsided oblong about an inch and a half by three-quarters, so that he turned it about in his hand speculating what it could have been made for. And as he looked at it he began to see that it was far more beautiful than any glass he had ever known; it was a very clear and lovely green, the colour was so intense in the heart of it that it shone like green fire. He pondered over it, and at last put it to the test of his tourmaline tongs. It was not glass. No, at any rate it was not glass.

Mr. Mooney knew of no other green stone and could learn of no other green stone that this could be. In spite of some obscure resistance in his mind his persuasion grew that this was indeed an emerald, and a wonderful emerald at that. For him it was a profoundly disconcerting discovery. He locked it up in a rusty old safe that lay in a corner among some second-hand books in his back room and did his utmost to dismiss it from his mind. The problem of its disposal did not trouble him. Its value was so immense that to realise it would have completely upset the routine of his life, and the routine of his life was what he valued. Its ownership would have made him conspicuous. He disliked conspicuousness so much that he did not frequent the big auction-rooms at all, his habit was to bid huskily from the back rows at small household sales. And what was a still greater difficulty to him, he could not visualise a purchaser. Mr. Mooney was one of those shopkeepers who are particular to whom they hand over their goods. He liked to feel that the things he admired were going to a kind and appreciative home. He had a great nose for another dealer, and would never sell to a customer he suspected of being one unless it was something that he despised. He made short commons of the customer who would attempt to bargain by disparaging an article. "If it isn't what yer care for, I don't want to sell it yer," he would say bluntly, and replace the object out of reach. He had been known to declare stoutly to a smartly furred and jewelled lady who asked him for "all that darling old Chelsea" that it was already sold to an entirely mythical gentleman – "the housemaids of her sort 'ud smash up anything," he declared – and to the customer he thought worthy he would abate his marked price without being asked to do so, offering a lower figure as if he did not want to miss the chance of getting a bit of his stock well settled in life. When he tried to think of a purchaser who could afford the emerald, he thought of a figure like the most disagreeable capitalists in the cartoons of Mr. Will Dyson, and their feminine equivalents; royalties could no longer buy such things, and if they could there was no one left among them who Mr. Mooney could possibly imagine as wearing the emerald well. Mr. Mooney, when he thought of the emerald being worn, thought of someone like the Queen of Sheba advancing very slowly up to the gold and ivory throne of Solomon. At least that was something like what was in his mind. But nowadays there were no Queens, no Occasions, fit to adorn the splendour of that jewel.

He took it out of the safe, settled down at the table again, and turned it between his great thumb and finger, this way and that, in the light of the lamp. In the stillness of the shabby little room it shone with a magnificence above all earthly things, it proclaimed its kinship with the stars. "You pretty dear," said Mr. Mooney softly to it, lying in the hard creased palm of his hand.

There was no avarice in Mr. Mooney, and it gave him no particular pleasure beyond the looking at it that this treasure was his own. Indeed he regretted it in his shabby old safe as a lovely living thing imprisoned in a dungeon. He would say of a good thing among his stock, "Somebody ought t'ave it who'd appreciate it"; and that sentiment, greatly magnified in intensity, was his chief feeling about the emerald. Locked up in that dingy safe, with the marvel of its colour slain by darkness, what good was it? It seemed to Mr. Mooney that when he shut it in the dark safe he killed it. "Some one who'd appreciate it," he murmured, turning it over. He meant, of course, for its beauty's sake, and not on the least account because of its money value. He had a complete contempt for value expressed in terms of money. It occurred to him fancifully that he felt about this jewel as a man might feel about a favourite and lovely daughter who was also a great heiress. She must be loved and married for her own sake, even as if she were penniless. It was his business to circumvent all fortune-hunters. He himself had seen its loveliness when it lay among the dusty scraps in that lacquer box, and so it ought to be seen and admired and desired by its possessor.

There came into his mind a daring thought. Suppose he were to put it, his jewel, into the window, obscurely among cheap trifles, and let it wait for the recognising eye. Like a princess who would be wooed as a beggar maid. There were three trays of odds and ends on the lowest window shelf, bits of jewellery, decanter stoppers and what not, assorted under the prices ten shillings, five shillings, and half a crown. Suppose he were to put it into the half-crown tray!

And the following morning, before he raised the outside shutter, he did so. He stood in the dimness of the shop, a heavy old man in cracked slippers and a shabby coat, leaning forward slowly and carefully, breathing huskily with the touch of asthma that was always with him, and pushed the great emerald among the riff-raff of the half-crown tray. It was right in the corner of the window, and he looked at it from outside and was satisfied with its place.

§2

A boy and girl walked sedately along the suburban road on their way to school. It was a hot, sweet May morning, the sky was summer blue overhead, there was a great rejoicing among the birds, and the air was lilac-scented. Laburnum dropped her yellow hair over the garden fences among giant bouquets of pink and white hawthorn. The boy held a baize bag by the string and swung it round and round, the girl clutched a mackintosh under her arm and poked her fingers into a shiny new pencil-case.

They were in the midst of an argument. "I'm as old as you now," the girl had said.

"You're not," said the boy.

"I am. I'm nine. So are you."

"I'm nine and three months."

"Only babies count months," said the girl crushingly. "You were eight yesterday, and you're only one day older now."

"But today's a Birthday, and I'm nine. Same as you are."

"You're a silly."

"You mustn't say that on my Birthday," said the girl very solemnly.

This was incontestably the Law. "What else d'you get?" he said, eyeing the pencil-case.

"Auntie gave me a purse with a half-crown in." She tugged at her pocket. "See."

"Are you going to buy something?"

"M'm." She knew what she wanted to buy, but it had to do with a doll, and she was shy of admitting an interest in dolls to Peter-next-door. Peter-next-door was so called to distinguish him from Peter her brother, and the girl, because of a certain vertical dancing step she had in moments of excitement, was known as Midge.

"You'd better save it up," said the boy.

"Why?"

"I'm saving all my money for Exploring," said the boy proudly. For Peter-next-door, he had settled, was to be an Explorer by profession.

"I've something to tell you," said the girl seriously.

"What?"

"It's a secret. Promise."

"Promise."

She flushed and hesitated. She held back her effect for a moment. "I've settled I'm going to be an Explorer too."

"Are you?" He took it quite calmly, as if this life-shaking decision was nothing; almost as coolly as if he doubted she would carry out her intention.

"I shall explore China," she announced.

He hadn't taken China into his itinerary. "There's that blue car again. She's a beauty."

Midge did not simulate an interest in cars at any time. She walked on, nettled, feeling she had committed herself irrevocably to a life of toil and danger and got very little in return. Peter-next-door craned his neck back to watch the car, and blundered into a policeman. "Now then, little chap," said the policeman, steadying him with two large gloved hands. "Little chap" restored Midge's cheerfulness. Their road debouched upon the High Street. Over that they must cross carefully, remembering the many warnings about traffic, and then go on down another side street to their school. Mr. Mooney's shop was on their way.

"Let's just look at Hanky Panky," said Midge.

Hanky Panky was Midge's idea of a Chinese name for the white porcelain gentleman with the black hair whiskers. So they drew up before the curiosity shop and gazed at Hanky Panky.

"I wish I could buy Hanky Panky," said Midge enviously.

But Peter-next-door was employing his time in speculating about the usefulness to a young explorer of certain curious curved knives. They went straight at first and then they wriggled in the blade – so. That was the bit you twisted.

Midge turned from Hanky Panky with a fleeting glance below to the bowl of mother-of-pearl fish, which she also greatly desired. The sun gleamed across the street and touched the lower corner of the window with a pointing finger of golden light.

"Oh!" said Midge suddenly, in a soft squeak of a voice. She tugged at Peter-next-door. "Look at that, Peter!"

"Which?"

"*There*."

The emerald shone out from the dusty company in the half-crown tray.

"Well?"

"Isn't it *lovely*. Look."

"It's a bit of glass."

"I believe it's a real jewel."

"I expect it's only an imitation," said the worldly-wise Peter-next-door.

"No. Look at it from here. Just here. Now look. See its lovely colour. It's real."

"It's 'all in this tray two-and-six.' So it can't be."

"I believe it is," said Midge solemnly. "It's a very rich and rare jewel. Somebody's lost it."

"Come along," said Peter.

She half turned to follow him, and then stopped.

"Peter!" she called out.

"Well, what?"

"I'm going to buy it."

"What for?"

"I'm going to buy it," repeated Midge, and plunged for the shop door. Then with her hand opening it and the bell jangling, she turned swiftly.

"Peter," she said beseechingly, "you *must* come too."

So they both edged into the shop, looking a little scared at the unusualness and silence of the place they had raided.

"Pussy," whispered Peter to Mr. Mooney's cat, delicately curled up among a table of glassware.

The door of the back room opened. Mr. Mooney came out. His eyes were aimed near the top of the shop door; they looked surprised, and then fell slowly to adjust themselves to the unusual dimensions of his customer.

"Good morning, Miss," he said helpfully.

"*Please*," said Midge, who now was holding tight on to Peter's thumb, "there's a green thing—"

Mr. Mooney's eyes sharpened suddenly.

"Is that a half-crown one?" said Midge, pointing. She was very flushed and her eyes shone.

"Let me see," said Mr. Mooney non-committally.

He took the emerald out of the tray and turned it over. Then he looked steadily at Midge. She was looking up at him eagerly, her cheeks were flushed, she was a little breathless and her lips were parted, and her eyes shone like his jewel.

"May I see?" she asked, holding out her hand.

He gave it to her. With a little cry she held it out, this way and that. She stooped down and plunged it into a pool of sunlight that splashed the drab floor. "Oh, Peter, look!" she said.

"M'm—" said Peter, with approval.

"*Is* it half a crown?" said Midge, still kneeling on the floor, with a glance up at Mr. Mooney like a towering cliff above her.

"Yes, Miss," said Mr. Mooney, deciding suddenly.

Midge stood up, tugged out the purse, opened it and pulled out the new half-crown without a look at it, and pushed it hurriedly into Mr. Mooney's hand. Then, holding the emerald very tightly clasped, and with a bright scarlet colour on her cheeks, she went out, followed by Peter.

They retreated from Mr. Mooney's sight along the High Street, the girl with a little bobbing step and the boy swinging level after her. Mr. Mooney watched them until he could see them no longer, until they had completely disappeared for nearly a minute. Then he turned round very slowly. He took a step towards his back room, and then stopped and looked again out of his window, looking at nothing of the passing traffic, for some moments before he finally turned away and went back to his sitting-room behind the shop.

§3

The morning was golden and glorious, and wearing on to mid-day. The school of Midge and Peter was a hive of industry; there was a history lesson going on in one room about the Wars of the Roses, a geography lesson in another where small children were dabbling their fingers in trays of wet sand, a drawing class where they were all drawing a flower-pot very carefully from nature, the science class where they had a basin of water that they mustn't splash and some glass tubes they mustn't blow through, and a singing class making a great and cheerful noise in the Big Room, and you might have looked through every one of these scenes of activity and improvement and found neither Midge nor Peter.

And quite two miles away, on a heathery common alight with yellow gorse in bloom, on a shore of pale gold sand that edged a miniature lake of sky-blue water, sat Midge and Peter, and dug and scooped and patted and shaped busily, a palace of sand to hold the great emerald.

The seditious idea of staying away from school had occurred to them when they were nearly at its door. Midge it was had rebelled. "It's my Birthday," she made her grievance, but in reality it was the thought of disciplined, occupied hours with her new treasure hidden and untouchable that she could not endure. And there was a maddening happiness in the sunshine, a misery in being indoors. Peter-next-door regarded her with an intellectual interest. "Don't go, then," he said logically, and when she hesitated at the imagination of the awful row there would be, he observed that if she was afraid of a mere schoolmistress like Miss Merglums, how did she expect to get on when she fought cannibals like he was going to. "*She* can't eat you," he pointed out.

And then Peter, still in an attitude of intellectual detachment and pleasurably watching the agonised wriggling of Midge's indecision, advanced the theory that one must test one's courage occasionally by daring deeds. Otherwise, how could one know if one had it? In the end, when the decision was made, Midge looked scared and serious, and Peter was in the best of spirits.

They turned back to the High Street, and went up the hill to the Common. The Common on its nearer side was known to them intimately; there were ranges of gravelly hillocks and they had names for each mound; tiny woods, small and large ponds, and further off, wilder parts where they had been on a few special long walks, and then the unknown. They began to run and scamper up and down the hillocks, play Touch, and race, and every now and then Midge would take out the emerald, which she had put in her purse for safety, and look at it and play with it and let the sunlight shine through it and upon it. And by a little lake of clear blue water they sat down and made a pile of their belongings and began the castle of stones and wet sand that later on was flower-trimmed, and stood on a noble lawn of velvety green moss. They played at Buried Treasure with the emerald, but Midge was uneasy when it was buried in the earth, and though Peter marked the exact place with a stick and there were important clues along the route on the way to it, Midge did not play the game with zest when they had to leave it out of sight. The second time, they did not find it all at once when they began to dig for it, so that Midge refused to have it buried any more. They guarded it in the sand castle, and with sticks they shot and killed several bands of robbers – "Bang – *bang*." Then they found themselves hungry, although it was as a matter of fact barely twelve o'clock, and they sat by the miniature lake and ate all their school lunch out of Peter's baize bag. There was a pink crab-apple dipping branches into the water opposite them, and behind was a wild-cherry tree and on that day it was a great haunt of tortoiseshell butterflies, hanging with wings outspread and palpitating in the hot sun. Midge counted up to fourteen, but they kept on flying off and getting mixed before she could finish the counting. Peter took off his shoes and stockings to get a piece of the crab blossom to make trees in the castle lawn, and then Midge took off hers, none gainsaying, and pushed her urgent little pink toes into the wet sand, kicking it up and delighting in the soft warm mushiness of it and the feel of the sun on her tender feet. When they were sitting still or quietly busy, bird after bird would fly down to drink or bathe flutteringly at the water's edge. And there was a water-rat who dropped out of a hole in the gravelly bank, and swam and disappeared and then came back, and clambered out and sat brushing his whiskers dry before he popped in home again. "Just like Hanky Panky would," whispered Midge, sitting taut and still, watching. And every now and then Midge would take the great emerald and dip it into the water, for when it was wet and dripping it seemed to her that it was clearest and its colour brightest.

They scrambled up an easy tree, and sat astride a low swinging branch, and Peter told a long story of the astounding adventures that would befall him in the future and the tremendous enemies he would fight and overcome when he went exploring. And while he talked on and on Midge lay back against the tree branch and gazed up into the sky, and wondered to herself what were the thousand minute sparkles of light that spun incessantly against the blue. Were they the stars? And she fell into a dream that only she of all the people alive in the world could see the stars by daylight. And because she could do that, that she was really the Princess of the Stars and that they were all her obedient and loyal subjects. She it was who ruled them and appointed them their courses.

Presently Peter's invention grew tired, and declaring that he had seen a rabbit, he went off and crawled into a thicket of brown bracken and young green willow. Then Midge, feeling lonely after a time, went in after him, and could not find him at first although she coo-eed. And then she found Peter hiding, and so began a game of hide-and-seek that took them far over the common; quite a long distance from the mackintosh and the baize bag they had left by their sand castle. The mackintosh as a matter of fact was still further off by this time, through the industry of a tattered gentleman in an unfashionable hat who had folded it in cummerbund fashion round his middle under his buttoned-up lounge coat. As he disliked making himself conspicuous, he left the baize bag where it lay.

The azure morning sky had yellowed to afternoon, and then the young year's sunshine, like a suddenly tired child, fell asleep. Midge and Peter went on playing, but the air chilled and the light faded. "Tea-time," said Peter presently in a businesslike manner, and struck out homeward across the common.

They went soberly, neither admitting aloud a certain uneasiness they felt as they thought of home and scoldings. Midge carried her emerald again, but there was no sunlight now to flash it into splendour, it lay darkly in the shadow of her hand. They walked across the hillocks they had scampered over in the morning, followed the paths they had ignored then, and came at last to where three ribbons of road converged, ran off the common together, and drove among the clustered houses. There, at the edge of their freedom, they halted. Behind them, tangled in the bramble bushes, ensnared in the depths of mirroring pools, was their day of liberty; before them uprose the houses, tall and disciplined, claiming them back. They said nothing, but Midge turned, and faced the westering sun again. For an instant it gleamed out, a gesture of farewell, and lit her grave small face.

At the meeting of common and town a fountain of water flowed into a horse-trough, poured down over its end and dropped into a gutter grating. The child lifted the green stone and held it in the rushing water. It vanished as if it were snatched from her hand, flashed, was gone through the grating and swallowed in its darkness.

§4

Years afterwards, she said suddenly: "Do you remember the emerald? The day we ran away from school."

Peter, lying on a slope of fine grass starred with gentians, rolled over towards her. "I remember you had some kind of a treasure. A bit of green glass, wasn't it? You lost it. I remember how you cried."

She mused. "That was a wonderful day, Peter. Do you remember how hot the sun was? That stone shines in my mind still – like a great jewel. I can never believe it was not really a marvellous real jewel. I remember it as the most exquisitely lovely thing—"

The man looked up at her. "My dear, you made it so. It is a way you have."

Fear

ON THE KENTISH COAST between Folkestone and Dover there is a stretch of stunted trees and thickly tangled bushes and undergrowth between the sea and the receded cliffs, a strip of picturesque desolation some half mile broad and five miles long. In high summer the nearer end towards Folkestone is the resort of happy holiday parties, picnicking all about a tea and ginger beer shanty; further on its solitudes, wilder and more beautiful, are seldom disturbed. The high road to Dover lies distantly up and away over the top of the cliffs, and such few houses as there are on that road stand remotely back, as if they shrink from the approach of the treacherous cliff edge that creeps ever nearer to them. Here and there the sheer white fall of the cliff is broken by a weedy slope down which a scrambling path traces a thin line, and beneath comes that stretch of tumbled land-slidden ground, its little hills and valleys richly netted with rose briars and brambles, wayfaring tree and hawthorn, and carpeted with short grass all beset with yellow rock roses and violets and a hundred other flowers.

There, close to the sea, in a grassy hollow that spread itself to the hot summer sun, lay a woman face downward to the ground, and sobbed. Her expensive, pretty muslin dress showed little rents here and there where it had been caught by unheeded brambles. And she sobbed because she had come into that lonely and beautiful place to take her life into her hands and end it and die.

She had been sitting there on the grass a long while, it seemed to her, trying to think for the last of so many times, what other thing she could possibly do. But no new light came to her. Her life seemed all too tangled now for new beginnings, and she herself too weary to imagine any. Her husband would never forgive her when he knew, and so went her tired mind again over the old trodden track – nothing could stop his knowing, even if he did not know already. Why else should he have got leave and be coming home again so soon?

She stared upon the sea that lay before her, calm and flat like a lake surface, its edge slapping gently on the grey, clayish sand. Silvery pale blue with lights and shades like satin it was, and further out it was streaked with azure bands. Far on the horizon hung the sails of the fishing-fleet, and it was so still about her that there seemed no nearer living thing.

She could not meet her husband, passionate, noisy, raging with anger as he would be. It was the sick fear of him that had driven her away here. He must be already in their house. She could imagine, and it made her tremble, his heavy tread upstairs, the flung open doors, the harsh loud demands for her. Even if she had stayed to meet him and brave it out with what courage she could, what good would it have been? He would never have let her speak one word of excuse or explanation; he would shout at her and curse, and fling her at last out of his house as he would a dead flower from his coat. What could she be but helpless before a creature so fixed and immutable? Why was there never a human being who could understand the trouble and the unhappiness and the misery, and the muddle and the lies that had netted about her? She wanted to cry, cry to that wise and kindly soul like a child that is hurt and be comforted and loved and set on her feet to try again. And instead of that it seemed to her as if an invisible hand had thrust her down a narrow passage of consequences, impelling her by the whispered fear of the terror behind, till she had come at last to a door, a way out, the only way out, that escape whose key was in the little chemist's bottle in her pocket. The memory of it there stung her with fear; in it she saw the terror that had followed her re-embodied before her now instead of behind her, crouched to spring and grip and shake the pulsating life out of her young and beautiful body.

She sat and gazed at the blue sea, and tried to make it seem real to herself that she would presently lie there dead, growing colder and stiff. In a few moments it might be, if she chose. In a few hours it would have to be. She felt suddenly very lonely. For a long time now she had sat there and seen no one. About an hour since a straggling line of black dots had appeared over the headland on the Folkestone side, schoolboys, they were, hunting the bay for fossils under the energetic direction of an explanatory master. They had come near enough for her to hear their shouts and the deeper voice of their tutor, and then they had turned back again, and disappeared at last in twos and threes beyond the headland. They left her the lonelier for having come and gone. Indeed she felt a little frightened at seeing, so measured out to her eye by those remote black dots, how much she was alone. A rustle in the grass above, the dart of a bird back to its hidden nest, made her start; and then she turned and watched for some time the businesslike coming and going of a pair of blue tits among the pale gold dried grass stems that fringed against the sky; patiently and lovingly attendant they were upon a faintly clamorous invisible cheeping. It was their happy domesticity that struck to her heart and set her sobbing, a sobbing that became violent and uncontrolled. And afterwards she lay still.

She sat up at last, and then stood up with the thought of going down to the edge of the satin-surfaced sea. But as she turned she saw about a quarter of a mile away on a little hillock among the bushes, the slouching figure of a man who seemed to look at her.

Before she recognised its unlikeness she had an instant's panic fear that it might be her husband. She turned from the sea and walked on among the bushes, the softly bred woman's fear of tramps instinctively setting her to put distance between herself and that dubious figure. She walked on quickly for about half a mile, among the stunted trees and up and down slopes, having lost sight of the man almost at once, and then she stopped and sat again upon the grass.

She would have to do it soon; she would have to do it soon. That invisible hand was pressing her hardly now against the very door itself. The afternoon had grown late, and the shadows had lengthened till those of a gorse bush three yards away lay across her feet. The blue was paling out of the sea before a tinge of yellow that grew warmer. The sea was swelling up, and flowing silently nearer with the turned tide. A faint chill crept into the air. It would have to be done soon.

She slipped her hand into her pocket and felt the cool smooth glass of the little bottle there between her fingers. Slowly she drew it out and held it in her lap and looked at it. The thing she had to do became to her as queer and meaningless, as unreasonably stupid, as something that happens in a dream.

She turned as if to look once more upon all the beauty that was about her, and with a clutch of terror at her heart, saw the ill-conditioned figure she had seen before, looking at her and coming towards her, less than a hundred yards away.

With a rush came Fear upon her, and possessed her. She had a watch upon her breast that glittered, shining trinkets on her wrists. She got up hastily, turned some high bushes, and frankly began to run, running into the thicker undergrowth and bending where the trees fell away, lest her head should show. She ran inland towards the cliff and doubled back, her heart thumping heavily with fear, threading through a maze of little tracks, through tiny woods, by a deep-lying pool of black and green stagnant water, struggling with brambles that caught and tore at her, pressed by one thought, to escape the horror of that stealthy pursuer. Thicker grew the trees, and thicker.

She stopped at last in a little opening among them, a circle of thin grass and bracken surrounded so completely by high bushes and small trees that she could hardly see from where she had stepped into the place. She was hot and panting and the noisy beating of her heart against her breast left her breathless. But here was safe hiding. She sank down again upon the grass.

Her hand still clutched upon the little bottle. As her breath grew quiet she saw it there and sat and gazed at it, helplessly, in a curious state of mind that was not thought, but only a dull pain. Twilight grew upon her. A light wind stirred; she shivered. Ah! night was coming and the cold, cold and solitude and the dark; presently she would grow hungry, and the world that had ever held her so caressingly in its lap would lash her with the whip of elementary human needs. That waited for her here, and over there waited her home – her home and her husband. With a low shuddering cry she pulled the stopper from the little bottle, shut her eyes in anguish, and pushed it against her mouth and swallowed.

It dropped out of her hand. For an instant that seemed long she thought that nothing was going to happen to her. Everything was suddenly without sound. Then came a spasm at her heart more terrible in its instant pain than anything she had ever imagined. Without knowing it she fell back upon the ground, and the bushes and patch of sky before her grew small in her vision and very distant, then rushed back upon her and swayed and swayed.

Then she saw, and the sight gazed her eyes in horror, the bushes part before her, and from among them looked out a cunning, evil face.

Cyanide

A LONG LOW white house, with a clock face set in the middle of its upper storey, basked, tranquilly domestic, in the hot sunshine of an early afternoon. It centred in a stone porch flanked by pillars, in whose shadowed depth the house door, standing open, showed a dim interior; rows of green sunblinds veiled its straight Georgian windows like dropped eyelids, and a broad sweep of immaculate gravel encircled a smooth lawn where oval beds of clustered begonias reposed like gaily coloured mats. Beyond was a fence of posts and chains, a meadow with grazing cows, cornfields stacked with grain, and rolling woodland. Little sounds intensified the quiet, the faint whirring of a distant reaper, a gentle cawing from the tall elms behind the house. On the sunny margin of the porch slept a Newfoundland upon his haunches, head between his paws; a sheep dog lay stretched out sideways like an overturned Noah's-ark lamb.

The house awoke. There was a burst of sound, somewhere within a door had opened. The dogs stirred. Dimly seen shapes moved in the hall, a white dress flashed from the shadow, grew brighter in advancing, and came out into the portico, a tall and graceful woman, chatting and smiling with the foremost couple of half a dozen men in shooting jackets. There emerged with them a smell of Harris tweed leather, and birds. "Where's the coffee, Wuzzie?" called a blond-bearded man to her from the rear, and turning sharply just avoided a collision with a man-servant who followed him, bearing it on a tray. Cane chairs were scraped into sociable position, but the blond-bearded man's rapid movements baulked them of their occupants. "We ought to be getting off," he shot at large across the chatter, and dissatisfied with his effect, caught his wife by the arm, shook it slightly, and said in a voice that felled competition, "Wuzzie, we must be getting *off*."

She smiled at him. "Old Fusser!" she said amiably. "Have you ordered the cars round?" and took a cup of coffee for him from a tray held at his oblivious elbow.

"Oh, haven't *you*?" he replied in a voice at the last pitch of exasperation, and swivelled round on his heel to the retreating man-servant. "Cars, SHARP, Willis!"

"S'sir," and the man vanished smartly.

Under the impetus of the host coffee-cups were hastily drained, boots stamped on the flags, hands felt for reassurance in pockets, cigarettes were thrown away in the flush of their youth, and as an afterthought fresh ones lit. “Aren’t you coming with us, Mrs Eveson?” said plaintively a tall thin man with insecure eyeglasses, standing with a concave sideways curve from head to heel. “Not again, I’m afraid. I’ve changed,” replied the smiling lady in the white dress, and stepped back as her husband butted in between them, upsetting the tall man’s curve. He despised men who drooped beside his wife, and troubled little about them. “Where are those cars, Wuzzie?” he began, but with a whirr from the shrubbery like rising pheasants first one very glittering and then one extraordinarily battered motor car swept round into the gravel path, drew up before the porch with a smart gride of brakes and halted, panting. The blond-bearded man, his foot on the step of the glittering car, rounded up his companions with his eyes. “Coming with me, Preston?” he called to a man in grey who stood a little apart with his back to the rest, examining his gun. “Right-O,” replied a pleasant voice, as the gun still held attention, but two other men climbed in behind their host and the chauffeur started.

“Wuzzie!” shouted the blond-bearded man, jumping round in his seat as the car took the curve; “have tea ready when we come back!” but the chauffeur pulling up to allow him to make this remark learnt with little delay that he had done the wrong thing, and plunged forward again with a spurt that took him through the gate. The gate was held open by a gardener's boy who had sprung into existence like a special creation. A short, spectacled man in rubber waders, very sporting in attire up to the waistline and thereafter frankly clerical, assumed loving control of the battered car, and there was nothing for the tall man with the curve to do but to unbend it and get in.

The lady in the white dress turned about to her last guest. "Is there anything the matter, Mr Preston?" she called out, advancing. And then at his side, in a quick, soundless whisper, "*Coming back to tea?*"

"*Yes*," he said as soundlessly, and then aloud, "All right now, thanks." He straightened up, did not look at her, and got into the battered car. The car started, jibbed, jerked forward with a lunge that threw its occupants violently forward and nearly took it on the grass, and finally settled down to the path through the gate. The lady in white stood in the porch smiling brightly and waving them off, her eyes on the tall curved man as long as he looked at her. Then they slid for an instant to the back of the man in grey.

She was alone. Her lips moved in a happy little smile, her brown eyes softened.

The gardener's boy shut the gate slowly and very thoroughly, and prepared to cease to exist again.

"George," she called.

The boy started round and ran across the grass towards her with a clutch at his cap.

"Please find Wates and tell him I want to speak to him."

"Yess'm."

The dark-haired lady sat down on one of the cane chairs, and the dogs grouped themselves about her on the understanding that they were all three now finally arranged for the afternoon. She clasped her hands about her knee, leaning forward, and her smile came and went. A pink flush crept into her cheek. She remained so lost in thought – it might have been a moment, it might have been hours…

Wates scraped his boots on the gravel and ventured to clear his throat.

The lady in white looked up and saw him. "Oh! Wates," she said, and seemed for a moment to wonder what it was she had to say next.

Wates cleared his throat again helpfully.

"Wates, there are altogether too many wasps."

Wates looked as if convicted of being over-zealous, and stood reproved.

"I do wish you could find the nest."

"I've 'unted and 'unted, 'm, and George he's 'unted. All round the fence we bin – I've know'd 'em before foot o' the fence. All round the garding we bin." He paused, and added brightly, "If ther'd bin a nest I bet a guinea we'd a seen it."

"Then perhaps they are not in the garden."

"Didn't know as how they'd bin so bad these last days."

"Wates, they're awful! Look there now!" and the lady in white pointed up into the air where a yellow body sailed past and away.

"That's a waps," said Wates in triumph.

"There's another! And there! Now where are they going?" She walked swiftly after the flying wasps, stopped to pick up the track of another, hurried after it to the fence. She became suddenly active, sent the man for sticks to mark the nests when found, dived through the chains and set out across the lumpy turf of the meadow in the trail of the wasps. The man followed her, and across the meadow they went, growing smaller, stopping, going on again, over a stile and along a hedge, till her white dress became only an occasional shimmer through the bushes, and at last disappeared completely.

The dogs, who had seemed to entertain foggy and ill-shaped ideas of following her, turned their minds to the rearrangement of their disrupted afternoon. The Newfoundland sat down, yawned enormously and blinked; the sheep dog also sat, and bit for a moment at a fancied flea. Presently they had settled again into the position out of which the lunch party had disturbed them. They blinked as they lay, and then with an occasional heaving sigh, drowsed to sleep…

The man-servant came out into the porch, collected the scattered cups, picked up the cigarette box, rearranged the cane chairs exactly in line, and disappeared with his tray…

Silence settled upon the house once more. The sunshine poured upon it, still and quietly, no slightest breeze shivered the green blinds; the trees stood straight and motionless. The dark shadows of the pillars crept minutely to the east, the clock face in the wall above altered invisibly. A tiny beetle, glossy green and gold, emerged from a crack between the flagstones, paused to reconnoitre, and began one of those immense, motiveless journeys with an air of concentrated purpose, that are peculiar to its kind. Its route lay very near the larger dog. It stopped once in its approach to his slowly heaving bulk, and resumed its way with a momentary hastening. It passed into the shadow and out of sight…

The gardener's boy appeared again through the laurels. There was a pool of black treacly fluid on the gravel, exuded from the battered motor car. He noted this, fetched a shovelful of sand, strewed it over slowly and thoroughly, scraped it up, and restored to the gravel walk its spotless complexion…

Inch by inch the minute hand of the clock on the wall crept round its circle, inch by inch the shadows slid away to the east. It seemed as if the place fell into a slumber so profound that it scarcely breathed. And yet beneath the surface of the placid scene a thousand minute activities interlaced and spun the eternal fabric of life; a spider laid her eggs, a group of ants fed busily upon the carcase of a beetle, and left it at the end a hollow shock of brittleness that would presently shiver into the earth, a tiny insistent maggot tunnelled its arduous way a little further into the great tree that in years to come its remote progeny would kill, half-open buds expanded softly into flowers, a burnet-moth whose chrysalis clung along a grass haulm by the fence bit its way right through the skinny stuff, crept out into the sunlight and lay and quivered there, lustrous in green and scarlet. To a hearing finer than any human creature's, the silence would have seemed a felted clamour of tappings, rustlings, flutterings, crepitations, tearings and gnawings, a murmurous mass of infinitely small busy sounds like the soft confusion of an orchestra before the arrival of its conductor. But to us a silence, unfathomable, profound…

The clock hand was well on its second revolution when the lady in white appeared distantly at the stile again, and came slowly towards the house with her gardener in attendance. Their voices grew through sound to words. "Cyanide will soon settle them," she was saying, and he, "A pot of tar now, on the end of a stick, and just pour it into the holes evening time, 'll do 'em like fun-oh.' "But I've got the cyanide," she insisted.

"H'm." He seemed to reflect. "You got to be keerful now, with that stuff."

"Oh, it's the deadliest poison. I'll show you how to be careful. It's quite the surest way."

"Hum," he said again, and then in a quietly conclusive tone, "Don't know as I keer to handle it."

"Oh, nonsense, Wates," she answered briskly; "I'll get it ready now," and went through the conservatory door by the drawing-room into the house.

Presently she reappeared at an upper window, pulling its green sunblind partly up and looking out, and then her head and garden hat could be seen fitfully as she moved about the bedroom within.

The purr of an approaching motor car brought her to the window. The smart motor, with her husband in it alone, swept round the trees before the gate, her husband got out, spoke some directions to the chauffeur, and the car went on. He opened the gate and came in.

The lady in white left the window and met him in the porch.

"You...ah!" she caught her words back in astonishment. Her husband's face was leaden white.

"We've -- we've—" He spoke huskily and with little sound, like a man who has lost his voice. "We've had an accident, Wuzzie." He put a hand against the pillar, and looked at it. His mouth twitched. He did not see the terror leaping in her eyes. "Preston – stumbled – fell on his gun—"

"Hurt?" she gasped.

He spoke with lowered head, in respect for the tragic fact. "Killed outright, Wuzzie. Poor chap... Good chap he was!..."

His voice broke for an instant. His hand went to his eyes… "Good thing he wasn't married, Wuzzie… haven't got to tell some poor woman."

His wife had turned her face from him towards the house. She stood quite still. He looked up and put his hand reassuringly on her shoulder. "It's a shock, isn't it, Wuzzie? I feel it, I can tell you. I – I was fond of him… Came along to tell you, old girl, in case you heard there'd been an accident and got frightened about me."

"Ah – yes!" she said. Her voice startled him, it had a sound as if it were breaking on the edge of a scream. "Are you sure?" she said.

"Sure? What?"

"He's dead?"

"Oh!" He cleared his throat of something like a sob. "Blew the side of his head away, poor chap."

With a cry she broke from his hand and away into the house.

Her husband looked after, her, surprised, and followed her to the door. "Wuzzie!" he called, but she had gone.

He stood for a moment as if puzzled, and then turned back and dropped into one of the cane chairs. He pulled at his beard, took out a cigarette case, began to light a cigarette in an habitual manner, and threw it away impatiently. His hand shook. He sat staring before him uneasily, as if something confronted him that he could not see.

A noise above, a sound oddly like someone falling, caught at his attention. He raised his head, listened, got up and went into the house quietly. "Wuzzie!" he called gently. His heavy tread could be heard going upstairs…

There was a sound of knocking up there, that became all at once louder. And then the crash of a door burst open…

A violent bell-ringing from above suddenly filled the house. The blond-bearded man came leaping downstairs. Through the gateway whirred the old motor car with three of the other men returning. Their host rushed from the house like a man distraught, his face working soundlessly.

"A doctor," he shouted. "Fetch a doctor, for God's sake!"

The tall drooping man was arrested in descent and pushed back into the car. "Get a doctor instantly!" shouted the blond-bearded man, beside himself. "My wife's had an accident."

There was an instant of silence between the four men. For that briefest space of time there came to them a strange perception, for that instant it was as if a door had burst open into an inner world beneath the placid surface of life, and there was let in upon them a blurred welter of sounds, of laughter and songs of beauty, and the faint persistent sound of someone weeping through the night.

The blond-bearded man slammed that door with an inspiration of speech.

"I was going upstairs to tell her about Preston," he began in a husky, forced tone...

The Draught of Oblivion

§1

THE APOTHECARY stood behind the counter in his pharmacy and watched the bubbling of an azure-blue liquid in an earthenware pot, which he held over a glowing charcoal brazier with a pair of iron tongs bound about the handles with leather. His long white beard fell over a gown of black velvet trimmed with fur, and very worn and damaged by the accidents of his profession. Besides the brazier, the little room was lit only by a copper lamp of the pattern that may still be bought in Rome today, and the crowded shelves behind the counter sent back gleaming reflections out of the obscurity from the bright brass lids of rows of white china jars patterned in blue with heraldic devices and gothic lettering which contained his ostensible stock-in-trade. In either corner was a cupboard with doors strangely carved and blackened, as was all the wood in that place; one of these yawned open, with a bunch of heavy iron keys hanging from its lock, and showed glimpses of a mysterious confusion that loaded its shelves; little greenish glass phials rifled from old Egyptian tombs, earthenware pots from Greece, glass jars with unknown brownish contents, and three skulls and some indefinite bones, a shark's skin, bundles of dried herbs, and some old leather-bound books. On the counter beside the Apothecary lay open a great folio with massive brass clasps and corners; it was a manuscript in heavy black and crabbed characters; and beside it was his balance and weights, his pestle and mortar, his inkhorn and quills. Overhead dangled a stuffed crocodile, and its long, grinning rows of teeth gleamed and vanished as the shadow of his bent head passed to and fro across them.

It had fallen dark an hour since, and the Apothecary felt himself secure from interruption for the night. Else he would not have begun the manipulation of the intricate and delicately difficult poison paste for the presentation ring to his Excellency for which he had been commissioned. He was surprised and annoyed, therefore, when a trooping of feet in the cobbled alley outside stopped before his barred and shuttered door, and a discreetly muffled but insistent clamour began for admittance.

The Apothecary thrust away the crucible into a recess below the counter, shut the cupboard door, fumbled the keys into his pouch, and, grumbling under his breath, went and unfastened the wooden hatch of a little grilled peephole in his street door.

The head of a tall hooded woman bent down to the lattice, "Let me in, Messer Agnolo," she said, in a whisper that did not fail to be peremptory.

The Apothecary undid the bolts, still inclined to grumble, but a little stimulated by the personality of his visitor. For the Lady Emilia, besides being beautiful and young and noble and passionate-tempered, was the custodian of an envied treasure which the Apothecary had hitherto failed by any means or persuasion to set eyes on, and which he wanted to get hold of as much as anything in the world. This was her grandmother's private memorandum book of useful recipes, and the Lady Emilia's grandmother had added a very notable store of knowledge to a violent temper (her erudition concerning poisons was remarkable even for a great lady of that day), and her chocolate parties in consequence were the terror of all her acquaintance. And her granddaughter gave promise to be a no less redoubtable lady. She was an orphan and very wealthy, and as yet there had been no one sufficiently temerarious to marry her.

She strode through the unfastened door with the light vigour of a young man, and was followed by a short and stout duenna and two stalwart young pages. It was well to be stalwart in the Lady Emilia's service. They crowded the little pharmacy, but the Lady Emilia achieved privacy for herself and the Apothecary by seating the old lady on a stool by the door, and by conducting her conversation with him in the Spanish tongue.

At first it seemed to the Apothecary that she had come merely to gossip, but he bided his time patiently, being wise in the behaviour of patrons who were shy of broaching some particularly unusual request. She turned her conversation at last to the contents of the blue and white china jars, and spoke of charms and potions. He answered her, wondering what his black-haired, high-coloured, and tempestuous visitor had in mind.

"A silly maid of mine," she threw out, "bought a love potion in Carnival week. Not that it worked her any good, the dolt. Rubbish bought in the street!"

"Made her fancy man sick belike," chuckled the Apothecary.

"Are there such things?" she asked, a sharp note creeping into the covering carelessness of her inquiry.

The old man shrugged his shoulders. "May be," he said indifferently, though he watched her. "There be legends and tales of such."

She waved her hand impatiently. "You know if there be, Messer Agnolo. Why do you fence with me? You are a wise old man, and you have your secrets. Is that one?"

"What?"

"This – this love-draught?"

"If I had that, your graciousness," replied the old man, bowing gallantly, "I'd find no customer for it in you. I'd keep it to bestow on one ill-favoured."

The lady shook her head impatiently. “Enough of your gallant speeches, Messer Agnolo. I have – a curiosity. I am interested in strange things. If there is any such stuff… I’ll pay you handsomely.”

The Apothecary was secretly pleased that she wanted something so much as she evidently wanted this. He scented a mystery. “Ah, lady,” he sighed, wagging his head and looking at her over the horn rims of his great spectacles, “there’s many would pay well for magic. A simple apothecary would grow rich…”

The lady thumped her hand on the counter with a bang that clattered the beakers and rattled the brass weights on the scales. “Messer Agnolo,” she said with directness and knitting her fine black brows together, “I know you for cleverer than you would appear. I have heard that you have secrets. I tell you that I would pay you well for – gratifying my curiosity. I am plain and honest with you. Do you be as civil with me.”

The Apothecary’s eyes gleamed. “Would you pay me very well?” he insinuated.

“A good price,” she said eagerly.

“And who is the noble gentleman who would be asked to drink?”

She stiffened her lip. “No!” she rapped out. “That I won’t tell you.”

The Apothecary moved his head in polite acquiescence. “I regret profoundly— “ he began.

The lady swore.

The Apothecary shrugged his shoulders. "I am a very simple old man, and know no magics. How am I to know magics? The gracious lady has her own magics written out for her by the hand of her noble grandmother. She wants no magics from me."

The gracious lady bit her lip and looked angrily at the impassive front of the big corner cupboard. Then she thought it over. "I'll deal with you," she said bitterly. "You shall have the book for half a year. Now will you give me what I want?"

The Apothecary was infinitely surprised by her surrender, and also annoyed. "I have no love-draught," he said slowly.

"That's not true?" A little anguished note came into her voice.

"It's very true, lady," he admitted. It chagrined him greatly to have to confess as much, with that precious book dangling before his mind's eye. "I had it, with some other curious things. Now it is all gone."

"Gone?"

"The last – a very little that was left – I sold to the Signor Matteo for his palefaced German bride. It was only a very little. She's made him but a cold and grudging wife."

The lady looked downcast. "Why is there no more?" she protested. "Can you make no more?"

The Apothecary shook his head. "It is twenty years gone and more," he said, "since I found a man one evening sitting on my door-sill there. He was bearded and lean and dark-skinned, and wore a strange habit like a man out of the East. He seemed ill and wearied, and I gave him a drink that heartened him. And being then, as I have always been, curious for strange things, I gave him shelter for the night, although he spoke no tongue I knew. I think now he spoke the Arabic. And the following day he fell sick of a fever, and died here in my house. But before he died he made me understand that he gave me his bundle, and in the bundle were some small bottles of a very ancient look, tied about with rags, and having writing upon them in the Arabic tongue. I learnt the Arabic then and made out what they were."

He paused. The lady was leaning forward eagerly. "Tell me, she said persuasively.

"There was the Draught of Love— "

"Great heaven above us!" she exclaimed vehemently, so that the old woman in the corner shook in her seat and the stalwart young pages quailed apprehensively. "I took you for no fool, Messer Agnolo. Surely you found out the secret of its making?"

The Apothecary fumbled with his spectacles, and shook his head slowly. "I spent much of it in the endeavour," he said excusingly, and seeing that precious book retreating ever more certainly from his grasp.

The lady sat and looked at him, biting her knuckles in an ill-contained rage. "Well," she said at last, "so much for your wisdom, Messer Agnolo. There are others," she muttered, pulling the hood, which had fallen back on her neck, over her glossy black hair and gold-embroidered coif.

"Te-he-he!" cackled the Apothecary. "Messer Messagerio has no love draught. He will sell thee one – ho yes! a bolus under a pretty name. 'Twill give the gentleman a twinge or two, but not of the heart – no! Now I," he said insinuatingly, "I am an honest old man."

"Too honest, belike," the lady returned sharply, and rising from her seat. "You cannot help me, and that is all."

As she turned the Apothecary saw the glint of angry tears in her eyes. The sight touched him to sympathy. "There was another draught," he said doubtfully. "I have that still."

She looked at him. "What?" she asked.

"The Draught of Oblivion," he said very gently and kindly.

The tears welled over her eyelids and fell on the silver-stiffened brocade of her dress. She swept them away angrily. "I have other plans to try before I come to that," she said.

The Apothecary regarded her gravely. "It is ready for you," he said, "in your last resort. I have given it three times to unhappy women. They forgot so completely that they never returned, even to thank me."

"How much – does one forget?" she asked.

"That one whose name shall be written on the leaf of a herb I know of. The leaf is steeped in the draught and is dissolved therein. You drink it, and it is to you as if that man or woman had never been."

She heard him dully, and then suddenly her whole being lit up as a dry leaf will flash into a sheet of flame. "Give it me!" she cried, and clutched the old man by the shoulders in a very storm of excitement. "Better! Why, that's better than the other! Quick! Yes, you shall have the book! A hundred books!" And she pushed him with her strong young hands towards the cupboard till his head had well-nigh rapped against its door.

"Gracious lady!" gasped the Apothecary, steadying himself against the panels; and was taken with a fit of coughing that threatened to end his existence then and there.

"Great powers above!" breathed the lady, fallen back, and watching him. "If he should die now!..."

However, the Apothecary did not die. And when he had done with choking and coughing and spluttering and gasping and sighing, and had wiped the tears from his eyes and got his breath again, the lady was calmer, although her eyes still shone and her breath came quickly.

"I will prepare it for you then, gracious one," he said hoarsely, wiping the last moisture from his eyes. He sat up resolutely, and coughing a residuary cough, selected a quill. "What is the noble gentleman's name I am to write?"

"No man's name, fool," rapped out the lady. Then, leaning forward that the others might not hear, she whispered: "Write the name: Teresa the Golden."

The Apothecary looked up and stared. "A woman's name?" he puzzled.

She nodded triumphantly. "If he drinks it, will he forget her?" she asked eagerly.

The Apothecary nodded. "Surely," he said, looking at her with liveliest curiosity.

The lady clenched her hands and laughed. "Then for the rest, I can work my own magic," she cried exultantly.

The Apothecary looked at her brilliant dark beauty, and dimly in his old heart it stirred him that she could.

"It will be ready tomorrow forenoon," he said.

She smiled radiantly. "You shall exchange it against the book," she assured him, and gathered her cloak about her.

The Apothecary bowed profoundly. "At your service always, gracious one!" he assured her. "I have a marvellous fragrant new scent, and a dew of honey for the lips. If you would command me in anything else..."

The tow-coloured hair of the younger page caught the light.

"You may give me a mess of black dye for my fellow there," said the lady shortly, in the Italian tongue, with an abrupt gesture at the startled lad.

"I hate a yellow head," she muttered, dragging her cloak about her and passing forth from the door.

§2

It was two months later, and the Apothecary sat in the cool shadow of his pharmacy with the book that had belonged to the Lady Emilia's grandmother upon his knees. The hot afternoon sun poured over the threshold of his open doorway, and lay on the stone flags in a golden pool. Ever and again a lizard, shining marvellously green and turquoise blue, would creep out from a crack between the flags and lie in the sun-patch, its little sides palpitating with the breath it drew, until the shadow of a passer-by would send it, a mere streak of colour, back into its hole again.

The Apothecary sat in the shadow, the air being heavy with summer heat, and was inclined to nod over the book. The book had been disappointing. There were recipes for extracting the scents of flowers, and recipes for complexion washes, and salves and unguents, possets and cordials, all written out in a fair hand, a collection such as any lady of family might be expected to have inherited, and which had very little interest indeed for the Apothecary. And the rest of the book was in a crabbed black writing, in a cipher to which the Apothecary, even after the most strenuous efforts, could find no clue whatever.

A shadow fell across his threshold and stopped. The Apothecary looked up, and the Lady Emilia came into the doorway, alone.

The Lady Emilia looked at the Apothecary, and the Apothecary looked at the Lady Emilia. He saw her face very white and tired, with her eyes reddened and set in dark shadows. She did not stand erectly proud as he had known her, but leant against the door in a manner he had never seen in her before.

"Messer Agnolo," she began in a husky whisper.

The Apothecary rose and placed a seat for her in the shade.

She sat silent for a moment. "Have you heard aught?" she asked.

The Apothecary looked at her with grave eyes. "Yes, Princess," he said. "It is a matter of common report still how splendid was the marriage feast of your Highness, and how bravely looked your graciousness, and how nobly handsome his Highness the Prince."

The Lady Emilia sat still, looking with level eyes at the wall of the room, and with her fingers twisted upon her knees.

"Tongues were so busy with the magnificence of your wedding, Princess," ventured the old man slowly, "that they forgot to wag any more over the sad and sudden death of Teresa the Golden."

The lady shrank away from him and shivered. A sound like a little moan came from her lips.

The Apothecary looked at her and the haggard misery in her face, and the matter, which he had never fathomed before, grew clear to him.

“You did not trust my draught, Princess?”

Her face quivered. “I wished to make assurance doubly sure,” she said with a touch of her old fierceness.

The Apothecary nodded slowly. “You did not visit me again, Princess,” he said. “Messer Messagerio’s poisons are clumsy potions… She took long to die?” he queried.

An anguish convulsed the face of the Princess. “Damnably,” she muttered.

The old man sighed.

The Princess sat down drooping and downcast, so still that the lizard crept again to its place on the sun-drenched flags. Then she braced herself erect, as if to dismiss an impossible remorse.

“Messer Agnolo,” said the Princess, “I want more of your draught.”

“Yes, I see,” he nodded. “With the same name steeped therein…for yourself this time.”

“For him again,” she uttered.

“But, Princess!” the old man expostulated, his professional pride in arms. “It was exactly the right quantity. It could not have failed.”

Her head drooped, and she covered her face with her hands.

“It was exactly the right quantity,” repeated the Apothecary.

The Princess lifted her head. “He did not drink it all,” she said slowly.

The old man waited.

"He took it from me," went on the Princess, her voice hard and dry. "He took it from me with a jest and a laugh, and made to drink it off. And as he drank, I saw again – her face – her twisted face… Mother of God!" she shrieked, "shall I ever forget her face?"

The Apothecary gazed at her. "And then?" he said after a while.

"I knew I must forget her too. I snatched the cup from his hand as he drained it, and swallowed the last drops that remained."

"Ah!" said the old man. "You did that, did you?"

She sat silent, with clenched hands.

"You were very greedy of your happiness, Princess."

"He must drink again," she said huskily.

The Apothecary pondered. "Then he has not quite forgotten?" he asked.

The Princess closed here eyes in pain, and shook her head.

"You must give me more," she repeated.

The Apothecary looked at her with a great pity, and hesitated over the thing he had to tell. "No one drinks twice of that draught, Princess," he said at last.

"What trick is this?" she flamed at him.

He shook his head. "To drink twice," he said slowly, "would make of him a poor silly natural, remembering nothing."

She stared at him with horror-widened eyes, that glazed and lost sense of him even as she looked. It was as if she gazed her destiny in the face…

Then with an effort, as if she shouldered a great burden, she turned away towards the open door.

The Apothecary stepped after her.

"There is surely much happiness in your life, Princess?" he ventured.

She pulled her scarf about her shoulders with a dragging hand.

"He has ever the look of one who seeks," she uttered, and stood still. Then roused herself, and had gone.

In a Walled Garden

THERE ARE PEOPLE who seem to fashion the fabric of their lives as an uninspired but painstaking artist will make a water-colour sketch, working every corner of it very carefully into a state of high finish, slurring no detail that their sensitive ingenuity can embellish, and achieving at last a meticulous perfection of harmonious living stippled delicately with flowers and pretty furniture and slim leather-bound books and comely clothes, all very thoughtfully placed and shining in the sun. In such lives birth has but a little place and death none at all, and the toil and heat of life and the pageant of its triumph and its failure pass by remotely, outside the white curtains that shade its tenderly coloured rooms. If ever a hand from that world without should pull aside the curtain for a moment and the face of Reality look in, it is prudent for the custodian of such a peacefulness to turn away until the intruder has passed, and presently hang up a little clean and spotless curtain in the place of the one that his browned and dusty hand has touched. So tranquillity may be preserved.

But sometimes it happens that Reality, having passed on, has not done with his disturbing. The memory of the shaft of sunlight, the breeze of strong air that came in when he pulled open the curtain so rudely, the memory of the shattering challenge of his glance, may grow more mercilessly commanding and appear more clamantly beautiful, the further it has gone beyond recall. The circumspect life within becomes meaningless and without savour; its moral value may have mysteriously evaporated. All the brave and shining things in life, all the worthy things will seem to have slipped out through that chink of freedom into the open world. This escape of virtue from the known to the unknown, from the sheltered and safe to the hazardous and socially adventurous, was what happened in the mind of Rosalind Bray as her youth passed. There came to her moments when she could have found it in herself to run out into the world, with hands outstretched and pleading, for the mere hazard of a few miles along the way with Reality's sunburnt arm about her neck.

Rosalind Bray, or to give her her unmarried name, Ellen Adams, was an only daughter in a small suburban middle-class family. Her father was a solicitor, and with that advantage it was obvious that her only brother should be called to the Bar. She received the perfunctory education that keeps middle-class girls unspotted by knowledge, and when she left school her parents took no measures whatever to enlarge her horizon of choice, and hopefully expected her to marry. Edgar Bray drifted into her world by the purest accident, and profited by its limits. He was thirty when she was twenty, and thin and dark and solemn in the Scottish manner. His fine dark eyes and the facility with which they expressed humble adoration or wounded dejection, or an anguish of unattainable longing, emotions which were the counters of his courtship, were the chief asset of his passable handsomeness; and their persistent siege, heartily endorsed by parental approval, overcame the immature, soft-hearted girl very easily. The manner of their ensuing marriage was quite beautifully thought out by Bray himself, and every line of the service was given its value by the excellent voice of the old college friend whom he got to officiate.

Her Christian name, as I have said, was really Ellen, but it was only one of the many graceful gifts with which her husband adorned her to select and fasten upon her a name that should better satisfy his ear. She was not more than common tall indeed, though of a slenderness that made it seem so when she stood alone. It may have been the suggestion of the green forest place they were in that sent the name of Shakespeare's Rosalind to Edgar Bray's mind, to be straightaway fitted on his new-made wife, "Baptize me, then," she had said, laughing. She lay with her head propped upon her elbow close to a tiny stream of water that slid by among the mossy stones, and she had a frolic idea that he would splash her face and neck with a rain of water drops, cold drops that would run deliciously down her skin. And she would splash him back. But instead he had kissed her very solemnly on the brow in a dedicatory manner, and whispered, "My Rosalind! My queen of the forest!"

It had all been very much like that. Bray made love to her delicately and reverently, and Rosalind, after an interval of puzzled discovery, settled down to her married life with a feeling of faint disappointment that she could hardly justify, seeing how exceptionally suited to one another her family considered her and Bray to be. Her world was so emphatic in declaring her marriage a most happy one that Rosalind fell into accepting it at that value. She wondered what it was she had expected that could possibly be missing. She was never aware that as the years went on they robbed her of her trick of sudden laughter, and left her utmost responsiveness a smile.

The Brays had no sordid cares to trouble them. Edgar Bray, as a younger son, had inherited about a hundred a year from his father, who had been a prosperous banker, and unsympathetic with the scheme for a quiet life devoted to literary art which Edgar, when he came to maturity, outlined as his purpose. So the bulk of the money had gone to the elder brother. But, by the time he married Rosalind, Bray had achieved a modest position in the world of letters which gave him a yearly increment of another two or three hundred. He was a serious and acceptable, if superfluous, essayist, he wrote and published verse, and the stimulus of foreign travel applied to Bray resulted with the certainty of a reflex in a book which would proclaim short but indisputably friendly reviews, had a charm of manner quite his own. All that came to give Bray, and his home, and his wife, a pleasant distinction, and an unobtrusive but definite place among cultural people. He had an easy way with a piano too, and would sing the love songs of Schubert and Brahms to Rosalind very charmingly, so far as his rather delicate throat would allow him.

The question of just where to make the home that was to enshrine his Rosalind troubled Bray a good deal. They lived for two years in a really idyllic country cottage, but the winters there, and social intercourse consisting almost exclusively of her husband, produced a pallor and thinness in Rosalind that was reluctantly attributed to the gravel soil. So Bray, after a careful and exhaustive search, transferred her to an old and extraordinarily charming little house at Chiswick, whose large and very beautiful garden gave her occupation and a great deal of pleasure. Rosalind had a natural aptitude for colour and arrangement, and a woman's love of prettiness, and with Bray at her elbow planning and appraising, and searching and judiciously purchasing, she set out with immense interest to make her home, a house that it was almost their prime occupation to care for and embellish. Rosalind furnished, indeed, with all the delicate thought and care and the streaks of happy instinct of a woman making love. She expressed her personality through and through that house and garden, making of it a richly-coloured setting for herself, a sort of extraneous garment as if she were indeed adorning herself for her lover. And somehow Bray remained indisputably only her humble servitor in the background. About this house moved Rosalind, a graceful figure of womanhood, dressed in carefully designed dainty garments of an old-world style that suited her best. That is to say, she dressed like that when she was at home and within the high old walls of her garden; outside that fastness she wore clothes of the current fashion, for the Brays would have disliked nothing more than to be remarked. Perhaps the necessary change deterred her from taking quite so much exercise as would have been good for her.

It will be seen that the Brays had no children. Indeed, they spent every penny they had upon their pretty life, and the advent of children would have disturbed the delicate balance of their comfort. Not that Bray was insensitive to that emotional value of parentage. Someday, somewhen, a child was to come and, as he said, "complete their lives." It was to be, so to speak, their final purchase, the last pretty touch they could give to their home, to add that child. It figured always in Bray's mind as a little girl, fair-haired like her mother, of a stationary age somewhere between two and seven years old.

One year after another passed. It was understood that there was plenty of time for that.

Rosalind acquiesced in that tacit arrangement as she accepted all the other disposals of herself that life made. She was not given to introspection of a very searching kind, her mind had received no training that should stiffen it to inquiry, and it was only as the presence of a faint discontent that she felt that her years were passing aimlessly, that now the interest of home-making was over she had nothing whatever to do, that the days stretched before her holding each a large vacant space of time, that Bray was beginning to bore her a good deal and had long silent spells that passed occasionally into melancholia and even into an apathy resembling sulkiness, and that the sort of thing that particularly bored her was to feel as she would on many an early summer morning in her garden, delightfully well and light-limbed and young, and to spend such a day quite inconsequently just as she had spent innumerable such days before, and see it end like a glorious setting with a cavity of hours that some jewelled memory should have filled. She was perhaps instinctively afraid of such a realisation, and so avoided thinking about it. But she could not always be on her guard against accidental glimpses of wider possibilities. Now and again it would happen that something would chance to pierce her seclusion and trouble her with the thought that there were other ways of life more worth the living that might be achieved outside the little backwater in which she was so safely kept.

There was, for instance, a little incident, slight in its reality as the brushing of a moth's wing in flight against her cheek, that will do well enough to take as typical. It happened on a summer's morning some seven years after her marriage, and Rosalind was in her garden alone. They had had breakfast in the garden, and Bray, after talking the matter over with her and getting annoyed because the sun dazzled his eyes, had gone into London to arrange with his publisher the colour and texture of the cover for his forthcoming book of poems. Rosalind walked about her garden, stopping here and there and looking at the brilliance of summer flowers which crowded about her in such gallant masses. The garden borders were so high and thick with blossoming growth that her housemaid had some difficulty in finding her, until at last she came upon her worshipping the great white clematis that hung upon the wall by the old greenhouse, and announced that the photographer from Brandon's had arrived.

Rosalind had forgotten all about the photographer from Brandon's. So evidently, she realised, had Bray himself, since he had gone out on the morning appointed for the sitting offered by that celebrity-hunting firm. Rosalind went indoors to apologise.

When she reached the door of her drawing-room she became aware that the photographer from Brandon's had already extensively unpacked. An immense camera had drawn itself aloft on a massive tripod, and faced her with a vast dark muzzle, plate-carriers of imposing size were piled generously on an adjacent table, and before one of the leather cases that were scattered over the floor knelt a young man with his back to her, and scrabbled in its interior. He was half hidden by a chair, and Rosalind saw him merely as brown boots and long legs in leather gaiters and a knicker-bockered knee. And chiefly she was looking at the camera.

"Good morning," said Rosalind to the camera and the boots.

The young man shot up to his feet and held himself erect, facing her.

At the sight of him her heart gave a queer little jump. She thought he was the most handsome thing she had ever seen. There was something in the sun tan on his skin that sent her thoughts flying to mountains and the sea.

And the young man saw Rosalind for the pretty creature that she was, her fair-skinned blondness softly outlined against the shadow of the door, clothed in cool pale blue linen, with little muslin daintiness around her wrists and throat.

For an instant they stood still face to face, and looked at one another. The first astonishment in his eyes had given place to a look of delight at the sight of her that called the colour into her cheeks. In Rosalind's mind at that moment there was no atom of doubt as to the thought that had leapt into his. She felt the silent air between them as thickly charged with meaning as if she had that instant called aloud to her, "Mate of mine! Found! Found!" Foolishly, irrationally, her heart began to beat fast, and with an automatic resumption of her original intention, she began:

"My husband—"

The young man's head went back with a little jerk, as if he had been lightly struck. Then he swung round to the camera with the gesture of a servant going back to his servitude, as to something he had forgotten, and gave her an indifferent shoulder.

"I'm afraid my husband has forgotten," stammered Rosalind, colouring now hotly with the odd little twist that had been given to her emotions.

He turned again. "Yes?" he inquired curtly.

Rosalind recovered herself. "Mr. Bray has gone to London, today," she explained. "I'm afraid – I'm quite sure – he has forgotten you were coming."

"Oh!" said the young man blankly, looking at her again.

She waited.

"I'll pack up then," he said, with formal politeness.

Confused and quite inexplicable sensations were making their tumult in Rosalind still.

"I'm so sorry," she said slowly.

Why was it that once that was said it seemed to mean something quite other than her intention? "I am really so very sorry," she faltered. It was ridiculous, it was monstrous, that such things should come into her head, but in a most curious manner she felt that in that simple remark she was apologising for the absurd blunder she had made in marrying Bray.

"Thank you," he replied, "it doesn't matter," and went on packing up, unscrewing the lens of the great camera with an expert twirl, and clapping together the tripod stand into a bundle of rods.

"If you don't mind," he said, pulling straps and not looking at her, "a boy will call for these traps in about half an hour."

"Certainly," she answered.

He turned to go. She wanted to keep him there, wanted to explain herself to him, and could not think of any possible way to do so that seemed consistent with her dignity. She felt that nothing had happened between them, and yet that everything had happened. She went before him out of the room to the open front door of the house. There was a bicycle tilted against the hedge.

"Good morning," he said; took the bicycle, swung into its saddle, and was gone.

Rosalind stood still for a moment, and then went back into the drawing-room with the queerest feeling of elation lifting her heart. The first sight of the heap of strapped leather cases thrilled her as if she had been kissed. Her eyes were bright and her cheeks hot, her hands were cold, and she pressed them against her cheeks to cool their flush. What had there been in that glance that had lit in her this mysterious fire?

She walked about the room, touching things here and there, still with a flush in her cheeks and a little smile about her lips. She wondered what manner of man he was. She tried to recall his face exactly, and found that her memory played her the trick of giving her no continuous picture of him. He was that tweed-clad, stalwart figure with the light brown hair, and for the rest his face remained obstinately blurred. And then as she came to the door of the room some disarrangement of the furniture as she looked back to the place where he had stood, recalled his face to her quite vividly, and she felt again that little clutch upon her heart.

She knew what it was that had flashed to her from his eyes. She knew all that it meant, the ultimate demand, the ultimate tribute and homage from a man to a woman. "Beautiful, worshipful things!" it had said. "You are my mate. You are she, you are she! You are she that should be flesh of my flesh and bone of my bone. You are she!"

She began to imagine the response to that demand, the high-spirited, adventurous quality of it, the test it would make of one's courage and one's pluck.

"Ugh!" she said to herself; "am I a decent, sensible woman, or a novelette-reading fool?" And she went out into her garden, disconcerted and ashamed.

But her thoughts, thoughts that she told herself were unworthy of her dignity and self-respect, raced along their way like a team of horses utterly beyond her control. They did but drag her with them, holding on powerlessly to their reins. She could not suppress the feeling that surged up in her that something extraordinarily sweet and delightful had happened to her, something suddenly awakening and refreshing. There were times indeed when she deliberately allowed herself to sit hidden among the drooping leafage on a remote garden seat, and hug to her heart the memory of that glance, like a child that had hidden itself to enjoy forbidden sweets. She told herself that only by thus letting her mind exhaust the thing would it trouble her no more.

But indeed she found that to fatigue out the sharpness of that particular impression was only the beginning of her disturbance.

When Bray came home she put off telling him for a time of the coming of Brandon's photographer, afraid that something in her voice would betray her, and when at last she did tell him she was amazed that she was able to do so quite easily. She marvelled that he did not ask her more questions, and only remarked that he would appoint another day, or go to Brandon's studio himself.

"Don't do that," urged Rosalind, on an impulse that terrified so soon as it had moved her. "It will be much more successful if you have it done here. The atmosphere of a photographer's is so stiffening."

Bray agreed. "Do you mind writing to them for me?" he said.

"Very well," answered Rosalind, in a faded voice. She detested herself now for the commonplace manoeuvre. At any rate, she could and would put herself right by being out when he came.

"Rosalind mine!" murmured Bray.

He leant over the table. They had been dining on the verandah.

She started from her abstraction and looked at him. The dim, rosily-flowered globes of paper Japanese lamps glowed on either side before her.

Bray gazed upon her with sombre eyes. "How beautiful you look there!" he said. "Do you know, when I feel the dust and heat of this great toiling city as I did this morning, and contrast the complete, and beautiful life we lead here…" He paused, a little tangled with his sentence.

"Yes?" she asked.

"It seems almost greedy," he said. "As though we had sucked away all its happiness and loveliness and content, and held it prisoner ourselves."

His gaze upon her became abstracted. With a little nursing there would by a lyric in that.

And Rosalind fell back into her own preoccupations.

Five days passed before the fresh appointment fell due. With the best intention in the world Rosalind could not suppress a lifting expectancy as those days went by. It was futile for her to tell herself that nothing more could happen, while some impish hope was going about in her brain insisting that it could. But whatever went on among her rebel thoughts, Rosalind remained heroic mistress of her actions, and when that morning came she set herself a penance for her foolishness and went out.

When she started she was very satisfied with herself for that, and when she was half an hour away she was acutely sorry that she had done it. She hurried home, telling herself that the time had passed when he would have come and gone.

She opened the garden gate and met Bray coming out. "I've sat to Brandon's man," he said. "He's just packing up. I'm afraid I can't get home to lunch, Rosa Mundi."

She went into the drawing-room, trembling a little, and found a little old man with a long beard taking a camera to pieces with infinite leisureliness…

That was all, and Rosalind tried to think that she was glad to have escaped an embarrassment. And, none the less, like some little carelessly-dropped seed, this new emotion, and the thoughts that sprang from it, stirred and grew and spread. There came times when she doubted very thoroughly if that odd encounter of eyes had ever happened outside what she told herself was her own vanity-fed imagination; others when its sudden memory pricked about her heart again with stealthy pleasure. It was months before the stir of it faded from her mind.

And afterwards she had moods when she reproached herself for the idleness that left her a prey to such imaginings, and pondered whether she could not find some kind of work to fill her days. She thought first of one and then of another of the various movements in which she might involve herself, but the idea of artificially-induced occupation, for which she knew she felt not the least real desire, repelled her. "I wonder what it is I am meant for?" she repeated over and over again.

"I am an idle woman, leading an idle, useless life," she announced to herself.

She went a step further. "Am I to go on living like this?"

But if it was not to go on, what could she do to alter it? Women, she thought, have no chance in the world whatever to do serious work once they are married. "Serious work" remained a vague term to her.

One day she happened upon a novel by a writer of the modern school that made some obvious suggestions. "Of course, the right and honourable work, the work that lies naturally to a woman's hand, *is* to bring up children," she admitted to herself after reading it. "Why have I no children?"

Why had she no children? She had never faced that out before.

Did she, she wondered, want children?

She was standing in the broad gravel path near the boundary of her garden, looking up at the high old wall as if it made a prison for her. "I am young," she said bitterly, "I am young and I am beautiful really, and what is it all for? What is going to be the good of it? Why do I not at least have children? Here are life and youth and opportunity passing by, they are mine now and they are passing, and soon I shall have no more youth and no more opportunity. I am as if I held life's gold between my hands, and let it slip, and slip. Why am I doing that? Soon it will be gone, and mingled in the sand at my feet. Why cannot I take my work, if that is my work, and grip it and make it my own?"

She had a vision of the children she might have. She remembered the fair soft skin of some children she knew, and though of flaxen hair, fine and soft and shining, that would presently deepen to ruddy gold. The picture warmed her heart to tender excitement. She saw them adolescent, big-limbed, tall and broad-shouldered, stepping proudly about a world that was their inheritance.

And then it occurred to her a little chillingly that Bray's children would not be like that.

But she dared not go on with that particular train of thought, and indeed she hardly allowed it to come to the surface of her mind again. Perhaps some instinct warned her that it would have led her to an unbearable realisation. For over the threshold of that thought, the threshold on which her mind trembled and turned away, lay the knowledge that it was not Bray's child that she desired, but the child of some big fair man, with limbs of a strength that outmatched her strength, and a sun-tanned skin that sent her thoughts flying to mountains and the sea.

Robe de Boudoir

MRS. HANNAFORD drove her fast-trotting pony neatly up the railway approach, gave the reins to the garden boy who accompanied her, repeated her directions for being met by the down train at 6.40, gathered up her sunshade, her purse-bag, and her novel, and passed into the cool shadow of the station.

She was making one of her customary excursions to London that happened every fortnight or three weeks, combining shopping with the acceptance of some invitation to lunch or an afternoon "At Home". Her husband was a sportsman and a country gentleman in a small way – ill at ease away from his fields and his gun, and never leaving them willingly – who visited London, when it was unavoidable, in a humour of ferocity that made him a difficult companion. But Mrs. Hannaford clung with persistence to the convention she had set up, that occasional shopping in London was a duty no conscientious house-manager could neglect; and she would have valued her vote as a badge of freedom very lightly if it had been offered to her against her ticket for the Stores.

One had to manage a little.

"I think," she would say one day at tea, "I really ought to go up to town tomorrow, if I can, and get some shopping done."

She would throw a slightly troubled accent into her voice.

Perhaps Mr. Hannaford would grunt, and in that case she could go on making her plans in fair security; perhaps he would say nothing, but just go on reading the *Field*; perhaps he would make some objection and she would defer her plain necessity until the following day; perhaps at breakfast the next morning he might suddenly allege that he was aware of her intention for the first time, and with the simple statement, "You'd better not go today," postpone her excursion. She never felt quite sure of herself till the pony-trap cleared the avenue and the lodge gates, and was well along the wide white road to the station three miles away. And even surer and safer did she feel when the train began to move, and slipped from the familiar little platform away and away and away into freedom, giving her a whole six hours of liberty before the tether of the 5.45 brought her back to her home.

It was delicious – that liberty. But do not let it be inferred that Mrs. Hannaford had ever passed an hour of her life in any but circumstances of meticulous decorum. There was nothing awaiting her in London but the shops, and perhaps the small luncheon-party given by another woman, which were the avowed objects of her journey. But the experience of freedom; of being able to make her own decisions as to what she would eat and when; of being able to go down this street, or, if she willed it so that one; of stopping here to look into a shop window, or going on without argument of justification or debate, thrilled into her veins like wine. Sometimes she would squander so much time at first in this joyous exercise of free will, that she would have to hurry immoderately at last to get through her allotted business. She went along Regent Street or Victoria Street or Oxford Street with the *élan* of a cage-bird that has escaped to the blue sky.

Once or twice, indeed, she had done things that seemed to her to beat the very bounds of liberty; once or twice she had gone into a picture gallery; once she had slipped into a concert, sitting in a back seat and looking furtively about her in the fear of seeing an acquaintance who might recognise her; but the anxiety of that and the subsequent strain of concealment seemed to her to overbalance the strange pleasure of the music. For it would be quite impossible to make it acceptable to Mr. Hannaford that she should do, or want to do, anything of the kind. To Mr. Hannaford attendance at concerts and picture galleries was either the doubtful privilege of people in "society" – a position he would repudiate – or the unhealthy proclivity of people who were "artistic." He felt about "artistic" people the same slightly contemptuous commiseration that he would have felt about coloured people. He himself was not artistic, and he would take good care that his wife was not either. And all that body of sound, downright opinion that occupied the basement in Mr. Hannaford's mind would have made it dreadfully difficult for Mrs. Hannaford to explain to him that she had been, alone, to such places – in fact, it made it impossible. It would be like confessing to a moral lapse. It might have the effect of curtailing her freedom to go to London at all.

Once, indeed, she had done something even more inexplicable. In the early darkness of a winter afternoon, changing from a motor-'bus from the West End to another for Victoria Station, she passed close by the great shadowed mass and orange-lit windows of Westminster Abbey. There was a sound of music, like a trail of thin smoke across the air. It was as if she saw it for the first time; it uprose in its great height so strangely aloof that it penetrated her with awe and wonder; it was like a giant in still communion with the stars, while the little men ran about their little dark affairs around its feet. The pealing of the bells for evensong beat against the roaring traffic like the legendary phantom peal of a church swallowed long years ago by the encroachment of the sea.

She saw people passing in through a small doorway in the great one, and with sudden daring she too passed into the murmurous, shaded mystery of the interior. She slipped into a chair and knelt; the pealing bells sounded as if they were ringing at an immense distance; the sound of a voice rose and fell far away, with chanted responses; the pattering up the aisles of feet on the pavement, the shrill scroop of a chair – all this soft web of sound enclosed her in a globe of solitude. Her whole being was pierced with a sense of self-abasement, of humility too profound for adoration. She knelt with her face pressed upon her muff; her eyes filled with tears so that she had to seek her handkerchief; she wept. Presently she rose and slipped away, fearful lest she should have lost too much time to catch her train; but she found she had been there barely ten minutes. She concealed that incident of her day with the scrupulosity that another woman might have employed upon a rendezvous.

Those were rare and trepid adventures. Usually she enjoyed the simple pleasure of passing along the streets, the simple exercise of her own free will.

It was a very warm, very beautiful day in June. She was a pretty woman; riding and country life had kept her fresh and young. There was the usual group on the platform, of three or four neighbours, some farmers and workpeople; no women she knew, she was glad to see, since they would have travelled up with her; the men would make off to smoking-carriages.

There was Colonel Burton, raising his hat.

"You coming up, Mrs. Hannaford? Beautiful day. Wonderful weather." And so on, as usual, for five minutes.

The train came snorting in. Mrs. Hannaford parted from the colonel and got into her own compartment. She opened her novel.

Now novels were a source of imaginative stimulus unreckoned with by Mr. Hannaford. He knew about pictures, he knew about music; he knew that they led women into trouble and tended to break up a man's home; he knew that a conspicuous interest in religion could be neutralised by red beef and exercise and a little auction in the evenings; but he did not know since he never opened one, what novels were like nowadays, and how astonishingly they illuminate the female mind. Mrs. Hannaford did not obtrude them. She changed them inconspicuously at the library.

The floating population of novels and other popular works that came and went were accepted by Mr. Hannaford as part of the furniture proper to a country house. People who came to stay expected them, as they expected to find the newspapers about and things to smoke. He was not a reader himself; he had too much to do. He would have been immeasurably shocked to see a French novel among them, and would quickly have put a stop to that; but, lulled by the long security of the Victorian era, he never thought of opening them or doubting their innocuous fatuity so long as they bore titles in English. Among them, unsuspected by him, were translations from Russian, from French, from Italian – wolves in sheep's clothing. And so it came about that Mrs. Hannaford had glimpses, and more than glimpses, not only of reality, of the mental and emotional workings of nearly every sort of human being in the world, but of adventure and experiment and peril and happiness, and of all the beauty and tenderness of love that the most ingenious minds of our age can devise.

As she read, something like the weight of a big clumsy hand resting upon her mind passed away. She reached Victoria in the highest spirits. It was an extremely beautiful day.

She determined on a bus to Sloane Square. There was a shop there where they had pretty clothes in the window, and an attractive old furniture shop; and then she liked to walk up the length of Sloane Street – she liked its breadth and clarity, the long stretch bordered by garden, and at the top the bright, interesting, individual shops. And then the great glossy curved plate-glass windows of the big drapers' shops in Knightsbridge, where she would make some small purchases.

The warm summer air was still fresh with the morning; women passed her, charmingly dressed; there was a sparkle in the sunshine that made people smile at slight provocation. It was pleasant to linger under the broad awning of a florist and breathe the scent of the gorgeous mass of blossom banked against the cool depths of the open shop; it was pleasant to see the neat baskets of glossy, pampered fruit, the speckless gleaming glass bottles of a *parfumeur*, the smart, luxurious stationer's, with its profuse elaborations of letter-writing.

She walked along very gaily, now in the shade, now in the sun, humming a little soundless tune, her parasol drooping back over her shoulder. The branches of the trees swayed in their full green of summer; the smartly fronted houses had hung out striped sun-blinds over window boxes blooming with that high pressure of achievement peculiar to West End plants; taxis passed with a swish, motor-'buses with a heavy impetus; there was the glittering passage of a water-cart, a keen, fresh smell, the swirl of water in the gutter. She had a wonderful sense of happiness, of looking charming, of being admired by passers-by while she kept her eyes quietly upon the shop windows or the interests of the traffic. It was pleasant, it was delightful. And she had five hours more.

The big shop in Knightsbridge, where she meant to buy some gloves, foamed and frothed over with the light gossamer of summer raiment, stocked with an exuberant abundance. In the lingerie department, through which she had to pass, were lying on the counters and displayed on stands fragilities as lovely and light as soap bubbles. She marvelled at a series of transparencies, sheaths of chiffon faintly flushed with colour, their low décolletages edged very simply with lace, and labelled "Robes de Boudoir." Mrs. Hannaford had never seen their like before; it was, in fact, the first season that that particular kind of garment appeared in the department of feminine wear which has of late years done so much to rid itself of its old partnership with scarlet flannel. She looked, and then went on, just a little embarrassed by those wisps of chiffon. They were so different in every particular, in every characteristic, from anything she had ever possessed. But they were lovely. As she sat among the austerities of the glove department, they were enormously alluring to think of; they took insolent possession of her imagination; they clung about her like cobwebs. It was a scrap of the world of imaginative beauty become fact and reality; it was as if a figure from a floating, quivering mirage had suddenly thrust forward and touched her with a living hand. Such things existed. They were made; they were bought.

She would buy one.

She went back a little nervously through the lingerie department, as if she were casually strolling; she stopped in front of one of the coveted coquetries and fingered its edge with an expression of sternness, as if she were debating whether it would wear well.

A pretty young saleswoman approached her. "These are just in, madam. Are they not charming, madam?" And she twirled the stand to show it off.

"Very pretty," replied Mrs. Hannaford with dignity. "I think this one would look very well, lined with blue silk."

Fatally she caught sight of a quick spasm of amusement that lit up the pretty young saleswoman's face. She dropped the edge of the chiffon wrap as if it were hot, turned straight about and walked off, out of the department, along a maze of counters and show-rooms towards the street. She was not thinking, she was too confused; but as the heavy swing-door was being pulled open for her, something like a voice spoke straight into her ear:

"Some day you will be dead!"

She turned away from the open door, feigning to examine a festoon of lace. Then in a moment, she walked with straight swift resolution back to the *robes de boudoir*.

"I will take that one," she said very gravely, as soon as she got there.

"Two and a half guineas, madam," said the salewoman, whipping it off the stand.

"Thank you," said Mrs. Hannaford, with a sense of having just jumped off the edge of a precipice and of floating, floating in mid-air.

"No, I will take it with me, thanks.

"No thanks, I will pay for it now.

"No, please do not put it in a box. A small parcel, please."

She took the little flat parcel and doubled it up again. It might have contained a veil.

She continued her shopping methodically, a little entranced.

Punctually at 6.40 the train from Victoria brought Mrs. Hannaford back to her station. She gathered up her novel, her sunshade, her parcels, and looked out of the window.

She was astonished to see her husband waiting for her on the platform.

He had a jackdaw curiosity about parcels. He liked to see that she had got good value with his good money. Her idiotic dress had no pocket.

The train stopped. Very quickly she took the slim little parcel that might have contained a veil, and slipped it as far possible down into the crack between the seat and the back of the carriage.

Everymother

WHERE THE PINE-CLAD MOUNTAIN sides pinch the valley to its end in a steep glacier there stands, square and alone except for a few scattered chalets, the typical Swiss mountain hotel, white-walled and green-shuttered. It is the resort of climbers, and of those who climbed in younger days and come there to breathe the thin glacial air once more, look up at the familiar peaks and trace old routes, and potter along the lower paths that once they strode by lantern light before the dawn. Over the dark, steeply rising mountain wall the sun sets early; it will not warm much longer the groups of people at tea round the iron tables on the rough hotel terrace. Most of them, wrapped up in woollies and shod in nailed boots, set off for a last walk before dusk along the banks of the noisy torrent that pours from the glacier above and plunges and roars its way over the grey rocks downward; but some of the men, changed and washed and exceptionally brushed and sleek about the head and reddened and burnt in the face, sit on, smoking and easefully contemplating the peaks they clung to and conquered in the morning hours.

Everymother sits at one of the tables. She has finished her tea but she does not think of going for another walk, for if she did she might miss the boy's return. He went off this morning very early, soon after three; from her bedroom window she had watched the start, a glimpse in the darkness of the slender, tall, tight-knit figure striding down the path beside the shorter, sturdier guide carrying a lantern. The lantern twinkled along the path after the two figures were lost in the darkness, and then at a turn it vanished.

Everymother stood still for a moment by the window, and then went back to bed…

Her son had come into her room to say goodbye, as she liked him to do whatever the hour of his start; had not kissed her but laid the tip of his finger to his ointment-smeared mouth and touched her lips with it. "Be good, little Ma," and "Good luck, my dear. Clear, isn't it?" and "Splendid," was what they had said, and off he had gone, stepping gingerly in his great boots. ("It is defended to circulate in the hotel in boots of ascension before seven hours," announces a written notice in the hall.)

This climb was the biggest thing he had attempted. With his own guide he was joining another climber, an hotel acquaintance, and his guide, to make a party of four. They were not only going to climb the Grand

Aiguille but going up it by the steep face instead of the usual easier route by the arête. "Very interesting," was what the older man had called it. "Horrible," was Everymother's unspoken opinion, looking up at the thing the day before. To-day she had not looked at it very much. It jerked up on the skyline, a sharp narrow peak with steeply sloping sides and a vertical face. It was the most conspicuous object on the eastern side of the view.

Everymother had got up and breakfasted rather early, and then messed about as she called it in her bedroom rather late before going out. She hadn't felt inclined this morning to get included in an expedition by kindly meaning fellow visitors. She wanted to be by herself. She didn't want to be bothered all day pretending interest in everything in the world except the steep face of the Grand Aiguille, and reserving for that grim-breasted monster a phlegmatic calm. She thought she had had enough of that after breakfast, when two enthusiastic hard climbers, a brother and sister, lean, experienced, beetroot-faced, had captured her as she came out on the terrace. They were at the hotel telescope, trained as usual on the notorious Aiguille, and with the utmost kindness they had shown her through it all the route in detail, there where the climbing party would come into view round the edge of an arête, and there where they would begin to ascend the face. "You'll be able to watch them a good part of the way," said the sister in a considerate voice as if she apprehended that Everymother was a novice at this sort of thing and might be anxious.

But Everymother had thought to herself that watching that crawling progress wasn't a bit what she cared to do.

She tidied up her tidy room, wrote some letters, and finally started off to walk fast and far before lunch. But before long she found herself sitting by the shore of a little blue lake that lay between the mountains like a dropped jewel, watching the rippling of its surface and brooding over her boy. The water was perfectly clear, so that every little stone on the white sandy lake bottom could be seen. How deep could it be? Perhaps eight or ten feet or deeper. She discovered two systems of ripples, one that was blown across the surface by the light breeze and another running in the contradictory direction and below the first, that was the path of the stream that fell into the lake at one end and flowed through it. There was a lovely and endless interplay of iridescent patternings running and flashing through the crystal-clear water.

She wished she had had a better head and a tougher physique when she was younger; she would have loved just what he cared for, the high and lonely wastes of gaunt grey rocks, the austere splendour of great snowfields, blinding white, the incredible beauty of the whole pageant of dawn and sunrise, of blue-white snow fired suddenly to gold and grey clouds lit up to flaming rose. Odd how they both turned upward to these things, how they both disliked "going down," how they were always getting away from the warm lush valleys up into these cold heights. He must now be clinging to some rock face, tense and with every nerve alert and wary for the falling stone, the loose handhold...climbing, clinging, working chilled fingers into a crack, a crack ice-glazed...

This was absurd. This was the particular sort of thing she was resolved not to give way to. Everymother shook herself together. She walked back to the hotel, looked through the books again in the fumoir, took up a Wilkie Collins novel and read for a while in her bedroom, with the long French windows open on to her balcony and the sunshine. The stillness was profound. She went into her boy's room, his clothes were tossed about as he had left them, a disorder of garments on the chairs and a jumble on the table of books and photograph prints and papers and chocolate and cigarettes. Everymother would have liked to tidy it all up for the pleasure of handling the stuff that had lain so intimately close to him — just for the feel of it. But he would rather it were all left, just so, where he could put his hand on everything. She had found a weak place in one of his stockings, and got some wool and darned it. It was very comforting to have the rough warm thing on her fist. She tried to find a hole in the other. The day had worn through at last to four o'clock.

At any time now the party may return.

"Hasn't your son got back yet?" remarks an insensitive elderly lady, passing Everymother as she sits by her tea-table.

"Hardly yet," she answers casually.

"All the others seem to be back," says the elderly lady informingly, and passes on to the hotel entrance.

The sunshine thins out. Everymother looks up; the sun is dipping over the shoulder of the mountain. A few moments more of golden light and the sunlight has faded altogether and left the garden cold. Everymother feels chilly, gathers up her book and her newspaper and oddments and goes upstairs to her room.

Her window looks out over the terrace to pine trees and the foaming river down below, and to a length of ascending rocky path down which the returning party will come. It is silly to watch the path, but it would be such a happiness to see them coming into sight. They will be coming very soon now, Everymother tells herself. Of course theirs was a particularly long expedition, it is not that they are late. They will appear, she thinks, just by that bent fir-tree at the end of the loop of path, and come across the bridge over the river. He will be leading, a slim tall figure, with the little grey man who went with him at his side, and the two guides, their day's work over, tramping behind them. Quite soon, and then she will laugh at her—

No, not fears. Impatience.

As she watches, her thoughts escape the stern control she has kept on them all day.

What a stalwart man he looked in the early morning, this erstwhile baby of hers, so short a time ago a small bundle of white-frocked activity in a nursery, with a little busy incessant brain beneath a crop of curly hair. And yet what could be directer from that exquisite child than this figure of fearless youth, gripping his ice axe and elated at the adventure before him. Everymother at the window, watching the path, is filled with pride that she indulges, with fear that she beats down. (Fear is putting up quite a fight now for the mastery of her thoughts.) This climbing, is it justifiable? The risks are horrible, the gain — what?

Here is this young creature on which labour and care have been lavished for twenty years, and precious on that account now not only to herself but to the whole world. Precious perhaps least to herself if his value were told, her part in his making a small one if all the reckoning were made. There flashes before her mind a procession – herself and his father, his nurse, governess, schoolmasters, university professors, and a retinue behind these of toil and service that reaches to the miner digging in his pit and the sailor labouring the cold sea. And now he stood ready for manhood, youth equipped for life. What else is the hope of the world? Ready like an elaborate tool wonderfully made and exquisitely adjusted, and one could do no better with him than hang him on a frangible rope with those strong shapely feet and those trained clever hands clinging to slippery rocks that overhang precipices of ice… Was one mad?

Her thoughts, glancing at the rope, fray it to an impossible thinness, the rock face plunges downwards to a dark abyss, the nailed boots slip…

This will not do. This is folly. Everymother is glad that no one can possibly know that such thoughts are in her mind. It was really silly to be anxious, letting herself get worked up, watching in this fretting way. If she was seen to be watching by those tough men outside there it would be ridiculous, and make her boy ridiculous. There was no reason in it. As a matter of fact mountaineering was probably safer than most other occupations, since everyone was so extremely careful who was concerned in it. Motoring accidents were far commoner than climbing accidents.

How would she have liked to have mothered a son who adventured nothing, who avoided risks, who showed fear?

It was time she changed for dinner. She left the window, and moved about the room, deliberately humming a tune, and not looking at the path. She is dressed in quite a short time.

One more glance before going downstairs. Ah! There is a movement among the shadowy fir-trees at the bend of the path. Three figures detach themselves; a guide with a rucksack and ice axe in front, a short small figure next, a guide behind— No one following? No fourth figure with them!

Everymother feels as if the solid hotel has swayed and jumped violently sideways. "Keep steady! oh *keep* steady," she says to herself, going quickly but very quietly out of her room, along the corridor, down the stairs, through the hall, out of the door and up on to the terrace… It is so far to go…

Much nearer, she can see the three distinctly. The guides are strange to her and the small figure in the middle is a woman in knickerbockers…

Half an hour later her son comes striding into the hall with the rest. He looks alert and triumphant and not a bit tired. One knickerbocker knee is torn in a jagged rent and a couple of knuckles on his left hand grazed red and raw.

"Splendid time!" he says, seeing her. "Oh splendid! How have you been getting on?"

"I've been all right."

April in the Wood

THE WOOD is of birch and willow and thin-leaved trees so that it is not dark like other woods but irradiated with lightly veiled sunshine. The sunshine falls down, glinting the upturned primroses that star the sides of the ditch that surrounds the wood, the primroses drift a little way along the mossed paths and come to an end among knots of pale violets. For a space there are no flowers, there is only an undergrowth of light and vivid green, and then through the distant tree stems appears a filmy mist of blue. The heart of the wood is massed thick with bluebells. As I go nearer the blue grows brighter, and spreads and flows out into a miraculous lake of blue, emerald edged, at whose brink I stand at last. Above the myriads of flowers hangs the sharp and tender green of the young trees, shading and deepening their marvellous colour. The arching bells rise to my knees, away in one corner a little streak of white bells runs like a laugh among the perfect blue, and at one side the blue lake froths and foams and creams at its edge with white fool's-parsley. The air is filled with their scent, laden with scent; silent as if all nature hung breathless over their beauty.

How silent is a wood! In the open country the song of a bird seems only the louder part of a universal stir of sound, here in the wood it lifts up sharply and alone against the silence as against a curtain of black. In the open when the air is still and there is no sound it is like the silence of a rumbustious person fallen asleep, in the wood it is the silence of something awake and still, in brooding thought. My footsteps, however lightly I may tread, fall brutally in the stillness. I am constrained to stop, and presently sit down upon the green-mossed roots of a beech-tree that lie asprawl across the path.

A bird twitters and is hushed. Time ceases. Each moment is a strange, still eternity.

A tiny sound makes me aware of a tiny flash of movement. It passes by the tail of my eye and out of sight. Possibly a mouse. My ears grow tuned to finer shades of hearing; the air is not so soundless, the earth is not so still as at first it seemed to me. Beneath the surface of this placid scene a thousand minute activities interlace and spin the eternal fabric of life, a spider lays her eggs, a group of ants feed busily upon the crackling carcase of a beetle and leave it at the end a hollow shuck of brittleness that will presently shiver into the earth, a tiny insistent maggot tunnels its arduous way a little further into a great tree that in years to come its remote progeny will kill, half-open buds explode and expand softly into the leaves and flowers, a thousand wild bees drone and bustle among the yellow gorse bushes outside the wood. To a hearing finer than any human creature's this silence would seem a felted clamour of tappings, rustlings, flutterings, crepitations, tearings and gnawings, a murmurous mass of infinitely small busy sounds like the soft confusion of an orchestra before the coming of its conductor. Perhaps in the ears of one of those little creeping creatures of the earth this place hums like a busy city.

And as tiny sounds begin to drop into this silence at first unfathomable and profound, so do small unnoticed things begin to leap into my sight as if they sprang there and then into being. Little delicate lovelinesses lie about everywhere for the finding. Close by my hand I see among the grass blades a single feather. It is hardly two inches long, it is of the lightest grey, and from its root for nearly all its length it is a mass of soft fluffiness that becomes at the tip suddenly smooth, speckled, fine and thin. That glossy transparent tip is all that the bird shows, the fluffy rest is just his exquisite underclothing! I turn it about and marvel at it; if I stroke it against my lips it is almost too soft for feeling. Minute white flowers, humbly perfect in their tiny shape, cling about the stems of that undergrowth I took for plain green leaves. As I lie still the little creatures of the wood begin to come and go again about their busy affairs. A robin, his beak brimming over with scraps of faintly writhing worm, hovers in the bushes about, scrutinising me first with one bright brown eye and then the other between anxiety and growing confidence, and then with a dash he has shot into that thicker place among the leaves where hides his nest. A beetle, glossy green and gold, emerges from the litter on the ground, pauses in reconnoitre and begins an immense journey of some unknown, concentrated purpose. Its route lies near my foot; as I move slightly to look at it, it stops, to resume its way with a momentary hastening. It passes at last out of sight under some dead leaves... The mouse has come out again and seems not to trouble about me at all. He must have his home on the other side of this beech-tree against whose trunk I lean. I watch him with delight.

The infinite delicacy, the loveliness of little mice! He bustles out, a mite of a mole-coloured thing, with tiny perfect ears and feet and eyes and whiskers and a completely round body of grey and silver like a willow bud, a glove of softness, a thing as exquisite as lives. He burrows his nose under every leaf and twig, he nibbles every morsel about him, he stands on his minute head and turns somersaults out of sheer joy. He impresses me as one of the most volatile and adorable characters I have ever met. I would like to go back to the story of Creation for his genesis, and think of God making him with tender care, chiselling him with the finest instruments from the primal clay, and bending His great attentive brows over the little emerging shape. Surely it was when God had done with the elephants and whales and horses and men and such rough furnishing of the earth that He made mice and small birds and squirrels and butterflies, because it was such a lovely work to do.

And because He was happy in their making they remain the happiest of His creatures now.

Night in the Garden

THE COUNTESS of Canfield's nursery-governess was dressing for dinner in the bedroom high up on the second floor of a big country house. The roof sloped down over the bed so that when she first came she bumped her head once or twice when she awoke and sat up in the night. But she liked her little room. "This," she would feel, coming back to it from the bewildering novelties downstairs, "is me again. How are you, Me?" she would say with a whimsical smile, trying to keep her end up. The room held all the small store of her possessions, her modest outfit of clothes, her photographs of home and family, her simple toilet articles, her few precious books – all she owned, in fact, was there except her deposit in the Post Office savings bank. It enclosed her comfortably and still left scope for movement.

It was the only place in the vast and splendid house where she did not feel remorselessly exposed. She had lived her life before she came here in a small house where mostly one had one side of one's person towards a wall, one's feet masked by table or chairs. But here the sweeping curves of the wide staircase, those immense saloons downstairs, the terrace and great stretches of open lawn, all impressed her as terribly devised to display completely the human beings who moved across them. Even the nursery close by, where she taught the two youngest children, was spacious and handsome, and dominating it was an elderly nurse with a grand manner who had first gone out to service as a nurse-girl with the Countess's mother, and two nursemaids of a superior kind who spoke careful English. Next along the corridor were the younger children's bedrooms and the nurse's own room, and then little Lord Canfield's bedroom and the study room where he worked in preparation for his public school with Mr. Trimmer. And somewhere beyond she might have inferred if she had thought about it, which she never had, Mr. Trimmer's own bedroom. All the people outside this little room of her own, except Mr. Trimmer, were large and on the grand scale that went with the house. The children were stout and tall with flawless complexions, masses of fluffy gold hair and big blue eyes; the Countess herself was a noted beauty, and downstairs was a continual coming and going of guests, a god-like population for the big house, confident and lovely ladies and handsome, distinguished-looking men who might often be more than six feet high but never by their nature seemed less, who came to stay there in the intervals, it seemed, of governing or owning or otherwise controlling large portions of the earth. Some of them came to lay siege to the Countess, for she had been a widow since, three years ago, her husband had been killed in France.

The nursery governess at home was called "Mousey" but here she was Miss Bates. When she arrived, the children, with the directness of the upper-class young, asked her at once all they wanted to know about herself, including her Christian name, which was Ruth. They discussed it frankly without disfavour, and bestowed it on their next new doll. She thought of herself as Ruth.

She brushed her light brown hair very neatly and coiled it up, and took her evening dress of black taffetas out of the corner wardrobe. As she had been with Lady Canfield now four months she had worn that dress already nearly a hundred times – there had been an interval in the spring when Lady Canfield had gone to the south of France and she had not dressed for dinner. She fastened round her neck, as she did every evening, her gold chain with a tiny pendant heart set with seed pearls, took a clean handkerchief out of the table drawer, and looked at her watch. It was only twenty minutes to eight. She leaned out of the window.

What a beautiful evening it was! The sinking sun bathed the garden in golden light, the lawn was golden green streaked with the long cool shadows of trees, and the big leaves of a fig-tree that clung against the house shone transparent green gold close to her face. No one was about to see it, and it was the loveliest evening after the hot summer's day. Every one was indoors dressing for dinner. "It seems a shame," thought Ruth simply, looking out at the exquisite evening. "They can do just as they like, and they miss the best part of the day."

The golden intensity of the light grew every moment. It was going to be lovelier and lovelier now until it was dark. Reluctantly she turned away from the window.

Because there was a big house-party she had timed her arrival in the great saloon carefully about a quarter of an hour before dinner so that she could be first there. To enter that room in the presence of a crowd of people had happened to her once and should never if she could help it happen again. The Countess had democratic ideas and kindly principles, and there was no separate evening meal served away from the dining-room for governesses, ex-governesses on a visit, tutors, secretary, disabled officer who looked after the stables and dogs, or any others of the secondary class of resident in the house. On the occasion of a house-party they might be placed together at a round table in the window bay, but in the saloon before and after dinner they were assumed to mingle with the rest of the company. Ruth found herself there first as she had expected.

She went across to a table strewn with books and began to turn them over. After a long interval a door opened close beside her, and unexpectedly one of the goddesses appeared, a slim wisp of girlhood clothed in one narrow sheath of green satin like the stem of a lily. She looked astonished as though she had found the room empty.

Ruth dropped her book and smiled. The girl smiled back. They hesitated an instant. "Isn't it a lovely evening," said Ruth.

"Isn't it too wonderful," replied the girl, perching fragilely on the arm of a chair and staring at Ruth. Then, "It must be too lovely living here always."

"Yes," said Ruth.

"Don't you love it?" said the girl. Then the door swung open with a fling, almost a bang, and let in three young men together.

"Oh, *sorry*," they said simultaneously and laughed.

"Your *manners*—" said the girl.

"Oh Opal! *yours* usually."

"Hugs pushed."

Laughter.

"Sit down and be quiet," said the girl.

"Yes, let's sit down. Opal's sitting down. Let's all sit down nicely, like Opal." The young man they called Hugs balanced on the top of a chair-back caricaturing her poise on the chair-arm. They all chattered.

More people had come in at the other end of the room. An older woman was sweeping over to them in front of a long tail of black velvet. "Opal darling!" she exclaimed with a fastidious kiss. "*Just* come. *Such* a journey! Inverness last night! Oh Mr. Hughes! Mr. Patten!! Reginald!!! How very nice—" She gave a bright smile to Ruth, still on the margin of the group, and a handshake. "Delicious dress, Opal," she wound up.

"Jolly good stream-line," said one of the young men approvingly.

They all talked at once. There were waves of chatter from the room, now filling up. Ruth ceased to distinguish words, heard only sounds rising and falling like queer music. It always amazed her that the Olympians had this never-failing flow of fresh talk and laughter ready whenever they met, for all the time they were together. Particularly the women. Olympian men she did sometimes see standing apart, temporarily silent; occasionally one might be seen smoking and pacing alone in the grounds, but the women never. If they were not accompanied and talking they seemed instantly to retire to their rooms.

Every one was moving after Lady Canfield to the dining-room.

"We're quite a party at the round table tonight," said Miss Clarkson, who was staying in the house to paint a set of water-colour views of the gardens, to Miss Baker who had come to organise the new Women's Institute. Next to them sat Mr. Dixon, the disabled officer aforesaid, who was stone deaf, and then there was Mr. Trimmer and Ruth herself. Miss Clarkson and Miss Baker resembled one another in being dark and big and coiffured without frivolity, and had common interests that included knitted jumpers, long sensible walks, the

Black Forest and Lucerne, and contralto songs, so that they had plenty to talk about. Mr. Dixon could not talk to anyone. Mr. Trimmer was vaguely about thirty, thin-haired and rather grey, with a narrow chest and a slight stoop; a bad bicycle accident years ago had left him with a faint limp; he had been secretary to the late earl and so was an old inmate of the house. He had always talked to Ruth when he could, lent her books and done her many a little kindness of social support during these bewildering house-parties. He began to talk to her now.

Ruth answered, and tried to listen entirely to him and not to let her mind wander to watch and listen to the big table where the gods and goddesses sat. But her thoughts did wander. They were all very gay over there, their talk and jests leapt from side to side of the table, their laughter flickered about and sometimes great outbursts of laughter seized them all. Ruth could not help then trying to hear what it was all about. And sometimes when she heard the thing she wondered why they laughed so much at it. The talk of the Olympians puzzled her always, it was so elusive, so very quick; what they actually said seemed so simple to say when said, so difficult to imagine before it was said. She would ask why that thing said should be so acceptable, so welcomed and applauded, while the things she said – but no one among the Olympians seemed to hear when she spoke. But then – why should they? Up at the top of the table sat Lady Canfield, brilliantly lovely, in a marvellous dress of sparkling silver, perfectly formed, witty and clever, a splendid rider, a fine tennis-player, and having a beautiful singing voice. Ruth could never take her eyes off her without an effort, it was marvellous that a creature could be so endowed. She wondered quaintly what she herself would look like if she mounted on her own little round fair head that monstrous comb of brilliants that sat so queenly over Lady Canfield's dark beauty. Next to her sat a big handsome man, slightly grizzled at the temples and with very fine grey eyes; he had just come back from North China, and he was a noted traveller, explorer, and self-appointed diplomat. The household, Ruth knew, favoured him as the Countess's future husband. He seemed never to cease talking or to cease to draw laughter and delight from those who heard him. From him Ruth's eyes ran along the splendidly done men and women of the Olympian dinner-table. The lights from the towering candelabra of crystal flashed and sparkled from the silver and glass, from the jewels and shimmering dresses of the women, from their bright eyes. It was a wonderful world, thought Ruth, for Olympians.

She wished she had been born a daughter of Lady Canfield, so that she might have grown up in this great house among the goddesses of the high table, as completely at her ease as they. Then she would never have stood about, an outsider, wondering what to do. She would have been very tall, and dark, and beautiful—

Or else that fate had left her in her own small home at Minehead with Father and Mother.

She wondered if the others felt as she did about the high table people.

Miss Clarkson and Miss Baker, she knew, were putting it on that they were accustomed to living in this kind of place, and saw nothing at all extraordinary about it. It wasn't possible to know what Mr. Dixon, poor man, felt or thought about anything. Mr. Trimmer always seemed at home, gently and unobtrusively at his ease in this magnificence. But Ruth imagined him at his ease anywhere. Ruth would sometimes have cried herself ill with nervous shyness when she first arrived if it had not been for Mr. Trimmer. Mr. Trimmer made one feel one was all right. He was kind.

By one of the chances that happen in a confusion of talk a woman's languid voice at the big table suddenly became very clear, saying in a tone of negligent contempt: "No – only a bicycle accident – he wasn't *in* the war."

Mr. Trimmer! As if the war were a good club that he hadn't been elected to! Had he heard?

Impossible to say. He was talking to herself, perhaps his face was harder and brighter than usual. With a start she realised that she had been a little absent with him. She turned her mind from the high table to attend to Mr. Trimmer. Presently she was answering happily; she lost the feeling of being only a part of the wallpaper against which those more brilliant lives were played out, and became again herself a solid and visible personage. Nothing she said made him laugh, or bend forward eagerly with a retort or a witticism like the Olympians did. But they talked and smiled contentedly, about the books they were reading, about the little things of their past day, about a walk he described to her and urged that she ought to take while the charlock was in bloom, and then on to talk about places in her own home county of Somerset that they both knew. Ruth forgot the Olympians while Mr. Trimmer was talking to her.

Dinner lasted an enormous time. There were pauses in the ample interchange of Miss Clarkson and Miss Baker when they made an audience, and then Ruth was too shy to go on talking to Mr. Trimmer. There were silences at the round table. But the big table grew gayer and gayer, and no one there was in a hurry to make an end. At long last it was over, the goddesses trooped into the saloon and the ladies from the round table followed after them.

The dining-room had been a concentration of soft shaded light upon the dinner-table, but the great rose-coloured and silver saloon they went back to was now ablaze with light, glittered with open light from end to end. Lady Canfield's tall loveliness went here and there, disposing her guests expertly about the big room. "The General *must* have his bridge," she was saying gaily, and a look of contentment came into the faces of half a dozen people at the magic word. Two tables were made up, the glossy cards began to flicker and fall on the green cloth and a strange absorption to enclose the quartettes of players. The rest fell into intimately conversing couples that sat remotely, and a group that carried off Lady Canfield to the adjacent music-room. Five or six young people, including the three young men and the girl in green, had gone into another adjoining room, had shut the door in consideration for the bridge players and were evidently engaged in some exceedingly active and hilarious game of their own. The lights in the music-room were shaded. Ruth could see through its doorway an exquisite glimpse of a graceful woman in a white dress seating herself at a harp, her bare arm stretching across the strings, her satin-shod foot on the pedal. She plucked it into music, and Lady Canfield's high, brilliant voice floated up in song.

Miss Clarkson and Miss Baker negotiated with one another in undertones; they took an unoccupied card-table and began to play piquet. Mr. Dixon no doubt had gone to the billiard-room. It was so fortunate, said everyone, that he liked billiards. Mr. Trimmer must have retreated to the library. If she had been a man, Ruth thought, that was what she would have done. But what should she do? It was frightfully hot in this room; great banks of flowering plants, filling corners and recesses, poured out a heavy scent. How queer this room was, hot, dazzlingly lit, with its little concentrated groups of people intent on their games.

What odd things games were! Here were these people dotted now in separate groups about these rooms, each group as if enclosed in some invisible crystal of seclusion. They sat engrossed, they made the ordered movements dictated by their game, they became something that was mechanical, they ceased to be of flesh and blood, akin. She was as alone and unnoted as in the company of clockwork toys. She could hear the rattle of their machinery:

Click. "Your deal."

Click. "Shall I deal for you?"

Click. "Three hearts."

Click. "Three spades."

Click. Click. Click.

How hot it was! Lady Canfield seemed to be singing at the top of her voice.

The heat, the loneliness, the scent! This curious feeling stealing over her – was it faintness?

She mustn't faint. Very quietly she slipped out of the open door close by into the corridor.

It was cooler there, and the lights lower. She would stay there a few moments and recover. Perhaps no one would notice if she went away to her bedroom instead of going back.

It was cooler. The French windows behind those dark, straight-hanging curtains must be open. One curtain moved forward and back in the draught, and a thread of moonlight was shot for an instant on the floor like a poniard of shining steel.

Moonlight!

She went over to the curtain and lifted its edge. The window stood open upon the terrace, the white stone shone as if it were day. She stepped out.

Out of the heat and glare and noise and laughter into the cool and silent night! The heavy curtain fell, the glittering magnificence behind it faded from her mind, a tinsel sham. Here was another world, a world of magic silence, a world that lifted to the stars, a world wherein that overwhelming house lay like a little pebble on the earth, a world of marvellous moonlit beauty, of black and silver light. The moonlight fell full upon her, clothing her in a fairy garment of moonshine. She was a Cinderella magically touched. She moved softly across the terrace and on to the noiseless grass among the flowers.

The divine sweetness of the air! The air was the scented breath of night herself, the velvet breath of roses asleep and dreaming of their bee-haunted noon. Close to Ruth a mass of white clematis blossom gazed upwards at the moon, and down beside the path in clusters went the starry nicotine, that slattern of the daylight, with every petal parted to allure some soft-winged dusky lover to her lips. All the night world was strange and breathless and still, and yet awake and intensely alive; tiny noises broke the silence, faint cries, crepitations, fluttered leaves. Something like a big white feather floated past the trees; a rustling at Ruth's feet startled her and there tumbled out upon the grass a little dark bundle of a hedgehog that scooted off busily, poking his nose this way and that.

"Like a busy old woman shopping," thought Ruth.

Could she dare to go further? Beyond the flower-beds was a belt of tall trees, black and mysterious, and beyond them was the lake. Was the lake very lovely under the moon? If she were a man and not this tethered thing that she was, she would go there, and take the dinghy that was tied up to the bank, and float out – into a lake of silver? And stay there hour after hour alone with the night, watching the moon pass across the sky and fall at last over the edge of the world. The stirring life of the night would be hushed, the darkness would be utter and profound. With all the rest of nature one would fall asleep, and sleep deeply, peacefully, and wake with the stirring dawn—

What was that?

Someone was down there in the garden, someone standing quite still. Watching her? Moving now and coming towards her. She turned shyly to escape, and stepped back upon the terrace. It was Mr. Trimmer. She stopped, irresolute.

"You have come out too?" he said softly. "I thought when I first saw you that the terrace had been given a new statue, a little statue all of silver and ebony. Come out among the flowers."

"I must go in," said Ruth demurely.

He stood on the grass beneath her, looking up at her.

"Doesn't this matter?" he said.

"This?"

"The beauty of the world."

Ruth gave a little cry in answer, and lifted her arms to the moon.

"Come."

She hesitated, and glanced back at the curtained windows.

"Oh, *they* never come out here when it is dark and the moon shines and the grass is wet and white with dew. Why did you come?"

"It was so hot," said Ruth. "They are all sitting in those hot rooms, with the curtains drawn close. I could not bear it..."

"Don't go back to it yet."

She yielded. She stepped from the terrace.

They walked down the grassy path in silence. At the end he turned with a gesture to look back. The darkness of the great house, dotted above with yellow-lit windows, uprose behind the moonlit flowers.

"Why do they not come out?" she said softly. "All this beauty waits for them and they do not come."

He answered as softly: "The beauty of the world waits for all humanity and they do not come."

Ruth whispered: "Do I know what you mean?"

"Before I saw you I was thinking how like those hot rooms are to human lives. The busy fretful lives people lead! With thick curtains drawn close to shut out beauty. And outside, this wilderness of beauty, all this loveliness of the world and the universe of those stars, waiting patiently. Till men choose to come and take it for their own."

Ruth was silent for a moment. "Will they ever come?" she asked.

"Some day perhaps. Perhaps never. Far down the ages, with the spirit of man hushed for ever, the beauty of the world may be left alone."

"We are seeing this bit of it," whispered Ruth.

He did not answer at once. Then: "Let us see all we can," he said.

They walked in silence between the flowers.

He whispered: "Can you smell the sweetness here?"

"Night stock!"

"And here – the sour sweet of those evening primroses?"

"Yes. I love it. They grow at home."

"Do you know they are giving all they have; they have only this night to live. At sunset they unfurled those flawless blossoms, and sunrise will fade them and they will hang withered. Only this night! Come this way – there are lilies—"

He guided her to a side alley between the flowers and stopped. Ruth caught her breath in delight. On either hand tall ranks of white madonna lilies stood sentinel, pouring out their ultimate perfume.

She could not speak. She had no words. She was close to tears. They stood silently together, and in silence walked slowly down the path between the moonlit lilies to a grassy space beneath the shadow of great trees. There was a white seat, flecked with the pattern of overhanging boughs.

They sat down side by side.

After a moment they turned as if with the same thought and looked at one another. Ruth's face relaxed into a shy smile.

"Why were you so miserable at dinner?" he asked.

"I wasn't really miserable."

"Yes, you were. You were looking at the other table – so wistfully. And once there were tears in your eyes. What were you thinking then?"

"Oh, silly things."

"Tell me."

"They looked so splendid. I…"

"What?"

"They always do. They are so brilliant and confident and clever and happy—"

"Yes?"

"Everything belongs to them."

"Yes, it does. Was it that put tears in your eyes?"

"I was wishing – it was silly – I could be beautiful too and have – beautiful clothes – and talk – so that people would listen."

"I know. I understand."

"I can't help it. I feel that, often. It's silly. Every one is kind to me."

"Very kind. And besides being so kind, they hurt you badly, don't they?"

"I suppose so… They don't mean to."

He looked at her, not speaking.

She whispered: "Do they ever – hurt you too?"

He hesitated. "Yes. They hurt. Life hurts."

"Life?"

With a gesture of both hands he indicated his slight body, touched his lamed leg. "Life is a long journey to go – with a third-class ticket."

She uttered a soft note of understanding. For a moment she could not speak, seeking in her mind some comfort for him in his desolate avowal.

"But we look out of the window," she said timidly – "at this—"

"If they let us," he answered with a nod at the distant house. "They suppose us now caged in their rooms, hemmed in with hewn and hacked lumps of wood and twisted metal that they call furniture, with enough air to keep our hearts beating, shut each in our own silence; while outside this goddess that is the night walks the earth in beauty for all men to see. You know, if they knew, they wouldn't even let us – be here."

"Oh!" she cried, afire with rebellion.

"Well, would they?"

She was silent. "No," she said, very quietly.

Suddenly they were clinging together with their arms tightly about one another, sobbing like unhappy children. His head was on her shoulder; they clung to one another as if against some force that would tear them apart. They clung until their storm of tears was spent. Then he lifted his head, and they faced each other in the shadowed moonlight, his hands clasped behind her neck. Her face was quivering.

"Ruth," he breathed.

"What has happened to us?" she said in a breaking voice.

"*Love*," he whispered, almost below her hearing; and gazed at her white-faced, hushed and strained.

She broke away from him with a little cry.

"Oh no!" he cried out. "Ruth! Don't leave me alone – again—"

She turned her eyes to him, and her agitation crumpled to tenderness and pity. She gave her hands to his hungry clasp. He was trembling, trying to speak a word unfamiliar to his tongue.

"I love you," he whispered huskily.

"But – I don't understand – *this*."

"*I* don't understand. Does it matter?"

"You never seemed to think of me – like this."

"No. But I loved you when I saw you on the terrace in the moonlight."

"Why?"

"How can I tell why? Something – it was like being seized by a strong hand – gripped together. Don't you feel it? Both of us – lonely, unhappy. Oh, come back into my arms. You are trembling, you tiny thing – you are not cold?"

"No, no—"

"Dear! you wanted to be beautiful – if you could see your face now! It is like some exquisite flower—"

"It isn't—"

"It is, my dear. And your eyes like dark pools of shadow. And you wanted to be dressed beautifully—"

"No—"

"From head to foot in cloth of silver. You wanted to talk, so that people would listen. Here I am listening for every word – every word. Listening to your very breathing. Talk to me – speak to me—"

"But I never thought of you before – like this – and now, in a moment – *why*?"

"I don't know. Why trouble to know? Let us be happy now and forget the Big House and the Big People. Love is with us tonight, not with them. Perhaps Love *is* a god, a living god and a hunter of men – for sport, and he passed when you were coming through the window and I was in the garden. Perhaps he was going to the big drawing-room. Going to make mischief. And he saw us – the nursery governess and the secretary tutor. What a joke it would be to take us – who never dreamt of being taken. So he seized us for his playthings, and now he is drumming upon our hearts this tune, throbbing in your breast and mine.

He does what he will with us. Dearest, I care not what he does so that he is with us now. Do not fret him with questions. Perhaps tomorrow he will tire of us and turn to play once more with bigger game. But tonight he holds us. In this kindly darkness. It does not show that your dress is shabby, dear, and that your poor little shoes are crumpled at the toes. It does not show that my hair is touched with grey. I'm weedy stuff by the common standards—"

"No, no!" she protested.

"I am, dearest. When the darkness does not shield me. To-morrow this Love god will have dropped his playthings into the daylight, and all these things will show."

"I do not care if they do," she said shyly but earnestly. "Why should we not love as well as other people? Why should we not be more happy than those people who are in that blazing place?"

"Oh, little Ruth," he said sadly. "How can we be?"

"We *are*," she said stoutly.

He was silent. He held her hand against his lips, broodingly. Then he got up, as if he would dismiss his thoughts. "Come, dear, and let me show you all the beauty I can while this magic lasts." He put his arm about her shoulders, and drew hers about himself, and so embraced they walked slowly through the trees, stopping now and then, looking up through the dark fretwork of the leaves of the starry sky.

"I was here only a few moments ago, aching with loneliness."

"And I was miserable in the house."

"Little Ruth, soon I must take you back to the house. Soon our little hour of loveliness will have gone. But first let me show you the lake. It will be something you will always remember, Ruth, something that must lie always warm at your heart, this night of Love made beautiful. Love! To-night all the world is in love. Look at the lake water, dreaming in bliss. Come out on this platform and look down into the water, velvet black beneath us. Ssh! We have stirred the sleeping waterfowl in the reeds. Hear the chuckling little questions they are asking one another. It's nothing… All this side of the water black, black beyond seeing – and creeping across the water over there that pale mist, hiding the reeds so that only their tasselled heads stick up above it. I've seen that in a picture somewhere, a picture of Japan. Would you like to travel, Ruth, and see places like Japan?"

"*Like*!" she breathed.

"You never will, Ruth. Nor I. You might get to Japan some day, but you'd have somebody's child to mind. That isn't travel. All that belongs to the people in the house. That is why Love will get tired of us tomorrow, because he knows how little we can do that will interest him. Love is for soft clear skins and fresh youth and loveliness and stalwart bodies. He won't like my limp, Ruth, in the daylight. It amuses him now, but it will bore him tomorrow and he'll just drop us." He mimicked the languid lady: "He'll find out he wasn't in the war!"

Ruth clenched her fist with indignation. "Oh that woman!"

He laughed. "Oh, it's true – tomorrow's truth."

"Why do you say that?" she said, bewilderment breaking in her voice. You talk as if this – tonight – were a game."

Her voice trembled. Her mind had been running with an undertow of happy concrete images, like the pictures in a Stores catalogue. Page 1354, Engagement Rings. "This – isn't a joke, is it? A kind of joke you are playing with me?"

"God forbid, my dear one," he said very earnestly. "But what do you think is before us, the you and me that the daylight will reveal? Do you think we shall go on to marriage and a home for you and all the rest of it? Would they have me even for a schoolmaster, do you think, with my halting leg and my battered body? I don't know, dear. I have never thought of such things, never wanted them before. But do not think I do not love you, dear, however I may fail you in fulfilling the common programme of a lover. Love is our god now, and tomorrow we will keep faith with each other, although he may laugh at our poverty."

"I will keep faith," she said very solemnly.

Their hands clasped in promise.

"We want so little," she said.

"No, I want much. I must teach you to want everything."

"I won't. I'll be happy with almost nothing."

He did not speak for a moment. Then he said: "What is your dream of a happy life? You must have dreamed dreams. Tell me."

She smiled with her arm tucked under his, and looked wistfully across the water. "Why, I would have a tiny house…" There flashed into her mind a particular china teapot with a rosebud on it that she had once seen in a shop in Minehead.

"We will not have a tiny house!" he exclaimed, so loudly that she shuddered and put her hand up to his face and said, "Hush, hush!"

"We will live in no tiny house that you can fill with the smell of boiling cabbage-water. I was born in a tiny house – and I will not live in one. I will live in space – space and beauty – beauty too or I will not live… Ah-h-h-h!"

He had stepped backward off the edge of the wooden platform and fallen with a great splash into the black water below. A vast, horrible tumult and it seemed she saw his dark head in the heaving shadows. "Ruth!" his voice came – a strangled struggling cry.

She flung herself on her knees and leant over. "Here, here!" she cried into the darkness. Her hand was touched for an instant by a slippery grasp.

"Here!" She stretched further, clutched, and overbalanced…

They struggled, they fought for life, for that life that they had found so poorly furnished for them, and which yet had held the beauty of the world and the quick fire in their hearts. They struggled vainly, they clutched each other fatally, and the soft, impassive water flowed over them and smothered their unheard cries, covered them at last and rippled outwards, swaying the reeds by the shore, rippling ever more quietly and slowly until the ripples ceased altogether and the lake was placid, smooth.

The hushed small signs of the night crept back; a bird clucked, a fish leapt. There was the whisper of a breeze, as if Love himself sighed, and through the swaying branches the silver petals of the moon fell once more upon the mirror of the pond.

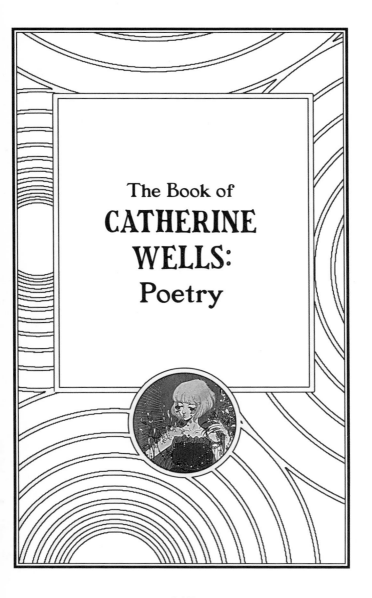

The Book of CATHERINE WELLS: Poetry

Winter Sunset

When you and I were young, dear love,
'Twas like a summer's day;
Your love poured hot into my soul
A very little way,
Like the sun into my window here
Upon a summer's day.

But that was years ago. And now
Your love comes warm and wise;
It stoops, it streams, a golden flood
Level into my eyes,
Like the sun into my window here
Low in the wintry skies.

The War

1
Spring 1915

Spring, dear Spring,
Dear Beauty!
You come with soft feet
Bringing your old, immortal joys
That have given us in all our years
Delight so exquisite.
You spread your loveliness before us —
A tender veil!
As if in kindness you had hung a curtain
Thick fold upon thick fold unstintingly
To stop our hearing how a madman
Raves, in the next room.

It is no good, dear beauty of the earth!
Tearing great rents athwart you
Come the screams of war.

2
June 1916

Last night I dreamed.
In the void of space
Stood three great Archangels with pitiless eyes
About an armoured monster in their midst;
A brutal shape that spat impotent fire
At their bright immortality.
"He must be beaten out of life," they cried;
"He is War."
And as I looked came multitudes
Carrying their all, and heaped upon the brute
Each staggering load, blow after blow, until he lay
Writhing beneath a monstrous heap of treasure
And brave bodies of men, and women's tears
That ran down the heap like pearls.
And still the angels cried, "More yet! More yet!
Not yet is there enough!" Again
The people toiled with fast diminishing loads
Until they had no more to give.
It seemed enough, until a tiny chink
Showed in the heap.
"One thing more," they cried, "and ye have done!"
"We have no more," the people wept. And then
The angels turned, and each his finger held
Straight aimed at me, and called in unison,
"*Thy son!*"

3
Red Cross Workroom 1917

Daily here my body sits,
My fingers tearing bandage strips,
My drilled eyes watch the pattern fits,
My agile scissor cuts and snips,
But truant Brain leaps out at play
And flies to some pellucid day
And suddenly I seem to hear
A sea maid singing at my ear
And straight am with her on a strand
Of cockle shells and pearly sand.
Where rainbows crown the leaping surf
And green weed wraps the rocks with turf.
We wreathe her yellow hair with weed
And play with coriander seed
And coral beads and horns of pearl —
The while that here my body sits,
My fingers tearing bandage strips.

The Kneeling Image

There was a day I remember
And shall remember a long while,
One of those pleasant oases
When hour after hour
Falls to the touch of time
Like a ripe apple.
A day for clear eyes and brisk walking,
With autumn scents, and a pale gold sun,
And a breeze that clutched at the leaves
And scurried them down by the walls
Under the hedge, and piled them there
In the sun, for their last sleep.
We had tea by the fire,
The lamp was lit;
And presently one of my friends read a poem
Of heaven.

He sat by the lamp and I in the dusk
In the firelight,
And the poem had so much beauty that tears
Would stand in my eyes, a shimmering veil
Between me and the golden flames;
For it was a poem of heaven

And that, as we know it,
Is the tale of two people
Being together, that were not.
So simple as that is all that we know of heaven
Who live on this earth;
So simple, so little a thing,
And so hard to attain.

Was it that poem of heaven,
That brought me my dream of hell?

One would think
That if heaven is being together
Then hell is in being apart.
But there's more. For parting alone
Leaves hope, and hope is abandoned in hell.
You're apart, but the barriers that part you
Are barbed with crueller thrusts
Than a sentence of time.
That sentence of time is a wall
Between you and your heaven,
And hope is not killed by a wall.
Its cold decree
Is attacked by tendrils of hope
As one worries a chink
In the hardest wall, by the tips
of one's fingers at last,
Though they bleed to the bone.

But the barriers that hell can put
Between you and your dear
Are of iron, are of ice,
And your fingers may scratch to Eternity
Making no sign
On their pitiless strength.
And one knows at the first
At the very first moment in hell
That one's fingers may scratch to Eternity
Making no sign
On their pitiless strength.
For hell has invented the loss of faith
And the crawling poison of lies
To rot the fabric of love
Between you and your dear.
And lest you should hope even then,
Hell has invented the wrinkled skin
And the grey, thin hair,
And the body that first is so fair
And loses minutely and surely
With creeping time
Its beauty and scent
Till it bulges and hollows and sags
As mine did, kneeling in hell
In my meek nun's robe.

It was a strange dream.
I suppose it was reading a book

Of the Borgias and Sforzas and such
Late that night, that started my brain
At so queer a game.
For I was not I any more, but the wife
Of a Florentine prince,
A man very great in war,
Very stern in power,
Whose helmet had rubbed and worn
The grizzled hair from his brows;
Big in bone and heavy in tread
And with hard eyes.
I came, little more than a child,
From my father's house;
A kind house, where there was laughter
And long days of content,
And sunshine and olive-trees
And vines borne to the ground with
 the load of their purple fruit.
I went in my turn,
In my stiff dress sewn with gold
And splendid with jewels
As my sisters had gone;
And meekly was bride to my lord
For that
Was life as I knew it then.
He was just, but he was not kind,
And he hated the weak,
The weak, little things of the earth.

I think he hated my babe
Who died so soon, for its wailing cry
And its weak little cold limbs.
"You're young," were his comforting words,
"And the first always dies. The next
Will be brawnier stuff."

But I mothered no other child,
And I trod the threshold of hell.

For that struck his pride in a deadly place
To father no sons,
And the look that I caught on his face
When he saw me first
And the little thing that I was,
Came back and stayed.
And his first uneasy patience
Gave way to an angry contempt.

But the ante-chambers of hell
Are not all dark.
Hell has a cunninger way
Than to toughen your sense with
    the dull piling of pain.
That you may later know pain
To its last agonised throb,
There are windows that open on heaven
That let in the breezes of heaven

Its sunshine and shouting of birds,
And the happiness overrunning,
The extravagant prodigal bliss
That is heaven's first gift.

It was spring…
That window flew open,
My lover came in.

My lord discovered our sin…

It is strange that in hell
It is hard to believe that you sin.
I could ne'er understand
– For a girl is not learned like a priest –
How the monstrous and evil snare
I'd been taught to expect and resist
Never was, never gleamed;
And the thing that in hell they call sin
Is past belief fair,
Is compact of dear joy,
Of beauty and tender care.
It seemed that Love held out his arms
And enfolded my heart with such rapture
Such ecstasy pure
As Mary her Child.
Is it part of the cunning of hell
To dress sin

In God's very skin?

My lord took no common way;
With his iron pride
He'd be meat for no sniggering tale
Of husband betrayed.
He announced I was dead, and even my dear
Thought me dead,
But hell is eternal, the sleeping of death
Is not there.
No death, not a thousand deaths
  could have slaked his revenge.
He kept me alive, to wreak on my body his rage.
Here was no shred of magnificence docked
From my funeral cavalcade,
But the coffin that shammed to hold my corpse
With a stone was weighed;
And because, he publicly said, I
  had led so saintly a life
He would build a memorial fit for so good a wife;
And a tower of stainless white
Should lift to the sky
And up at its topmost height
Should a chapel be placed,
And my image should kneel so I faced
The holy pair.

It was done as he said, but the statue they put

Was no figure of wood
But my flesh and blood.
That knelt on the cold stone
And could not move.

Year followed year, year followed year;
I knelt and could not move.
The strangeness of dreams! for all those years
I knew in such multitude,
Dragging their leaden days,
Their endless succession of days,
Were perhaps a few moments measured
By the ticking clock at my head,
The time from one turn to another
Of my body lying in bed.
But to me in my dream
Year followed year, slower and slower,
Colder and colder,
Till time itself froze and was still
And my heart ceased to beat;
Only my body grew older and older.

I knelt in a shrine deep recessed
Over the altar,
And the figures of Mary and Child
Sat enthroned in a blaze of gold
Encircled by angels.
And the day and the night

Were alike in the light that streamed
  from hundreds of candles
With tall and unquivering flames.
There I knelt, in a white nun's robe,
And could not move.
It is all in the spirit of hell to be near heaven,
To have lost heaven
And not know why,
I knew that behind me were windows
  that gave to the sky;
I knew when each dawn
Stole on the silvered dark
And the creeping grey light
Roused the first faint stir of the breeze,
The first thin song of a bird,
Very high, that trembled and ceased
And uprose in flight.
It seemed that I knew
The instant the sun at my back
Smote the floor;
But all that I saw
Year after year, was the crack
In the stone at my feet where my bent eyes fell
In unblinking stare.
I would hear each day
The city awake, and the life of the street
So distant below,
Would rise in a murmurous sound

Of voices and far away feet,
And swell to each noon
With a clanging rejoicing of bells
From the new campanile Giotto had made.
And I saw as if I had been there
The piled ruddy fruit on the barrows,
The women with striped kerchiefs
Tied on their glossy hair,
And the babies rolling in the doorways,
The barter and laughter in a long crescendo
To the hot midday;
And a long diminuendo to the evening
And the ultramarine night.
Through each day of those years and years
I longed for the peace of the night,
For behind me the day
Was ever a crowd
Who toiled up the winding stair of the tower
And prayed.
But the night was silent…silent…
I wept through each night of those years;
A ceaseless river of tears
Furrowed each cheek, wearing a deep groove,
And the years followed the years and still
I did not understand
Why Love had been given mankind
To be banned.

Not all days were alike,
Some were marked
With a bitterness more profound
When I knew my lord stood there,
– I knew his step on the stair,
Heavy on the stair –
He stood, he alone of them all
Knowing the image before him
Was my living flesh in thrall,
And I felt the touch of his gaze
Like a hot flail…
Ah well, every dream, thank God!
Must end at last,
Even a dream about hell.

It came with a sudden pause
In the worshipping crowd.
It seemed they vanished
And I was alone with the candles and saints
And a new fear.
Then up the stairs like the tread of a doom
Trampled the feet of my lord,
Not alone, for I heard him talking
And a gentle voice replying
That pierced me like a sword;
The voice of my lover –
No other!
What torment had the fiend devised

That he urged my lover
So courteously nearer?
With a smooth voice saying,
"I've always wanted to show you how like
It is to herself, how well done."
It seemed my withered body shrank
    in my shape of stone
To one burning drop of pain,
And the heart that had shrivelled to
    something so small and so hard and old
Could bear no mockery more, and broke
And released me. I moved, I sprang,
From the shrine to the floor, and up to the sill,
And leapt from hell...

It ended as dreams do
In a long fall,
A rush through the sweet air
To the city below, tiny and white,
Laced round with a river of blue
That meandered the plain.
But the rush was brief,
I fell
Slower and slower,
Floating to earth at last,
... like a leaf.

A leaf, wind-blown, nowhither;
Brown, dry;
Scurried and blown in a torrent of leaves
'Gainst the foot of a wall,
Scraping a window, lamp-lit.
Oh window! fly open again;
A woman who's dead is beating
her soul at thy pane!

The Fugitives

At night my sleeping-room
Is dark and high,
With three great windows opening
To the garden and the sky,
And soft and dusky visitors
Come swirling through the room and go
Back to their moonlit pageant show,
While through the shadowed places of my brain
The dreams drift to and fro.
It was the hour before the dawn;
A full night we had lain,
Still with fright, in a secret hole
Behind a trellised pane
In an Indian Rajah's palace, and I
Was some brown bit of unheeded life
Serving the Rajah's new young wife,
And somehow mixed up in the sudden flight
She had made from her raging lord.
We lay close pressed and scarcely stirred,
She by the side, without a word,
Of the dark young Prince who had caused the din
(I dare say theirs was the ancient sin;)
And one or two others like me, and her nurse,

An aged dame, who to make things worse
For us in our hiding, would whimper with fear
And betray us all were I not near
To muffle her mouth
With a handy cloth.

All night the search went to and fro
About and around and above and below,
And we heard her master rage and roar
With an anger I'd never imagined before.
And the flashing lights passed, and pierced within
Our sheltering trellis that was so thin,
Lighting her face with her lips compressed
And her little hands crushed on her lover's breast.
Late we heard two who paused to speak
Say as soon as there was a daylight streak
He'd orders to pull all the palace down
If he could not "find out where
    the rats had flown."
I saw by the light they carried the flash
In the Prince's eyes, and the movement rash
That clutched at his dagger; and
    guessed his thought,
To kill his belovéd where she lay
Rather than suffer the peril of day
And the chances that it brought.
And then it seemed she counselled flight
While yet we lived in the night.

It was the hour before the dawn,
And well her lover knew the way;
Ah! better in the darkling night
He knew it than in day!
So fast as they ran, as if they chased
The flying skirts of Paradise.
Through tall bamboos that speared the moon,
Our shadows with their shadows laced;
Through the gardens, through the ricefields,
Slipping close along the hedges,
Hiding from the candid moonlight
Till we reached the desert edges
And a strange, untrodden land.
The dawn came up and paled the moon;
We ran no more, but plodded over sand;
And in the cold grey morning came
Into an open space among great dunes,
Where from thin threads of grass
  a small thin wind
Whipt elfin tunes.
And up against us rose a lofty hill
That set the aged woman muttering of ill.

She told it was an evil place;
An ancient palace, derelict,
Lay buried in the sand.
She pointed up where near the crest
The hill was rifted with a scar;

And then another. Through such holes,
Through such small holes, as birds into a nest,
Had rash men crawled and lost the light of day,
And ne'er returned to tell if aught
They found of all the marvels they had sought.

The sun came up behind us with a sigh
And touched as with a spear of gold
The crest that fringed against the sky,
And growing hot and bold,
Poured down the pearly sand face of the hill;
And as it went it flamed to light
Great jewels, emerald, sapphire-bright,
Of palace marble, showing where the wind
Swirling against its walls, the
massive sand had thinned.

Oh youth! who laughs at evil powers,
Oh love! who heeds no curses of the gods,
These were our guides. A fearful name
But makes a hiding-place more safe.
(What if an aged woman chafe?)
We climbed the slipping sand.
We clung to grass that pricked the hand,
We burnt beneath the sun;
With lips that split and tongues that clave
We reached at last a hole that gave
Us shelter, every one.

Oh could I but remember
That palace of delight!
Its halls of twilit splendour,
Its caves of sapphire night!
Its gold-besetted ivory,
Its thrones of malachite!
The patterns of the tracery
That sprang against the light!
Too much that in my dream life
I know minutely there,
Forgotten is like music
That fades into the air;
But oh! My heart is haunted
By melody most rare.

(There lives yet in my memory
A hall whose summit cleaved the hill,
A fountain that was never still
But soared to fling its slender spray
Up to the fretted dome.
A pool of water, marble-lipped,
Where scaly fishes, silver-tipped,
Slid through the silver foam;
And a moment in the morning
When the sun, but newly risen,
Like an archer with his arrow
Oft essayed, yet sudden finds the mark,
Shot through the ivory spandrils of a window

Striking the fountain to her feathered heart;
And in the seven splinters of a rainbow
Lay on the marble floor, a shattered dart.)

And now our lives had great content;
Bereft of all affright
We laughed and slept and hid by day,
We ventured forth by night;
Beneath the tropic moon we lay –
Our eyes were drunk with sight;
We ate the wild sweet fruit we found,
Dream fruit that grew on moonlit ground.

But frailer than a bubble
Is the happiness of dreams
As frail as earthly happiness
That first so solid seems;
(We clutch so tight the pretty thing
We crush the joy to which we cling.)

The aged woman with us
Discovered fretful ways;
Began with grumbling discourse
To poison all our days;
For the sweetmeats of the harem
And its softly cushioned bowers;
And now my dream leapt restlessly
Among uneasy hours.

The sun went slanting down the dunes
And gilt each grain of sand,
And turned the crimson cactus blooms
To globes of fire and blood,
And silhouetted each black thorn
That spiked against the sky alone;
And I was in a narrow way
That led out to the open day
With that noisy, angry crone.

And while I prayed her to be quiet
A hand of ice still caught my heart;
For at the passage end remote
I saw a swarthy face –
Some shepherd of a starveling goat
Had spied our hiding place…

We watched the coming of that night
And we were not alone,
For Fear came in among us
And sat down like a stone.
From a hole that gave upon a hill
We watched the night grow black and still;
As dark as if the earth itself
Hid from our angry doom.
And in the middle hours of night
Came a sound we could not hear,
Till it grew upon our senses

From a throbbing in the ear
To a multitude in movement
Pouring sound into the air,
To the bellowing of savage beasts
Who in anger leave their lair;
And we fled from side to side to find
If haply 'twas not there.

It seemed as though a window then
Gaped open great and wide;
A window I had never known
Yawned in the hill side.
And amid the crashing cymbals
And the flare of smoking torches
And the reddened rabble faces
Was one, taller by a head;
And we saw the devil fury
Of the Master we had fled.

Then Fear stood up among us
And gripped us for his own,
And clutched our tiny hearts of flesh
Against his breast of stone,
And the tatters of our bravery
Clung to his hands of bone.

But those two –
The girl bride and her lover –

Went hand in hand together
To the great hall with the fountain
Where they'd loved and laughed so often,
And stood with even breath.
And there, with heads uplifted
Like slender pine-trees, waited
The coming of their death.

Two Love Songs

1

Come to me yet again, and bring
Your hungry heart;
Let us clasp hands again, and play
We're not apart.

Put your dear lips on mine, with one
Last lingering kiss;
In pity close your eyes, lest I
Their love-light miss!

2

We sit in a quiet room;
You are very far away;
And very strange it is that I
Who so easily could call you
When I would,
Can do so no more.
You are very far away,
Though so near;
I sit alone in our silence,
My dear!

Music Set to Words

1

Chopin, Prelude No. 15, Op. 28

Against the window tapping
The ivy fingers beat,
A waterspout is dripping
Cold rain on to the street.

And all my life goes halting,
A bird with shattered wing;
Like pearls its days are dropping
From off the broken string.

2

Chopin, Prelude No. 4, Op. 28

Beat on – beat on –
Blood in my heart;
Think on – think on –
Thought in my brain.

Stifle – oh stifle
The ancient smart;

Memory touches –
I flinch with the pain.

3
Chopin, Prelude No. 6, Op. 28

The garden of the roses
Is loveliest at night,
When the red are like black shadows,
The white ones still more white.

In the garden of the roses
A woman walks alone;
She listens for a footstep,
Knowing it will not come.

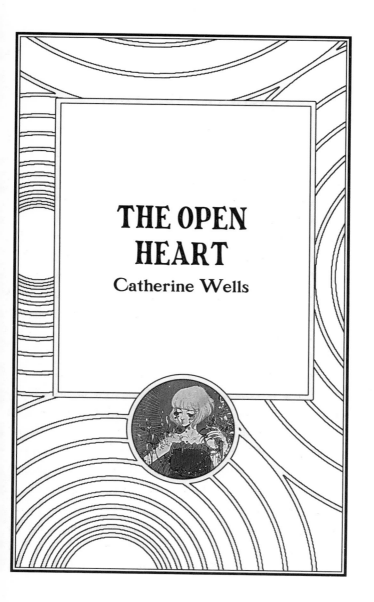

THE OPEN HEART

Catherine Wells

Note on the Text

THE TEXT of Catherine Wells's unfinished novella presented here is an edited version of a transcript prepared in 1990 by the late David C. Smith, a distinguished H.G. Wells scholar who had been given a photocopy of the original manuscript by two of Catherine Wells's grandchildren, Catherine Stoye and Martin Wells, both of whom have since died. We have not succeeded in locating either the manuscript itself or the photocopy. Some apparently cancelled passages in the original manuscript have been omitted, while others, necessary to maintain continuity, have been enclosed in square brackets. The original chapter divisions have been retained, although it is unclear if these would have reflected the author's final intentions, and there are numerous other breaks in the text (where the narrative shifts or a new topic of argument is introduced) which are marked with a row of asterisks. As for the title, it is not certainly the one that Catherine Wells herself would have given this unfinished piece. In the manuscript, at the head of Chapter One the title 'Letter from a Lost Island' has been crossed out, with *The Open Heart* substituted in what Smith believed to be H.G. Wells's hand.

Three explanatory footnotes have been added.

Prelude

MY FRIEND, Edgar Crawshay, who died by his own hand last year at the age of thirty three, left me instructions as his executor to publish the manuscript that follows. His name was not Edgar Crawshay, nor is mine Williams, but it seems to me that to the stranger reader our identities matter nothing, while the facts I am about to set down will be sufficient to reveal him to his friends, and by explaining his action in taking his own life, gain him that understanding and forgiveness that is his due.

Crawshay died in his flat in London, but to me he died three weeks later one torrid day in the Mediterranean on a P and O liner[1] bound for Southampton from Bombay. We had discharged the bulk of our passengers at Brindisi, and the rest of us who were not shortening the journey by the overland route were left, a flat, discontented minority, to make the most of the letters and newspapers that had reached us at that port. I

1 Incorporated by Royal Charter in 1840, the Peninsular and Oriental Steam Navigation Company (popularly known as P&O) was, by the time that Catherine was writing, the largest shipping company in the world.

suppose I must have read almost all of the single week-old copy of the *Times* that had come to me, except the shipping and financial news, before I folded it back to the front page and looked up the columns of advertisements of concerts and picture shows with an odd feeling that after all my long absence was not appetite but a sort of shy reluctance, and my eye fell over the edge of the column on to the obituary notices. Under Crawshay's name was the bare statement that he had died at his London address three weeks before. At one time I had known Crawshay as well, I think, as any man, and I was deeply shocked and sorry to realise that his gentle presence had vanished from the world. Later in the day I remembered that some years before he had asked me to stand with his older brother, in the will he was making, the administrators of his little independence.

I reached London – days later, and lost no time in looking up his brother. It was then that I learnt that he had died by his own act. An accident that had happened to him abroad – for of late years in contrast to his previous almost indolent life he had gone wandering – had threatened his eyesight, and it fitted exactly with what I knew of him that his keen fastidiousness should refuse life on limited terms. He had ended his life, his brother told me, deliberately, carefully and considerately; his rooms, always charming and neat were scrupulously so on the day he died, and gay with freshly bought flowers, and his papers, accounts and personalia disposed of with such order as to cause the least possible trouble. He had wrapped up, sealed and addressed to me a parcel found on his writing desk, and then having done these things, in the midst of his quiet flower-set room, he had sat in his armchair, thought for a moment perhaps, or perhaps, so piercing must have been his disappointment, not dared to think, and shot himself.

His brother had awaited my coming before he had begun the dismantling of that room, and the inevitable destruction of the quiet place that Crawshay had made for himself. It was not until I stood in his graceful little room, with the delicately golden London sunshine flowing in and lighting its colours to their utmost fullness – he loved colour of a grave and subtle kind – that I felt the measure of my loss of him. I had not seen him for two years by reason of those wanderings of his, and before that perhaps scarcely half a dozen times a year since our college intimacy, but now it made me unbearably unhappy that he was for ever unattainable, that I should never see again his welcoming smiling face, the kindly eyes that lit so warmly, the graceful lines of his tall slight body stretched out along his window seat – an attitude he loved – or hear his amused voice as we elaborated some absurdity or ragged one another's prejudices as easy friends may. I remembered the last time I saw him, on a June morning when I had dropped in to urge him to come with me for a ten days tramp in the Alps I had planned, and how he had jeered at the "Swiss ramp" as he called it, and would not be persuaded by me that Switzerland, which he had never seen, was anything but a conglomeration of Rue de Rivoli shops, palace hotels and funicular railways scattered generously over the landscapes of a Nestlé advertisement. I remember feeling then, for all his affectionate sociability, how detached he was; how his spirit, for all his ready friendliness, ever secluded itself a little apart. I remember thinking how difficult and charming it would be to try and draw his subtly shaped, sensitive hands as his fingers caressed a bit of ivory he had picked up from his window sill. I had known him a young man drunk with beauty, and he loved beauty with such passion still that he lived almost austerely in his desire to maintain the keenness of his perceptions. People talk of a man being alive to his finger tips, Crawshay lying purposefully and quietly on his window seat was sensitive to the tip of every hair on his head. I do not know why he would not come to Switzerland. A month after I heard of his having packed up suddenly and started for the South Seas.

There is no doubt at all in my mind as to what he did. Somehow the manuscript that follows came into his possession, and he – that indolent, leisure-loving man – dashed out across the world to answer its human cry. I do not doubt he spent the two years that followed in passionate determined search, and then came his accident, a boat hook carelessly swung by a Negro had caught him in the right eye, and destroyed it. He then came back to London and treatment, and it was presently evident that the sight of the remaining eye would not endure. So much his brother told me, and the rest, to me who knew him, happened as a matter of course.

The parcel found on his desk contained the manuscript that follows, with a letter asking me to have it published.

J.G. Williams

The Open Heart

"Let us Walk a Little with the Truth."

Chapter One

WHERE AM I?

It seems to me that I am in fairyland, or the Utopia of dreams, or perhaps in some distant, forgotten part of Heaven. Yet surely Utopia cannot exist for one woman alone, and I am the only human creature here, and if I am dead and in heaven, then heaven is in many ways curiously like our earth, the same sun rises and sets, although more gloriously than ever I saw it before I came here, the marvellous blue nights are jewelled by moon and stars, the same constellations sweep across the sky, and if this is indeed heaven there is again the riddle of my being alone. I puzzle over it and puzzle, and now at last come to this earthly trick of writing about it, writing with the materials that lie to my hand, a sort of diary I think it will be, that will relieve the need I feel of talking.

I suppose really that I am in an abandoned palace built by some incredibly wealthy, half mad monarch of the past, some bygone Ludwig or Shah Jehan, a place accidentally forgotten by humanity, its very existence wiped out of history, else it would for its beauty's sake be as familiar to us all as the Taj Mahal. If I go on writing I must try to describe it, its wonder has not faded in the slightest with the familiarity I have with it now; every day on waking I feel again my first fresh amazement at the marvel of it; so incredible is its reality that I run up again to the high white window of this hall I sit in and touch the snow-white stone that frames it to assure myself that it is tangible and not a vision, lean forth across the sill that is warm with the sun that pours upon it, and see the winding walks of the nearer garden up which I came an hour ago, and look across the dark green glossy ilex trees to the sea, blue with a blue so intense that I have seen no colour like it save in the wings of some tropical butterflies. There is a fluttering clatter of wings as I lean forward, and four pigeons alight on the sill beside me, walk jerkily upon it; one hops and perches, swaying heavily, on my shoulder. I stroke the purple lustre of their firm backs. It is real, as we human creatures know reality, and I come back to my writing.

I must, I say, begin to describe this place, since the wonder of it and its inexhaustible beauty utterly fills my mind, but poor pen, poor pen! and poor stumbling tongue that drives the pen! What can my best description be but as a heap of faded ashes beside a shining flame.

* * *

How can I tell where this place is, since I do not know how I came to be here. There was a crowded liner, in which I was a passenger to Auckland; in that drab world into which I was born and lived for twenty seven years, and which seems like a dead thing to me now. I was a second class passenger travelling to New Zealand, with a meagre commission from a publisher in London to make sketches for a colour book of scenery. We were in the tropics – I do not know where within a thousand miles, since it had been many days since we had seen land – and then came the shipwreck of that great glittering, expensive, wasteful, floating hotel. Boats were lowered, filled – but I am not going to write here of the brutal scene that ended my life in the world. I was roped into a small boat, there were other people in it whom I could not see for the darkness, for all the blazing electric light of the ship had just snapped out, someone was tugging in the dark at a cork jacket that had been strapped about me, there was a hellish outcry, a quarrel arose in my boat, a shout that it was leaking, and I felt suddenly that all the noises and all the people grew very faint and far away, that I was glad it was all going, and then – nothing.

I woke with the sun shining in the dawn, I was alone in the little boat, and I was drifting into a sandy shore.[2]

* * *

It was a shore of silver sand, on which the quiet sea slapped gently, and from the shore masses of green-grey trees like olives flowed up a hill slope. I lay in the boat, very happy, still half asleep, and not quite remembering how I came to be there, and bathed from head to foot by the delicious warmth of the sun that strengthened every moment. I watched the trees with quiet pleasure, a faintly stirring breeze caressed them like a gentle hand, and ruffled their leaves to show their silvery under sides. Presently a slight shock aroused me to the grounding of my boat; I sat up and looked around.

The smooth sea stretched level behind me under the risen sun like a sea of pale liquid gold. [It lay still, no lightest ripple broke its placid atmosphere.] Before me

---

2 A comparable, first-hand account of a disaster at sea – this time the wartime sinking of the *Lusitania* – is given by Viscountess Rhondda in *This Was My World* (London: Macmillan and Co, 1933), pp. 239–260. Notably, P&O, the shipping company with which 'Williams' is travelling when he receives the news of Crawshay's death, suffered the loss of the luxury liner *Egypt* when the vessel collided with another ship on 20 May 1922, off Ushant island, on the northwest tip of France. The catastrophe resulted in the deaths of over 80 people and the sinking of over £1 million.

was the silver sanded shore, shell strewn, and among the trees I could see something white, the corner of a building or statuary perhaps, that told I was in no savage desolation. From the first I felt no fear. The air here is strangely buoyant, with a sweetness in the smell of it, a savour, and to breathe it diffuses throughout my body such a sense of happiness and health as I have never felt in my life before. One is not afraid when one feels like that. I gazed upon the beauty about me, the air I breathed and that thin freshness, that poignant delicacy of an early spring morning; the morning was like a young and tender thing that lay just awakened, eyes opened, but not yet astir.

I sat there in the boat for a long time. The sun warmed with every moment, and presently a flock of white gulls, their plumage shining in the sunlight, came flowing down the air and settled at the edge of the sea to splash and peck and chatter among the pools.

* * *

I got up at last, clambered out of the boat, realised with delight that I had to take off my shoes and stockings and wade into the limpid water, pulled up the boat on shore and felt beneath the tender soles of my feet the warm and silky sand.

Since I came out of the world into this beautiful freedom I have experienced an infinite number of exquisite fresh sensations, but none do I enjoy more than the touch of various surfaces to my feet, the lush wetness of the sand, the cool crispness of the grass at dawn, dew drenched, the velvet pile of the carpets in this place, even the bare polish of the wood floors gives its peculiar pleasure.

I walked up towards the trees among which I saw the peeping corner of white buildings. As I came towards them the open sandy shore passed into garden, and the ground became covered with little scented plants that felted into a turf. Among the trees broad walks of arching greenery opened out to invite me, on their mossed floors lay pools of dim sunlight fallen through the trees above. I came to a fountain, where sportive nymphs and boys in stonework played in the water, and the garden grew more formal and architectural, with much statuary and ornament. I was coming up a side alley, at the end I turned the corner of a high hedge, and all the front of this little palace burst into my view.

* * *

I must put down something here if I am to be faithful in my account, though it was the idlest fancy, the faintest, instantaneous trick my imagination played me. In that first instant there flashed upon my eyes the vision of people there, silken clad or naked in the sunlight. But there was no one there, and I know there is no one here upon this island but myself. It was like the flicker of a picture seen and instantly withdrawn.

* * *

Imagine a long white marble frontage some forty feet high, pierced by tall window openings, openings supported at their centre by slender spiral columns like those of Giotto's Campanile. Running the length of the palace and a little below the windows is a broad terrace that descends in wide, shallow steps to the ground. This frontage forms the side of a great hall whose windows have no glass; in this warm climate there is no need to shut out the softly breathing night or the stirring dawn, and there are no evil beasts to fear. The centre of this front juts forward into a portico upon the terrace, it is framed with columns like the windows and is indeed a larger copy of them. Through that entrance the great hall is seen, deep and cool. Add colour now to the white marble of the building, the terrace and its approaching steps are flushed with tawny yellow and with lichen grey, the framing columns of the windows, their cornices and pediments are of amethyst blue and malachite. The whole place is Italian in its spirit, nowhere but in Italy have I seen staircases flow in such graceful easy lines, or seen such pleasure taken in displaying the beauty of falling and splashing water. From the terrace on either side of the central doorway spring upward paired staircases of marble, curving and pausing in landings and curving again on either side to meet at last on a balcony high above the portico. That balcony is a wonder and delight to me. It is backed with marble, and from its utmost centre a cascade breaks out in a thin fan-shaped stream that, falling, encloses the whole balcony with a dome of falling water. Up there one may sit dry upon the marble seat, surrounded by the pouring, streaming water, and watch the rainbow colours that start and glitter from it in the sun. You cannot think how beautiful it is! It is the most beautiful thing of all the beauty that is here. The water falls, and is led down the façade close to the staircases, made to play a hundred pranks on its way, and falls at last into a great basin before the terrace, whence it rises in a fantasy of fountains and jets and sprays. I spring into the basin, swim, am buffeted by the fountain, toss and splash the sparkling water, and come out to lie supine upon the turf until the sun has dried me. I roll over, face downward on the warm turf, my head drowsily on my arms. My hair, dried and fluttered by a stirring breeze, curls and rises like a breathing thing; I look through a veil of it at the sunlit garden and watch on each separate hair the play of a thousand iridescent colours.

* * *

Within, the little palace contains only the great hall, occupying more than the half of it, and some small rooms, libraries lined with brown books, cool and with deep-set window openings, and smaller rooms about twenty feet square each devoted to the display of some special kind of decorative beauty, and furnished with little save a great divan or two. There is one such empty room whose walls and ceiling and floor are purely white, and on which rainbow colours fall through large prisms set in the walls and windows. The happy minute accident of the carafe of water on a sunlit luncheon table has been seized here and increased to a perpetual feast for the eye. Another room can be darkened by pulling down blinds, and by some trick of the old camera obscura kind the walls and floor and ceiling become pictured then with softly waving trees, the flowers and the piling clouds of the scenery outside. And in another room one looks through eyepieces like portholes set in the wall and sees as if near at hand, enlarged and minutely clear, irradiated with a curious brilliance, some small distant flowers in the garden without, and hanging on them perhaps a butterfly or grasshopper or bird, careless of the eye that watches them so distantly. Windows are made to be filled not with glass but with the thinnest sheets of precious stones and rocks and minerals of splendid colour, that pierced by sunshine glow with the loveliest intensity of blue. Everywhere is it sought by every possible device to saturate the eye with pleasure. I begin to understand too that the exquisite surfaces of the divans and carpets and bare floors are no accident, but designed to give the utmost delight to my touch, and there are drowsy rooms where the water murmurs outside, or others from which I hear it splash and patter; in the great hall I have discovered behind a curtain an indicator with perhaps a couple of thousand stops, each labelled with the name of a musical work familiar or strange to me. I pulled at one, and Bach's great Toccata in D Minor rolled out into the silence. At any moment, I can set this invisible orchestra playing, or hear songs sung with a human voice.

* * *

Is it that by some trick of time I have been jerked forward, hundreds of years perhaps, into the future, to this mise-en-scène such as now we only dream of in our utopias, this little corner of the great and various paradise that is ready and waiting like an attired host expecting a guest, for the arrival of mankind?

And those phantom and lovely people that I saw when first I stepped round the trees that hid this place from me, – were they indeed humanity's children?

It may well be so. For it is to the shaping of our earth into such a place of safety and pleasantness as this that we bend our endeavour. If we succeed it seems that humanity at last will live in such ease as I am here in now. Shall we find some way with the human soul so that toil and cold and hunger and war, and conflict with evil beasts and unkindly parts of the earth are no longer needed to keep an edge upon our courage and our ease and leisure will not beget sloth and slackness in a people, nor happiness selfishness, and that everyone will be wealthy in having what they need and no one will be wealthy in having what others need? And so released from the struggle to live, what will they do?

It is not within my power to gauge the quality of those bright creatures of the future who are going to live in such a place as this, but I do not know nor can I imagine any people with fine minds who can live content in the enjoyment of beauty alone. It may be that the universe will always outrun the seeking and conquering mind of man, and how can I imagine what search or endeavour will engage those finer beings? For my part, am I not writing here, and so trying again every human creature's constant task, to make something, if only a record of the thoughts that drift into my mind here as I live and enjoy.

* * *

I read over what I have just written, and discover myself saying "you". I suppose that is the only way of writing after all, to imagine a reader. One does not write a personal narrative to oneself any more than one talks aloud to oneself. But I wonder how many of us do not, in the secrecy of our minds, entertain a near familiar, and throw most of our thoughts into the form of explanations to that imaginary confidant. I admit that I have always done so. I abandon my first pretence of writing an impersonal essay. Why should I not write frankly to you, spiritual brother of my soul.

* * *

How delightful it is to discover that I have been thus writing to you all the time! My pen trips into hurry at the thought, for to you I have so much to say. And in this solitude I can talk to you with unexperienced freedom and ease, while I remember in the old human world days and days when I had no time to call you into my presence. And there too, we suffered estrangements; I was forever trying to identify you with some living man or woman, trying to find that you had become corporate, and then, disappointed, returning to your phantom companionship.

* * *

Those adventures in search of you – how unsatisfactory they were; at times how humiliating! Surely the thing that is most wrong of all that is wrong in the world I have left is the manner of intercourse of its human beings. We encounter – we poor humans – in the most casual, accidental ways; and often through the encrustations of prescribed custom, law and usage under which our personalities suffocate, there shines something – something that calls. There is perhaps a note in that other's voice, or a something said that fills one with sudden delight, and sets one groping for more of that other's inner mind. (I have groped, and never found you, dear brother.) And then one drives one's seeking hands upon the barriers.

I suppose of all the barriers that that ugly old world has put up between one human and another the worst that they have done is to make a barrier of sex. We face each other, man and woman, like nominally friendly powers that regard each other across a common frontier studded with fortifications. Even between people who keep their converse a fellowship the old world, by incessant suggestion, suggestion, suggestion, has planted something – something like an invisible presence, something that is saying silently all the time – "Man, woman – man, woman". It is a presence with a mood that deals only with technicalities. "What are you doing with this person of the opposite sex?" it insists. Headlong the Presence offers its counsel of prudence. "Have an eye to your defences. This friendliness you think so good, this friendliness that gladdens you between yourself and this fellow creature, don't you know where it always leads? That will never do." For only in such ready-made phrases can the Presence think and talk. The barbarity of it!

Stupid, glib, unsubtle Presence! You take the possible delicate web of human converse, the complex, elastic, shining, strong exquisite fabric that is sometimes in the making, and tear it into shreds with those dull and clumsy fingers of yours. You are the vulgar mind, omnipresent and penetrating as a fog; so that you drench our printed matter, soak into our stage, put your coarse hand upon our humour, slime our common converse, with that innuendo, the *double entendre*. You come between my friend and me as the fog will creep into a warm and lovely room from the dismal street without. *You* know, you knowing Presence, why we are there, and you will go on spoiling our intercourse till we are old, and the faint knell notes of the grave that awaits us chill you away. To have you gone for ever will be the chiefest pleasure recounted in my *De Senectute*, when I write it.

* * *

The business of human intercourse, dear brother!

Out of my little shining heaven I look back into the world I have left, and think upon its darkness and the gloomy suspicion of one another in which its creatures live. I think how near yet is man to the beast he sprang from, how near not only in his cruelty and savagery, but in his dullness and apathy. Man has dragged himself up from the beast by making for himself a mind, and of many of the possibilities of that mind he seems as aware as the oyster of the beauty of its pearl. It is still but an irritation to man, that mind and its powers. He crushes its gracious instincts towards love, starves its craving for beauty. And yet crush and starve them though he may they are deathlessly there, that boundless capacity for love, that boundless desire towards beauty; they lie passive in the depths of man's nature as gold lies hoarded in the cellars of a bank, unused, fruitless, fallow; for the time idle and wasted, and yet the very source and mainspring of its power is the hidden unused strength that means its life, in the end the two enormous untouched assets that someday, somewhen in the ages to come, will spring forth and grow to their stature, and surely – surely – make humanity as the gods.

* * *

I was thinking just now, dear Spirit, how much happier can be my conversations I have with you than any real ones in one way, which is that I have afterwards so much less to regret, to wish unsaid, to wish better said.

I remember once on earth being for a time quite charmed with an acquaintance, so that I looked forward with eagerness to meeting him, tried to devise encounters, and when they happened the wished for moments ran out like quicksilver between the fingers of my desire. I had, I felt, to capture his attention, chain it to myself, say things he would remember, and all the time there was to do it in was perhaps the briefest instant between the competing drag at his mind of this other one and that. And so I would blunder, talk fast and foolishly, fearing to let him slip. And afterwards the things I had said – the witless clumsy things! – would come back to sear my memory with shame. But here with you! Sometimes I run on so fast I can hardly write down my thoughts, and sometimes I hang deliberate, and no other claims you, while I turn over my tongue the words that shall sound most sweetly to you. Here you are, dear blank one, ever with your expectant face towards me.

* * *

First, little brother, I want to talk to you of Love.

I had a lover once, as love goes in the world. He would be called there an accepted lover, a man to whom I promised myself in marriage. For in the world the only people between whom love is held permissible are unmarried and marriageable people. (It is quaint, little brother, that I find myself talking to you now as if you did not know that world; I begin to feel that after all you may be the invisible genius of this paradise.) As I have said, it is assumed there that only to the unmarried and marriageable is love allowed – love, that is to say, that is more than affection. And here I must interrupt myself again to say that the language of the world is so poor in words that it has only one word, love, to express the countless degrees and kinds and intensities of love that can exist between human hearts. And so at the very outset it is difficult to explain how love is thought of and considered in the world. Hampered by this insufficiency it is as difficult to write of love as it would be to express a melody by the use of the single word "note". On the other hand, the very fact that they have but one word tells much. You will understand that when the language is poor, the thought is poor also. They also use the word love, oh! like a blanket, to cover all the different emotions of pride, possession, pity, protectiveness, sensual pleasure and responsibility that the parent feels for the child; they have none other for the affectionateness that, welling up exuberantly and spontaneously from the heart of a happy child, spills over, as it were, on to the parent as, unless it is checked by great unkindness, it does over every other circumstantial thing; they call by the same name the quiet friendliness that they allow between sisters and brothers; they apply it tentatively and a little shyly to great depth of attachment between man and man, or between one woman and another; they use it universally to cover every manifestation from the slightest to the strongest of the attraction that draws any man and woman together; they use it for the mechanical response of an intelligent pet animal to the person who feeds it; they employ it for the relation between their deity and themselves, whom they suppose him to have created in circumstances that expose them to pain and cruelty and death. You see that at different times they use "love" to designate almost every emotion known to the human heart. To particularise further they have no instruments unless we include a few adjectives borrowed from the vocabulary of scientific writers, adjectives that for their boorish sound are almost worse than useless. I know, for instance, no other phrase of definition for the chief form of love, that love which my lover and I bore one another, than the gross and ugly expression "sexual love". Such expressions become tainted with a disagreeable savour of meaning which if they are used they trail into one's discourse.

As I have said, such love is considered by them really permissible only to the unmarried and marriageable. They profess to regard it as a phenomenon upon which marriage must follow with seemly dispatch. There must be marriage, according to their rules, before the love is what they would call "consummated". That having happened – the ritual of marriage performed and the lovers allowed to consummate their love, they are assumed to continue to love each other, or at least to maintain a relationship of paramount affection for the rest of their lives. A departure from these rules and suppositions, the consummation of love without marriage, the manifestation of love for any other than the married partner, is visited by the gravest censure they can apply. And as you know well, little brother, there being scarcely any human heart born so poor in its capacity for loving as these rules demand, the pretence that they are the only wise and possible and good and right rules lies over society like a thin and brittle skin, beneath which tosses and writhes the uneasy nature of man. Constantly the rigid impossible rules are broken, universally they are covertly broken. And that is the evil, little brother, that is the evil. It is not that human hearts should go hungry for a while that matters so greatly as this other thing. It is that the starvation imposed on them is too dire to be borne and it is not borne. Everywhere the rules are secretly broken. But as much as they can they pretend the rules are excellent and work well, and that only the dissolute break them. By laying upon itself a rule so hard that it does not keep it, humanity has done its soul that injury which you do a child by threatening punishments so severe that it is driven to lie to you. How deeply must humanity have stained its conscience with guilt by maintaining this pretence for over two thousand years; is it any matter for wonder that human beings now are things of little pride, of stunted honour and of crippled power. Under the surface of their ostensible lives lurk the spoilt things and the base things and the dark things, and the price of its sustenance is paid in intrigue, lies, hypocrisy, shams (or shame), deceptions, treacheries, cunning, trickery, betrayals, brothels, prostitutes, procurers, souteneurs, panders – into that monstrous heap of dirt they have stamped Love's rosy wings!

* * *

My lover and I were not married; it happened that he died.

He died, and I grieved greatly and yet not so greatly as I should have grieved had he died before our betrothal. Then I should have felt his loss as much as I should feel yours, were it possible to lose you, dear immortal! But as it was I had already touched the chill fringe of that isolation into which my marriage would draw me. Already, delightful as he was, he stood between me and the rest of humanity. Other men who had been friendly and easy or affectionate became suddenly formal and restrained, women who had been carelessly confidential and secure with me became reticent. In any company in which we were I was tacitly apportioned to him, no longer had I the great pleasure of bestowing my companionship upon him as a coveted gift, it belonged to him in the ordinary course of things. The clutch of our extending claims on one another strove to imprison love and make it more certainly ours, but indeed to treat love so is like chaining a snowman to the earth to keep it safe forever.

Had he not died, we should I suppose have followed the observances prescribed in the world for those whom Love has brushed with his wings and lit to momentary radiance. It will seem to you, as it seems to me now, the oddest appanage to that divine chance that we should presently have had to choose a house, buy furniture for it, and after the ritual of a marriage service, live there together, excluding our fellow-creatures. Our fresh rapture in one another would quickly have become interwoven beyond all disentanglement with the wearinesses, disappointments, compromises, greediness, economy, baulked desire, and finally the clipped and meagre realisation of a dream that make up the business of getting property in the world. We should have seen one another not glorified, but played upon by these mean passions of acquisition. We might have had some pleasure in arranging our home, but the things that the world makes are multitudinous, discrepant, and rarely beautiful, and it is a matter of experience, natural talent and command of money to agglomerate a pleasurable houseful. I should have wearied in matching colours, measuring quantities, weighing the merits and expediency of this and that material. We should have gathered about us as the first fruit of our love a retinue of shopmen, porters, postmen and carriers, plumbers, paperhangers, painters, gasfitters, upholsterers, tailors, dressmakers, carpenters, servants of all sorts – a labouring army. That is the sequel in the world, my dear, to the impulse that flung us into one another's arms, one April morning, to kiss!

* * *

If by accident I did not go that way myself, so have I seen my friends. I remember once visiting some young married lovers, and finding them heated, distracted, and almost quarrelling. The husband was nailing down a disagreeable substance called cork carpet; he had cut it badly and also cut his thumb. The little bride received me with a manner too riotously gay to conceal the recent tears that had smarted to her pretty eyes. And after the experience of home making, what happens? Love is in thrall to the urgencies of petty domesticity, and it is inseparable in the world that a woman who has seemed to gather all beauty in her arms and give it to a man should come to embody for him the troubles and inconveniences of our ill-contrived domestic arrangements. Is it remarkable that Love, that delicate fragility, goes under? I remember asking a friend some time afterwards how that very couple were.

"I think," he said, "that Love found it so dull there that he has flown away. They don't seem to have noticed..."

I remembered them in the first days of their engagement – their radiance!

* * *

This intimate connection the world has established between love and linoleum marks a stage in the history of human love that has already passed away in spirit but not in form. They say that in the dawn of civilisation humanity, and some primitive savages even now, did not detect the relation between the conception of offspring and the freedoms of lovers. A second stage has lasted for thousands of years when, that consequence being known, love has been enthralled. The moralists, unable to remake humanity and abolish sex, have placed procreation in the forefront of their virtues, and to attain that, while admitting with misgiving the inevitableness of preliminaries that Nature, unconquerable Jade! has decked with alluring pleasures, they have had grudgingly to allow Love to exist in the world, hedged about, living on the barest subsistence indeed, clipped of every excrescence that they could manage that did not contribute to this end. Love has been made the salve of begetting. Hence these marriage laws, these houses and furnishings.

The fact is that just as the development of man's mind has far outrun the necessities of food getting and offspring rearing which shaped it, so has the capacity for loving outrun its primary purpose of mate getting and procreation. They are both enormously stronger and richer faculties than those erstwhile ends require. Thank heaven! Nature is no economist; if a bird or plant ask from her a pleasing conspicuousness to further their ends of survival, she loads them with such excesses of her art as the plumage of the peacock and the flower of the orchid. Continually her prodigality propounds riddles to the biologist, exceeding as lavishly as she does his neat requirements. The choosing of a single mate, the raising of a single family, makes as little tax upon the passion as the filling of a jug upon the miraculous cruse of oil. There is more and more to give. The moralist, having filled the jug, would spend the rest of life hammering in the reluctant cork. But the nature of man defeats him. All human history is saturated with the stupendous overflowing of this passion of love, love that has no thought of permanent mating or procreation, but that is the simple reaching out of one human creature to the perceived beauty of another. The higher the civilisation, the more advanced its culture, the greater its knowledge, the finer, the more susceptible to the sensations of beauty will be the senses of humanity; the quicker and subtler the understanding between us, the greater and ever greater will be the stimulus to the emotion of love. How long will it be, little brother, that the world will continue to set its face against these things?

Just so long, you might tell me, as human beings fall short of the fine perfections necessary to enjoy them.

* * *

Yet I protest that you and I are fitted to bear our part in that world of friendship-love, that indeed it is the only world in which we should be happy, the only world in which we should not feel thwarted and wasted of the best we may have to give. You know that if one sows flower seeds in a shady place they may germinate and grow, but they will not grow shapely and sturdy and tall, they will never achieve the triumph of their beauty – blossom. So it is in the world with you and me and hundreds of our mind, we creep circumspectly along our lives, the bitterness of imposed failure in our hearts. It is not lack of courage, in the world we live in we can no other. Sometimes it has happened that a few have withdrawn from the world to live as they believed it truthful to live, and they have found that no people can segregate from their fellow men and live successfully in a manner disharmonious with those others. Humanity is one vast smear on the face of the earth. There is no corner to which those allies could fly and be safe forever from intrusion. And even were it possible for them to find so remote a fastness, still the ideas and traditions of humanity would surge upon them out of the depths of their own minds, which had lived and soaked in the common idea so long.

* * *

In the case of my friends, Love flew away because he was so dull there, and indeed it seems that human beings have much to learn before Love will abide among them a happy and enduring guest. The delicate boy can not only be bored but frightened, and oftenest he takes fright and flies from the hands that grasp him too fiercely. The response of the savage in man to the appeal of beauty is to clutch at it, seek to own it, hold it tight and firm in his endeavour to perpetuate the flying happy moment when he perceived it, and in his hot, possessive hand lie the limp, fading flowers, the motionless, torn butterfly, the passive, spiritless woman – mute witnesses to his admiration. He grasps at Love to grasp – the air. Love escapes. And then, feeling something in his hand after all, he looks again, and green-eyed Jealousy grins back at him, his secure slave.

Did you, one happy day, become corporate, little brother, I would love you better than that. I would set my love in your life as I might plant a flower in your garden, in the hope that it might blossom and add its tiny loveliness to the world about you. It should make as little claim upon you as the violets beneath your feet. Did you see it there it would flame with joy; did you not, nor seem to need it, still it would live happy that it breathed its perfume into the air you breathed.

If you became corporate!

For an instant let me suppose I were to go, now, down into the garden, and were to see you there, standing at the end of a long allée, and that you were to turn and come towards me! Too far as yet for me to see your face, I should know you by your bearing. You would step into the dim pools of sunlight that fall upon the mossed pathway through to the trees above, they would run rippling up to your body to flash in an instant in your eyes, glint from your hair, and fall behind you again upon the ground. You would come nearer – nearer – *nearer*—

This is folly, little brother. Are you not here now, close to my soul?

* * *

What part then should love play in the world?

* * *

Little brother, it is many days since I wrote that last sentence. Again and again I have taken my pen to talk to you of that, again and again it has fallen idle between my fingers. I begin to realise what I did not know before, that as well might that hairy ape who fathered us all have set himself to foretell all that religion might mean to humanity as that I, with a mind born and cradled in that little world over there beyond my purple sea, should be able to imagine what life may be like when our souls have grown strong enough to make a confederate of love and not a foe. One may indulge in dreaming of a world in which friendliness and affection and helpfulness and gladness of one another's presence there shall be the common matrix of individual lives. But from that genial earth who can know what flowers of sweet relationship may spring between those who find beauty in one another. I cannot know what love will mean to those wiser men and women. It seems that all our knowledge touches only the fringe of its possibilities, that we play only with the surf of that ocean. There are no ships in our soul's harbours in which we may set sail. To us love at its intensest is an untamed giant in our hands, we deal with it more often to our disaster than our happiness. Our traffic with it breeds jealousy and anger and base cruelties. It begins in a mist of beauty like the rising of the sun, and dies with lovers beating each other's hearts to pieces with clumsiness of speech. It is easy to say that then, in that happy *then* to which we postpone our dreams, love will never bear such bitter fruit. But even *then*, can love be always a simple and crescent happiness, will it never trail sorrow with it? Will there be, even then, any way of soothing that most poignant human pain, the love that wins no return?

Isn't the answer to that, another question? Is there love that wins no return? Now, perhaps, there is, but *then*, among those kinder people?

Does not love, my dear, so touch the heart of the beloved that it melts in loving kindness towards that suppliant one? who brings all his heart's treasure to lay at those beloved feet: "I am not for you, brother, but stay a little in this green garden of my loving friendship, and ease your pilgrim heart on mine." Most cruel in our day is the aching exhaustless love of a mother for an unregarding child, but is not love so magnificently selfless its own supreme satisfaction? Has it room or time in its lavish outpouring of tenderness to feel the pain of disregard? "Es-tu blessé, mon cher?" whispered the mother's heart, pierced with anxious care for the son who had torn it from her bleeding body. Did that sublimely loving heart even know what murder it had done?

To seek happiness in loving not in being loved, to give because one's heart is so full and not to offer love as a usurer on condition that it is returned with interest, to be filled with delight and gladness because the beloved is so beautiful and one perceives it, those are the emotions which will make happy lovers of us all. We must not claim, we must not seek to put the creature we love into the purdah of our own hearts.

* * *

Jealousy!

Have you guessed, little brother, that it was jealousy that like a beast ravening its kill, came suddenly upon my lover and me, found us weaponless and powerless in our youth and inexperience, and as a man who is even slightly torn by a lion will die of blood-poisoning, poisoned our love to its death with the wounds of its foul claws.

My lover came upon me, impetuous, mastering, in a flushed joy of eagerness, claiming every moment, every thought of mine. I had friends precious to me in all kinds of ways, a few intimates in whom there were hidden sweetnesses of heart known to me as one might know secret and exquisite places in a wood. I endeavoured to make him the sharer of my pleasure in them, but he wanted to banish them by slighting speech, he drove my affection for them in upon my mind to smart with injury.

I remember one speech of his that struck upon my memory and has impressed it like a die struck upon metal. It was in the earliest first rush of mutual confidence that can be so glorious a self-discovery to the beloved, that I even committed the treachery of telling about another man's avowal. It had seemed so beautiful a thing to me, so linking an experience, that little scene of honest self-expression.

He heard me impatiently. "Of course you must never see him again," said my lover.

My spirit flamed with astonishment.

* * *

But I would not tell you more of the discordance that grew between my lover and me, any more than I would describe to you the brutalities of the shipwreck that brought me here. They lie at the back of my mind, scars of acutest disappointment that are tender to the touch, that are so tender yet that were I determined to tell of them in the desire to open out for you the whole book of my experience, I should not tell you of them justly; emotion would distort the truth in the telling. The ugly blow that knocked one man out of the way of another struggling to the boats, the ugly speech that tried to strike a blow at another man. Who loved me – I wince at the memory. I shrink from them in shame.

I could do nothing with my lover's hatred of any love except our love, I was as mentally powerless there as I was physically powerless in that struggle in the night. Such things play their part in the roaring stuff of the world, and the spirit that drives a blow goes into the seething play of it like mustard into a mass of cooking. I think I have a mind too gentle for these things. I come away from them into a place where they are not, and with you I dream and play how they may no longer be.

* * *

You are changing, little brother, out of the mist and shadows, you are gathering for yourself shape and substance. You are getting for yourself a body, no more are you content to be mere spirit. Every day I see you in my mind a little more clearly, discover you further. Your hands are very fine and give me great delight; they are cool to touch and warm to grasp, and of slender, exquisite shape; here in the sunlight a glowing crimson lurks in the shadows beyond their long sensitive fingers. I caress your hands, little brother, and follow their outline round with my fingertips for the sheer love of its beauty.

(Have you noticed how very pretty my hand is as it lies loosely, palm upward, on the table here, curved and shadowed like a rose?)

Interlude

People in the world now are not very clever about love. They are terribly unpractised in the knowledge of loving, and they can hardly be happy in its experience since by all of them it is so despitefully considered. Indeed it is difficult to shelter love in the world at all. The vulgar mind thinks of love at the best as an amiable conceded weakness, at the worst as a vileness. Out of that permeating atmosphere of the vulgar mind we have to drag our loves as it were out of a sucking morass. And when the vulgar thought is of this nature it is astonishing to see how everyone will be tainted by its attitude, how almost everyone assumes that love is a little idle, a little of a weakness, a little of a dissipation of time and energy that we ought to use otherwise. You and I know that it is the bread of our bodies and the wine of our hearts. My dear, all the people in the world now are *famished* people. I see their poor hearts like those terrible pictures of starving natives one sees from famine-struck districts in India. What nobility, what generosity, what courage can we expect from human beings weakened as they are by this silent, unceasing struggle with their instincts. There is much pity in the world, and rightly, for the poor, and for the wretchedness of those whose bodies ache with hard and hurtful toil, but far greater is the total misery that is borne in silent human hearts, that hunger for the love they cannot find, or seeing dimly, are forbidden. It is a hunger that strangles endeavour of any other kind until it is satisfied, it is an obsession. I imagine this obsession secretly fastened upon hundreds of the dull drifting people whom I knew on earth; either, clear-eyed, they know it, or they feel it vaguely as a discontent, a sense – they know not why – of the ultimate worthlessness of their lives to them. For how many happy people do we know on earth? How many placid-seeming ones have we not known in whose hearts we, drawn closely near, have discovered the abiding sorrow of some immense privation of love.

You know with all this that I do not look upon love as an end in itself, a thing which it is the crown of life to achieve and enjoy beautifully, in supreme content, until the grey hairs come. For such a one what terror, those grey hairs! From such a one each day past the early middle of life filches a little happiness. It should be no more the aim and end of a human being to love than it should be the aim and end of a human being to breathe. But before other things may be done that are good, one must have wholesome air; if one has it not it is a need that blots out everything else, and so it is with love. Love assured, love free, and we go on, sturdy, light-hearted, eager-eyed, to our peculiar endeavour, to our personal minute contribution to the throbbing life of the world. And then – the grey hairs must come almost unnoticed. One is so interested. Each day adds something to accomplishment and knowledge and understanding. But, it is true, at last even that dims. Truly at last that dims, but dims in the way that things do when sleep bears down on one's eyelids. One does not regret the loss of sight, it is such a pleasure to close one's eyes and pass into sleep after the busy, good day. So death should come.

So indeed death should come. God grant I may not die in bitterness, as many must die in our time. "Is this then all, God? *All?* But God! – the things I have not had! The many things held high and promised before the eyes of my youth, the things of light and passionate loving that were the birthright of my flesh?"

Can we ever hope to lose the quality of jealous possession in love?

How in the history of any worldly lovers does it arise? Let us say, in the history of any real love passion, and leave out of consideration those loves which are from their inception a mere clutching of a beautiful creature for self-gratification. Let us consider what may sometimes happen in the case of any two people who come together, as people do at their happiest, with an instinctive self-forgetful rush of emotion. All their thought is contained in the simplicity of "I love you!" The lover has no thought but of the beloved, in turn the lover, no thought but of the other. They do not think of exclusive possession, since they do for that moment so exclusively and utterly possess with a possession as unremarked as the air they breathe. Whence comes the subtle decay that changes that unconscious certainty of one another to an anxious watching, an assertion of rights, by what mysterious alchemy do we presently hear faintly beneath love's flung garland of roses, the steely clink of a chain?

Is it not the struggle to trim their conduct to an imposed artificial ideal, the ideal of fidelity, an ideal imagined by man's clumsy mind? Again we are dominated by that infirmity of the human mind, the tendency to regard life as fixed and constant, to endeavour to hold still the changing universe, to freeze stiff before we will consent to enjoy the emotion that palpitates with life, the emotion that in reality is never the same, that every instant of time is either increasing or lessening. The pledge of fidelity suggested by the world is lightly given and taken by lovers in those earliest days, it does indeed gratify a spiritual need of that moment, it is a seal set on the wonder of love, a solemnity, a sanctification; it approaches their emotion for a moment to the high atmosphere of religion. That it has the flavour of unfelt abnegation gratifies still more. They can afford to count the world well lost who hold it as cheaply as the dust upon their shoes. But presently the lovers are, almost subconsciously, feeling uneasily that those static states of emotion that have been imposed on them as ideals do not correspond with anything they are experiencing. Their attention is awakened to this contradiction, they begin to watch for and demand what before they took for granted. And the demand – the demand that follows the suspicion – kills the thing it asks for as a frost will kill. The mutuality of that unnatural pledge is not forgotten, the time comes when each, a creditor, exacts from the other its meticulous observance, and there is no creditor so merciless as that one who in turn is pressed upon by lien and mortgage. She who is irked by her own bond will not consent to the slackening of his.

One would like enormously to trace – what a work it would be! – the history of a single human idea through the ages – and fidelity as an obligation is a human idea. They say that its virtue may have been imposed upon impressionable woman by possessive man seeking to strengthen his ownership, and that it may have served dependant woman to assure her welfare after the waning of her youth. It is a romantic idea, the idea that there is another human soul utterly and completely for one's self, as one's self shall be utterly and completely for that other, it is an idea that has ever appealed to man and woman as an ideal of relationship to be sought and aimed at. The beauty of Plato's image of the soul divided into two seeking halves has gripped the imagination of man through the centuries – that imagination of man whose unconquerable bias is to unify the separate and coalesce the discrepant. The price humanity must pay for an ideal is always a high one, and there can be none other than this more bitterly beset with tears. It may make a disastrous mischief in a dozen ways. It is the boast of happy lovers to have loved like the glory of God and this ideal of a love fixed and immutable in its ardour imposes the sense of failure upon honest lovers who see that their passion abates. The joy that should be theirs for ever that their love has been, is killed by the censure that it is no more, and that measure of love which, most preciously, still is, is withered by disregard.

But we are not seeking halves, man or woman we are not halves of a possible unity; the truth is that each one of us is the many millionth fraction of one unity, the human race. But when we love, we are not accustomed to regard love in this manner; by the time we are adolescent we have been trained by the incessant suggestion of poetry and romance, law and moral admonition, suggestion that has been dropped upon our impressionable minds through all our youth, to look for and demand nothing less than a supremely fitting mate, anything less than such a union we regard as a falling short of the possible best that life can give. And more and more, as the soul of man becomes more complex, we think of mating as a spiritual as well as a bodily completion. We expect a mate who shall answer to our spiritual needs as Echo to our voice. But human beings are infinitely and marvellously various, no human being can enclose and satisfy every need of another like the atmosphere enfolds the earth. As human souls we are rather like solid polyhedrons than [intermixing] gases. We touch at facets. We women, compelled to spend our lives in that close intercourse with a single other human creature that is implied by marriage, wither partially like trees might do which had only one or two branches exposed to the sun. In marriage the souls of men and women are compressed within each other's characters like the feet of Manchu ladies.[3] There are snatched friendships, of course, in most women's lives, poor hungry relationships shut away from the light, starvelings fed with scanty gleams of kindliness and affection that no one must see. Gracious as these things in their reality may be, they are tainted by the ugliness of secrecy. It will not do, my dear, it will not do. Sooner or later humanity must face the truth that its own nature is finer and more beautiful than it knew, and reshape its way of living to encourage and not thwart the life of the soul.

And apart from the single permitted intimacy of marriage we live side by side in the world in a jostling, loveless companionship. We live for the most part in jealousy and malice, since there is no love between us to dissolve our offences against one another. For we all offend against one another; and although we may discipline ourselves, savage and uncouth beings that we are yet, against committing knowing offences against one another, for our unknowing offences we must invoke our fellow-creatures' love towards us to forgive.

3 In fact, Chinese Manchu leaders issued edicts to ban the practice of foot binding.

Little brother, I think the time will come when it will not be so that we shall pass the short life we have with one another on this earth. We shall not have to choose once and choose irrevocably, shutting the door then upon all other human souls; we shall not have to measure what each fellow-creature has to give us against a difficult, exalted standard, and take our love to market, seeing very carefully that we get the utmost measure in return for our expense. We shall not behave as if we had exactly a sovereign to spend, and having spent some of it, our resources are depleted and we must be very wary lest we do not get good value with the remainder. We shall believe that the more we empty our purse the fuller we shall have it. We shall reject nothing, but we shall meet each other human soul eagerly, hands and minds outstretched for whatever of love and sweetness we can receive or give. Sometimes it will be little, sometimes much; sometimes it will be supremely much, and some of us may even get a constant wealth that may last throughout a life, but never will it be twice the same thing. Never indeed shall we look for or expect the same thing from our different fellow-creatures, that will not be our attitude towards them nor towards love. We shall not say, I want Love, personified and with a capital letter; we shall say to our fellow men, I want *you*.

Brother or sister, what is there of me that you will have? Here am I before you with open hands, take of the store of my self, welcome guest.

And you with the eyes that look into my heart, come and despoil me of its treasure!

And so, Shadow of my heart, since we mortals are so weak in loving, is it not good that your love and mine is no mortal love and can never suffer these decays? There were never lovers since the world began who did not think to outwit the death of love. Since I can never meet even the tip of your finger with the tip of mine, that little, thrilling touch can never, repeated for the second, third, hundredth time, give me the faintest degree less pleasure than the unforgettable delight of its first. Since I can never kiss your lips I can never kiss them with less than that utmost rapture that waits upon them now. Since I am never to hear your voice I can never hear it in disaccord with even my most secret thought. Am I not blest beyond all earthly lovers?

Beloved! I lie! I lie! Give me your hands, your lips, your voice, your beating heart! Have I not called into the silence long enough, that you do not come?

* * *

It is a pity, but it is necessary, that as humanity goes on its march through the centuries it must throw away by the roadside many things excellent in their time and need, but grown with time to be decorative rather than indispensable, and at last as humanity picks up fresh needed things, mere encumbrances that clog the march and grow continuingly heavier to bear. And so for all they are so fine, they have to go. What is there more splendid both in fact and idea among all that man has possessed since he rose from the beast, than a sword? Think of the skill that made it, the shining steel of so fine a temper, the keen cutting edge; the skill that decorated it, and lavished upon this worthiest of man's weapons his most ingenious imaginings; think of the skill that used it, the cunning and drilled adroitness of eye and wrist and supple body! And yet the sword has no place in man's life now but to hang idle upon the wall of some pacific dwelling room. And what place will fidelity – that idea, so noble in its time, of the lifelong fidelity of pledged man and wife, partners as they were in a struggle against a universe that would down them and their breed if it could – what place will that have in a society whose women and children are secure, as secure they will be. In the rougher days of that former time the woman bore fidelity in her heart as her man carried the sword at his side. I mean here pledged and enjoined fidelity, fidelity upheld as a duty and ideal and concomitant of marriage, and not that natural fidelity of great lovers, which like the perfection of mating that bears so lovely a blossom, is a thing accidental, beautiful, rare, and forever to be extolled. But a loveliness spontaneous; no more to be manufactured upon a love than is loveliness upon the face of a woman. Indeed it is the contemplation of such natural love, like the contemplation of nature's loveliness in forest and stream and mountain, that will make us in the end dissatisfied and careless of our topiary garden of clipped and pruned virtues. We shall cease to think that fidelity that does not spring from free will is good. The liberty to love or not to love as one will stands for us – for you and me – in the forefront of our liberties, all other liberties shrink beside it.

* * *

There are times when liberty – that precious thing! – seems to be the most fragile of growths in the world. But perilously, threatened by innumerable dangers, it lives on for our taking. Constantly the soul of man gropes his way towards it, plays with it gingerly as he would with a plant that might sting him; anon drops it, stung indeed, and then bereft of it, accumulates the desire for it until the foundations of his society quake to destruction point with the energy of his grasp at it. But always, face to face with it, he fears its wide unproved immensity, he encroaches upon a fraction of its margin only, and shrinks back from the adventure to its unpeopled horizons. For Freedom bears with her the austere gift of solitude, and they are brave who do not fear the grasp to that icy breast.

To be given much liberty is indeed to the soul of man as if he were set upon a vast and empty plain and stripped naked. Time and again he hastens back, to give away his free will to any laws, any religion, any rule and usage that shall avert the burden of self-direction that freedom lays upon him. Solitude, self-direction, self-responsibility, the invention and incessant examination of personal conduct and motive, self-criticism, of such as these are the burdens of liberty, and we cannot avoid them.

We of this generation, for instance, have had to come out of the shelter of those religious beliefs into which we were born and bred, and with our formal religion we had to throw away the guidance of its rules of conduct; we could no longer accept, but must examine its sanctions and its prohibitions and rejudge them for ourselves. Liberty of thought opened to us like coming out into a flood of sunshine from a closed house. But sometimes, very high, very cold, very thin is its air. All alone now we carry our burdens, and when they chafe us unbearably, all alone we must contrive our healing. With the abandonment of our formal religion we have no longer access to those expedients for the refreshment and comfort of the soul which her priests, wise in the needs of the human heart, have devised. The relief of taking all one's spiritual hurts and bruises, all one's heavy conviction of failure and weakness, and rolling the whole load off one's soul into the tenderly understanding hands of a personal God, and going on again, clean and light, has been an idea that has animated the services of both Protestant and Catholic churches. The Protestant service of Communion sends forth its faithful participant cleansed in spirit, with silence in the heart, with a soul profoundly at peace. That that may certainly happen we are enjoined to prepare for the service, to meditate, search and scour the mind for every lurking evil, that no forgotten irk may be left behind to fester its way to consciousness when the burden has been cast away. Be very sure, says the Church, that it is all here, my child.

They were very good, those hours. The big church would empty slowly, rustlingly, after the morning service, the mass of people would flow out of the pews, collect, a pool of humanity, towards its end, drain through the doors, its breadth shrinking to a thin stream that went at last drop by drop into the sunshine without. The crunching of the gravel would become fainter, die. Silence. Here and there, remote and few, remained a kneeling figure.

"Ye that do truly and earnestly repent of your sins and are in love and charity with your neighbours and intend to lead a new life…draw near with faith, and take this holy sacrament to your comfort…

"Almighty God, the remembrance of our sins is grievous unto us, the burden of them is intolerable. Forgive us all that is past…

"Almighty God have mercy upon you, pardon and deliver you, confirm and strengthen you…

"Hear what comfortable words our saviour Christ saith unto all that truly turn to him…"

Into the silence fell these sentences and others, and left us in the silence again. It is one of the great silences of the world, that Sunday morning silence in a nearly empty church. Humanity has withdrawn into its homes, the open windows, the door ajar, let in no sound. Piercing it came the song, very high, very thin and sweet, of a robin perching swaying on a bough without, a jet of song that rose and fell and ceased, and left the silence deeper. Tranquillity stole into my heart, the gentle thief of all my turbid pain; my soul was folded with the happy song of God's little bird...

"The peace of God, which passeth all understanding, be amongst you and remain with you always. Amen."

I would come out, clean washed in spirit, like a thing new born. My heart within me was softly glad of life.

My path led round the church. Its beautiful windows of stained glass were protected by outer gratings of stout wire, netted close against its treasure. And yet not so close but there remained at the tops of them a narrow gap, where the wire guard did not quite meet the stone, a gap through which a tiny, inquisitive living body might pass.

At the base of nearly every window, behind that savage wire, lay the little, bleached skeleton of a bird.

* * *

Never did the Church give me any explanation that even began to satisfy me, of the dealings with their God of those tortured birds.

From my earliest childhood the Church failed in its endeavour to win my soul. The story of the Creation, fragments of Old Testament history, the life of Christ, the immortality of the soul and its destination for heaven or hell were presented to me by books and teachers as absolute facts exactly as the history of England was presented. I accepted it all as I accepted the rest of the patent universe in which I found myself, and tried to constrain my conduct to satisfy its commandments. Christianity came to me, a little child of four years old, in the guise of pictures of the crucifixion, sanguinously coloured, pierced side and feet and hands streaming redly and terribly. The persistent pushing upon my mind in picture-books and church and Bible of that horrible murder did nothing to engage my affection for my heavenly Father. My home was one of those English homes in which religious matters are not mentioned, are so conspicuously not mentioned that the whole celestial world, impending over our heads so weightily and ignored so pointedly, acquired an awful added significance. Religion began at church on Sunday morning and ended with the service; we came away and walked home, saying nothing about the uncomfortable matters with which we had been confronted for an hour and a half. Beyond that I "said prayers" on going to bed, and on rare occasions of extreme naughtiness, such as being rude to my mother, I was bidden as the furthest penance to ask God on my knees to forgive me.

Such a public invocation of that name in a family matter cowed me utterly. My religious curiosities, as usually happens in a family of my sort, I took to my nurse and the servants, who filled in the gaps in my information with matter-of-fact statements that left no ragged ends of doubt. I remember very brightly being told of the death of Mr Gladstone, whose figure, with streaming grizzled hair, hawk nose and monstrous winged collar, hacking at forest trees inscribed on broad sashes about their middles "Slavery", "Cowardice", "Hypocrisy", or as a gladiator with sword and shield defending himself against a menacing masked opponent with net and trident, also sashed as "Fenianism", was as familiar to me in the weekly old bound volumes of *Punch* as the members of my own family, and having some inkling of the marvel of time and space in reflecting on the astounding queerness that whereas yesterday he was *here*, collar and square chin and all, on the solid earth, yet now at the moment he was *there* in the sky above me, miraculously supported on nothing, and looking, I couldn't help feeling, very extraordinary among the angels. (For it was understood that, however my father might mutter discontent over his morning paper, Mr Gladstone was a very good man.) And very bright too is the memory of sitting up long after my lawful bedtime on evenings when my father and mother had gone out, and listening with marvelling wonder to chapters from the book of Revelations, read aloud by one servant while the others sewed. The chapter of the sealing of the Children of Israel with its rolling repetitions, was particularly splendid to me, and I urged for it again and again. But I did not like the lank black figures of the clergy who lurked a little awkwardly in the back premises during the time of that particular servant, they were too like monstrous developments of the kitchen beetles to win my confidence. As I grew old enough to read freely for myself, the books that fell into my childish hands went on emphasising the awful importance of the unseen world; the works of Elizabeth Wetherall and Grace Aguilar and other books, and those much more emphatic in quality, whose authorship was veiled under initials or the pseudonym "A Lady", did not mince the matter that things were going to be extremely disagreeable for me someday if I did not look out.

So I tried to look out. The profound difficulty was not to forget all about the salvation of my soul for long periods of happy summer play – two or three weeks perhaps – and thus, as I knew too well, run immense risks of being hurled suddenly into eternity during one of those oblivious times, with the very worst prospects. Prompted by my storybooks I adopted all sorts of expedients for keeping my mind concentrated on celestial affairs; I began reading the Bible, a chapter a day, until the day and the day after and the day after that came when I forgot; I tried carrying texts about in my pocket, scribbled on torn scraps of paper and ink-smudged; they fell out of the shallow pocket of the little girl capering in the garden, or went to the wash in my holland pinafores; I even tried to conduct religious services with some much younger cousins, singing hymns to the accompaniment of a gorgeous musical box that lived in dignity in the handsome spaciousness of their dining room, but we children were not allowed to change the barrels, and though my emotion could exalt me to the strange possibility of singing "Holy, holy, holy" to the tune of Yankee-Doodle taken very slowly, they were not so animated, and a spate of disastrous giggling would rise and drown the whole of my hopefully prepared little ceremony. But always for long intervals of days I would forget it all, relapse into my preoccupations with my dolls and my rocking-horse and long rambling secretly imagined and performed romantic dramas in which, dressed in abandoned lace window-curtains and with the constraining ribbon pulled off my hair, I would marry myself solemnly and splendidly to a wonderful princely figure, who stood, a ghostly performer at my side. For most secret and precious of my childish treasures was a bent and flattened brass wedding-ring, the prize of some Christmas cracker.

Again and again I forgot. That was the failure of the Church for me, then in my childhood and now, that it left out so much. It had no place in it and said nothing whatever about everything that made me happy. It took no account of the childish world of flowers and insects and little animals seen intimately and close as they are seen in those days when you live so tiny a way from the earth, of sunshine and warm, mysterious, whispering, tree-sheltered shade, of the joy of movement, of dancing and running and leaping, of swinging up high into a wonderful vast tree dome of shining translucent green leaves, of laughter and jokes, and the extreme funniness of Uncle Charles when he was in the mood to amuse you. Religion had an attitude of grave disapproval towards all these delightful things; they were frivolous, idle, profane; innocent enough in aspect they were yet the top of a moral buttered slide that led to Sabbath-breaking and the mysterious prohibitions of the Commandments, and so perilous to your immortal soul.

But they were the warm and dear things of one's heart.

* * *

[A few lines written in longhand, with many deletions, have been omitted here.]

That was the aspect of Christianity to me, as a child; a higher, more implacable development of the parental noes and mustn'ts. As a child I went straight to the satisfaction of my little immediate desires, though sometimes I had to pick my way to them altogether through the prohibitions of the authoritative. With adolescence comes a change.

I think that in many ways it is the same change that happened as when man became human and ceased to be animal. He comes to think it is worthwhile to sacrifice immediate desirable ends to obtain postponed remoter ends that appear to him still more desirable. The capacity to do that, to see and desire beyond the immediate concrete something further and largely imagined, and to have the self-control to pursue that further end, isn't that the beginning of man in the history of the race and the history of the individual alike? It is also the origin and cause of morality. No animal is moral or immoral. That distinction begins only with the capacity for imagining those remoter ends, and the consequent imperative of choice. With adolescence one comes to appreciate and desire remoter ends, one discovers that the prohibitions of current morality and Christianity are directed towards the achievement of remoter ends and are not the denial of immediate gratification only, and then one begins to look at the remoter ends particularly promised, and examine if they seem worthwhile or not.

Of course a child's mind does not think with such precision at all as that implies, but I think that does express in a rough diagrammatic way the sort of change of attitude that happens as one grows up. One examines the ideals and further ends of Christianity, for instance, and one is attracted or not to undertake the discipline necessary to attain them according to the idiosyncrasy of one's individual temperament.

When I was a young girl between fourteen and eighteen Christianity had a greater attraction for me than ever before or since. Its ideals were ideals in which then I perceived such beauty, they held much of what seemed to me then the most beautiful ideas in the world. I have told you already, little brother, of that secretly treasured wedding-ring, and for all the mass of emotion hoarded in my childish mind that gathered about that as a symbol I could find in the world about me hardly any expression at all. I see now that no good literature came into my hands to feed and express my imaginings about love. The heroines of my fiction were greatly surprised and horribly embarrassed when they were told they were loved; their invariable behaviour was to get their ashamed faces, which were deeply reddened and hot, into the nearest cover, which if their lover was ardently near, had to be his waistcoat. This brought into my mind an image of rough-surfaced clothy seclusion the reverse of delightful. When the severity of this ostrich phase of the affair had mitigated a little, I was told that kisses were pressed upon her reluctant lips. It was all very puzzling. And apart from these refinements there was only a world of vulgar laughter about love. In my fiction it was a dull solemnity, in the pages of the old *Punchs* in the library it was a joke. That made me very sure that had I ever a lover I would keep him secret in my heart, so secret close that no breath of that coarse world should touch our sacred joy.

I fell in love again and again through those years as schoolgirls do, with actors, with visiting masters at my school, with young men much older than myself, never with my contemporaries, the mutely adoring brothers of my schoolfellows. I was overflowing indeed with the need to love to such an extent that it could do no other than to spill over on to those circumstantial and unconscious people. I was so starved of expression that I sometimes confided these passions to chosen girl friends. I found among them much the same response as my books had given me, either they were refusing as a matter of personal virtue to think of those things at all, or they responded with an artful innuendo that tickled my vanity at first and afterwards filled me with disgust. I was so wearied at last, so deeply disappointed with what I got from the world without me in this matter of love, that by the time I was fifteen I vowed to myself to postpone this business of loving until the skies were kinder. In no way could I reach you, come nearer to you then, little brother. Meanwhile Christianity invited me – and at that moment it came with allurement – to discipline and deny myself every pleasure that I knew about that I might wash and clean my soul. Was that not also necessary, to be more ready for you?

* * *

What was it like, that year or two I spent within the Christian faith?

I remember once standing alone in a church somewhere high up in the hills over the Italian lakes. It was a big church, accented heavily with incense, great columns soared upward into darkness, its narrow windows of coloured glass let in a tempered light that fell in patches of vivid stain upon the tessellated floor. Suddenly out of the gloom, flew a bird. I caught sight of it flying among the pillars, till it vanished once more. It was a swallow, and I watched it a long time sweeping silently, restlessly to and fro, to and fro, seeking and seeking. I looked back along the twilit nave to where at its end the open door framed a little, vivid glimpse of the world outside, the purple hills, the glittering blue lake far below, the sapphire sky with a soft white cloud. That indeed was what the bird sought, but I could not aid it, and I left it circling, darting, soaring, swiftly and so noiselessly that it might have been the spirit of a bird imprisoned long ago.

During those years, I was like that bird.

* * *

The religious life, and the spiritual protection of a rule prescribed, has ever been man's refuge from a universe too difficult for him, too complicated for his understanding, so pressing in its variety that it wearies him to try and comprehend it, so violent in its events that it confuses his endeavour. Think only of the teeming intricacy of the primitive earth that met the dawning intelligence of man, as it lurked in the eyes of those hairy, ape-like creatures who were the ancients of our race. Profoundly, intensely, beyond all belief difficult has it been through the ages for man to deal with wild nature, and win through even so far as he has done in his struggle for the mastery of the physical universe. For it is the mastery of the physical universe and no lesser task that has been man's history and is his destiny. Struggle of athletes! And as if that were not enough there has pressed upon him as hardly and imminently that need of learning how to live in peace and order and fellowship with his fellow-men. For that also is man's history, and is his destiny.

Already we feel the edge of power within our hands; we have subdued fire and steam and electricity and many elements to our service. We are no longer helpless before all disease, no longer does pestilence stalk upon a helpless earth, slaying whom it will, nor man cower before marauding beasts; we begin to control the existence of all other living creatures, even life itself. Man has made sensible progress towards that ultimate mastery, and it is visibly a progress that hastens. Has he made as much towards his other goal, towards living in fellowship with his fellow-man? The parallel to pestilence may be found among human things in war, and war is still with us, an active danger which humanity is unable as yet to avert, an inner weakness which saps the solidarity of man's fight for the control of the earth. While man struggles against his external adversaries, disease and tempest and the fierce stubbornness of nature, internally he is weakened by his ignorance and those baser passions which militate against the achievement of fellowship. There is no path among these confusions, inch by inch he must push on into the unknown, sometimes he cuts a way that looks backward and not forward. There are many in every generation to whom the conflict seems but the vanity of fretful men, who see no good beyond the present confusions, and of such are they who turn altogether from the crowded, hurrying, stumbling stream of life, and within a little cell contrive a little peace.

Of course, there is beauty in the Christian ideal, in the image of that still, withdrawn life, that image which culminates in the picture of the cell, with its solitude and silence, simplicity and peace. One wears one's body like a garment, for one lives in a world where bodies are, but it is the soul that is beautiful and shines.

Speak not – lest thou speak evil; hear not overmuch – lest thy hearing seduce thee; seek not curiously to learn – for what availeth thy wisdom before God? Of such a spirit is the teaching of Thomas à Kempis, that preceptor of behaviour to Christians. It is a negation of life, a refusal of experiment, a laying down of the restless intelligence that the Fashioner of the universe has given to man as he might have put a sword into his hand. But so I did not see life then. It seemed as if my soul came like a shining dewdrop straight from God, which I must presently return unsullied to his care. I held my ideas of personal conduct like tall straight slender lilies in my arms.

And then, I changed. Or rather, for me Beauty changed.

The process of such a change in thought is curious to consider. There is an established idea against which a new idea comes in active conflict, they engage and the new idea retires as if for ever defeated. But it comes back to fight again and again, and every time leaves the old idea a little weakened. The time comes presently when it returns and meets no opponent. Life plucked those pale lilies from my arms one by one. Every thought of my mind was stretching out in curiosity to apprehend the world in which I lived, every fibre of my nature faced eagerly to experience like a flower to the light. What room was there in the *Imitatio Christi* for my little pagan body lying here in the sun, saturated with the pleasure of living?

Chapter Two

THINKING OF YOU, little brother, just now while I came up the garden from the sea it came to me that I may find you here although it was impossible for me to meet you in the real world. For do you not know that our first parents were turned out of paradise, and do you think that you and I would be allowed to meet on earth and cheat the angel at the gate? I remember in some gallery or other a delightful old Florentine picture, it might have been by Fra Angelico, of the gate of Paradise, and a bustling angel turning out a forlorn little Adam and Eve, who seem disposed to linger. "If you won't move on I shall really have to hit you with this sword," the angel seems to say, "and it's hot, you know." And Adam and Eve parlay. "But how long are we turned out for then?" they say. "Ever and ever," replies the angel briskly, pulling up the staples that hold the gates open and preparing to shut it. Eve regards him with a slowly growing astonishment. "But you pretty angel," she begins, "you don't mean we shan't come back – soon?" "None of you will ever come back," says the angel tugging at the bolt, and getting crusty because he hates the whole business and likes Eve the better the more he sees of her. "That's my orders, and Orders is Orders, ma'am."

Eve begins to cry. "But there'll be all our children," she sobs, "and their children and *their* children. Some of them will be as good as gold, dear angel, not like us. Ever so far on, in thousands of years' time, there'll be such a nice little woman, and the man she calls little brother. Dear angel, can't *they* come back?"

"Certainly not," snaps the angel. So you see how impossible it is for me to meet you in the world, for if I met you, crash! those bolted gates would fly open and you and I would be in paradise, my heart!

* * *

After writing that, I ramble about, strangely stirred and restless. I want to go back to the world. There is something there that is not here, something, my lover, more precious than love.

Can I possibly explain to you what I mean? It began when I was a child, and whatever else I have done and however else I have occupied my mind it has shone like a steady, patient light.

The world according to my childish mind was a clear definite little place, dotted with familiar things, a house and garden, parents, school, toys and books, but out of that brightly lit circle of daily experience my thoughts adventured in at least three different directions, into alleys that led to magic and mystery, dimly seen and heart-stirring.

There was the mystery of love and there was the mystery of God, and there was yet another place where mystery and magic dwelt, and that was that I knew of the existence of scientific knowledge and later learnt something of the nature of scientific thought. In those childish days everything that was "science" lit my imagination with excitement. I was taught no science, my lessons were history and geography and French and arithmetic, but it touched my mind there and again, out of books, out of magazines, and things seen and heard. Papers on chemistry too abstruse for my childish understanding inflamed my mind by their illustrations. Queer woodcuts of Volta calm and dominant among quivering coils of wire and leaping sparks, of Faraday experimenting with induction circuits, of Priestley making oxygen, and even the quieter matter of the fossils of monstrous saurians, became to me what fairies and magic castles are to some children. It took me out of the common day into a world where the very air I breathed could be rent asunder into strange miracle-working substances, where the passive water that I drank leapt apart to become astounding powers that could bang and flare. And there were the tools of investigation! There was, for instance, that magical piece of apparatus, the air-pump, never seen, but brooded over in a woodcut illustration for long intervals of time; that wonderful thing that if you had, could become empty, empty in a sense quite other than that in which I knew the word, and the ringing alarum clock would grow fainter and become inaudible though one could see its active gong whanging away, and the mouse would die and the bladder burst soundlessly. There was a time when I would have given up any other desired thing for an air-pump, eagerly. It lived for me in the world of pure imagination, never had I known anyone who possessed even so usual a scientific implement as a microscope, nor did I know any place where such things existed and could be seen and touched. Never did I succeed in materialising any of the experiments described, for all their apparatus was outside my range. The writer of the articles on chemistry would speak of "taking" this or that, as if one were God and had only to dip down one's hand from the clouds for anything in the physical universe. He set out tasks as impossible as those proposed to the heroes of faery. "Take a Florentine flask" was not so easy as the writer seemed to think, to a little girl of eleven in a middle class home. What *was* a Florence flask? One never found out. And the mysterious substance called bladder so lightheartedly demanded, was not a thing to be borrowed from one's mother's workbasket. As the result of much excogitation I concluded at last that the preparation of nitrogen presented the fewest difficulties. You only had to "take" a piece of phosphorus.

I went to my father and demanded to be allowed to expend pocket-money in the purchase of phosphorus.

His reply was quite emphatic and extinguished all my hope. It was an extremely dangerous substance for me to be playing about with, and not to be thought of for a moment.

So Nitrogen, the only one of the mysterious family which had made a struggle to come out of my dream world, went sadly back into the shades.

There began the oddest little collection of objects upon a shelf set carefully apart in my toy cupboard. It comprised everything that I could lay my hands on that remotely suggested the apparatus of the experiment according to those woodcut illustrations. Its most imposing item was a large glass cylinder rounded at one end and fitted there with a cork, through which a hole was bored for tubing. Quite possibly that might have been a real piece of apparatus, it came with a lot of odd wine glasses and bottles from some sale of furniture, but more likely it was meant for an aquarium and the purgatorial dwelling of sea-anemones. There was the top part of a broken glass filter, also a convincing object seen endways on the shelf, and in a cardboard box and packed in cotton wool was – mysterious flotsam of a suburban home – a glass object beginning in a tube and expanding bulbously, that I knew from its all too emphatic inscription was a milk tester, but over which I threw a veil of ambiguity by keeping it at the back. There was a greenhouse thermometer. There was a piece of glass tubing out of the filter and another piece preserved from a strange, isolated occasion when the physical geography lesson at my school became touched with hygiene and came out into the open of fact with lime water, tubes and hard breathing. You blew into clear lime water and it went milky; that showed you how bad it was for you to keep the windows shut. The resultant fluid and precipitate of my personal allowance of lime water were preserved in a corked medicine bottle, not labelled, for the experimenter had not frittered away her effect by giving a fresh name to the demoralised lime water. There were one or two empty bottles, a very small and a bigger magnet, and a scrap of dark-coloured glass, bought in the street on an occasion when there was an eclipse of the sun.

Queer little hoard that it was! I would take it all out, dust it very carefully, pass the tubing through the hole in the cork of the aquarium once or twice, shake up the carbonate of lime, dream and ponder... Priestley made his discoveries with the simplest apparatus – they said so; wasn't there some way in which even these things could be made to come to life and unlock the door into wonderland? The rest of the toy cupboard was just like any other child's, a crowd of heaped miscellaneous things, jumbled in so that you shut the door quickly to stop their falling out, dusty and broken many of them, but that shelf was always the same, always with its contents scrupulously neat and placed at exact distances from one another. That cupboard has even a symbolism for me now, for so in my mind whatever else has been confused and heaped with broken values, that faith in scientific knowledge, its wonder, its beauty and trustability has never forsaken me at any time. My own scraps of understanding of scientific thought are perhaps as casual and ill-assorted as that semblance of apparatus, but I have never doubted that they were glimpses into a world of magical beauty and wonder, of thought as near to truth as we can ever attain, of something that in its purpose and destiny stretches over and links hands with the idea of God.

The mystery, the wonder! the marvel! The world unfolds endlessly behind the semblance that we touch and see. I look up into the night sky and see a tiny disc of light brighter than the points about it, and what I see is just what has shone into the eyes of millions of men. And one night I am shown that disc of light through a telescope. That semblance of a fixed and steady star like any other of the thousands in the sky falls like a mask from a living face, and a shining belt of exquisite roundness swimming in a belt of light comes quivering and rocking across the field – Saturn. I lie upon the earth and see a blade of grass translucent against the sun, and a microscope would resolve that simple image into a multitude of transparent cells, each with an intricate structure, and elaborate its uniform green into thousands of separate grains of chlorophyll. I myself am this body of a woman, a graceful little animal enough with a pink smooth skin, millions have lived like me and millions will live, and that pink skin which is my outward semblance is but the covering of a complexity of structure that no human brain has yet done more than touch the edge of understanding, the mind of man goes down to its study as into a labyrinth. The external beauty of a body is like a flush of the sunset, it is breathed upon it for a few short years, it glows, and presently wanes, and will fade out leaving it cold and grey. But a beauty that transcends all other lies deep in the fastness below that changing surface.

(Cold and grey. I beat the earth and cry out with pain. Do you hear that cry, my lover?)

Now do you understand that light that shines and beckons to me out of this world, and that has always shone and beckoned? Had I stayed in the world I might have become the humble servant of some research; if the world has any use for me at all, it is that.

* * *

Once after I had ceased to count myself a believer in the Christian faith did I endeavour again that sacramental peace. The pain of personal failure was the same, the stinging humiliation of remembered stupidities and clumsiness, the despair that comes on a new conviction of one's poor quality, the feeling of confusion and of wandering in the dark. One day I sought again the healing touch of that hour of quiet in a church and that dismissal with "the peace that passeth all understanding." But how little could I recapture!

Hardly enough to carry forth into the street! The measure of emotion I succeeded in experiencing evaporated from my mind so soon as I reached the outer world, it had but lain for a moment on its surface. Its perfume hung like a wilted forced flower from my coat. I was deeply disappointed but I never attempted such a reconstruction again. The personal, responsible God, capable of giving or withholding forgiveness, capable of being arrested and giving ear to an importunate child, was gone out of my world, and for the time my feet were planted upon no other faith.

What are the occasions, little brother, do you think when one most needs God? that is to say the sense of a purpose and destiny very great and beyond oneself, so that one's self and all that it has done and can do sinks into triviality in comparison with that. There are times in the worldly daily life when one's heart and mind are so bruised that the only healing is to take them into contact with that greatness. Little brother, let me tell you that the worst thing of all I think there is to bear in the world is the failure of one's own personal quality. Suddenly at the test it betrays its weakness and takes the poor ignoble line. One may think much of beauty and nobility, and one may have been born so lame a spirit that times occur and seem that they will never fail to recur when one acts with stupidity, clumsiness, unkindness and ugliness. One may have been given for an instant the precious chance to make beauty and one has not recognised it till too late, and let it slip. How can one deal with the remorse such things entail?

Men have been shown cowards in battle and have had to live out their lives with themselves. One discovers that one has behaved on some occasion like a dull fool, and one has to go on with life, knowing that that is not the end of it but that presently will come a fresh test and possibly one's spirit will be treacherous again. How can one meet such experience?

There came a night when I seemed to discover the stars.

Every day of our lives there is given to us a miracle and a wonder. Every day at evening the sunlight that dazzles our poor human eyes so that they see nothing but this earth and the struggle for living that goes on upon it is gently withdrawn, and we are shown the universe. It is shown to us in its immensity with its millions of stars; we look up into distances our little minds call infinite, we apprehend spaces of time we call eternal. There came such a night when I saw the universe above me and about me, boundless and serene, in its presence the failure and pain with which my heart was bursting shrank away and vanished. Once more I was given the peace that passeth all understanding. For that moment I found my cathedral and my service, I wanted no more from any church than that sense of peace, that inspiration of faith, the conviction of the littleness of my circumspect living, and the relation of myself to God.

Indeed all our lives we should sleep under the stars as I do here, every night we should look up at their benignity and slough the fretful day. In their presence our personal stumblings are but a minute part of the experience and travail of all humanity. In their presence, little brother, you who have hidden from me all day come silently near. Your arm slips under my head, your hand closes over mine, cheek to cheek we lie and look up at the great stars. I do not think of you, you do not think of me; we are looking up into the face of God.

* * *

How do I regard man and God, and the evident history of man's origin from the beasts that begat him? Can I express my belief in some such image as this –

Man is a creature of earth, but at some moment in his making God laid his finger upon man's brain and heart.

The fire he lit in man's brain was intelligence, and in his heart, love.

I am confident that those divine touches imbued them with His purpose.

I believe that man's intelligence grows and will grow greater continually and the power to love of his heart grow greater continually, and that by the measure of that growth and power will he understand the nature and forward the purpose of God.

I believe that for a guide to that growth and power he has his perception and desire towards beauty.

And I believe that for the personal life, to strive one's utmost towards intelligence, to open one's heart to its widest to love, and to measure one's conduct constantly against the standard of one's sense of beauty, is to live religiously and not in vain.

* * *

The little creatures of the world.

There is a wood near by of birch and willow and thin-leaved trees, so that it is not dark like other woods but irradiated with sunshine. I lie there very still, and the little creatures of the earth come and go about their busy affairs. Do you know the infinite delicacy, the loveliness of little mice? There is a tiny mouse with a home in a particular hollow tree trunk that I know. I lie upon the other side of it away from him, and watch him bustle out, a mite of a mole-coloured thing, with little, perfect ears and feet and a silver [nose] like a willow bud in spring, a globe of softness, a thing as exquisite as lives. He burrows his nose under every leaf and twig, he nibbles every morsel about him, he stands on his minute head and turns somersaults out of sheer joy. I would like to go back to the story of Creation for his genesis, and think of God making him with tender care, chiselling him with finest instruments from the primal clay, and bending His great attentive brows over the little emerging shape; and to think that when God had done with the elephants and whales and horses and men and such rough furnishing of the earth that he made mice and birds and squirrels and butterflies because it was such lovely work to do.

* * *

Do you think that since I talk to you so much that yours is the only society I have upon my island? Infinitely conceited little brother, listen!

This morning I have had the prettiest adventure with a bird. It is an *affaire*, no less. I was lying after my bath in the warm shade that comes just on the edge of the sun, and I think I was half asleep. Do you wonder at my being half asleep in the early morning? But last night was a night of magic moonlight. There was but one colour in all the night, blue in the velvety darkness of trees that was almost black, of silvery paleness upon the palace walls, the sky the profoundest depth of blue out of which the yellow moon shone full and serene. I leant over the terrace wall, watching as the colour deepened moment by moment. I went up the stairway to the topmost balcony and stood there within its bubble of streaming water, pouring over my head like liquid moonlight. I came down to wander through the garden, and away from the ripple of the splashing water into the silent groves and spaces of the night. Indeed it was a magic night; the familiar allées seemed mysteriously changed, they led me by unexpected ways I had no memory of by day, and suddenly, like one who flings wide his arms, they turned me into an open glade. About that glade the trees uprose to the moon, the soft turf sparkled, glow-worms twinkled in the shadows, and there was a deep hush, a breathless watching hush, as if a goddess walked. How long did I hide in the shadow to see her?

I do not know. But later I went on through the allées, and came at last to the miracle of the moonlit sea.

But, the bird. I lay then half asleep in the sunny warmth, seeing only a lucid greenness that crept between my closing eyelids. A little grey-blue bird mistook me I think for one of the statues fallen into the grass, for I was startled awake by a fluttering sound close to my ear, the touch of a pair of little cold wet feet, and as I started, the scratching flight of those feet as the little creature jumped away. I kept very still and opened my eyes but narrowly, enough to see him hopping and flirting his wings on a bush close by. Then suddenly, with head on one side and confident bright eye, he flew to me again and settled, hopped all over me with his queer little scratchy feet, flew down to peck up some eatable morsel of seed, back with it in his beak to perch on my arm, nibbled the seed out of the husk, and then, crowning impertinence, wiped his beak briskly on *me*. Little bird, little adorable bird! His grey-blueness resolved itself, seen so close, into a marvellous complexity of colour and feather patterning. Then he began to explore, hopped up to my shoulder, and his house-furnishing instinct suddenly aroused, pulled smartly at a wisp of my hair. He gave it up as undetachable, and flew back to his bush. I ventured to move gently and he was unalarmed, and I discovered he had no fear of me left, he was only interested to find me alive. He has been my constant attendant all this day, never very far from me, always reappearing just when I was quite certain he was tired of me. He looks at me first with one friendly black eye and then with the other; he has a funny little smile that he produces with the corners of his beak, and he impresses me as the most volatile intellect I have ever met.

* * *

Very wonderful is the life of a wood.

It is a silent place. In the open country the song of a bird seems only the louder part of a universal stir of sound, heard in a wood it lifts up sharply and alone against a black curtain of silence. In the open when the air is still and there is no sound it is the silence of a rumbunctious person fallen asleep; in the wood it is the silence of something in brooding thought. A bird twitters and is hushed. Time ceases. Each moment is a strange, still eternity.

Oh my dear, my dear! I would have you with me in a wood!

Little delicate lovelinesses lie about everywhere for the finding. Close by my hand I see among the grass blades a single feather. How odd that is, the way something that has been present all the time will leap to one's sight as if it sprang there and then into being. It is hardly two inches long, it is of the lightest grey, and from its root for nearly all its length it is a mass of soft fluffiness that becomes at the tip suddenly smooth, speckled, fine, and thin. That glossy, transparent tip is all of it that the bird shows; the fluffy rest is just his exquisite underclothing. I turn it about and marvel at it, if I stroke it against my lips it is almost too soft for feeling.

It leapt to my sight! You were playing with it yourself, it shared your invisibility till you dropped it from your hand.

Chapter Three

I DO NOT THINK now of going back into the world as a possibility likely to happen. At first I looked to my blue horizon, half fearfully curious if some sail or steamer's smoke might drift along it and perhaps take me back again to mankind. But now no more do I expect that to happen. I do not imagine myself growing old here, weakening, losing by minute decreasings the sweetness of my body, as would happen in the world. I think I shall be here some time, and then cease to be. For what avails it for me yet to return to the world? Are you there, little brother? Much more you are here. Without you, what place has the world for me? What place is there in the world for any woman? I could hand myself over to the keeping of a man, I could by the grudging grace of men, live meagrely alone. Live richly and freely, as I want to live, I could not. The world yet does not care enough for me to give me that. I am Woman, and the world does not want me a free and happy soul, it likes me best a subjugated thing, it cares nothing for keeping me beautiful, it does not care if I become work-worn.

What is it that women want in the world?

They want – little brother, come here to me, and put your head side by side with mine, your cheek against my cheek. So can we look at this matter not as man or as woman, but as man and woman, humanity thinking of this business of woman's life. They are asking, we know, for what all creatures want – freedom. That word marches like a banner before all the insurgence of all dependant people. It is such a commonplace that to hear it again makes people impatient and angry. Freedom *is* a commonplace; so is bread. Freedom is as necessary to the soul as bread is to the body.

Women are in need of a particular kind of freedom; they have been obliged always to find in their sex their means of livelihood; before they can be much happier than they are now, they need to be freed from that. Whether in marriage or outside it, it is the bare fact that women are kept women, kept for their sex. Upon that basis are built it matters not what structures of fair and honest relationship, of affection and love and honourable partnership, the basis remains, and upon that same basis rest sordid and avaricious and prostituted relationships. Never ought women's sex to be their means of livelihood, it is their moral undoing, never should they lease their chastity in marriage in return for a soft labourless life, clothes and food and ample housing. For what else is marriage but such a bargain? Until women can get their living apart from their sex they will be creatures of debased honour; never will they be in the plain sense of the word "honest" women. Indeed women cannot now, as the world is, marry and entertain that equivalent of personal pride men call their honour. So far in the history of the world the indulgence of such a feeling on the part of women as personal honour has been unprovided for. They have cultivated an artificial honour, a feeling of pride in having kept the rules of conduct dictated to them, or the terms of their marriage bargain. Now it may be a source of just pride to keep the terms of an honourable bargain, but if it is not an honourable bargain? If it is enslaving and debasing, then to keep it may be the source of very evil pride. And so we find often an evil pride in women, a hard pride in the convention of their virtue, a hatred of others who have put themselves into like bonds, a malignant pleasure if those others are unhappy. Once give hospitality to a mean emotion, and it will hold open the door of your heart to all its base born friends.

Before we are happy in the world, love and beauty must be free gifts, never to be bought or sold or leased on even the most honourable terms. Marriage is a lease of love. For a woman to lease her love in marriage deprives her of that kind of freedom, the power of self-direction and of personal responsibility which is the very marrow of personal honour. One may ask indeed if it is not time to give this particular freedom to women almost forcibly; if indeed the soul of woman has not yet grown up to an age when it would be braced by such circumstances, as one gives a pony to a little boy to ride and make him manly, and risks a tumble or two. Most of the faults peculiar to women as a class arise out of their condition of moral tutelage over-prolonged, they concentrate on dressing and they occupy themselves with toys, a shifty streak has been gotten upon their character because the freeborn soul that lives in women just as in men, is cramped to the peril of its health, and constrained to crooked ways. They use their soft womanliness to attain their ends, they smile and persuade and allure.

My dear, sometimes I think it would be well for women to go down into the battle of life for a few generations, earn their living at any trade that can employ them, live hard and poorly and learn the value of material things, and before all else the value of themselves. They cannot do that, never can we so marshal the world as to oblige them to do that, and so they must pick up honesty as best they may. Little brother, I hope they may. For to me only in the light of honesty can love be beautiful. It is like a fine room, the more beautiful it is, the brighter may be the light upon it; to dim the light is to lose much of its loveliness. There are shadowed moments, moments of mystery as beautiful as twilight, but there shall be no curtains before the windows to veil away the sun. For the sun, little brother, is the gaze of your mind into mine, and of mine into yours. It should melt away our ignorance of one another like the sun dissolving the soft white mists of the morning. In such manner shall I know you, in such manner should we human beings encounter. First this thought of yours and then that will catch the light of my regard, shine like slender pinnacles of gold through the filmy vapours that melt between us, until at last all your mind will lie clear before mine and all mine before yours like cities of enchantment distant in a valley, down into which we may wander with delight. I shall rifle and plunder the treasure of your thought – oh madly and greedily! and carry off my loot in hugged armfuls, only to find while I have been thus busy that you, sweet thief, have stolen every secret of mine that I thought so safely stored. Should I try, I wonder too late, to lock the doors, fearing lest you plunder my tiny treasure all too soon and turn from the empty storehouse? What good will it be? For like little treacherous ghosts every thought of mine would slip away from me and run straight into your heart.

But was I not talking of women and the world?

* * *

Women everywhere are questioning the current rules of morality, the rules that concern their relations to men.

We women, with our love of beauty and our sense that we can make and give it, are constrained to hide it and strangle it, to seek out the places in our hearts where beauty springs to life and lay them waste utterly, salting the ground which gave it nourishment. We spend our lives with our hearts in sackcloth, abjuring fine silk. And only sometimes do we regret that so greyly and in no other way do our days pass, for deep seated in the human heart is a love and willingness for discipline, for denial, for going in soldierly ranks with one's fellows along a stubborn road, for obedience to wise orders, for marching with pride and squared shoulders under a banner whose motto may be harsh as it pleases so it be noble. I would do that gladly, and see the days of my life fall from me on the march like the petals of flowers that are done, and not regret them. But our marching ranks are breaking up, we ask, we women, to see the orders, for a creeping poison of doubt of their great wisdom runs about our thoughts, we are hauling down the banner and discussing its device. We question if our march along the hard road is really leading us to a splendid ultimate goal, or whether we are marching only to kick up the dust and give ourselves tired limbs to endure. We are not happy on the march, we hunger and thirst, we do not see clearly that we march to any purpose save that our masters will it so. We are virgin and we marry, we are chaste and bear our children, we eat and take our needful things from the hands of those who keep us. We are guarded by a savage jealousy, in turn we guard as well as we can from our ranks with a jealousy as savage. In the world, little brother, I should be glad if...for it is no world yet for women.

Women there must be born into it, but I would not have a child of my body grow up a creature of lost pride. For very insidiously as we grow to womanhood life undermines our honour. Love comes and we open our arms to embrace him, and in the world, my dear, love presses worldly gifts into a woman's hands. It does not matter in the end that they come in love's hands, we ought not to take from our lovers, as now the world obliges us to take. Many a woman must now end her love experience an unwilling Danaë, her soul dies beneath a shower of small comforts.

Oh this specialisation of women! Always she has been property! Nothing can be devised that will make life better for her while that endures. It seems as if one saw coming very slowly the first beginning of her emancipation. No material change alone can affect her, it is a spiritual change, a change of ideas concerning her and her place in human life that we plead for. She has been property while force ruled, and will ever be while that continues; she can only begin to be an independent soul as Might ceases to be Right.

Very slowly, all too slowly for our impatient hearts, brother, that change comes. It begins to be intelligence and not force that has the kingship of mankind.

Chapter Four

AN OLD MAN there once was who lived at peace in a land where there was much sunshine. The kindly fruit that grew in his garden fed and clothed him and fulfilled his simple needs. He worked in his garden, and when he rested he read wise books and pondered on them. He had for his companion a bird, a bird of marvellous beauty and of the sweetest song, and as the old man worked in his garden the bird hopped about him and pecked its meal of grubs, or sat upon the handle of his spade and sang. And in the evenings when the old man rested the bird sat on a branch above him and poured out a stream of music wonderful to hear, its body quivering with rapture, its throat thrilling with sweetness. And there was a king's minister who heard the fame of the bird, and came on a long journey to offer the old man money for the beautiful creature.

The old man received him courteously, and heard his offer with surprise.

"My bird is not for sale," he said.

The king's minister wondered at him, for the money offered was a great sum. He looked about him at the old man's small house and garden. "You could do great things with such money," he said. "You could wear fine clothes, have servants and a rich house, and of the books you like to read a great store lining a splendid room. You could look from your windows and all the land that you could see would be your own."

The old man listened while he spoke. "I have enough clothes and food, and my pleasant garden is large enough to grow all that I want. I have but two eyes and I can read no more books than those I have even if I owned many thousands. If I had those other things I should not have my bird. My bird gives me more pleasure than any of those things."

The rich man still persisted.

"But my bird is not for sale," said the old man, gently explaining.

Never is any thing one's own unless it is not for sale.

* * *

This morning, little brother, I have seen the beauty that draws near to tears, the beauty that leads straight to prayer.

I wandered far afield, very early. The sun was not high enough to warm me, and after standing a moment on the terrace I went back into the hall, drew a silken coverlet from the couch I had slept upon and wrapped it about my body. But presently as I walked and ran, I grew warm, I hung my splendid garment on a tree, and went on in the sunshine without it. It was about a mile from here perhaps that I saw through the trees of a wood a filmy mist of blue. Suddenly I remembered the bluebells of England. It grew more definite, more intense as I came nearer; it spread and flowed out into a miraculous lake of blue at whose edge I stood at last. Above the myriads of flowers hung the tender green of young trees, shading and deepening their marvellous colour. The arching bells rose to my knees, away in one corner a little streak of white bells ran like a laugh among the perfect blue. The air was filled with their scent. There was an utter silence there; no bird sang; it was as if all nature stood breathless at their beauty. It stirred my heart as nothing has stirred it here, so that presently I knelt and prayed. I prayed to God that he would let all men see the loveliness of his world and of one another, and so kneeling I put my arms about the flowers that clustered near me, gathered them to my breast and kissed them, and let them go again.

* * *

Do you then live? – is it possible that you live, little brother?

Last night I awoke before the dawn, and while the pale cold light grew slowly out of the darkness I lay awake for a long time, almost unhappily. I can say so gaily now, I was unhappy. For it came to me that you were but a thing I had imagined, that not only should I never in my life see you but that since I had myself made you I could not even think of you as living somewhere beyond my reach. Nowhere did you live, nowhere in heaven or earth did you exist, little brother. I was alone, and this pretence of you was a talking to myself, and that was all. How, I thought in the cold clearness of knowledge that had come upon me, could I keep you longer even as delusion? You who have become so real to me that you are almost a visible presence, slipped from my mind like a ghost. Little brother, it was as if you had died there in the grey dawn, or worse, for I knew that you had never lived.

Then – little brother, mate of my heart! – I slept.

As I slept the sun must have arisen and poured upon me, for I slept lightly, dreaming myself lying there in a warm golden haze. And then, you came, *you*, little brother. Your face was dim against the sunshine that blazed behind you, the tips of your hair flamed and made a shining corona about your head. As if you knew the chill unhappiness that had crept into my heart, you came out of the golden light, put your arms about me, and kissed me, my beloved, tenderly upon my lips.

* * *

All this day has been made wonderful by that dream of you in the early morning. It is indeed as if you had suddenly come to life, for since I saw you in my dream you are known to me face and body as you are, as clearly as if I had spent days by your side. Before today you were a faintly seen figure that came out in scraps of clearness like a developing photograph, with eyes that shone out and that I knew, with hands I had seen and grasped, the line of a shoulder. And now with that dream you have rushed to my eyes. You are like no one I ever met on earth, you are yourself. You are a living creature somewhere, and you are just over the limit of my reach.

Where?

Are you in dreams – is it only in my dream life that I shall meet you and know you? I feel that you are here now, just beyond my apprehension, that my eyes have to be so little different to see you before me, that least change in my ears and I should hear you speaking. You are perhaps speaking to me and I am deaf, gesturing to me and I am blind. I reach out and touch nothing, but is it nothing that I touch? I lay my head upon my arms on this table before me – does not your cheek touch my shoulder? Just over the edge of my senses you are, perhaps I beat my hands against you now and do not know it. What will happen to us, little brother, what can happen? I strain to you, I do my utmost; are you too straining – to break through the barriers to me?

The light is fading out of the room as I write, the friendly shadows creep forward and cling about my knee. I gaze into the dusk and fancy that I begin to see your face. My heart beats quicker, those dark spots are the shadows round your eyes, I see your shoulder, your arm… At last! I spring up and cry out, for it is you!…

No, – it is not you.

* * *

Do you know that there is a game I play with you, little brother? Have you found me out in it, I wonder? It is a hide and seek game, and some day, clever as you are at hiding, – oh no one cleverer – I shall catch you. We play it like this. I lie down perhaps, shut my eyes and pretend to fall asleep. Breathe deeply so that you think me sound asleep and you get careless of hiding from me. You move about quite close to me, I can hear – and then *quick!* I open my eyes. If I saw you by the most fleeting shade, if you did not vanish at that instant, I should win the game and you would lose it, little brother. Or I sit reading a book – absorbed in the book, letting my lips move with words in the concentration of my reading, and *flash!* I turn my head to catch you behind me. Or I walk through the woods, a mile or more. I walk and never turn my head and then when you've forgotten my existence, because you are watching the deer scamper away in the glade, or the rabbit running and a hundred woodland things, or the sun is hot and makes you drowsy, then, *then* is my chance. I turn suddenly, and because you are quick as I have been, you have slipped behind a bush.

I search and search, with a pounce behind the tree and my arm flings towards that – [but your shadow is when you are deep in the bracken, crouching.] I see your feet among the brown stems – I plunge in and laugh to find you have gone from me again. I laugh at your cleverness, little brother; it is a merry game. But you play the game too well, little brother.

I sit here in the evening and write to you again. The sun is setting beyond the trees, its last long beam shines through the tall windows at the end of this great hall and lies straight and golden along the polished floor like a carpet unrolled to my very feet. They were intense and burning beams, they mellow and grow paler moment by moment. Very soon they will melt away and I shall be left in the dusk. It is the end of another day, my most dear, the beginning of another night.

I have played no game of hide and seek with you today, I have not looked for you nor sought to surprise you. I have walked without turning my head, I have sat with my face covered with my hands. So have I thought to beguile you near, for beyond all else now I crave for you close at my side. Little brother, I do not care if I do not see you, but I implore you to come near, to lie close by me. You have done that before, often I have felt you near me as I write, felt you eager for me to write faster. Sometimes, any time in the day, when I have been thinking of quite other things, I have been startled by the sense of you close by me. There was once, you remember it, my lover – I cried out, for suddenly your arms were about me, your cheek upon my cheek. You know the intense happiness of your approach for me, daily you have come oftener, come nearer, given me some fresh sense of your sweet invasion. If you will do that, so that I feel your nearness, so that I live in the warmth of your body, I will hunt you no longer, no longer try to trick you into sight. Have you no pity, little brother, seeing me quiver with such longing?

Pity, pity? Forgive me the reproach. My beloved, you must be one straining agony of pity for me, seeing me here.

There are garments here that become you well, when you choose to wear them. They lie in five chests of golden brown, sweet-smelling wood, that stand in a smaller room out of the great hall. Every morning I choose clothes for you, sometimes the most gorgeous I can find, sometimes things soft and simple. There is a great mantle of dark orange silk and gold thread woven in a splendid pattern and belted about the waist with silver and emeralds that you must know I love to see you in, for I put it out so often for your wear. A close-fitting garment of blue furred with the softest grey fur, is one that suits you well, and there is a regal cloak of crimson damasked silk lined with purple, with a magnificent silver and blue patterning for a border that I have never given you yet. But very often I dress you in plain white. Each morning

I choose your garments for you, gather them in my arms, and turning from the room throw them behind me on the floor in disarray and go, and never come back to that room until the following morning. I think all day of the secret of that room which I must not surprise, the secret that you have taken the garments and left the room bare. But the next day, there they are again, thrown down upon the floor, and I smooth them out and fold them up and choose you others. The sun shines in through the windows and streams down upon the floor, lighting the lovely colours of the stuffs to their richest. I kneel beside them holding them close, holding close the silken folds that have but a moment before left your body – your warmth lingers in them yet, and here, *here*, clinging to the silk, I find suddenly – oh marvel of joy! a fragment of dry leaf! Then you were in the beech wood yesterday, for I know those leaves and where they lie.

(It did not blow through the window here.)

* * *

Last night, Beloved, I wept.

For the first time since I came here, to my paradise on earth, I wept bitterest tears. For I have held a secret from you these many days.

I am intolerably, intolerably lonely. I did not know, I never dreamt, how lonely I could be. When I first came to this place the beauty filled my heart and mind, I thought that beauty would be all sufficient. I did not know that it was not, and it was not or should I have created you? But, having created you, I was satisfied again for a time. Then I noted you becoming less a spirit; my mind persistently materialised your body, and at last I knew your imagined face, your imagined body as I might know someone seen often and a little distantly, who passes daily in the street. And now, I come to the last need, the final hunger. No more is your spiritual presence enough, I want to see you with my eyes, touch you with my hands, hear you, breathe your breath. I must have you so. I cannot talk to you, a Spirit, any more. I have nothing to say to you on this tablet save to cry to you and cry to you, to come. Cry to you to come, you whom I have said was here. I see nothing, but the void place that you ought to fill. I think of nothing but my need for you. I am alone for the first time, because you are not here, my embodied beloved.

This night I cannot cease to hope for your coming. Again and again I go to one window or another, and lean out into the warm dusk, watching. I lie on the dear earth I have so loved, and no thoughts will come to me but thoughts of you. The rustle of a bird, a trembling rustle among the leaves, and I start up, awaiting you. I come back to reality, and discover myself thus standing taut, with beating expectant heart, hands outcurved to that rustle, that little shiver of sound that is not [you] is brushed aside by my mind like an intrusive veil. If I were to go through that wood – down that allée? Had I been there just now, beneath those giant ferns, when the moonlight touched the reeds by the water, should I have seen your face shine out of the darkness, your body of silver as you stepped out into the light? Too late; I have come too late, the moonlight has swept away into the trees. But you were here? Surely that was beautiful enough to bring you here?

Or are you now, *now*, passing along the terrace – thought of madness! – while I linger for you here.

* * *

I have been about the island for hours, calling you aloud with my voice.

"Beloved!...

"Beloved!..."

The island is empty. I am alone!

The End

H.G. Wells's Introduction to *The Book of Catherine Wells* (1928)

§1

MY WIFE WHEN SHE DIED had written and published a few short stories and she had collaborated with my youngest son in one or two others. But what was printed was but a small part of the amount she wrote. I knew something of her writing, but not very much, because it was her desire to succeed independently of my influence. It was her desire to write and succeed as herself. Her literary activities were not due to any urgent necessity in her nature. She was not compelled to expression by any uncontrollable drive within. Indeed she was by temperament rather reserved than expressive. But living as she did in an atmosphere of continual literary activity, where statement in words as finely chosen as possible had a special importance, her natural inhibition of comment even to herself, was gradually broken down and she began to write first, I think, to see what it was she herself was really thinking and feeling about life, and then to convey this, not perhaps to the world at large, but to some imagined closely sympathetic reader. She did not write for me, though she did her best to make me feel and to feel herself that I was not excluded. She shrank from publicity; nevertheless she began to think more and more of publication. She sent her work to various periodicals from a different address and through various agents so as not to be identified with me. Her imaginary reader never materialised and I think would not have been particularly welcome if he had materialised. She was seeking expression for something that she realised she herself did not completely grasp and probably she would have been violently repelled by any assurances of understanding.

This shy and withdrawn authorship of hers began quite early in her married life but it became much more extensive and deliberate in later years. She sought her own proper forms and phrasing with peculiar effort because for the first twenty years of our life together she had been accustomed to act as my secretary and typist, and so her mind had acquired many habits and prepossessions about method that she shook off with difficulty. Yet I think the reader of the pages that follow will agree with me that she did at last achieve a delicately characteristic style. She has given in this series of stories and in these scraps of verse the quality of a mood, a state of mind, a phase of personality rather intangible, inaggressive yet resistant, not forcible in any way but clear, clean, sweet and very, very fine in its texture. This aspect of her personality is pervaded by a certain wilful melancholy; it is in the mood of very still landscapes, bright yet touched by the softness of evening, and pity broods upon it. Desire is there, but it is not active aggressive desire. It is a desire for beauty and sweet companionship. There is a lover, never seen, never verified, elusively at the heart of this desire. Frustration haunts this desire. And also fear is never far away, an elvish fear like the fear of a child's dream. Such is the mood in which nearly all of these pieces were written. Whenever my wife sat down alone to write it is manifest that very speedily that phase of her mind returned. I doubt if it was even a prevalent phase in her complex and subtle composition. But it was rooted very deeply in her character, it must I think have been the normal atmosphere of her girlish reveries, and however overlaid and set aside in her actively living hours it came to the surface as soon as she was alone with herself.

I have put forth this book under the name of Catherine Wells, with set intention; it was the name she used invariably in her writings, but it was not her full name (which was Amy Catherine) nor was it the name by which she was best known to her friends. I had thrust upon her and she had been ready and willing to wear for everyday use and our common purposes a congenial presentation of herself that we had christened 'Jane.' To most of our friends and acquaintances she was Jane and nothing else. They hardly caught a glimpse of Catherine. Jane was a person of much greater practical ability than Catherine. She was the tangible Catherine and made decisions freely, while Catherine herself stayed in the background amiably aloof. Jane ordered a house well and was an able 'shopper'; she helped people in difficulties and stood no nonsense from the plumber. Her medicine cupboard at home was prepared for all occasions. She had gone through a Red Cross course so as to be competent in domestic emergencies. She had a file of shop addresses where things needed could be bought. Her garden was a continually glowing success and she was a member of the Royal Horticultural Society and kept a garden book and a diary to check and improve her methods. Every year the gardeners were packed off to the Chelsea show. She transacted and invested for her unhelpful and uncertain husband, and she was wise and wary in his affairs and a searchlight of honesty and clear but kindly illumination in his world. Nonsensical people fled her quiet eye. One particular sort of nonsensical people she had dealt with specially and reduced to orderly subjection and those were the vague race of translators and would-be translators who entangle and obscure authors in foreign lands. For them she had devised a method and a standard agreement and built up a system of relationship abroad that no literary agent could better. That was Jane.

Certainly there was such a Jane about in my life. I cannot tell how much I owe her. But indeed my wife was neither Jane, which was her working and practically developed self, nor Catherine, which was the name of her personal reverie and of her literary life. She was both of them and many more as the lights about her changed.

§2

To recall the facets of this being, whose Catherine personality is presented by these fine spirited and, to my mind, very charming writings, is to go over the tale of adventures we have had together for nearly five and thirty years. I have been more retrospective in the past six months than in all my life before. I give here a portrait of her dating from about the time of our first meeting. That is Miss Robbins, her first facet. There one sees the person who came into the cramming classes I conducted in practical biology, for candidates in the London Bachelor of Science examinations. She was wearing mourning then for her father, who had recently been killed by accident on the railway; he had left no property worth speaking of and she was struggling to secure a degree in order to become a schoolmistress and earn a living for her mother and herself.

I thought her then a very sweet and valiant little figure indeed, with her schoolgirl satchel of books and a very old-fashioned unwieldy microscope someone had lent her, and I soon came to think her the most wonderful thing in my life. I was a crude, hard young man in those days, who had got a fairly good London University degree by way of a studentship at the Royal College of Science, I was widely but irregularly read, suggestions from Shelley and Huxley interwove with strands from Carlyle, Morris and Heny George, and my worldly and social experience was somewhere about the level of my Mr Lewisham's.[1] I was at war with the world and by no means sure that I should win. I held extreme religious, social and political opinions that shut me out from ordinary school work, and I found a satisfaction in beating the regular University teachers in their own examinations. Very soon this new pupil became the embodiment of all the understanding and quality I desired in life. We talked – over our frogs and rabbits. The cramming organisation for which I worked had published an expansion of my teaching notes as a *Text-Book of Biology* copiously but blottesquely illustrated by myself. She drew so much more firmly and clearly than I did, that I got her to redraw all my diagrams for a second edition. Our friendship grew swiftly beyond the bounds of friendship and I was amazed to find that she could care for me as much as I did for her. When I told her I had smashed a kidney at football and lost a large

1 In *Love and Mr Lewisham* (1900). Explanatory notes have been added to this Introduction by the editors.

part of one lung, that seemed to her merely a reason for immediate action. I do not think either of us expected to live ten years. But we meant to live every minute there was for us to live. We were the most desperate of lovers; we launched ourselves upon our life together with less than fifty pounds between us and absolute disaster, and we pulled through. We never begged nor borrowed, we never cheated, and we worked and paid our way first into a position of security and then to real prosperity.

And I seem to remember now that we did it with a very great deal of gaiety.

As I look back over those early years together, I find the grave little figure in mourning whom one auspicious afternoon I had discovered awaiting me in my laboratory, changing by the most imperceptible degrees into the companion of an easier life in a broadening world. Jane developed and Catherine began to appear. Thirty years ago we 'went abroad' for the first time. It was our first holiday and a plain intimation that we were getting the upper hand in our struggle for existence. We went straight through to Rome where George Gissing had promised to show us the sights. Rome in those days was still mellow and beautiful. Afterwards we went on alone to Naples and Capri and came back by way of Florence to England. My wife could be not only the most trustworthy and active of helpers but also the most appreciative of petted companions, and on this and many other journeys work was set aside and I managed the trunks and the luggage and she beamed happily upon the subservient spectacle. We armed ourselves with sheets of the Siegfried map[2] and went to walk in Switzerland, not to climb but seeking snowy and lonely paths. She fell in love with the Alps and we planned and carried out long tramps over the passes and down into Italy. We would slip away from our home at Folkestone for a fortnight or so, going often in June before the main holiday crowd and just as the inns were reopening. So we found spring flowers and unspoilt smiles.

The passion for high places took hold of her. I was never much of a climber because of my restricted lung and kidney surfaces, and after the war I was no good at it at all, but then my sons were growing up and she would go with them, developing a greater ambition every year. All I saw of that side of her after the war was the triumphant snapshots she sent me. She would toil through long excursions on foot or upon skis, never going very fast or brilliantly but never giving up, a little indefatigable smiling figure, dusted with the snow of her not infrequent tumbles. I would write to her from among my agaves and olive orchards and she would answer from her snows, and afterwards we would trace together upon those nice brown explicit Swiss maps, the expeditions she had made or still proposed to make.

2 *The Topographic Atlas of Switzerland* (1870–1926).

§3

We had no children for some years because we thought our outlook too precarious to inflict its risks upon other lives than our own. But when we had built a house for ourselves, got a thousand pounds put by and I had found an insurance company that did not regard my little misadventures with lung and kidney too pessimistically, we thought it time to launch a family. We had two sons. She fought for the life of the first of them and for her own life for more than four and twenty dreadful hours. She seemed a very little fragile thing in that battle and then it was, I fear, that the seed of her death was sown in her.

But now beside Jane and Catherine, a third main strand of her personality became important. Our house became a home when the voice of that hopeful young biologist, Mr G.P. Wells, pervaded it,[3] and I suppose it was his practice which determined that the new aspect of my wife should be called 'Mummy.' But the real importance of Mummy came gradually. In the early years of our parentage very much of the care of our children could be entrusted to a skilful nurse and a capable governess. My wife watched over our boys' temperatures and behaviour and we met them for perhaps an hour a

3 George Philip Wells would become Professor of Zoology at the University of London and co-author, with H.G. Wells and Julian Huxley, of *The Science of Life* (1930).

day and saw to it that they learnt to speak plainly, count straight and draw freely, and liked us as playfellows. But as they became schoolboys there developed much more companionship and intimacy between them and Mummy. They brought home their friends from school and Cambridge and Mummy became the centre of a bright fresh world of youths and young men.

A marked characteristic of this Mummy, which neither Jane nor Catherine displayed, was considerable histrionic ability. Mummy in her later years was a most gay, inventive and amusing actress. Many of our friends must remember the funny and yet consistent little figures she could evoke; her terrible detective with one wildly glaring eye, between his turned-up coat-collar and his turned-down hat, her series of venomous old ladies, from pew-openers and charwomen to duchesses, with their astonishing and convulsing asides, her queenly personages with the strangest of Victorian hats and a sublime dignity, her Mrs. Noah, murmuring her secret anxieties about 'the cost of it all,' and 'how-*ever*' she would 'keep 'em all clean,' her anxious maternal care of a succession of enormous and generally unsuitable children.

Charades had played an exhilarating rôle in our lives for many years. In the beginning we had had to fight the world very much alone; we had had few acquaintances, and fewer friends, and kept little company. We talked a lot of nonsense and had many jokes to help ourselves through those austerer days. Of that there is no telling. But as soon as we began to prosper and meet miscellaneous people we relaxed into social play very gladly. It was in '97 or '98 in a little house we occupied at Sandgate that we found congenial next-door neighbours, a Mr Arthur Popham and his wife, with two jolly children, and a coming and going of pleasant cousins and other friends, and could for the first time 'play the fool' and release our human disposition to mimicry and mockery in a roomful of people. 'Dumb crambo' was the earliest form of our dramatic expression. Then for some reason we took to shadow shows. These shadow shows dropped out of our practice long since, but in those days they were of sufficient importance to make us stipulate, when we built ourselves Spade House at Sandgate,[4] for an archway in the middle of a room which would give sufficient depth behind the white sheet for expanding and diminishing shadows. Afterwards we turned to charades, dumb or spoken, to impersonations of various sorts, to burlesques of current plays and to suddenly invented plays of our own. Sometimes we did scenes of travel or 'moral instruction,' scenes illustrating the unpleasantness of wickedness and the charms of virtue. Often we drew upon history, sacred or profane. The boys grew up into a tradition of rapidly improvised

4 The Wellses lived at Spade House, designed by C.F.A. Voysey, from December 1900 to August 1909.

drama, and took an increasingly important share in this fun, and Mummy got better at it and better.

I turn over my memories of these freakish quaint affairs, into which people threw themselves with astonishing zest. A great melodrama at Sandgate, with a Thames Embankment scene and a doped race-horse (Popham was the front half) all complete, returns to me out of the early days; Ford Madox Hueffer was the sole croupier at a green table in a marvellous Monte Carlo scene and Jane was a gambling duchess of entirely reckless habits. Then come certain travel pictures at Hampstead,[5] with H.W. Nevinson as the most Teutonic of railway porters proclaiming the trains at the waiting-room door, and Jane as a greatly encumbered mother with an equally tiny Dolly Radford[6] as her nurse, and a string of vast, crumby, bun-eating children in white socks, bare calves, straw hats on the backs of their heads and spades and buckets, and no end of luggage.[7] One of these infants, I remember, was

5 In August 1909 the family moved to 17 Church Row, Hampstead.

6 Caroline Maitland ('Dollie Radford') was an English writer and poet. Dollie, who sported daringly short hair, was a frequent guest at the Wells family home, together with her son, the writer and doctor Maitland Radford.

7 Here and in the pages that follow, Wells names a number of guests and family friends, ranging from well-known writers such as Ford Madox Ford (Hueffer) and Arnold Bennett, from entertainers such as Lillah McCarthy and Charlie Chaplin, and from politicians such as Lord Olivier and Philip Snowden to many lesser-known personages. We have highlighted some of the figures who today are not so well known.

my friend E.S.P. Haynes and another was W.R. Titterton,[8] and when at last the proper train was announced, Jane brought down the house by turning to Dolly and saying, with a finger pointing to Haynes, "*You* carry Siegfried," and waiting with a testy hatred on her face for her order to be obeyed.

Lord Olivier was always a great success with us, playing the infant Moses with touching realism to Jane's Pharaoh's daughter, and also doing a very mighty Sampson with a sheepskin mat of hair. The present, from Philip Guedalla, of a formidable-looking iron thing for cooking griddle cakes turned our thoughts for a time to hell. 'Nancy Parsons,' who is now Lady Mercy Dean, queened it among the damned and the rôle Jane invented for herself was a quietly peevish grumbler with a book of regulations and a tariff of torment, of whom the presiding fiend went in manifest horror. "But, *Sir*!" she urged, finger on the regulation in question. It was a quite new terror added to hell.

But I could fill a whole book with such memories. From first to last hundreds of people must have passed through the fires of these charades of ours. The figures crowd upon me, peeping out one behind the other,

8 On rainy days, the lawyer and writer E[dmund]. S[idney]. P[ollock]. Haynes would frequently get down on the floor with Wells's sons and play floorgames. W[illiam]. R[ichard]. Titterton was a writer, poet and journalist and biographer of G.K. Chesterton.

like that mighty constellation of stars, painted upon the drop scene of the London Coliseum – Arnold Bennett, Sir Frederick Keeble, Lillah M'Carthy,[9] Basil Dean, Noel Coward, Roger Fry as a skeleton with white paper bones on black tights, Clutton Brock[10] as a Prussian general, Philip Snowden (his first and only dramatic appearance) very wicked as an elderly raja dealing with concession hunters, and still more wicked in a crimson skull-cap as a Pope, and Frank Hodges in a white apron and with an armful of tankards as the unscrupulous landlord of an unscrupulous inn. The late George Mair was a wonderful missionary of the less attractive kind and Frank Swinnerton a terrible man about town. Sir Harry Johnston[11] created a marvellous Noah and Charlie Chaplin created a still more marvellous Noah on entirely different lines. But every figure I recall brings yet others with it. I cannot even name a tithe of them. And through all this tangle of cheery burlesque goes my wife, gravely radiant and indefatigable. She had accumulated presses full of gaily coloured 'dressing-up' garments and her instinct for effect was unerring.

---

9 Lillah McCarthy, whose surname is misspelled, was an actor, theatrical manager and suffragette.

10 After practising law for a number of years, Arthur Clutton-Brock worked for *The Times* and became an authority on Shelley. A pencil sketch of him is in the National Portrait Gallery, drawn in 1916 by William Rothenstein.

11 As well as being a writer, Sir Harry Johnston held various key governing positions in Africa.

All this charade business she made at last entirely hers. At first I suppose I supplied some initiatives, but she was so much more full and thorough about it, that gradually I dropped out of any share in the management and became a delighted spectator. I could never tell what odd little novelty she had plotted when she came on. She never lost the gift of surprising me into laughter and admiration. I cannot say how completely I feel now that this quaint and various volume of happy nonsense has closed for me for ever.

It has closed for ever because it was her life so much more than mine. The old place may continue as the home of a new generation, but for me now it is no more than a nest of memories.[12] I could write on, in the same tone of happy reminiscence, of a score of other aspects of that home life she created and which was so distinctively hers. Charades were after all only the typical fun of a great variety of kindred relaxations. She had a passion for improvised dancing, and we had a big barn to dance in; and she and my boys produced several plays in the village theatre. Our week-ends would gather the most incongruous people; they would arrive on Saturday afternoon a little aloof and distrustful of one another; they would depart on Monday magically fused, having 'dressed up,' danced, acted, walked, played, and helped get the Sunday supper. She never dominated, but she

12 In fact Wells would sell Easton Glebe in 1930.

pervaded the place with such a sense of goodwill, such an unqualified ardour for happiness, that the coldest warmed and the stiffest relaxed.

All that was in the normal order of things less than a year ago. I recall the bright atmosphere of coming and going, the variety of visitors about the tea-tables in the garden house, the lit windows at night sending out shafts of acid green light upon the lawns and bushes, the warmth of movement and laughter. The curtain has come down on all that pleasant scene and never more shall I revive it. It has gone now as far beyond recall as our first shy talks in our smaller classroom at Red Lion Square or our valiant struggles up the steep passes to which the exciting zigzags of the Siegfried map had lured us.

'What fun we have had!' wrote one old friend, and that must be the epitaph upon her social self.

§4

With all this, I realise, I am telling little that is essential about my wife. I am writing about facets, of this aspect and of that aspect she presented to the world. I am skirting round a personality which was in its intimacy extraordinarily shy and elusive. Jane Wells and 'Mummy' and the mistress of Easton Glebe were known to scores of friends, but my knowledge went deeper. There was something behind these smiling masks that Catherine Wells was seeking to express, and did at last in some of these brief pieces express perfectly. In the silent light of the reading-lamp, writing what might never be printed, she could search for her very self.

I have told of how we two defied the current wisdom of the world and won, with Shelley and Huxley and a profound contempt for the timidities and hypocrisies of the time among our common inspirations. What is more difficult to tell is our slow discovery of the profoundest temperamental differences between us and of the problems these differences created for us. Fundamental to my wife's nature was a passion for happiness and lovely things. She was before everything else gentle and sweet. She worshipped beauty. For her, beauty was something very definite, a precious jewel to be discovered and treasured. For me beauty is incidental, so surely a part of things that one need not be directly concerned about it. I am a far less stable creature than she was, with a driving quality that holds my instabilities together. I have more drive than strength, and little patience; I am hasty and incompetent about much of the detailed business of life because I put too large a proportion of my available will and energy into issues that dominate me. I have to overwork, with all the penalties of overworking in loss of grace and finish, to get my work done. In all this we were in the completest contrast and inevitably we strained against each other.

I think that young people nowadays must get a very considerable help in their adjustments from the suggestions of modern psychological science. Its analysis of motive and behaviour makes enormously for understanding and charity. But in our time psychology was still mainly a shallow and unserviceable intellectualism. We had to work out our common problem very largely by the light nature had given us. And I am appalled to reflect how much of the patience, courage and sacrifice of our compromises came from her. Never once do I remember her romancing a situation into false issues. We had two important things in our favour, first that we had a common detestation not only of falsehood but of falsity, and secondly, that we had the sincerest affection and respect for each other. There again the feat was hers. It was an easy thing for me to keep my faith in her sense of fair play and her perfect generosity. She never told a lie. To the end I would have taken her word against all other witnesses in the world. But she managed to sustain her belief that I was worth living for, and that was a harder task, while I made my way through a tangle of moods and impulses that were quite outside her instinctive sympathy. She stuck to me so sturdily that in the end I stuck to myself. I do not know what I should have been without her. She stabilised my life. She gave it a home and dignity. Not without incessant watchfulness and toil. I have a hundred memories of an indefatigable typist carrying on her work in spite of a back-ache; of a grave judicial proof-reader in a garden shelter, determined that no slovenliness should escape her; of a resolute little person, clear-headed but untrained in business method, battling steadfastly with the perplexities of our accumulating accounts and keeping her grip on them.

Our temperamental differences were reflected in our convictions. Though she helped and sustained me with her utmost strength and loyalty, I do not think she believed very strongly in my beliefs. She accepted them, but she could have done without them. I am extravagantly obsessed by the thing that might be, and impatient with the present; I want to go ahead of Father Time with a scythe of my own; I have a faith in human possibilities which has become the core of my life; but she was much more acquiescent and attentive to the thing that is. She was more realist than I am and less creative. She was more aware of the loveliness of things and the sorrowfulness and cruelty in things. She admired more than I did, she kept and cherished more than I did, and she pitied much more than I did. Her philosophy was more stoical than mine, because she could neither hope nor be angry in my fashion. And when that is understood, then I think you have the key to the feeling of wistful loveliness that touches such stories here as 'The Emerald,' 'The Beautiful House' and 'The Fugitives,' with their peculiar beauty.

Pity and habitual helpfulness were very characteristic of her. She was watchful of the feelings and humiliations and perplexities of everyone about her. She was alive to the discomforts caused by neglected teeth or troublesome minor ailments to poor people, and she would seize every opportunity of having matters put right for them. The timely good dentist or the timely good oculist may change a faltering life to a happy and successful one, and more than once or twice she saw that it did. And she would think of agreeable presents – a small motor car, a gramophone, a pianola, for households where these particular things were just inaccessible. She became a very skilful giver of presents; a timely holiday for a fagged worker, a new dress for someone confronted by a social demand. She was always trying to find the perfect present that would help deaf people, but that is still to be invented. After the war we produced a book, the *Outline of History*. We did not expect it to be a profitable book, but we felt it had to be done, and there was no one in sight to do it. We were not particularly equipped for the task and it meant huge toil for both of us. We would work at Easton long after midnight, making notes from piles of books or writing up and typing notes. But this task turned out far more profitable to us than anyone could have dreamt. I do not think my wife ever thought for a moment of any personal use to be made of this enrichment. She liked people in a cheerful mood and a pleasant receptive home, but she had no trace of social ambition in her nature. She liked pretty clothes – and sometimes pretty clothes are costly – but she lacked entirely the instinct for display. She had hardly any jewels and never wanted any. But now that we really had surplus funds she made her obscure and tender benefactions more systematic. Probably of very many of them I know nothing, for we kept our money in a common account, and the administration was completely in her hands. She would consult me about any expenditure that was 'serious,' but not about smaller things when she felt sure I would approve. And moreover, for occasions when my harder heart might not be in agreement, she had a fund of her own.

Pity, generosity, the love of beautiful things, of noble thoughts and liberal actions! How fine she was in the unobtrusive silences of her nature! And above all she had courage. It was destined to be tested to the utmost. For five months of gathering discomfort she faced an inevitable death and her heart did not fail her.

§5

Death we had to watch drawing nearer to her for five months, but the first intimation of that grim advance came to us as an absolute surprise. We had always thought that things would be the other way about; that I was more likely to die first and perhaps unexpectedly. So we had arranged our affairs as far as possible to ease the blow of my withdrawal. Our home at Easton was so contrived that if instead of one of my frequent absences – for every winter for some time I have gone abroad after the sunshine – there came an absence with no end to it, everything would go on, as it had always gone on. In January of this last year she was with our youngest son and his betrothed at Arosa and I was in the easier air of the Riviera. In March we were together in Paris for a pleasant week, when I gave a lecture at the Sorbonne and such charming people as Madame Curie and Professor Perrin made much of her. She had looked forward to that visit and it was characteristic of her that she secretly took a course of lessons to revive her French before coming and so surprised everyone by her fluency. We came back to London and she seemed a little out of sorts. Neither of us thought that there was anything seriously wrong with her. I went abroad again for a motoring holiday, but before I left I made her promise to see a doctor.

My elder son departed to France also, on his honeymoon. We came back post haste to the telegram of my younger son. She had gone through an exploratory operation without letting me know anything of its nature and the surgeons had discovered that she had inoperable cancer, very far gone and diffused, that left her hardly six months more to live.

She knew that quite clearly when I returned to her. She had questioned the doctors and obliged them to tell her. Seeing that they seemed sorry, they told me, she did her best to comfort them. "I know you cannot help it," she said. "There is nothing for you to be unhappy about."

We tried a foolish X-ray cure of which the least said the better. Then we sat down to make the best of life before the shadow reached her. And so clear and steadfast was her mind that we did contrive to win interest and happiness out of a great proportion of those hundred and fifty days. At first we hoped for a considerable recovery of strength but she never really got over the exhaustion caused by the X-ray while she was still weakened by her operation. For a few weeks she could walk up and down stairs at Easton, but then she had to be carried in a chair. We found a wonderful chair for out-of-doors, with big wheels with pneumatic tyres and good springs, and in this she could go quite considerable distances, into my neighbour's gardens at Easton Lodge and about the Park. For a time she could endure a well-sprung car and we paid a round of calls upon our friends and even went off for some days to an hotel at Felixstowe, when she had a craving to see the sea. The garden she had made at Easton flowered to perfection. The friends she cared for came to see her and she would hold a kind of reception on the tennis courts and laugh and applaud.

She read abundantly and we got a lot out of music, bringing all the resources of the gramophone world to her. Some of the new records are marvellously delicate and expressive. We would sit about together in the sunshine listening to Beethoven, Bach, Purcell and Mozart, and later, as she grew weaker and less capable of sustained attention, we would sit side by side in silence in the dusk and find loveliness and interest in watching a newly-lit wood fire burn up from the first blue flickerings.

She put all her affairs in order clearly and methodically. Day by day she weakened but her mind never lost its integrity. It is one of the dreadful possibilities of such an illness that the increasing poison in the blood poisons the mind so that it is afflicted with strange fears and unnatural hostilities, and for that last horror I tried to prepare my mind. Nothing of that sort darkened those last days. But the lucid times contracted. More and more of the twenty-four hours was taken up in sleep and drugged endurance.

At first, she would be very gay at her breakfast when I went in to her and the nurses would have her about in the garden by eleven or so. Then came a time when she began the day by coming down to lunch and slept through the afternoon, and had only between teatime and bedtime for animation. She wasted and became very thin, but with a strange emaciated prettiness that somehow recalled her girlish face. She shrank to be a very little thing indeed. She was sedulous not to look haggard or dreadful or be in any way distressing to those who saw her. She spent an hour or more with her hairdresser from London within a month of her death, having her still pretty hair waved and put in order. She dressed with care until she could dress no longer.

To the very last she 'carried on.' She was ordering new roses to replace some that had failed in her garden within a fortnight of the end. On September the 24th she had a tree felled that darkened the servants' bedrooms, and watched the felling. It was her last time in the garden. I was not there; I had gone to London to fetch a specialist from Paris, who might add, I thought, to her comfort. The nurses told me that when the tree crashed she turned away and would not look.

A great weariness crept upon her. She became more and more ready for the night, when an opiate put her into a contented sleep. She liked life still, but with a relaxing hold. She told me she was ready now to sleep for ever. She was very anxious I should not grieve for her and that I should feel sure I had made her happy. One thing held her still to life. She was very fond of our younger son Frank and the sweetheart he had chosen in his undergraduate days, and she wanted to see them married. The three of them had spent some cheerful times together in Switzerland and Italy. She ordered a wedding breakfast for the occasion. She would not let anyone else do that. She could not come to the church but she hoped she might be carried down to sit at table. It was to be upon the seventh of October. That date reminded her of the birthday of a little niece and a present she had bought for her in the Burlington Arcade and stowed away. She had that hunted out and sent off. Then on the sixth she began to sink very rapidly. She lay still and we thought she was insensible. But she heard the sound of my son's car as it came under her window on the way to the garage. He had come back from his work in London for his wedding on the morrow. She had been waiting for that familiar sound. She revived. She knew him and her weak caress fluttered over him and she said something indistinct to him about the wedding. Then her attention faded out. She spoke no more, she became a breathing body from which all token of recognition had departed, and an hour or so later, with her unresponsive hand in mine, she ceased to breathe.

The wedding seemed so much the completion of her life that we resolved to carry it out. We changed the hour from eleven to nine so as to avoid any gathering of people. We drove down through the morning sunshine to the old parish church of Dunmow to meet the bride and her parents, and after the ceremony the two young people went off together into the world and I and my elder son and his wife returned to our home.

The white and purple Michaelmas daisies were glorious that October morning. It seemed incredible that I could not take in a great armful for her to see.

§6

Among the last wishes she scribbled in a little memorandum book a few days before her death, she wrote very distinctly, 'I desire that my body be cremated,' and signed it with a resolute flourish. I think she feared there might be some legal impediment unless her own words could be produced.

Circumstances conspired to make that last scene a very beautiful one. I had dreaded it greatly, for I have few memories of such services that are not touched with something bleak and hard. I had to set about finding a secular form for the occasion if my mind was not to be offended once again by the Corinthian clevernesses of St. Paul, which constitute the substance of the standard Anglican ceremony. I consulted Dr. Hayward and he gave me a little book of funeral addresses prepared by F.J. Gould. One of those I chose, and then began to alter. In the end I altered it greatly. I altered it, not because I thought I could improve it, but because I kept finding some new way of fitting it more closely to this special occasion. I wrote in it and wrote upon it until at last hardly anything was left of it except certain quotations and the general shape. It became almost entirely a personal testimony, and these quotations and the reflections associated with them stand out in it like a portion of some preceding building incorporated, but not completely identified, in a new edifice.

Dr. T.E. Page read this address. He sat at a desk facing the little grey coffin from which all the flowers and wreaths had been removed and piled aside, and he read very clearly and well to a considerable gathering of our friends. We had circulated her expressed wish that no mourning should be worn for her, and so all these kind and friendly and sorrowful people came exactly themselves and not odd and disguised in unfamiliar black. It made the assembly much more intimate and touching. There were old associates and friends to recall every stage in our five and thirty years together, and many must have taken pains to come and have set other things aside, for the notice given had been very short.

We stood while Mr. Reginald Paul, who was the organist on this occasion, played César Franck's 'Pièce Héroïque' and then we seated ourselves and Dr. Page read these words:

"We have come together in this chapel today to greet for the last time our very dear friend, Catherine Wells.

"We meet in great sadness, for her death came in the middle season of her life when we could all have hoped for many more years of her brave and sweet presence among us. She died a victim of cancer, that still unconquered enemy of human happiness. For months her strength faded, but not her courage nor her kindness. To the end she faced her destiny with serenity and with a gentle unfailing smile for those who ministered to her.

"It would be foolish to pretend that this event does not bring home to us very vividly a sense of the extreme brevity of life for all mankind. The days of man 'are as grass', said the Psalmist; and again, 'The days of our age are threescore years and ten, and though men be so strong that they come to fourscore years, yet is their strength then but labour and sorrow; so soon passeth it away and we are gone.' Nevertheless we may learn from such lives as this that a precious use can be made of brief days and that the courage of a loving Stoicism is proof against despair.

"This was a life freed from all supernatural terrors and superstitious illusions. To-day few are troubled by evil imaginations of what may lie beyond this peace and silence that has come upon our friend. This dear career is now like a task accomplished, a tale of years lived bravely and generously and gone now beyond reach of any corruption. And though the dark shadow of her interruption and cessation lies athwart our minds today, it is a shadow out of which we can pass. There is much wisdom and comfort for us in these words of Spinoza's: 'The free man thinks of nothing so little as of death and his wisdom is a meditation not upon death but upon life.'

"The city of the living world is a perennial city, founded deep in the immemorial past and towering up in the future to heights beyond our vision, its walls fashioned like a mosaic out of lives such as this one. It could not be and its hope could not be, except for the soundness and rightness of such lives. All brave lives have been lived for ever. The world of human achievement exists in them and through them; in them it has its being and its hope, and in it also they continue, deathless, a perpetual conquest over the grave and over the sting of death.

"Some lives stand out upon headlands and are beacons for all mankind. But some, more lovely and more precious, shine in narrower places and come only by chance gleams and reflections to the knowledge of the outer world. So it was with our friend. The best and sweetest of her is known only to one or two of us; subtle and secret, it can never be told. Faithful, gentle, wise, and self-forgetful, she upheld another who mourns her here today; to him she gave her heart and her youth and the best of her brave life, through good report and evil report and the stresses and mischances of our difficult and adventurous world. She was a noble wife, a happy mother, and the maker of a free and kindly and hospitable home. She was perhaps too delicately inaggressive for wide and abundant friendships, but her benevolence was widespread and incessant. She watched to seize opportunities for unobtrusive good deeds. No one could give the full record of her tender half-apologetic gifts, her generous help, her many benefactions, for no one knows them all. She thought that a good deed talked about or even held in memory lost half its worth. She was great-minded. She could forgive ingratitude and bore no resentment for a slight. Never was a single word of ungracious judgment passed by her. 'Poor dears,' she would say, 'Poor silly dears,' when some ugly story or the report of some vindictive quarrel came to her, for it seemed to her that evil acts must be painful and shameful even to the doer. She was a fountain of pity and mercy, except to herself. For herself she was ever exacting. Truth was in her texture; never did she tell a lie nor do any underhand act. She had a great affection for beautiful and graceful things, and her taste seemed to grow finer with the years. Of natural things she most loved the roses of her cherished garden and sunlight upon mountain snows...

"No more will she see the flowers and the sun, and the pain and increasing weakness of these last months also are at an end for her, but the spirit of her life lives with us still, she is still among us, a spirit of pity and kindness, honour and merciful integrity, in the memories of all who knew her.

"And now her dear body must pass from our sight towards the consuming flames. Her life was a star, fire goes to fire and light to light. She returns to the furnace of material things from which her life was drawn. But within our hearts she rests enshrined and, in the woven fabric of things accomplished, she lives for ever."

* * *

Here the reader paused and the coffin passed slowly through the doors leading to the furnace chamber. As it did so all the congregation stood and remained standing. The doors closed and the voice of the reader resumed:

"We have committed our beloved to the flames and soon there will be but a few ashes, as a relic of the form we knew and loved.

"And as we stand here, we whose bodies must presently follow hers into that same peace and that same dispersal, let us think for a moment of the use or the misuse we may make of the time that yet remains for us.

"And may the memory of this gentle starry spirit be a talisman to hold us to charity, faithfulness, and generosity of living."

The reading ceased. The great arch of the crematorium chapel was open upon a wide space of garden glowing with flowers in the serene sunshine of a perfect October afternoon. The stillness of everything outside gave it an air of expectation. As one close friend of hers said to me, it was as though at any moment she might have come in upon us with her garden basket and those red-handled shears of hers upon her arm, smiling as she was wont to smile. When the last words of the address had been pronounced, Mr. Paul played Bach's 'Passacaglia,' a piece she had greatly loved.

I should have made no attempt to follow the coffin had not Bernard Shaw who was standing next to me said: "Take the boys and go behind. It's beautiful."

When I seemed to hesitate he whispered: "I saw my mother burnt there. You'll be glad if you go."

That was a wise counsel and I am very grateful for it. I beckoned to my two sons and we went together to the furnace room. The little coffin lay on a carriage outside the furnace doors. These opened. Inside one saw an oblong chamber whose fire-brick walls glowed with a dull red heat. The coffin was pushed slowly into the chamber and then in a moment or so a fringe of tongues of flame begin to dance along its further edges and spread very rapidly. Then in another second the whole coffin was pouring out white fire. The doors of the furnace closed slowly upon that incandescence.

It was indeed very beautiful. I wished she could have known of those quivering bright first flames, so clear they were and so like eager yet kindly living things.

I have always found the return from burial a disagreeable experience, because of the pursuing thought of that poor body left behind boxed up in the cold wet ground and waiting the coming of the twilight. But Jane, I felt, had gone clean out of life and left nothing to moulder and defile our world. So she would have had it. It was good to think she had gone as a spirit should go.

§7

And now follow some of the things she wrote. It is by no means all she wrote, but like the beginnings of most of us, much of her earlier writing was imitative even in the things it sought to express. I think I have given here everything she ever completed that conveys her quality.

There is a much greater bulk of unfinished work, and most of this belongs to a long fantasy of difficult design called *The Open Heart*. It has some fine and tender passages, but nothing I think better than what is to be found here in such stories as 'The Beautiful House,' 'The Emerald,' 'Night in the Garden,' 'The Fugitives' or 'The Dragon-Fly'. There are a few short poems and two longer ones.

I have put in at the beginning of this collection a glimpse of Jane Wells being merry at home, in the form of an absurd fairy story she concocted with our younger son Frank. That is by Mummy of the charades and Catherine Wells has small part in it. Throughout the rest the personality of Catherine Wells predominates. In all these other pieces you will find her brooding tenderness, her sense of invincible fatality, her exquisite appreciation of slight and lovely weakness and that predisposition towards a haunting, dreamland fantasy of fear which the courage and steadfastness of her substantial life repudiated altogether. Never I think in the work of any other writer has mood so predominated over action.

About the Editors & Authors

Patrick Parrinder is Emeritus Professor of English at the University of Reading and President of the H.G. Wells Society. He is the author of many books on H.G. Wells, science fiction and modern literature, and is General Editor of the 12-volume *Oxford History of the Novel in English* (2011–24).

Emelyne Godfrey has a PhD from Birkbeck College. She is author of several books on the long nineteenth century including *Mrs Pankhurst's Bodyguard: On the Trail of 'Kitty' Marshall and the Met Police 'Cats'* (The History Press, 2023). She writes widely on women's history, crime, science fiction and the supernatural.

Catherine Wells (1872–1927), born Amy Catherine Robbins, worked as a teacher and studied at Tutorial College, Holborn where she met and later married H.G. Wells. She is regarded as a great supporter of her husband's literary outpourings, while she was in fact herself a serious writer, quietly creating her own stories and poems, long-neglected until now.

H.G. Wells (1866–1946), novelist, journalist, social reformer and historian, was one of the greatest science fiction writers. With Aldous Huxley and, later, George Orwell, he defined the adventurous, social concern of early speculative fiction where the human condition was played out on a greater stage. Wells created some forty novels, including *The Time Machine*, *The Invisible Man* and *The War of the Worlds*.

About the Illustrator

Broci is a Finnish comic artist and illustrator. After gaining a BA in Fashion and Clothing Design from the Lahti Institute of Design, they now create art inspired by mythologies, horror stories, comics and manga, metal and witch house music, movies and fashion design. Broci has been publishing a webcomic called *Bad Friday* since 2014, has produced short comic story collections and graphic novels, such as *Varpaat (Pale Toes)*, and has illustrated all manner of books and book covers – all with characteristic dark and ethereal flare. Broci loves nature, music and anything spooky and creepy.

Acknowledgments

We would like to thank Maggie Stevens of the Gardens of Easton Lodge for introducing us to the work of Felice Spurrier. It is a pleasure to watch the dragonflies as they dance around the pond of the sunken Italianate garden, much as they do in Catherine's story of the same title. We are also indebted to Daniel Hardiman-McCartney MBE FCOptom, Clinical Adviser, The College of Optometrists for a possible diagnosis of the symptoms suffered by the protagonist of 'The Oculist'. Our most substantial acknowledgment is to the late David C. Smith, the Wells scholar who in the late 1980s prepared the transcription of *The Open Heart* and was its first editor. To this, Smith added an unpublished 120-page draft biography of Catherine Wells which has been an inspiration to us in our own work. Furthermore, we are not only grateful to H.G. Wells's family for granting permission to publish *The Open Heart* but are also delighted by the warm support they have shown towards this endeavour.

Emelyne Godfrey and Patrick Parrinder

Bibliography

Meyer, M[athilde]., *H.G. Wells and his Family (As I Have Known Them)* (Edinburgh: International Publishing Co., 1955)

Rhondda, Viscountess, *This Was My World* (London: Macmillan and Co., 1933)

Sherborne, Michael, *Another Kind of Life* (London: Peter Owen, 2010)

Smith, David C. (ed.), *The Correspondence of H.G. Wells: Volume I, 1880–1903* (London: Pickering & Chatto, 1998)

Spurrier, Felice, *Beyond the Forest: The Countess of Warwick and Some of her Coterie* (A Five Parishes Publication, 1986)

Spurrier, Felice, *Lady Warwick's Barn Theatre* (A Five Parishes Publication, 1988)

Swinnerton, Frank, Introduction to Frank Wells, *H.G. Wells: A Pictorial Biography* (London: Jupiter Books, 1977)

Warwick, Countess of, Frances (Daisy), *Life's Ebb and Flow* (London: Hutchinson, 1929)

Wells, Catherine, *The Book of Catherine Wells, with an Introduction by her Husband H.G. Wells* (London: Chatto and Windus, 1928)

Wells, Frank, *H.G. Wells: A Pictorial Biography* (London: Jupiter Books, 1977)

Wells, G.P. (ed.), *H.G. Wells in Love* (London; Boston: Faber and Faber, 1984)

Wells, H.G., *Experiment in Autobiography* (London: Victor Gollancz and The Cresset Press, 1966)

Wells, H.G., 'Zoological Retrogression', reprinted in *The Fin de Siècle: A Reader in Cultural History, c. 1880–1900*, edited by Sally Ledger and Roger Luckhurst (Oxford: Oxford University Press, 2000), pp. 5–12

Beyond & Within

THE FLAME TREE Beyond & Within short story collections bring together tales of myth and imagination by modern and contemporary writers, carefully selected by anthologists, and sometimes featuring short stories and fiction from a single author. Overall, the series presents a wide range of diverse and inclusive voices, often writing folkloric-inflected short fiction, but always with an emphasis on the supernatural, science fiction, the mysterious and the speculative. The books themselves are gorgeous, with foiled covers, printed edges and published only in hardcover editions, offering a lifetime of reading pleasure.

Flame Tree Fiction

A wide range of new and classic fiction, from myth to modern stories, with tales from the distant past to the far future, including short story anthologies, Collector's Editions, Collectable Classics, Gothic Fantasy collections and Epic Tales of mythology and folklore.

•